CREATED BY
DAN PANOSIAN

PRESENTED FOR YOU

DAN PANOSIAN
CREATOR, WRITER, ARTIST

PAT BROSSEAU
LETTERER

FULL COLOR! • 144 PAGES!

SLOTS TRADE PAPERBACK. FIRST PRINTING. JUNE 2018. PUBLISHED BY IMAGE COMICS, INC. OFFICE OF PUBLICATION: 2701 NW VAUGHN ST., STE. 780, PORTLAND, OR 97210. ORIGINALLY PUBLISHED IN SINGLE MAGAZINE FORM AS SLOTS #1-6. SLOTS™ (INCLUDING ALL PROMINENT CHARACTERS FEATURED HEREIN), ITS LOGO AND ALL CHARACTER LIKENESSES ARE TRADEMARKS OF SKYBOUND, LLC, UNLESS OTHERWISE NOTED. IMAGE COMICS® AND ITS LOGOS ARE REGISTERED TRADEMARKS AND COPYRIGHTS OF IMAGE COMICS, INC. ALL RIGHTS RESERVED. NO PART OF THIS PUBLICATION MAY BE REPRODUCED OR TRANSMITTED IN ANY FORM OR BY ANY MEANS (EXCEPT FOR SHORT EXCERPTS FOR REVIEW PURPOSES) WITHOUT THE EXPRESS WRITTEN PERMISSION OF IMAGE COMICS, INC. ALL NAMES, CHARACTERS, EVENTS AND LOCALES IN THIS PUBLICATION ARE ENTIRELY FICTIONAL. ANY RESEMBLANCE TO ACTUAL PERSONS (LIVING OR DEAD), EVENTS OR PLACES, WITHOUT SATIRIC INTENT, IS COINCIDENTAL. PRINTED IN THE U.S.A. FOR INFORMATION REGARDING THE CPSIA ON THIS PRINTED MATERIAL CALL: 203-595-3636 AND PROVIDE REFERENCE # RICH – 791035. ISBN: 978-1-5343-0655-4.

BY SKYBOUND™ AND image®

ARIELLE BASICH
ASSOCIATE EDITOR

SEAN MACKIEWICZ
EDITOR

TRULY AN INCREDIBLE DEAL!

SKYBOUND LLC. ROBERT KIRKMAN CHAIRMAN DAVID ALPERT CEO SEAN MACKIEWICZ SVP, EDITOR-IN-CHIEF SHAWN KIRKHAM SVP, BUSINESS DEVELOPMENT BRIAN HUNTINGTON ONLINE EDITORIAL DIRECTOR JUNE ALIAN PUBLICITY DIRECTOR ANDRES JUAREZ ART DIRECTOR JON MOISAN EDITOR ARIELLE BASICH ASSOCIATE EDITOR CARINA TAYLOR PRODUCTION ARTIST PAUL SHIN BUSINESS DEVELOPMENT ASSISTANT JOHNNY O'DELL SOCIAL MEDIA MANAGER SALLY JACKA SKYBOUND RETAILER REALATIONS DAN PETERSEN DIRECTOR OF OPERATIONS & EVENTS NICK PALMER OPERATIONS COORDINATOR INTERNATIONAL INIQUIRIES: AG@SEQUENTIALRIGHTS.COM LICENSING INQUIRIES:CONTACT@SKYBOUND.COM WWW.SKYBOUND.COM

IMAGE COMICS, INC. ROBERT KIRKMAN CHIEF OPERATING OFFICER ERIK LARSEN CHIEF FINANCIAL OFFICER TODD MCFARLANE PRESIDENT MARC SILVESTRI CHIEF EXECUTIVE OFFICER JIM VALENTINO VICE PRESIDENT ERIC STEPHENSON PUBLISHER/CHIEF CREATIVE OFFICER COREY HART DIRECTOR OF SALES JEFF BOISON DIRECTOR OF PUBLISHING PLANNING & BOOK TRADE SALES CHRIS ROSS DIRECTOR OF DIGITAL SALES JEFF STANG DIRECTOR OF SPECIALTY SALES KAT SALAZAR DIRECTOR OF PR & MARKETING DREW GILL ART DIRECTOR HEATHER DOORNINK PRODUCTION DIRECTOR NICOLE LAPALME CONTROLLER WWW.IMAGECOMICS.COM

TO MY
POPS

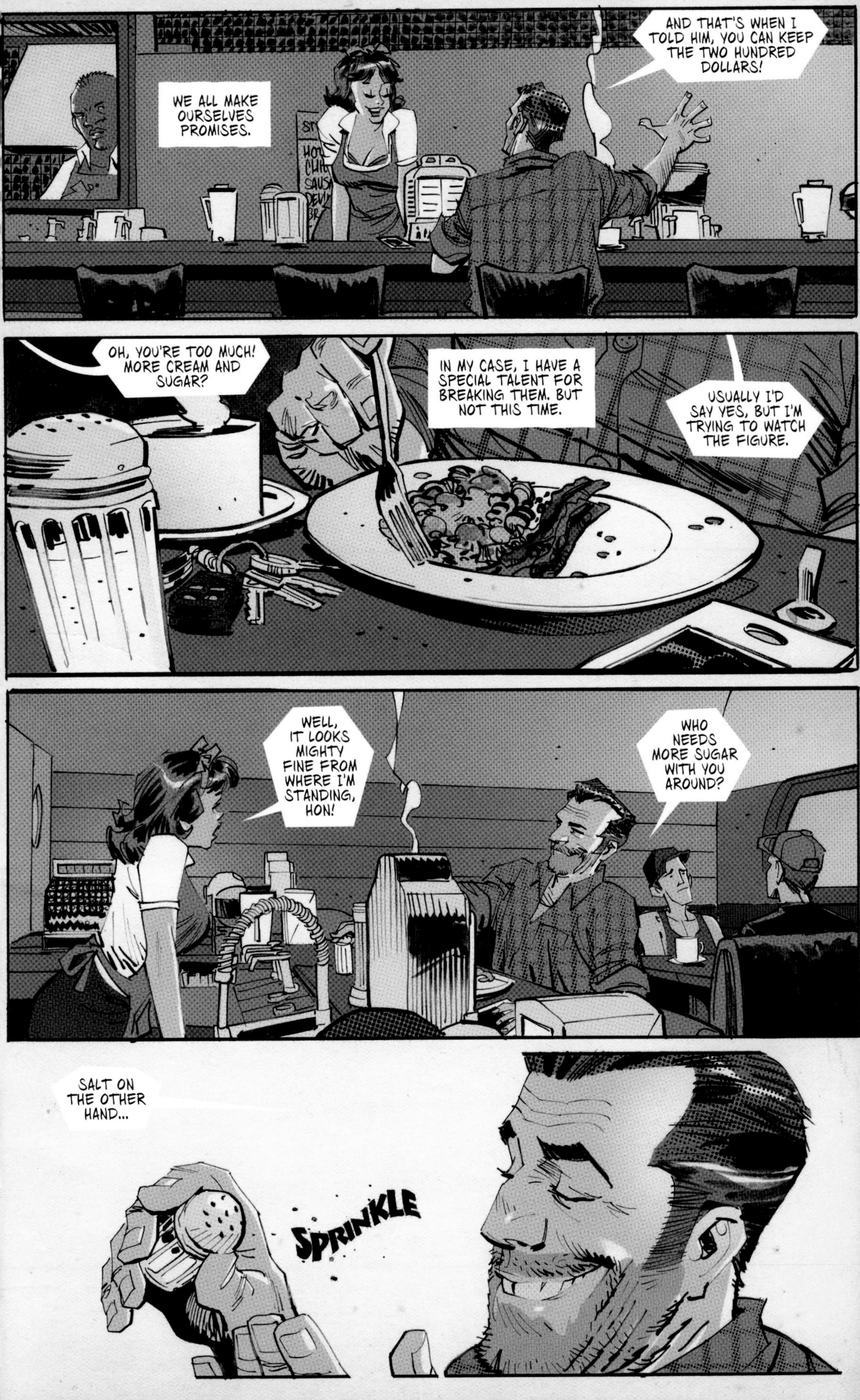
WE ALL MAKE OURSELVES PROMISES.
AND THAT'S WHEN I TOLD HIM, YOU CAN KEEP THE TWO HUNDRED DOLLARS!
OH, YOU'RE TOO MUCH! MORE CREAM AND SUGAR?
IN MY CASE, I HAVE A SPECIAL TALENT FOR BREAKING THEM. BUT NOT THIS TIME.
USUALLY I'D SAY YES, BUT I'M TRYING TO WATCH THE FIGURE.
WELL, IT LOOKS MIGHTY FINE FROM WHERE I'M STANDING, HON!
WHO NEEDS MORE SUGAR WITH YOU AROUND?
SALT ON THE OTHER HAND...
SPRINKLE

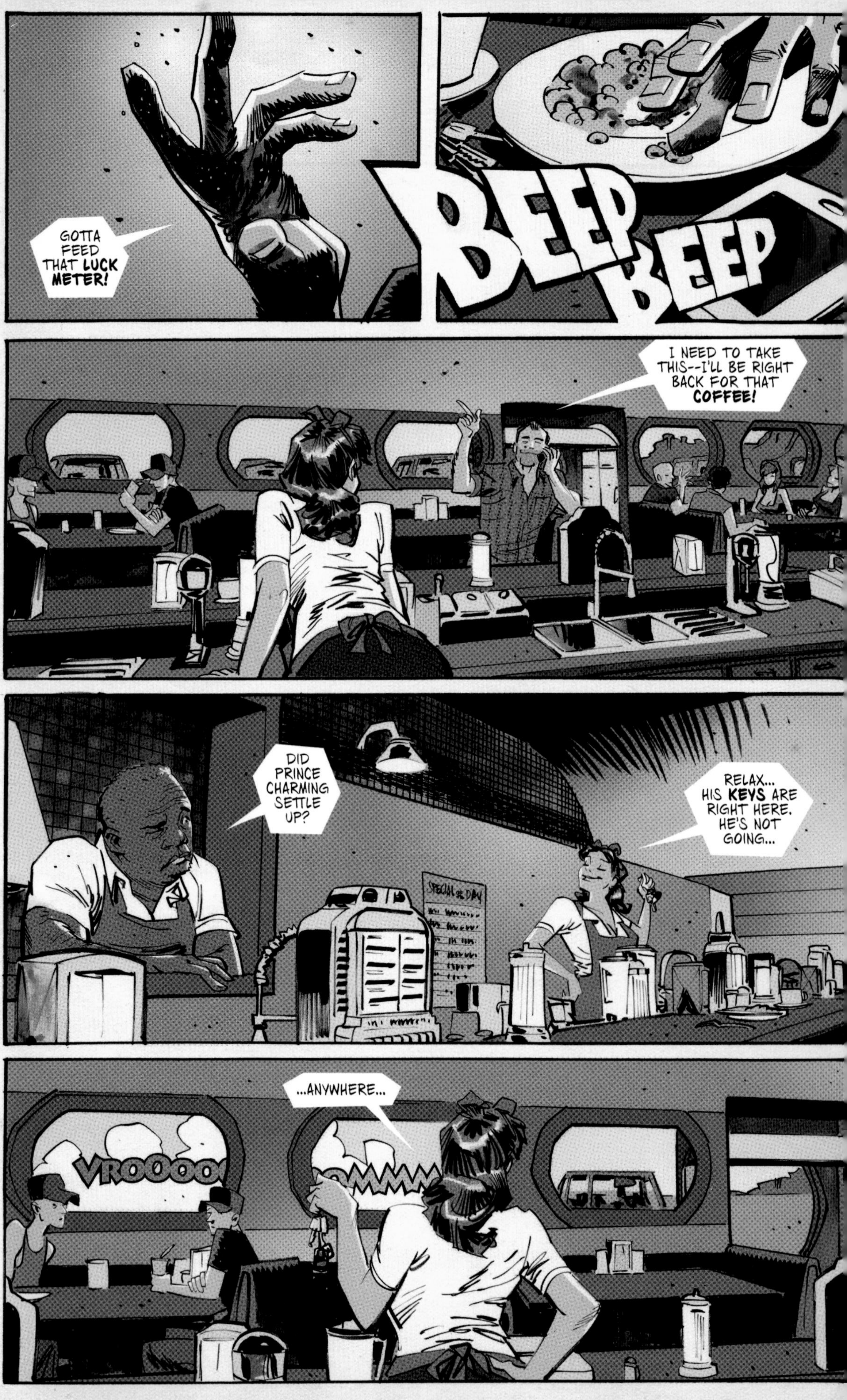

GOTTA FEED THAT LUCK METER!
BEEP
BEEP
I NEED TO TAKE THIS--I'LL BE RIGHT BACK FOR THAT COFFEE!
DID PRINCE CHARMING SETTLE UP?
RELAX... HIS KEYS ARE RIGHT HERE. HE'S NOT GOING...
SPECIAL OF THE DAY
...ANYWHERE...
VROOOOO
OMMMM

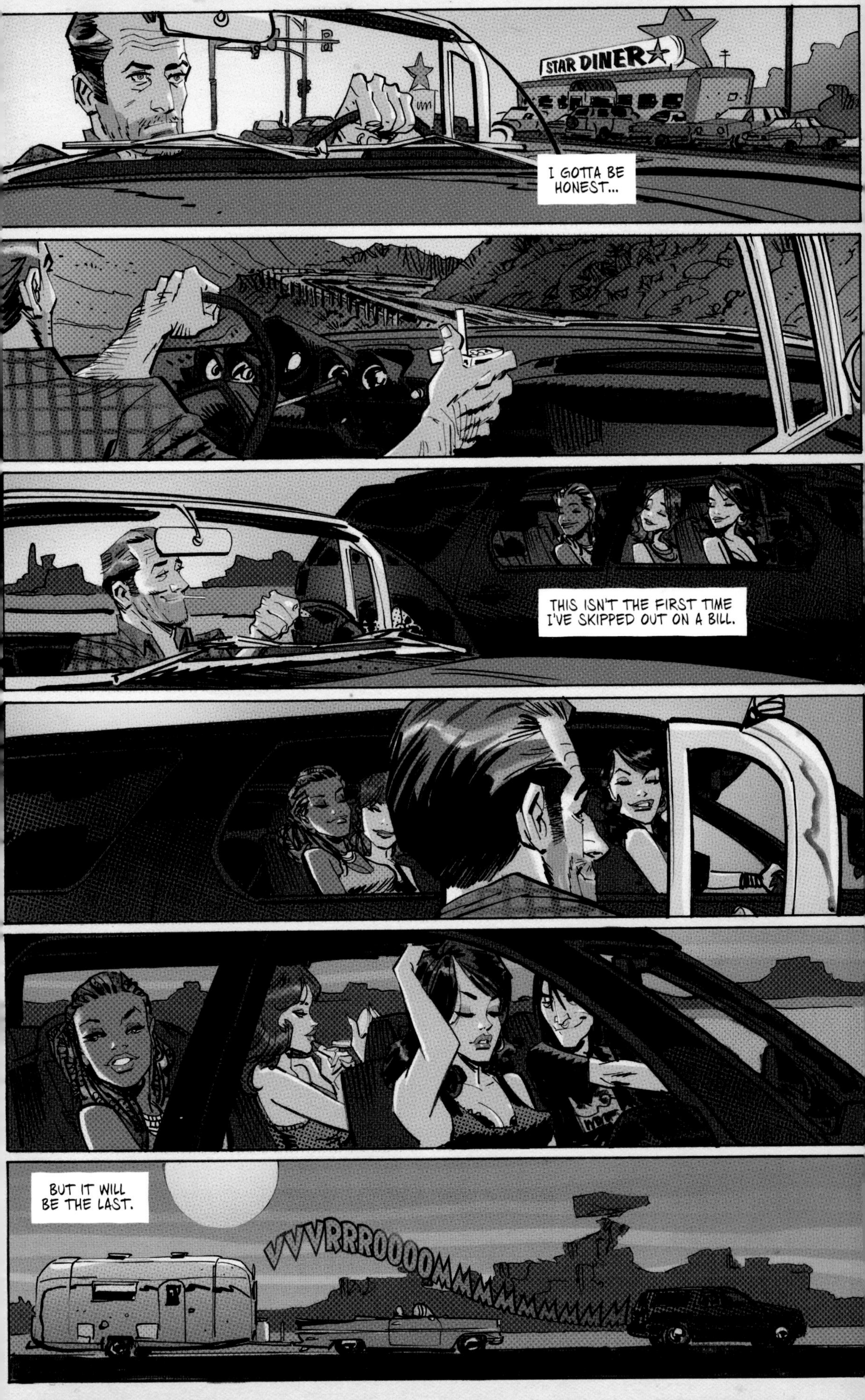
STAR DINER
I GOTTA BE HONEST...
THIS ISN'T THE FIRST TIME I'VE SKIPPED OUT ON A BILL.
BUT IT WILL BE THE LAST.
VVVRRROOOOOMMMMMMMMMMMMMM

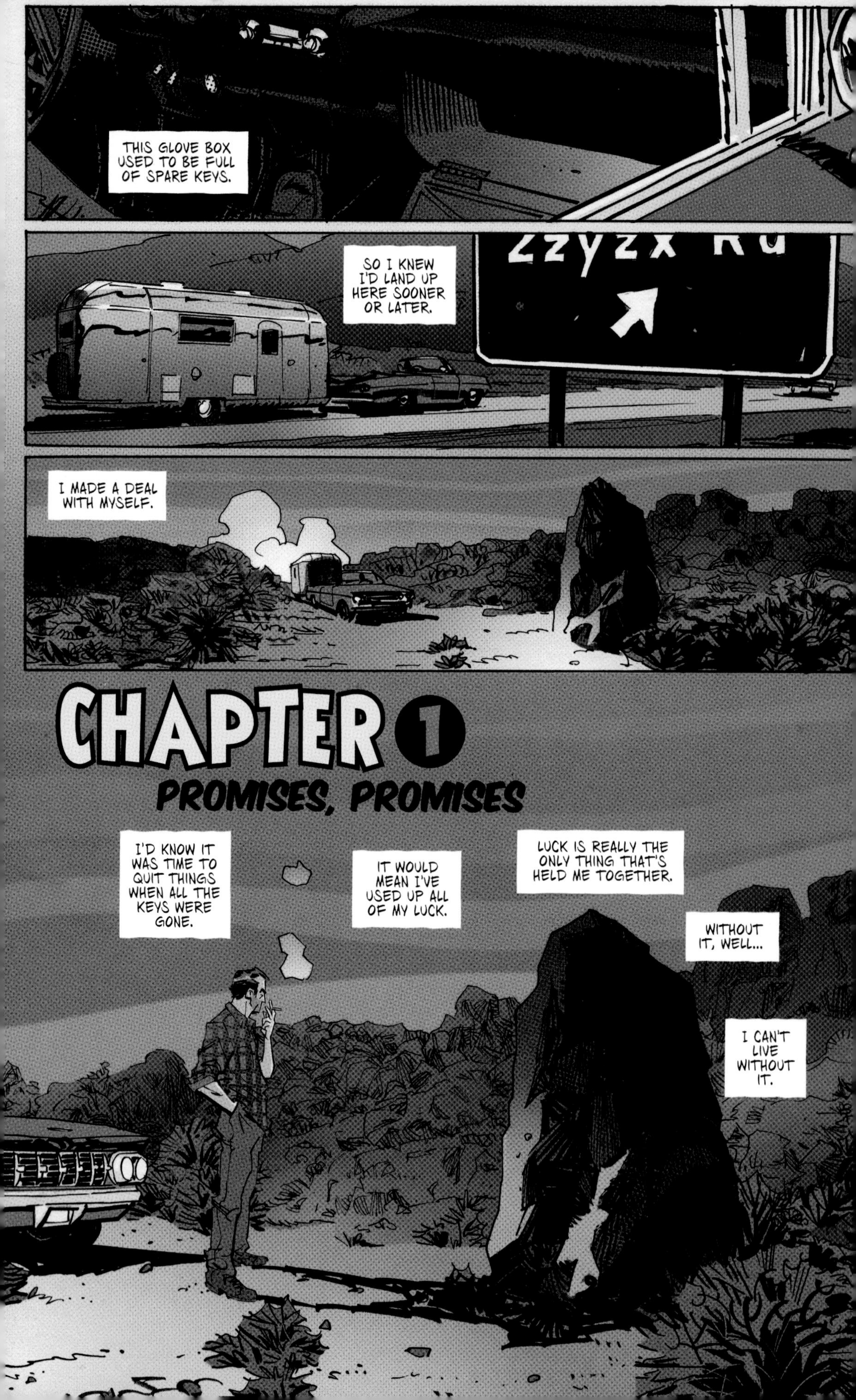
THIS GLOVE BOX USED TO BE FULL OF SPARE KEYS.
SO I KNEW I'D LAND UP HERE SOONER OR LATER.
Zzyzx Rd
I MADE A DEAL WITH MYSELF.
CHAPTER 1
PROMISES, PROMISES
I'D KNOW IT WAS TIME TO QUIT THINGS WHEN ALL THE KEYS WERE GONE.
IT WOULD MEAN I'VE USED UP ALL OF MY LUCK.
LUCK IS REALLY THE ONLY THING THAT'S HELD ME TOGETHER.
WITHOUT IT, WELL...
I CAN'T LIVE WITHOUT IT.

TURNS OUT I'M A BIT OF AN ASSHOLE.

MY FAMILY AND FRIENDS?

I'VE USED THEM UP, TOO.

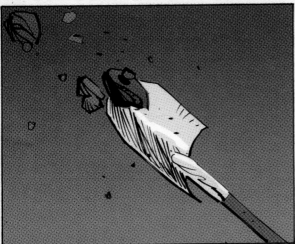

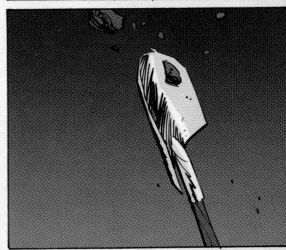

ASSHOLES TEND TO DO THAT.

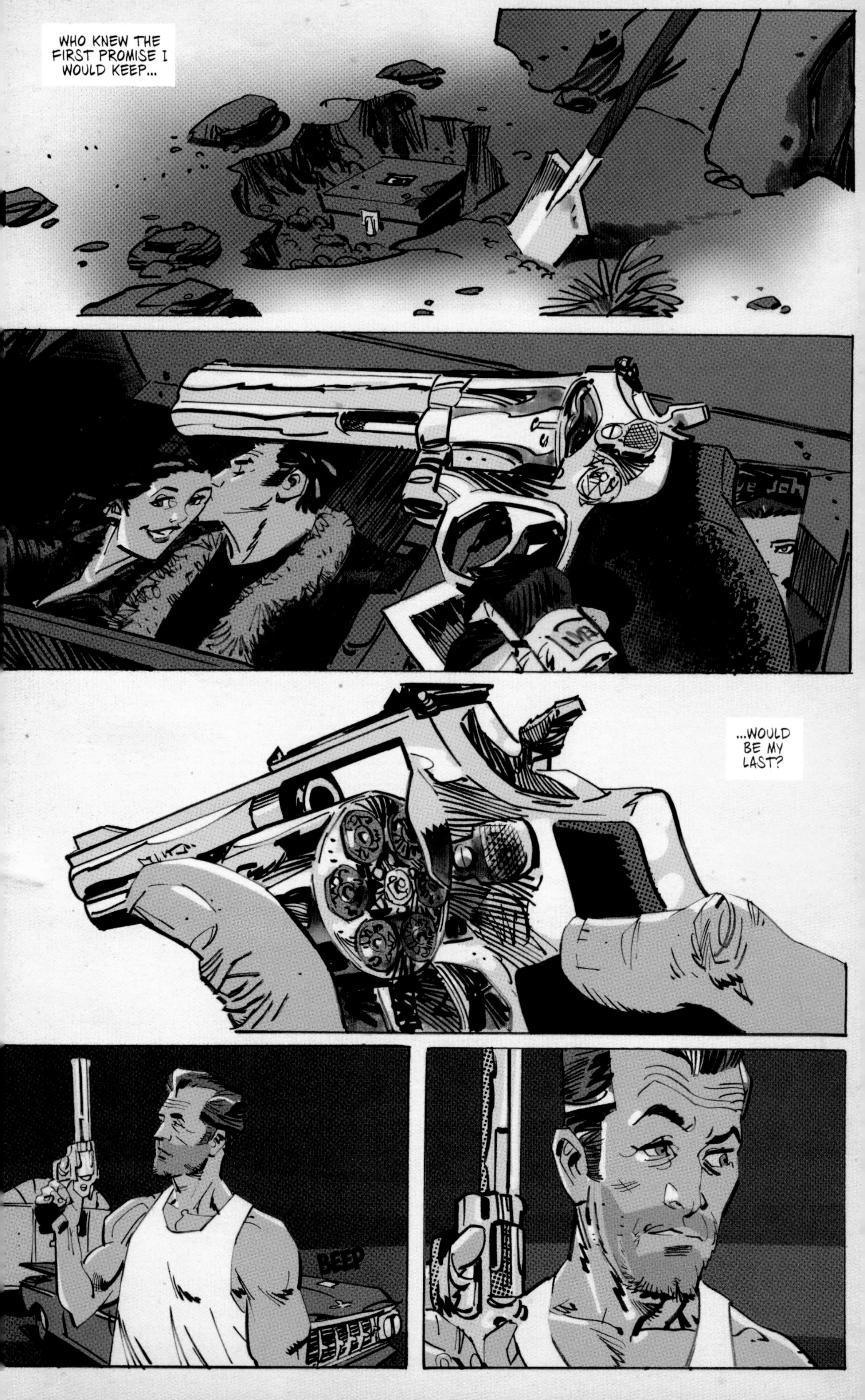
WHO KNEW THE FIRST PROMISE I WOULD KEEP...
...WOULD BE MY LAST?
BEEP

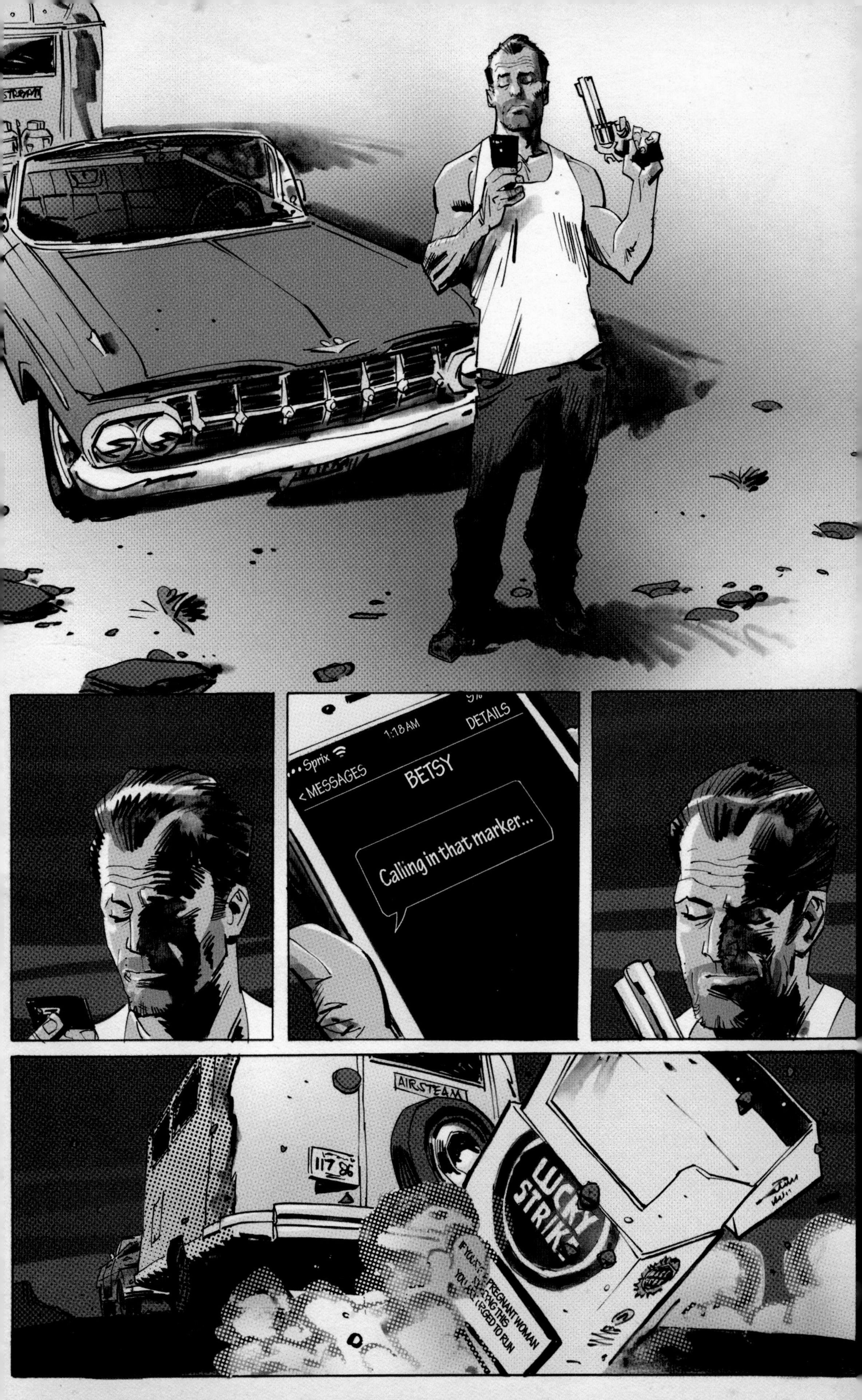
Sprix
1:18 AM
DETAILS
< MESSAGES
BETSY
Calling in that marker...
AIRSTEAM
117 86
PREGNANT WOMAN
THIS
TO RUN

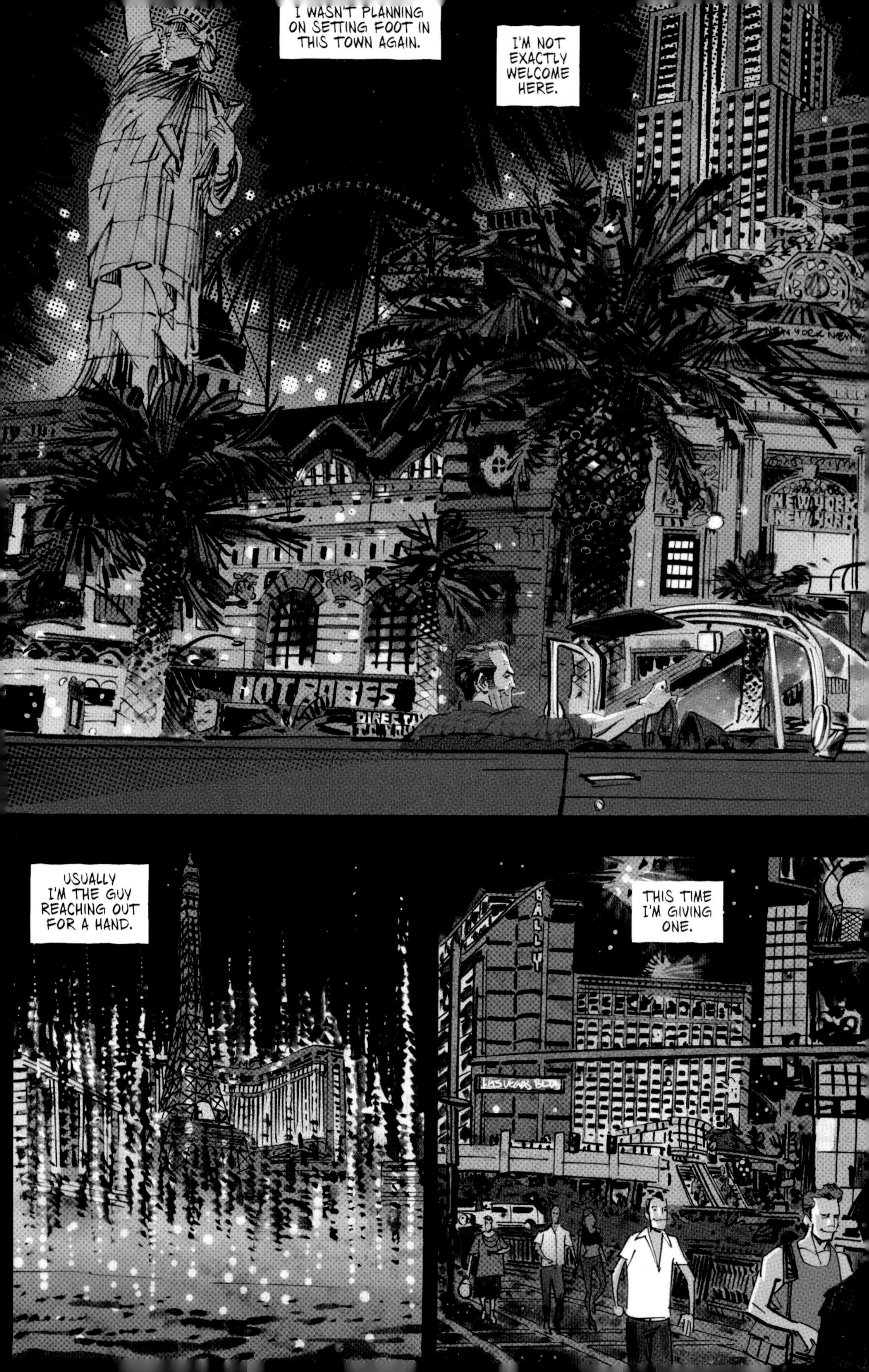
I WASN'T PLANNING ON SETTING FOOT IN THIS TOWN AGAIN.
I'M NOT EXACTLY WELCOME HERE.
USUALLY I'M THE GUY REACHING OUT FOR A HAND.
THIS TIME I'M GIVING ONE.

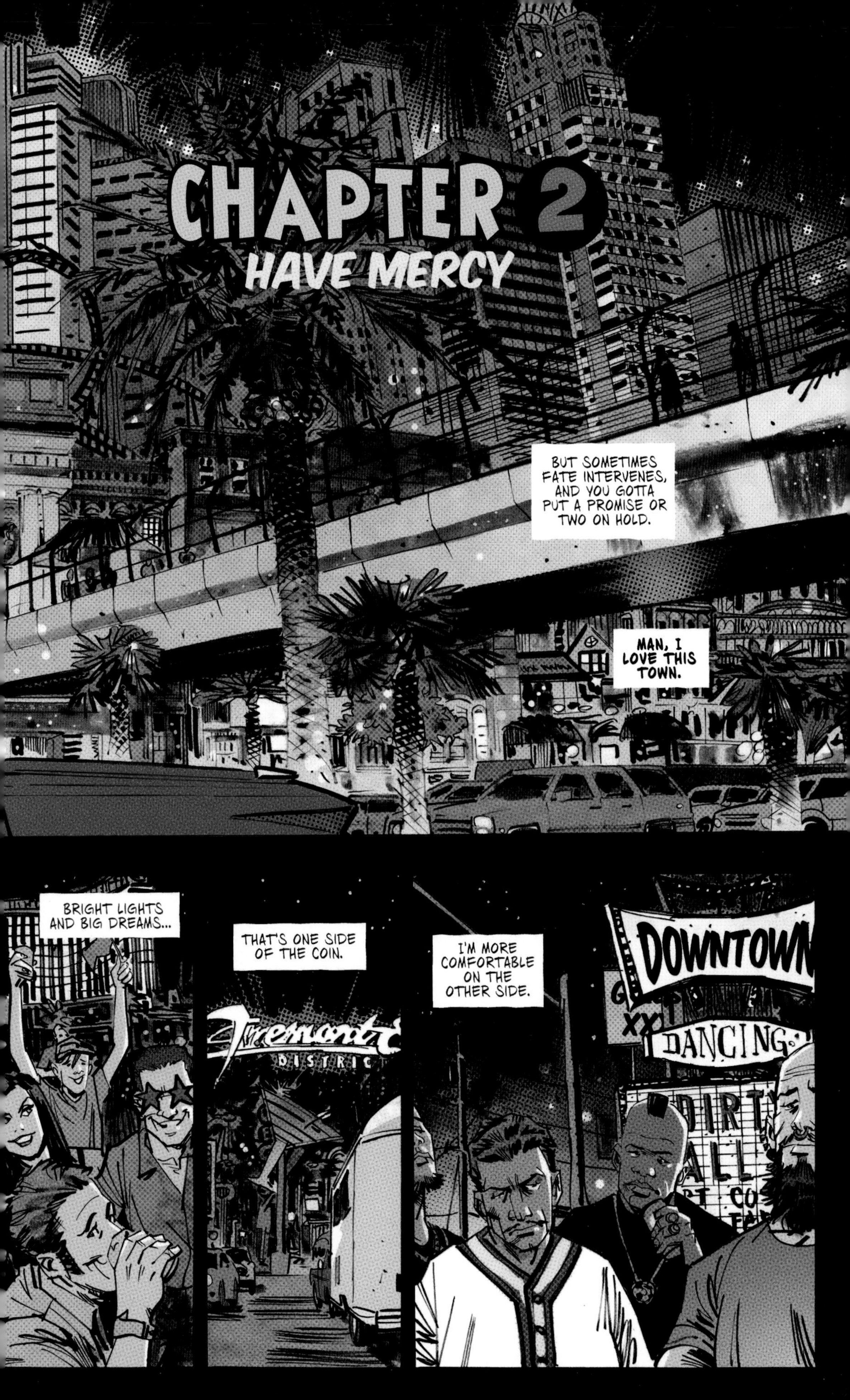
CHAPTER 2
HAVE MERCY
BUT SOMETIMES FATE INTERVENES, AND YOU GOTTA PUT A PROMISE OR TWO ON HOLD.
MAN, I LOVE THIS TOWN.
BRIGHT LIGHTS AND BIG DREAMS...
THAT'S ONE SIDE OF THE COIN.
I'M MORE COMFORTABLE ON THE OTHER SIDE.
DOWNTOWN
DANCING

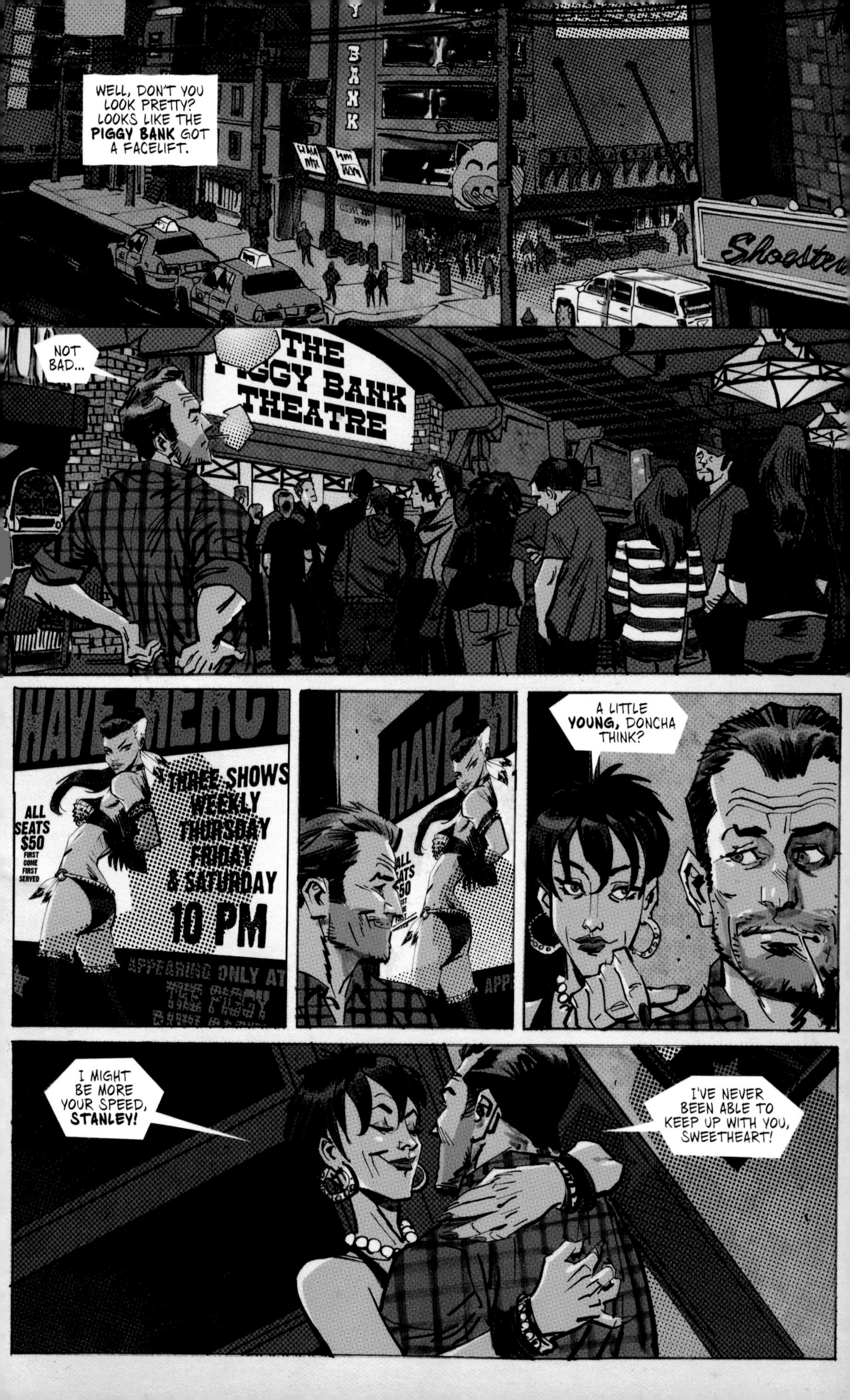

WELL, DON'T YOU LOOK PRETTY? LOOKS LIKE THE **PIGGY BANK** GOT A FACELIFT.
PIGGY BANK
Shoosters
NOT BAD...
THE PIGGY BANK THEATRE
HAVE MERCY
ALL SEATS $50 FIRST COME FIRST SERVED
THREE SHOWS WEEKLY THURSDAY FRIDAY & SATURDAY 10 PM
APPEARING ONLY AT THE PIGGY
A LITTLE **YOUNG,** DONCHA THINK?
I MIGHT BE MORE YOUR SPEED, **STANLEY!**
I'VE NEVER BEEN ABLE TO KEEP UP WITH YOU, SWEETHEART!

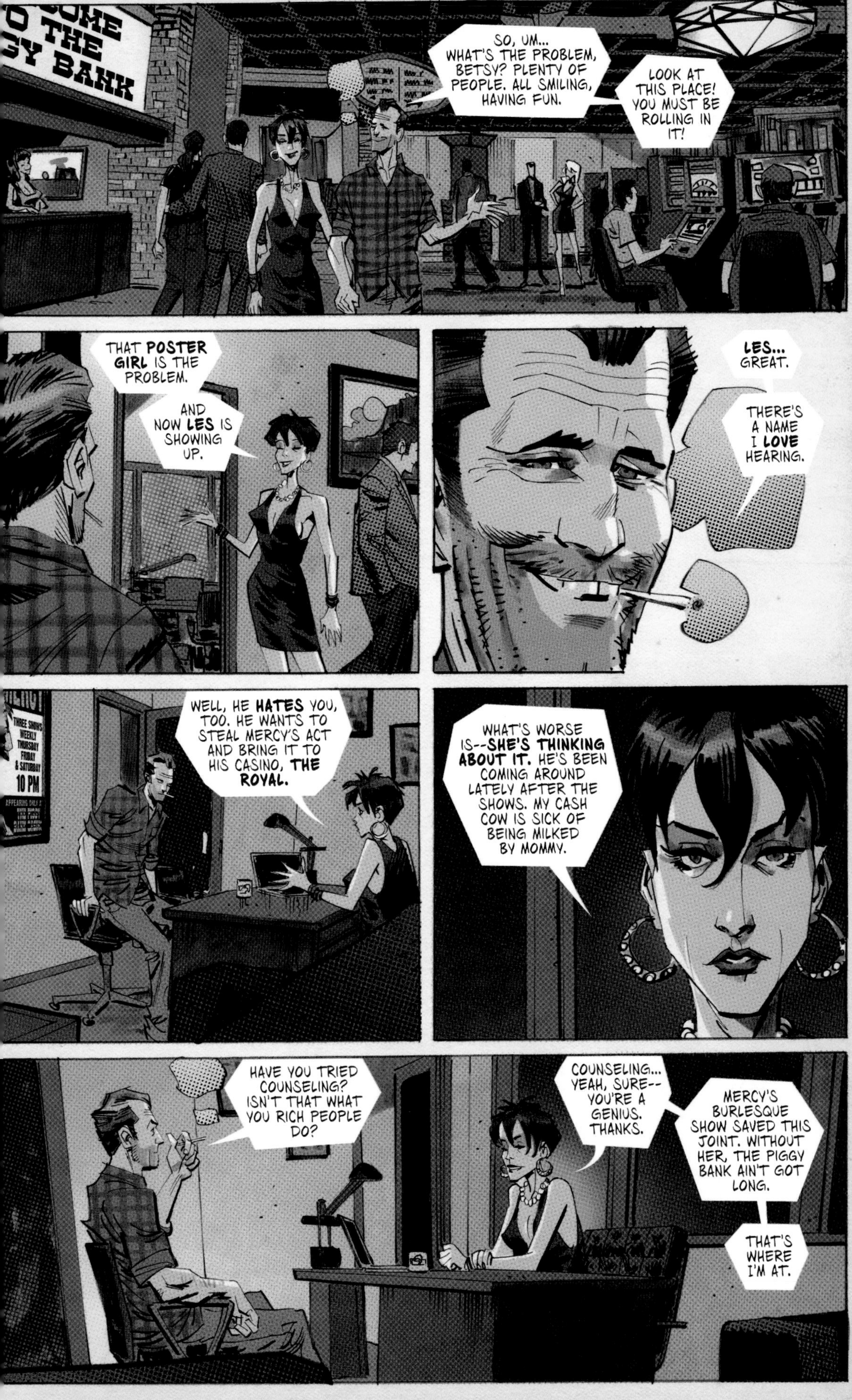

WELCOME TO THE PIGGY BANK
SO, UM... WHAT'S THE PROBLEM, BETSY? PLENTY OF PEOPLE. ALL SMILING, HAVING FUN.
LOOK AT THIS PLACE! YOU MUST BE ROLLING IN IT!
THAT **POSTER GIRL** IS THE PROBLEM.
AND NOW **LES** IS SHOWING UP.
LES... GREAT.
THERE'S A NAME I **LOVE** HEARING.
THREE SHOWS WEEKLY THURSDAY FRIDAY & SATURDAY 10 PM
WELL, HE **HATES** YOU, TOO. HE WANTS TO STEAL MERCY'S ACT AND BRING IT TO HIS CASINO, **THE ROYAL.**
WHAT'S WORSE IS--**SHE'S THINKING ABOUT IT.** HE'S BEEN COMING AROUND LATELY AFTER THE SHOWS. MY CASH COW IS SICK OF BEING MILKED BY MOMMY.
HAVE YOU TRIED COUNSELING? ISN'T THAT WHAT YOU RICH PEOPLE DO?
COUNSELING... YEAH, SURE-- YOU'RE A GENIUS. THANKS.
MERCY'S BURLESQUE SHOW SAVED THIS JOINT. WITHOUT HER, THE PIGGY BANK AIN'T GOT LONG.
THAT'S WHERE I'M AT.

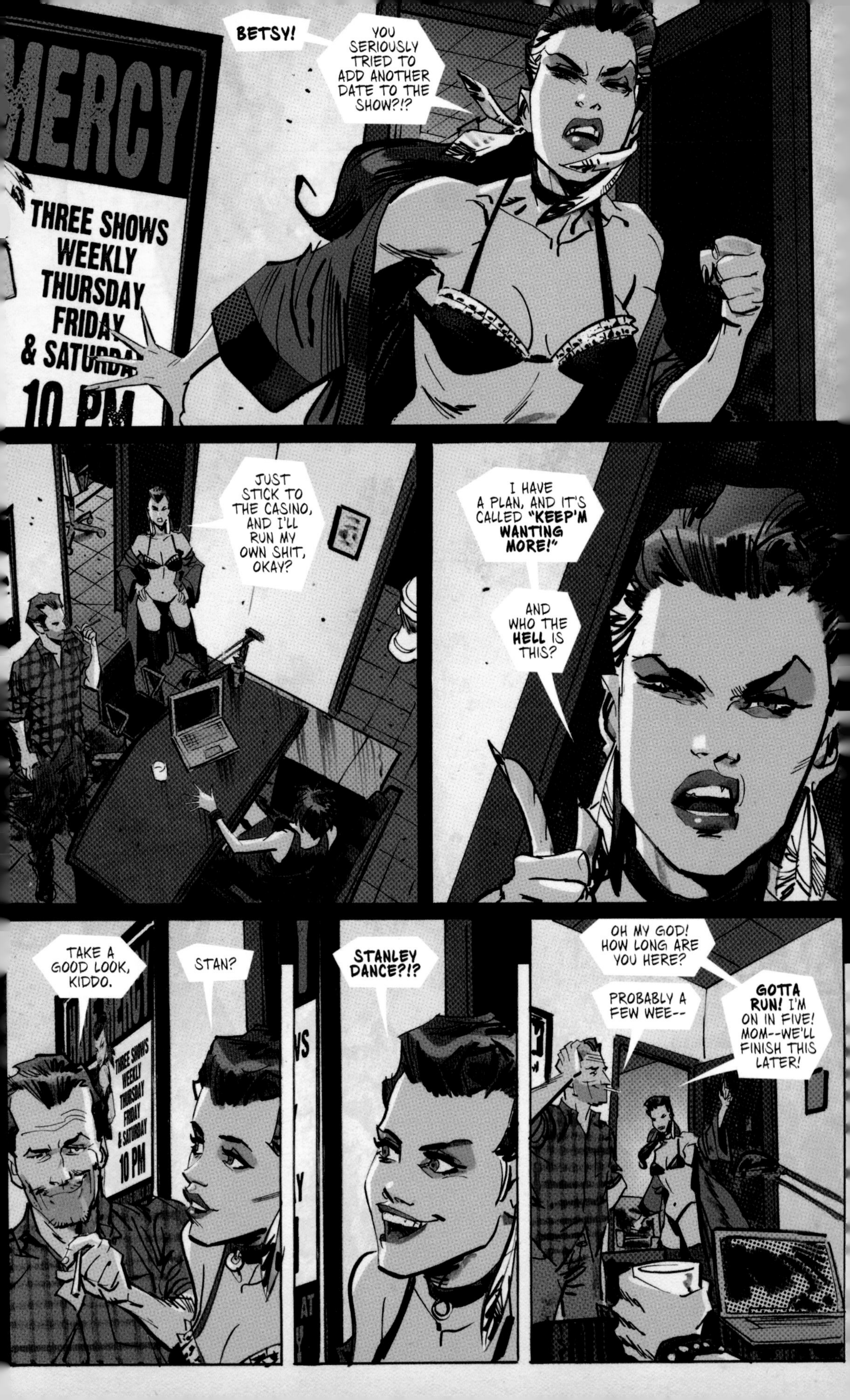
MERCY
THREE SHOWS WEEKLY THURSDAY FRIDAY & SATURDA
10 PM
BETSY!
YOU SERIOUSLY TRIED TO ADD ANOTHER DATE TO THE SHOW?!?
JUST STICK TO THE CASINO, AND I'LL RUN MY OWN SHIT, OKAY?
I HAVE A PLAN, AND IT'S CALLED "KEEP'M WANTING MORE!"
AND WHO THE HELL IS THIS?
TAKE A GOOD LOOK, KIDDO.
THREE SHOWS WEEKLY THURSDAY FRIDAY & SATURDAY 10 PM
STAN?
STANLEY DANCE?!?
OH MY GOD! HOW LONG ARE YOU HERE?
PROBABLY A FEW WEE--
GOTTA RUN! I'M ON IN FIVE! MOM--WE'LL FINISH THIS LATER!

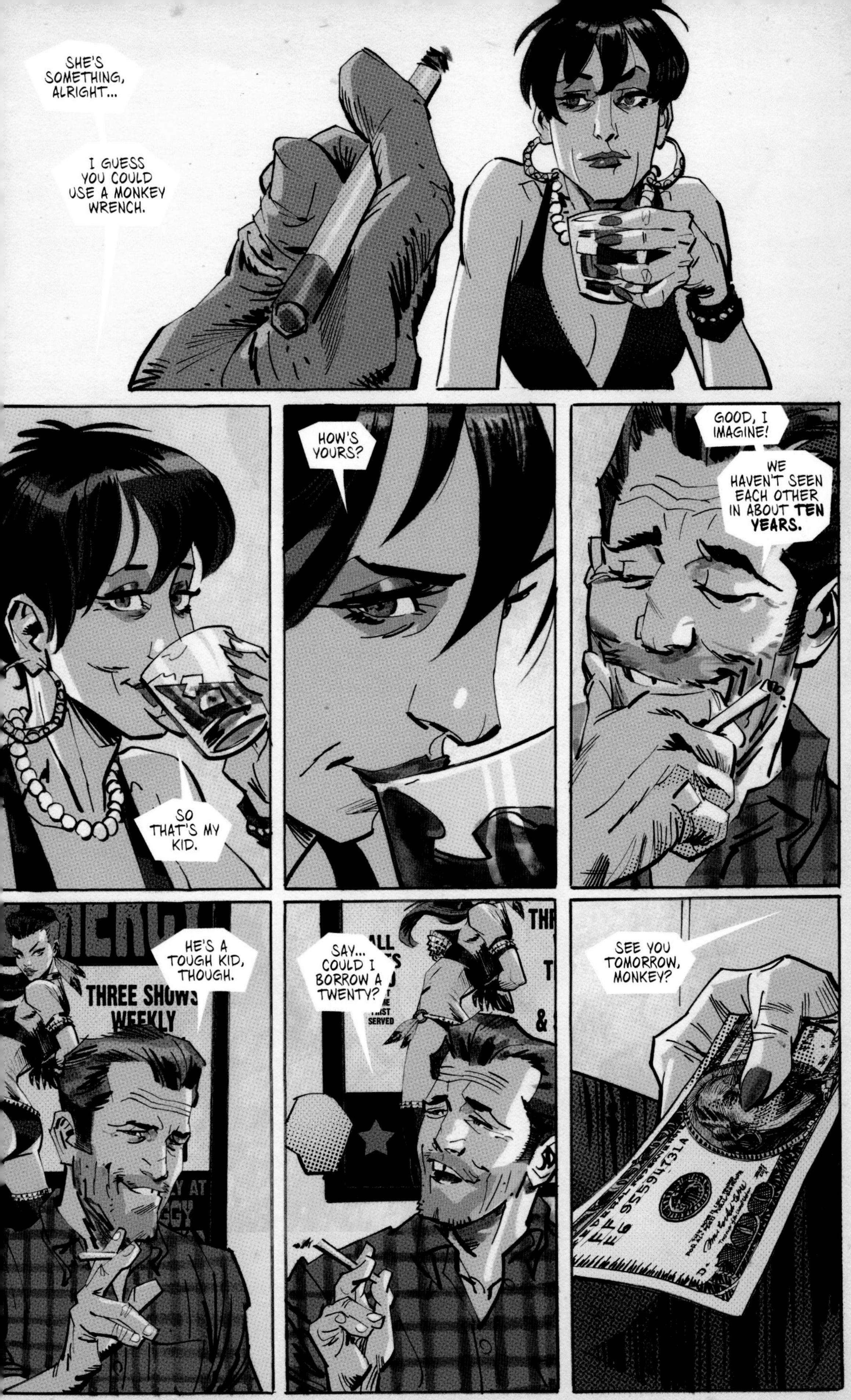
SHE'S SOMETHING, ALRIGHT...
I GUESS YOU COULD USE A MONKEY WRENCH.
SO THAT'S MY KID.
HOW'S YOURS?
GOOD, I IMAGINE!
WE HAVEN'T SEEN EACH OTHER IN ABOUT **TEN YEARS.**
THREE SHOWS WEEKLY
HE'S A TOUGH KID, THOUGH.
SAY... COULD I BORROW A TWENTY?
SEE YOU TOMORROW, MONKEY?

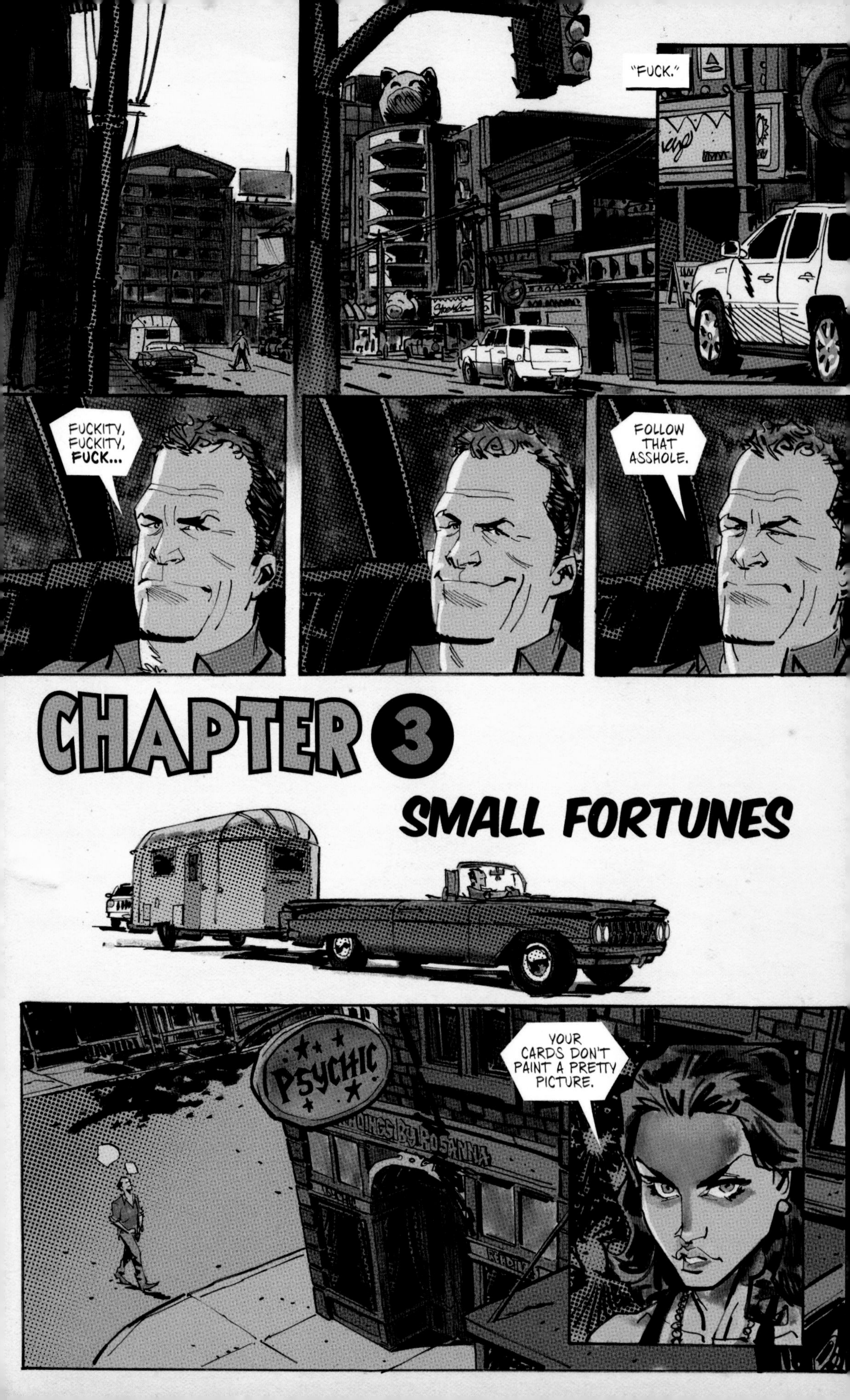
"FUCK."
FUCKITY, FUCKITY, FUCK...
FOLLOW THAT ASSHOLE.
CHAPTER 3
SMALL FORTUNES
PSYCHIC
YOUR CARDS DON'T PAINT A PRETTY PICTURE.

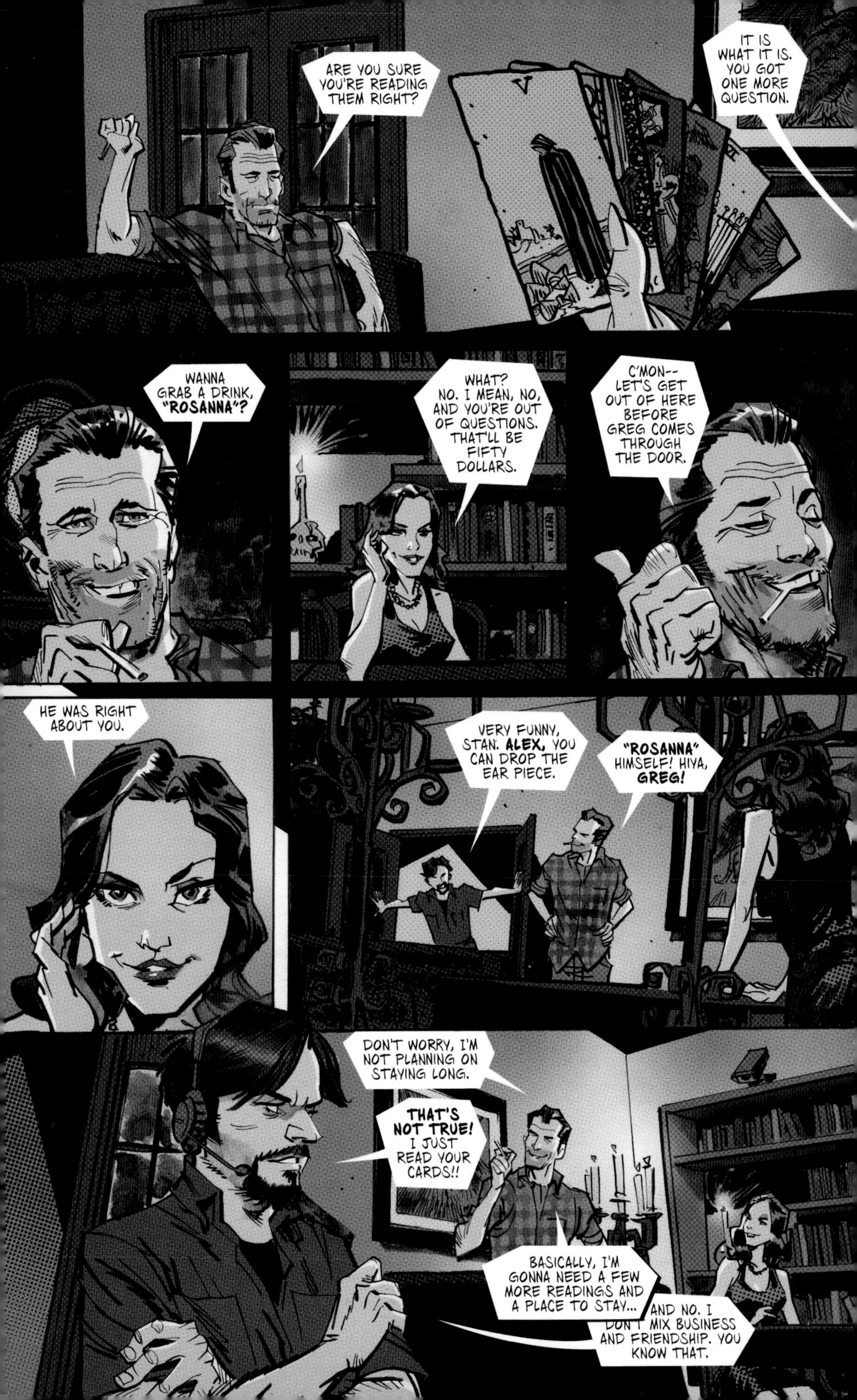
ARE YOU SURE YOU'RE READING THEM RIGHT?
IT IS WHAT IT IS. YOU GOT ONE MORE QUESTION.
WANNA GRAB A DRINK, "ROSANNA"?
WHAT? NO. I MEAN, NO, AND YOU'RE OUT OF QUESTIONS. THAT'LL BE FIFTY DOLLARS.
C'MON-- LET'S GET OUT OF HERE BEFORE GREG COMES THROUGH THE DOOR.
HE WAS RIGHT ABOUT YOU.
VERY FUNNY, STAN. ALEX, YOU CAN DROP THE EAR PIECE.
"ROSANNA" HIMSELF! HIYA, GREG!
DON'T WORRY, I'M NOT PLANNING ON STAYING LONG.
THAT'S NOT TRUE! I JUST READ YOUR CARDS!!
BASICALLY, I'M GONNA NEED A FEW MORE READINGS AND A PLACE TO STAY...
AND NO. I DON'T MIX BUSINESS AND FRIENDSHIP. YOU KNOW THAT.

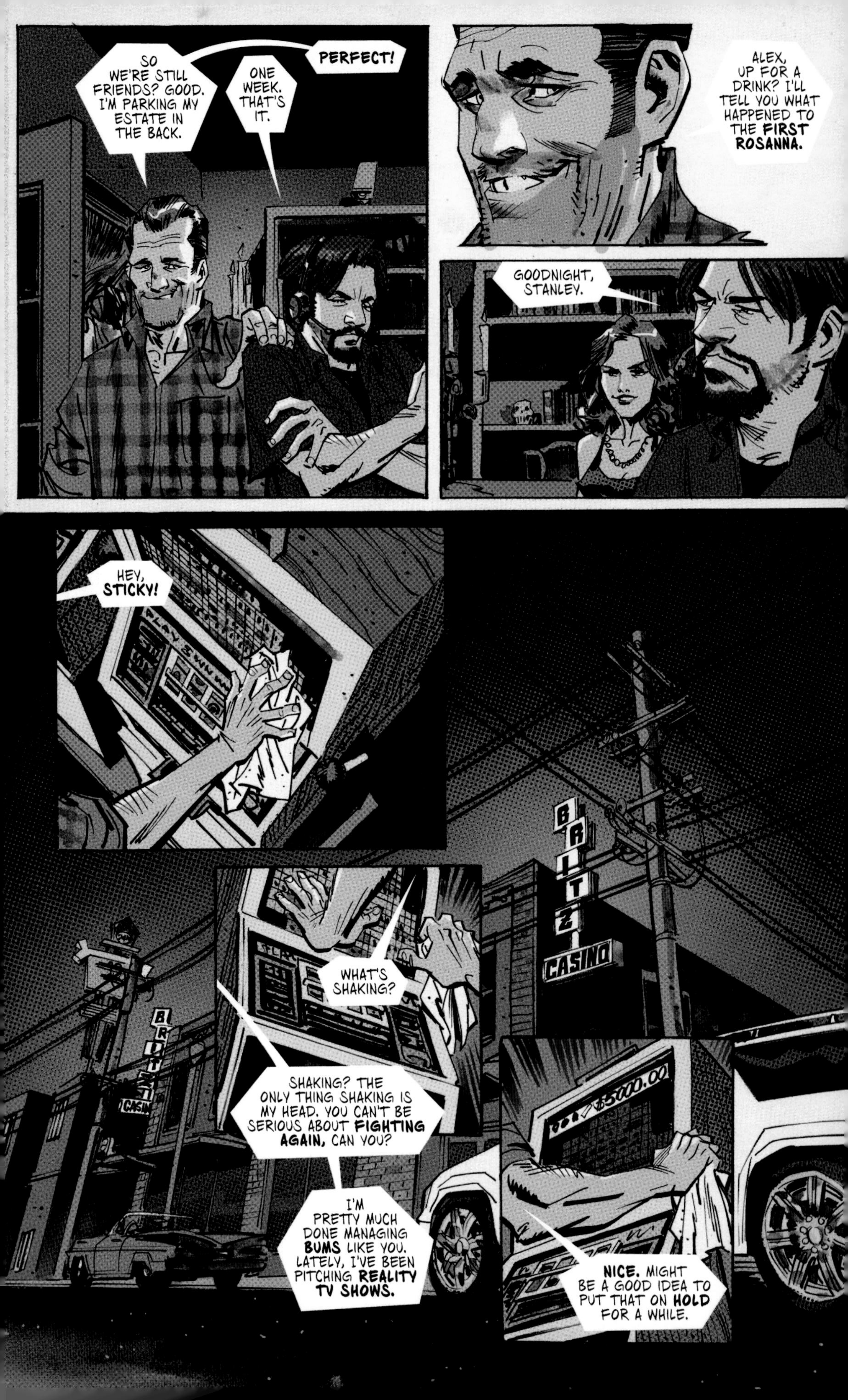
SO WE'RE STILL FRIENDS? GOOD. I'M PARKING MY ESTATE IN THE BACK.
ONE WEEK. THAT'S IT.
PERFECT!
ALEX, UP FOR A DRINK? I'LL TELL YOU WHAT HAPPENED TO THE FIRST ROSANNA.
GOODNIGHT, STANLEY.
HEY, STICKY!
BRITZ
CASINO
WHAT'S SHAKING?
SHAKING? THE ONLY THING SHAKING IS MY HEAD. YOU CAN'T BE SERIOUS ABOUT FIGHTING AGAIN, CAN YOU?
I'M PRETTY MUCH DONE MANAGING BUMS LIKE YOU. LATELY, I'VE BEEN PITCHING REALITY TV SHOWS.
$5000.00
NICE. MIGHT BE A GOOD IDEA TO PUT THAT ON HOLD FOR A WHILE.

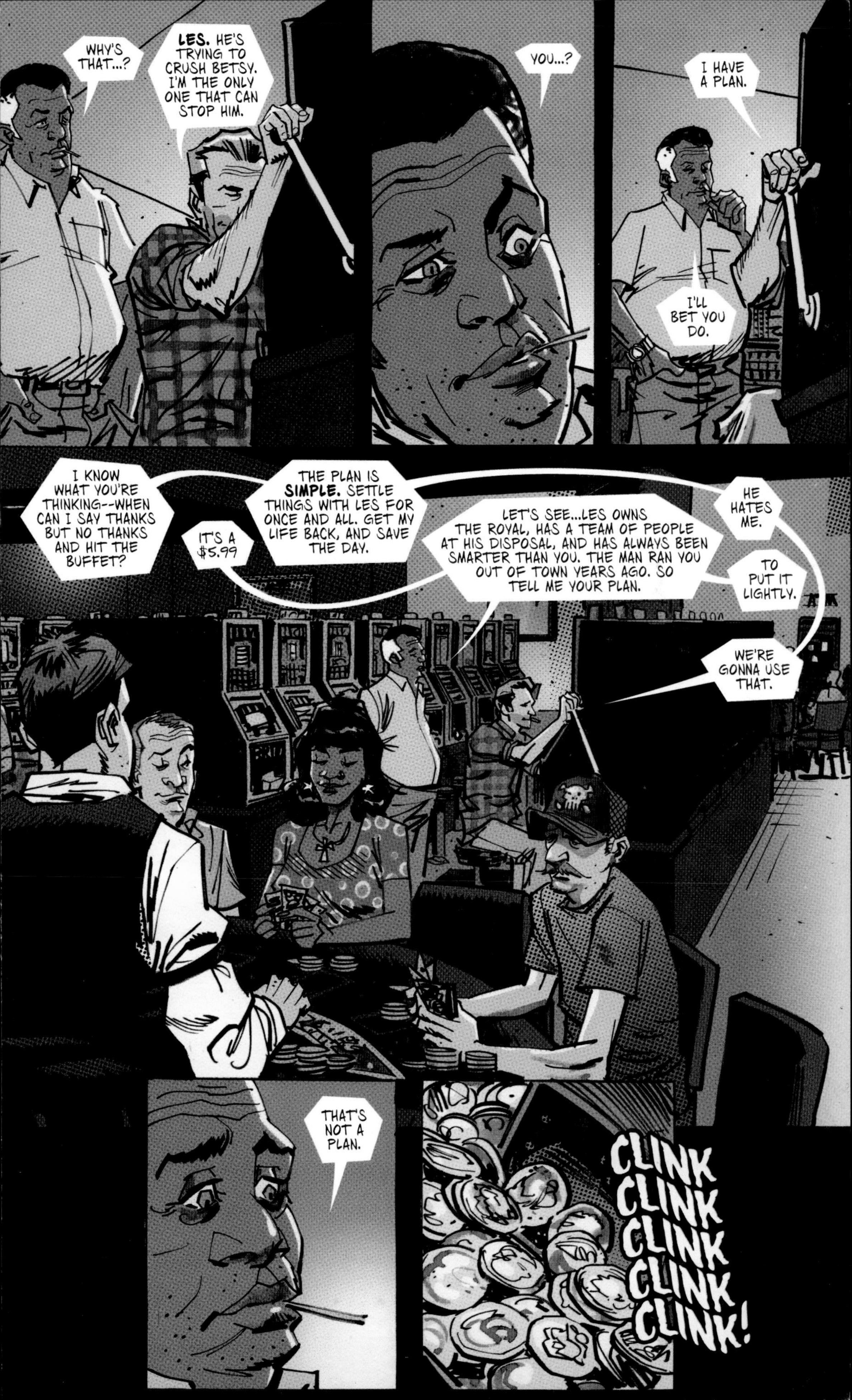
WHY'S THAT...?
LES. HE'S TRYING TO CRUSH BETSY. I'M THE ONLY ONE THAT CAN STOP HIM.
YOU...?
I HAVE A PLAN.
I'LL BET YOU DO.
I KNOW WHAT YOU'RE THINKING--WHEN CAN I SAY THANKS BUT NO THANKS AND HIT THE BUFFET?
IT'S A $5.99
THE PLAN IS SIMPLE. SETTLE THINGS WITH LES FOR ONCE AND ALL. GET MY LIFE BACK, AND SAVE THE DAY.
LET'S SEE...LES OWNS THE ROYAL, HAS A TEAM OF PEOPLE AT HIS DISPOSAL, AND HAS ALWAYS BEEN SMARTER THAN YOU. THE MAN RAN YOU OUT OF TOWN YEARS AGO. SO TELL ME YOUR PLAN.
HE HATES ME.
TO PUT IT LIGHTLY.
WE'RE GONNA USE THAT.
THAT'S NOT A PLAN.
CLINK CLINK CLINK CLINK CLINK!

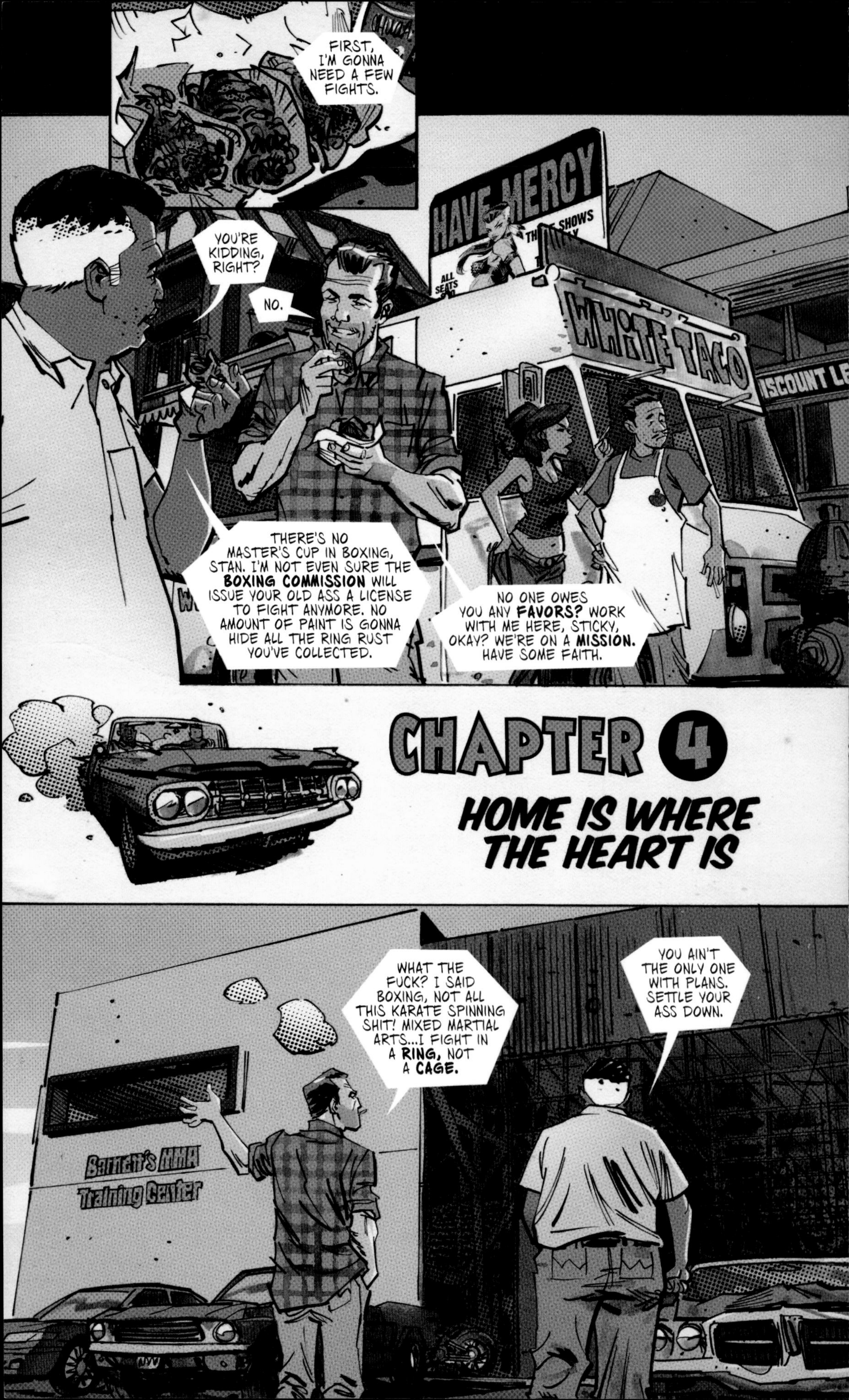
FIRST, I'M GONNA NEED A FEW FIGHTS.
HAVE MERCY
WHITE TACO
YOU'RE KIDDING, RIGHT?
NO.
THERE'S NO MASTER'S CUP IN BOXING, STAN. I'M NOT EVEN SURE THE BOXING COMMISSION WILL ISSUE YOUR OLD ASS A LICENSE TO FIGHT ANYMORE. NO AMOUNT OF PAINT IS GONNA HIDE ALL THE RING RUST YOU'VE COLLECTED.
NO ONE OWES YOU ANY FAVORS? WORK WITH ME HERE, STICKY, OKAY? WE'RE ON A MISSION. HAVE SOME FAITH.
CHAPTER 4
HOME IS WHERE THE HEART IS
Barnett's MMA Training Center
WHAT THE FUCK? I SAID BOXING, NOT ALL THIS KARATE SPINNING SHIT! MIXED MARTIAL ARTS...I FIGHT IN A RING, NOT A CAGE.
YOU AIN'T THE ONLY ONE WITH PLANS. SETTLE YOUR ASS DOWN.

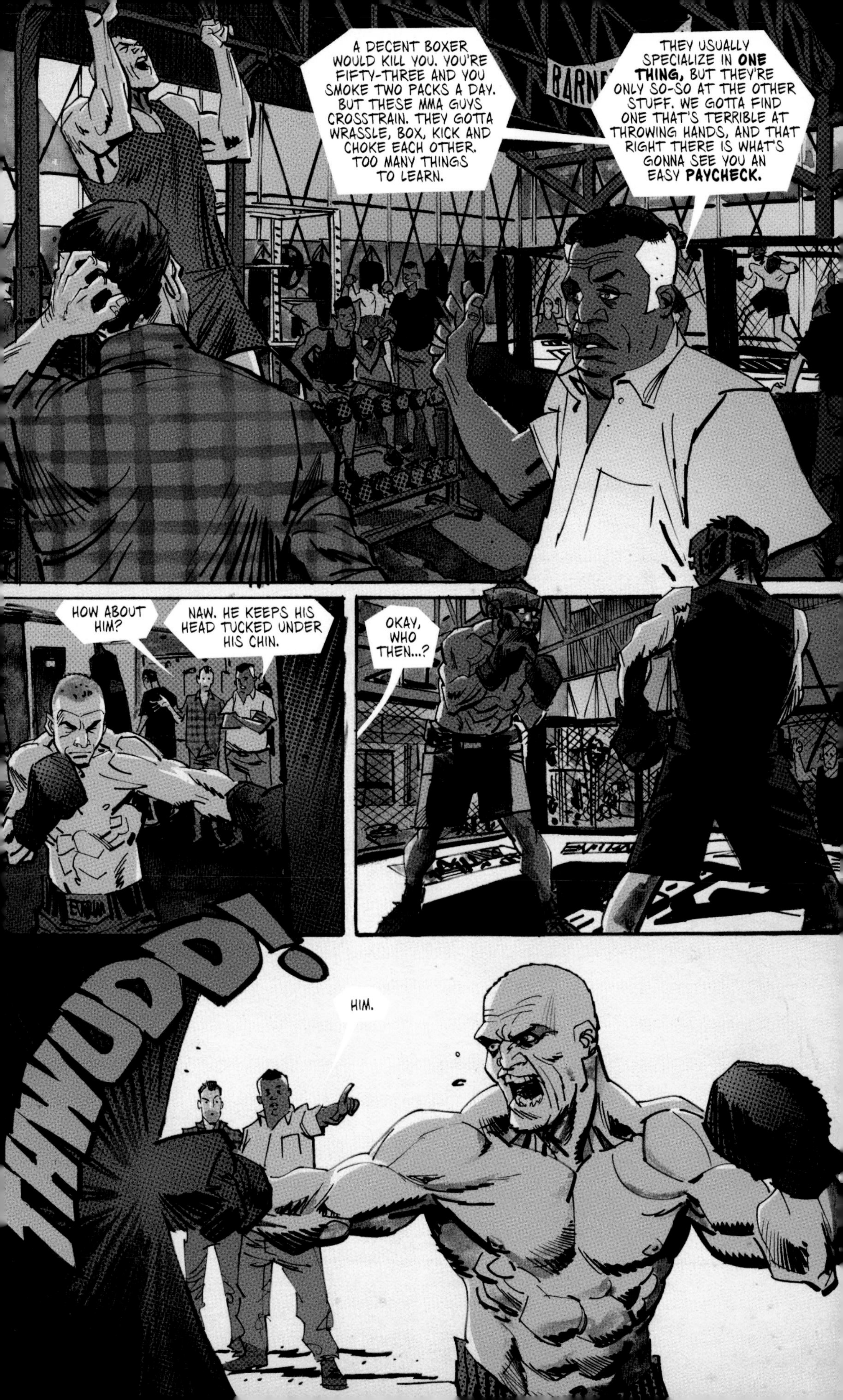
A DECENT BOXER WOULD KILL YOU. YOU'RE FIFTY-THREE AND YOU SMOKE TWO PACKS A DAY. BUT THESE MMA GUYS CROSSTRAIN. THEY GOTTA WRASSLE, BOX, KICK AND CHOKE EACH OTHER. TOO MANY THINGS TO LEARN.
THEY USUALLY SPECIALIZE IN **ONE THING,** BUT THEY'RE ONLY SO-SO AT THE OTHER STUFF. WE GOTTA FIND ONE THAT'S TERRIBLE AT THROWING HANDS, AND THAT RIGHT THERE IS WHAT'S GONNA SEE YOU AN EASY **PAYCHECK.**
HOW ABOUT HIM?
NAW. HE KEEPS HIS HEAD TUCKED UNDER HIS CHIN.
OKAY, WHO THEN...?
THWUDD!
HIM.

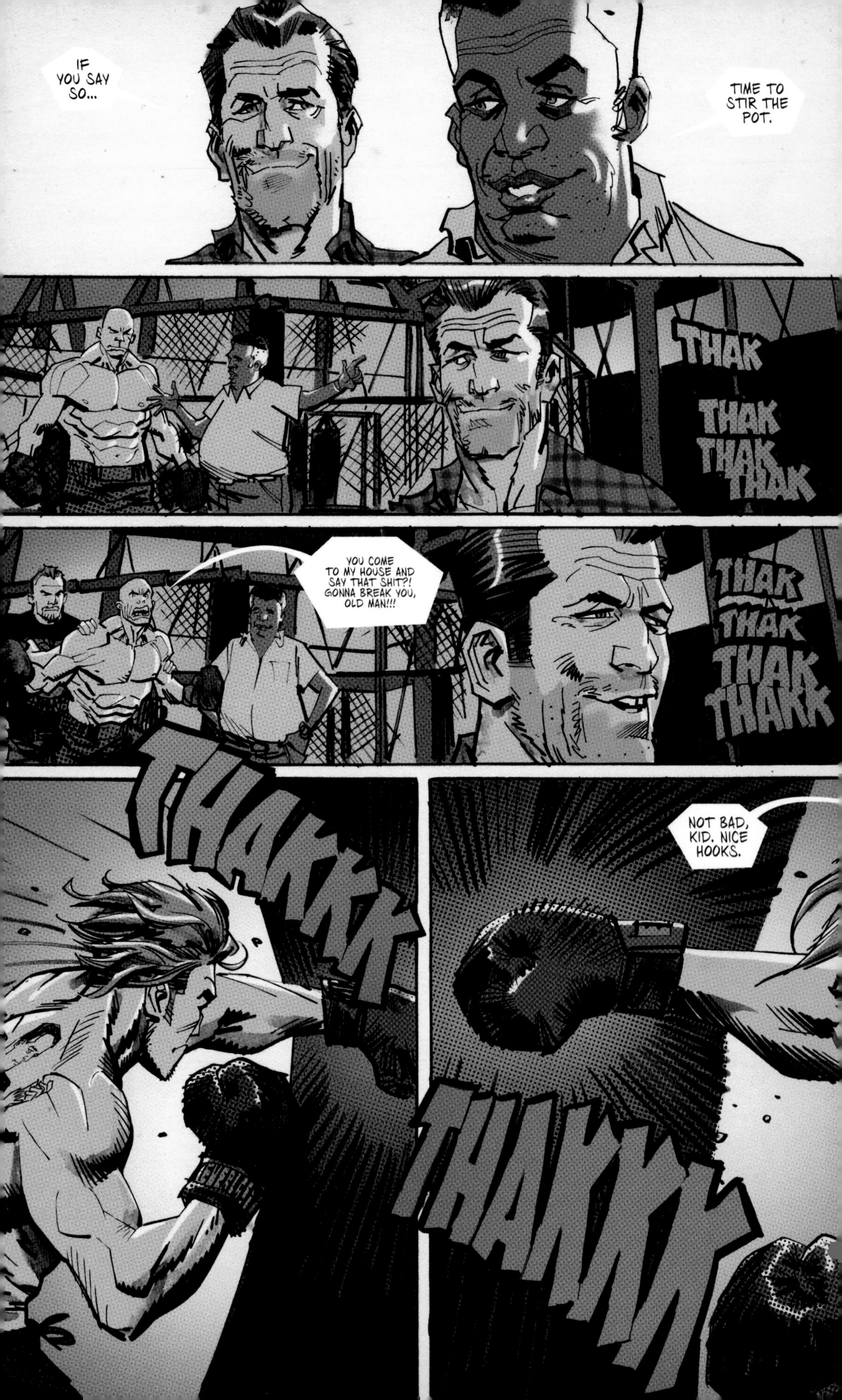

IF YOU SAY SO...
TIME TO STIR THE POT.
THAK
THAK
THAK
THAK
YOU COME TO MY HOUSE AND SAY THAT SHIT?! GONNA BREAK YOU, OLD MAN!!!
THAK
THAK
THAK
THAKK
THAKKK
NOT BAD, KID. NICE HOOKS.
THAKKK

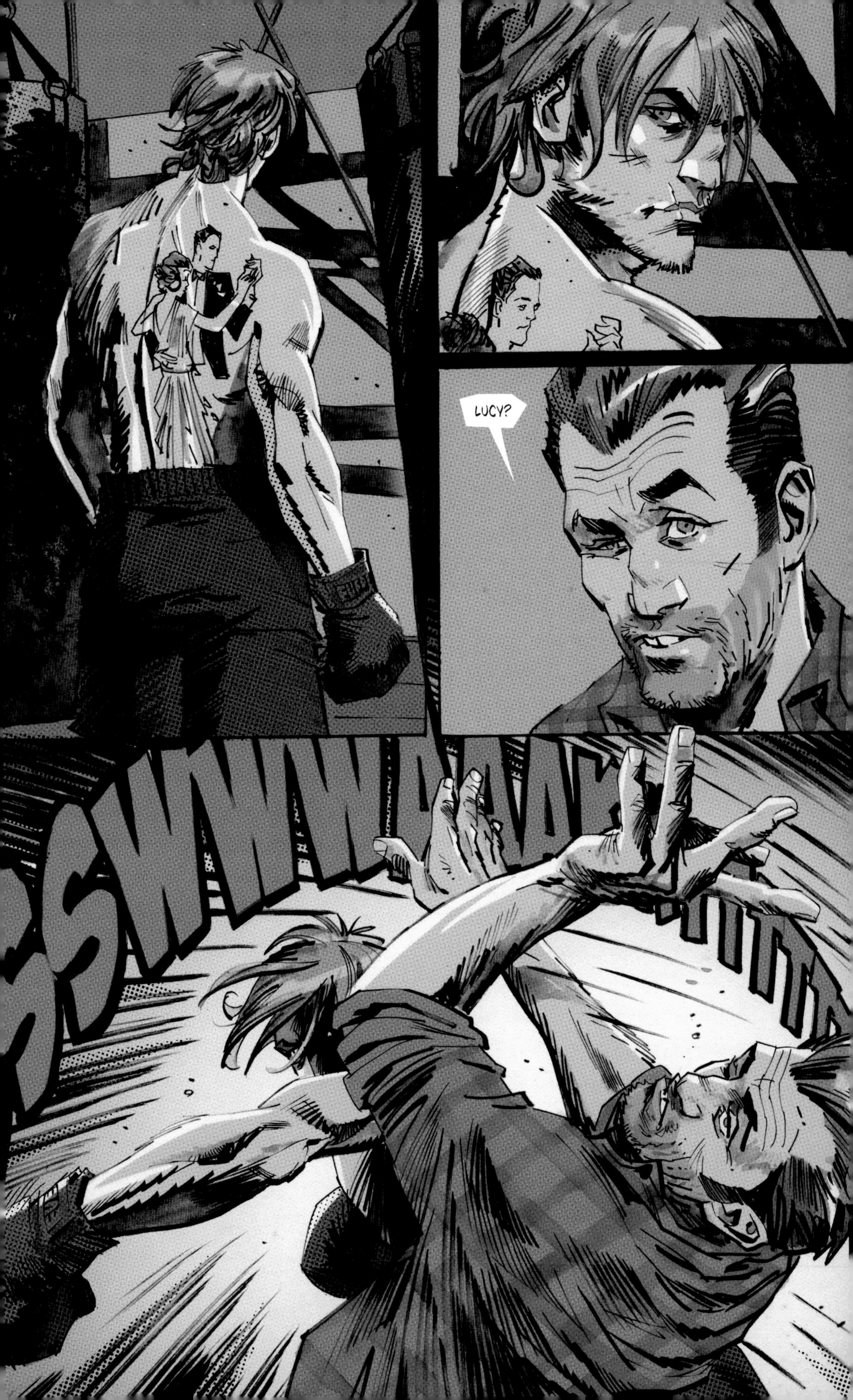
LUCY?

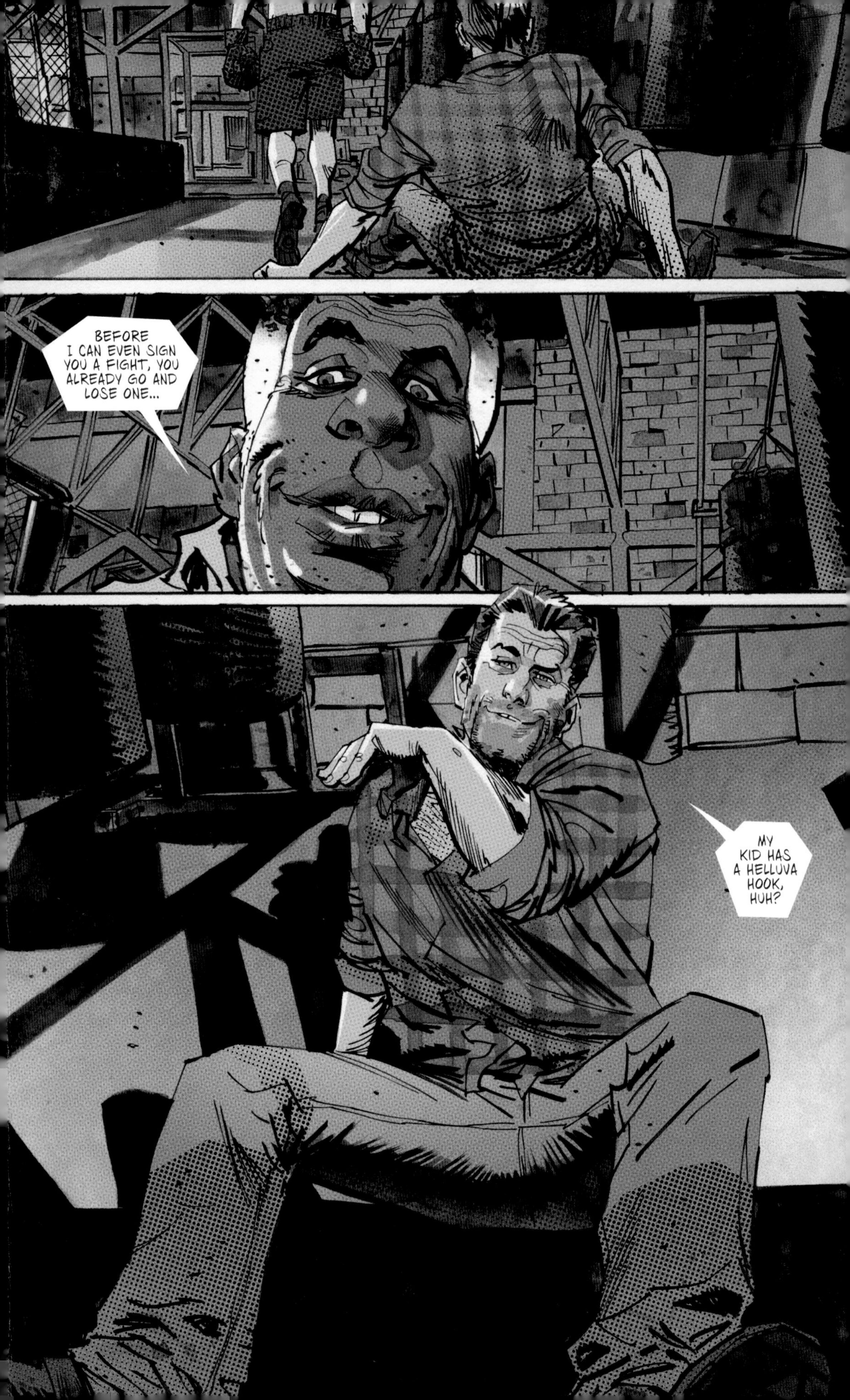
BEFORE I CAN EVEN SIGN YOU A FIGHT, YOU ALREADY GO AND LOSE ONE...
MY KID HAS A HELLUVA HOOK, HUH?

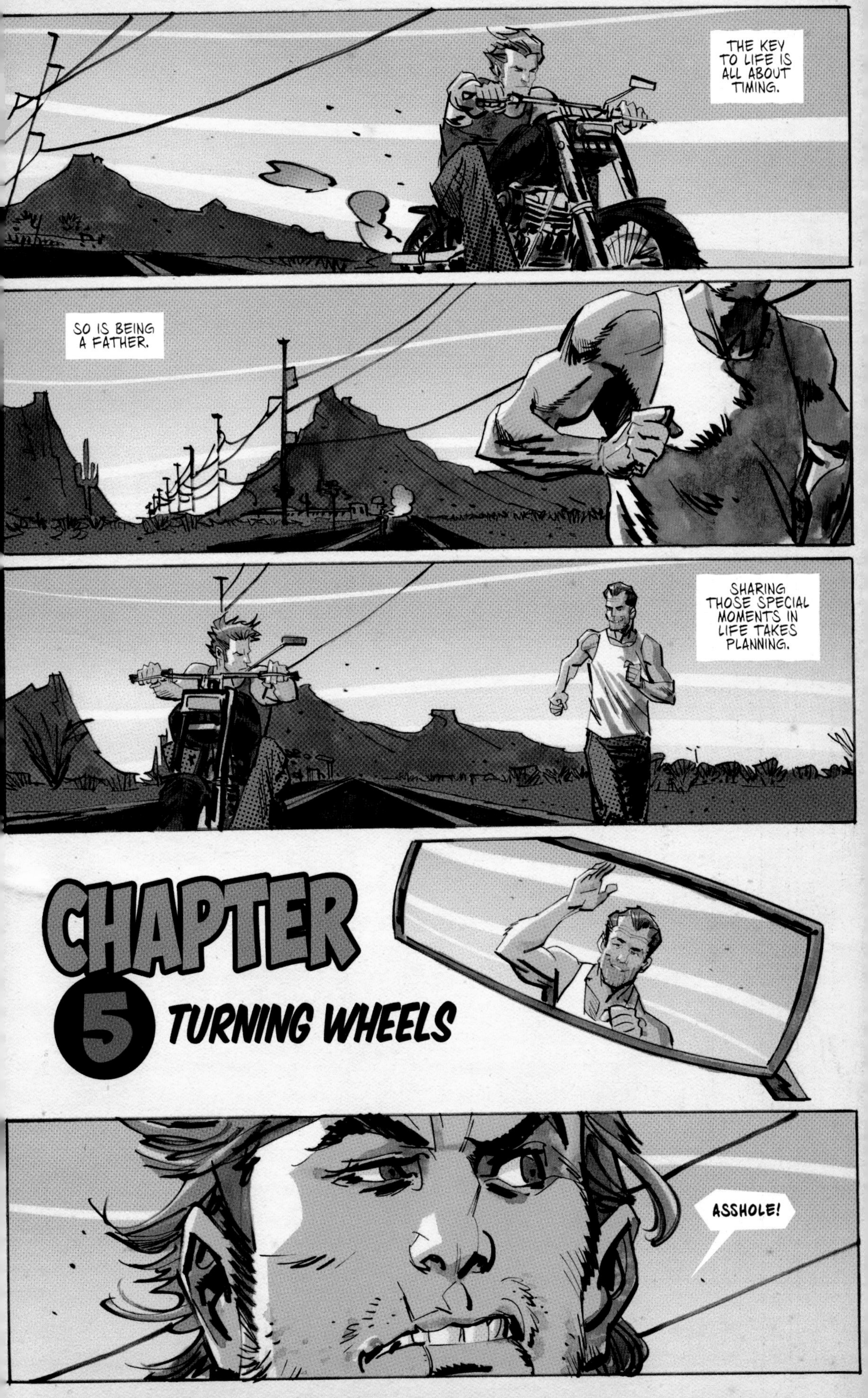

THE KEY TO LIFE IS ALL ABOUT TIMING.
SO IS BEING A FATHER.
SHARING THOSE SPECIAL MOMENTS IN LIFE TAKES PLANNING.
CHAPTER
5 TURNING WHEELS
ASSHOLE!

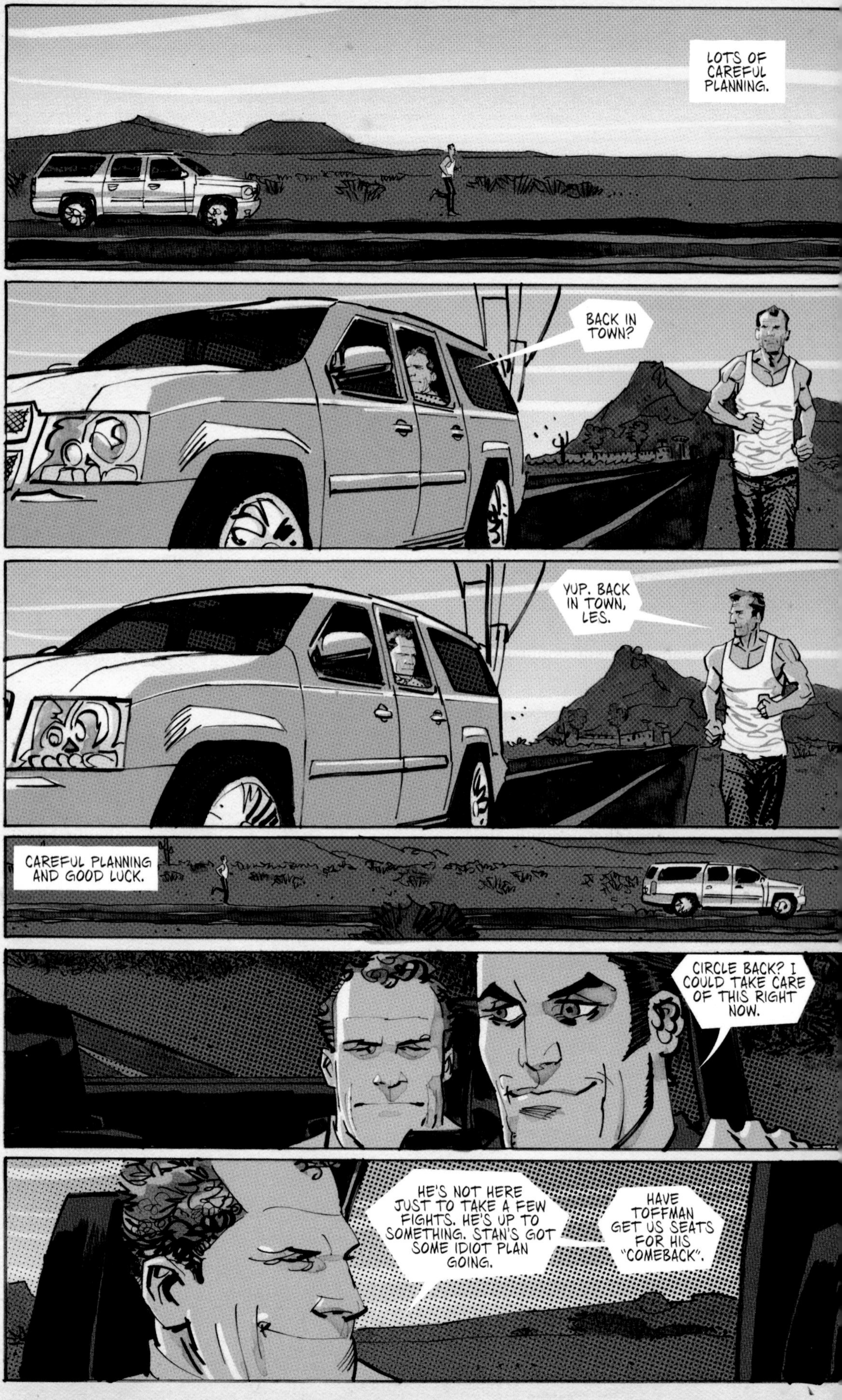
LOTS OF CAREFUL PLANNING.
BACK IN TOWN?
YUP. BACK IN TOWN, LES.
CAREFUL PLANNING AND GOOD LUCK.
CIRCLE BACK? I COULD TAKE CARE OF THIS RIGHT NOW.
HE'S NOT HERE JUST TO TAKE A FEW FIGHTS. HE'S UP TO SOMETHING. STAN'S GOT SOME IDIOT PLAN GOING.
HAVE TOFFMAN GET US SEATS FOR HIS "COMEBACK".

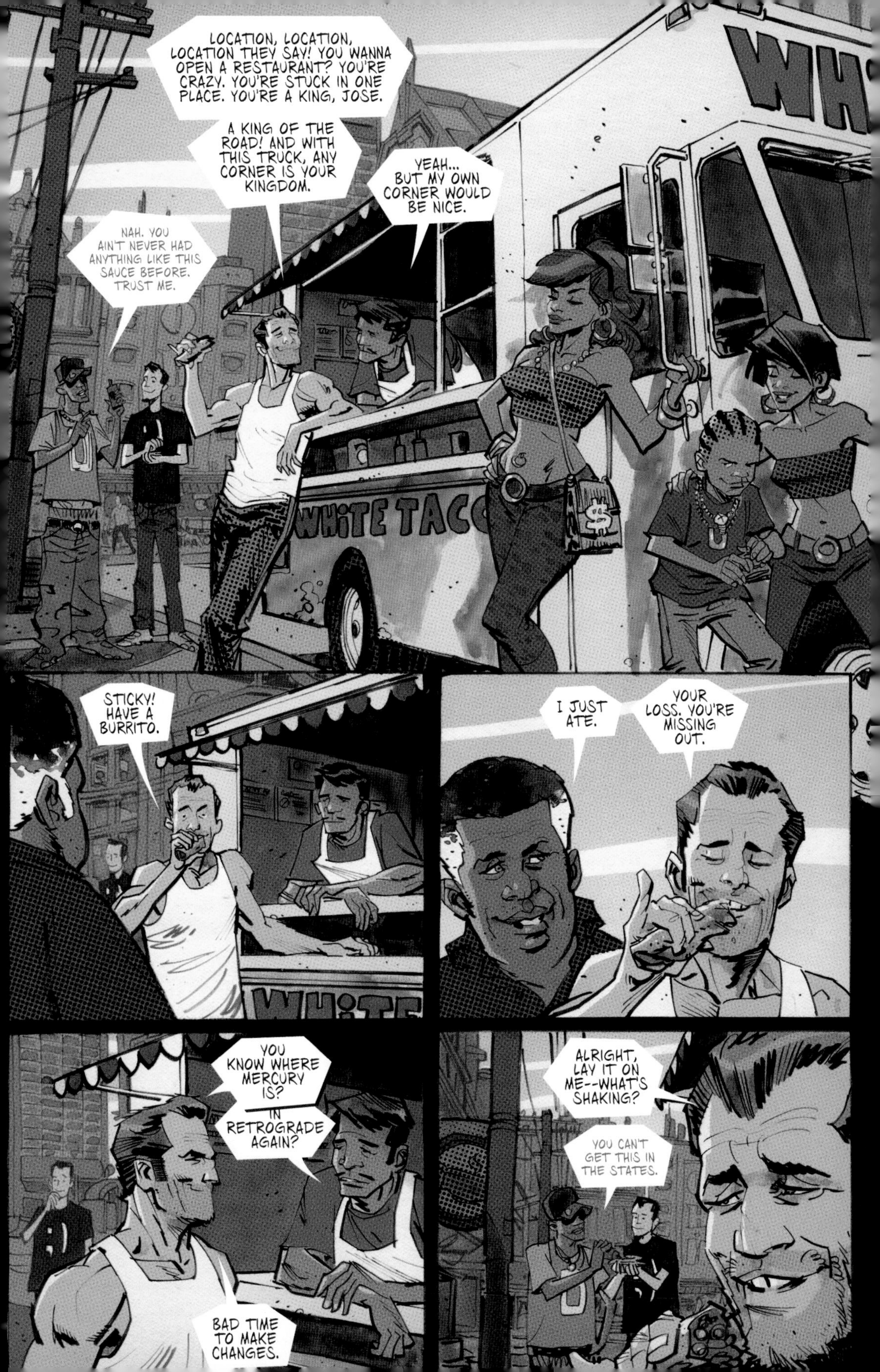
LOCATION, LOCATION, LOCATION THEY SAY! YOU WANNA OPEN A RESTAURANT? YOU'RE CRAZY. YOU'RE STUCK IN ONE PLACE. YOU'RE A KING, JOSE.
A KING OF THE ROAD! AND WITH THIS TRUCK, ANY CORNER IS YOUR KINGDOM.
YEAH... BUT MY OWN CORNER WOULD BE NICE.
NAH. YOU AIN'T NEVER HAD ANYTHING LIKE THIS SAUCE BEFORE. TRUST ME.
WHITE TACO
STICKY! HAVE A BURRITO.
I JUST ATE.
YOUR LOSS. YOU'RE MISSING OUT.
YOU KNOW WHERE MERCURY IS?
IN RETROGRADE AGAIN?
BAD TIME TO MAKE CHANGES.
ALRIGHT, LAY IT ON ME--WHAT'S SHAKING?
YOU CAN'T GET THIS IN THE STATES.

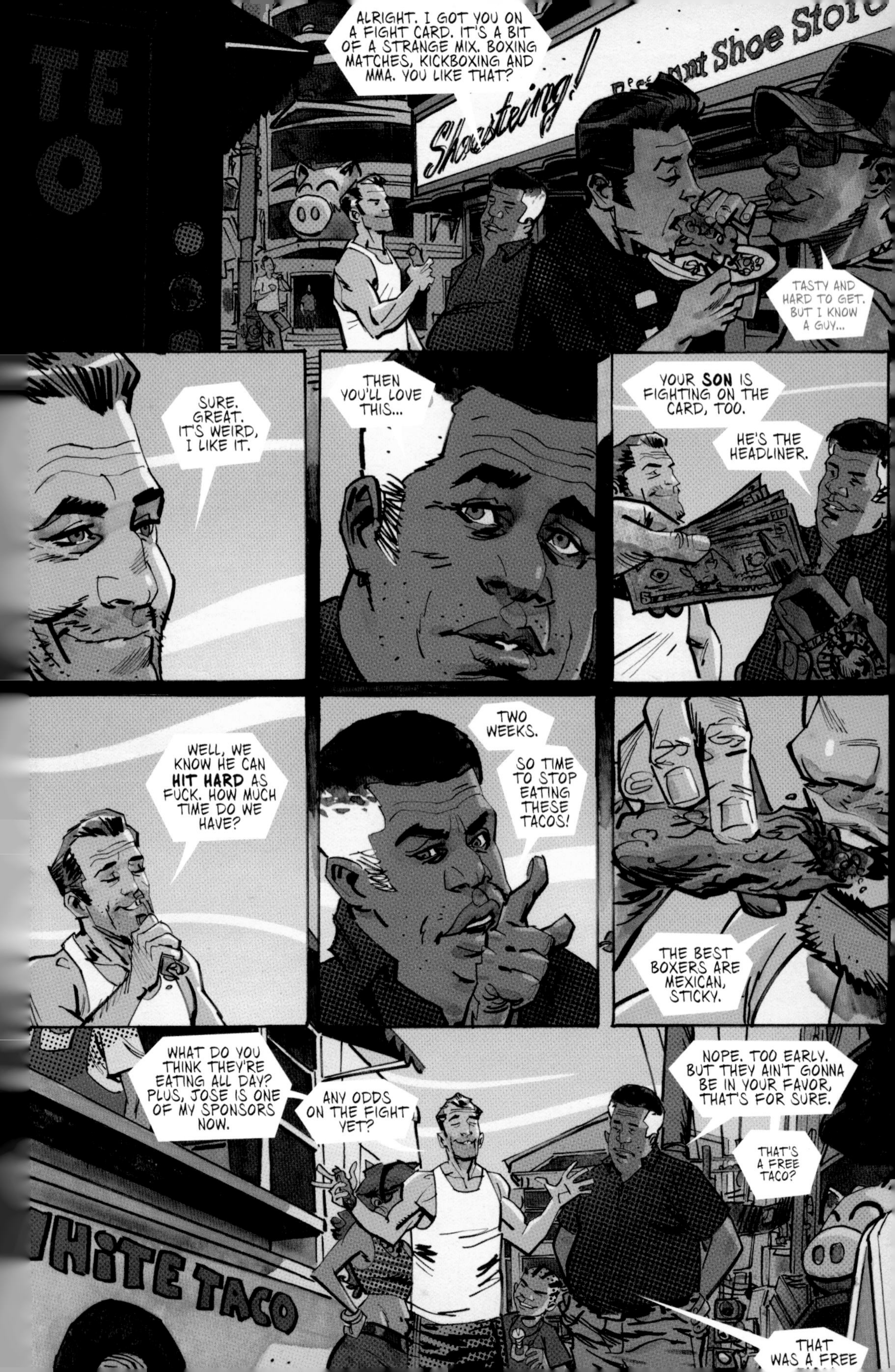
ALRIGHT. I GOT YOU ON A FIGHT CARD. IT'S A BIT OF A STRANGE MIX. BOXING MATCHES, KICKBOXING AND MMA. YOU LIKE THAT?
Shoe Store
Shoeshine!
TASTY AND HARD TO GET. BUT I KNOW A GUY...
SURE. GREAT. IT'S WEIRD, I LIKE IT.
THEN YOU'LL LOVE THIS...
YOUR **SON** IS FIGHTING ON THE CARD, TOO.
HE'S THE HEADLINER.
WELL, WE KNOW HE CAN **HIT HARD** AS FUCK. HOW MUCH TIME DO WE HAVE?
TWO WEEKS.
SO TIME TO STOP EATING THESE TACOS!
THE BEST BOXERS ARE MEXICAN, STICKY.
WHAT DO YOU THINK THEY'RE EATING ALL DAY? PLUS, JOSE IS ONE OF MY SPONSORS NOW.
ANY ODDS ON THE FIGHT YET?
NOPE. TOO EARLY. BUT THEY AIN'T GONNA BE IN YOUR FAVOR, THAT'S FOR SURE.
THAT'S A FREE TACO?
WHITE TACO
THAT WAS A FREE

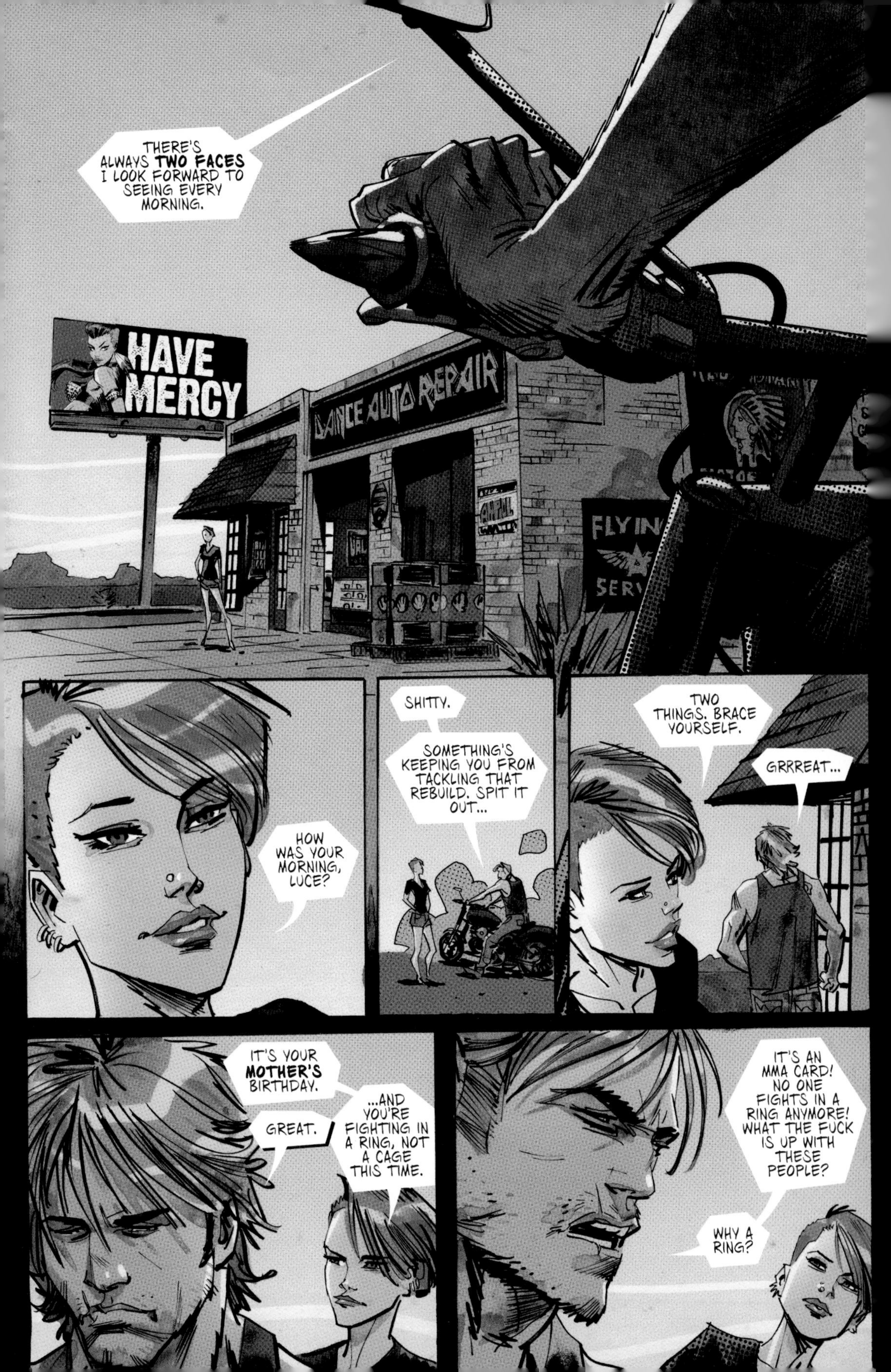

THERE'S ALWAYS **TWO FACES** I LOOK FORWARD TO SEEING EVERY MORNING.
HAVE MERCY
DANCE AUTO REPAIR
FLYING
SERV
HOW WAS YOUR MORNING, LUCE?
SHITTY.
SOMETHING'S KEEPING YOU FROM TACKLING THAT REBUILD. SPIT IT OUT...
TWO THINGS. BRACE YOURSELF.
GRRREAT...
IT'S YOUR **MOTHER'S** BIRTHDAY.
GREAT.
...AND YOU'RE FIGHTING IN A RING, NOT A CAGE THIS TIME.
WHY A RING?
IT'S AN MMA CARD! NO ONE FIGHTS IN A RING ANYMORE! WHAT THE FUCK IS UP WITH THESE PEOPLE?

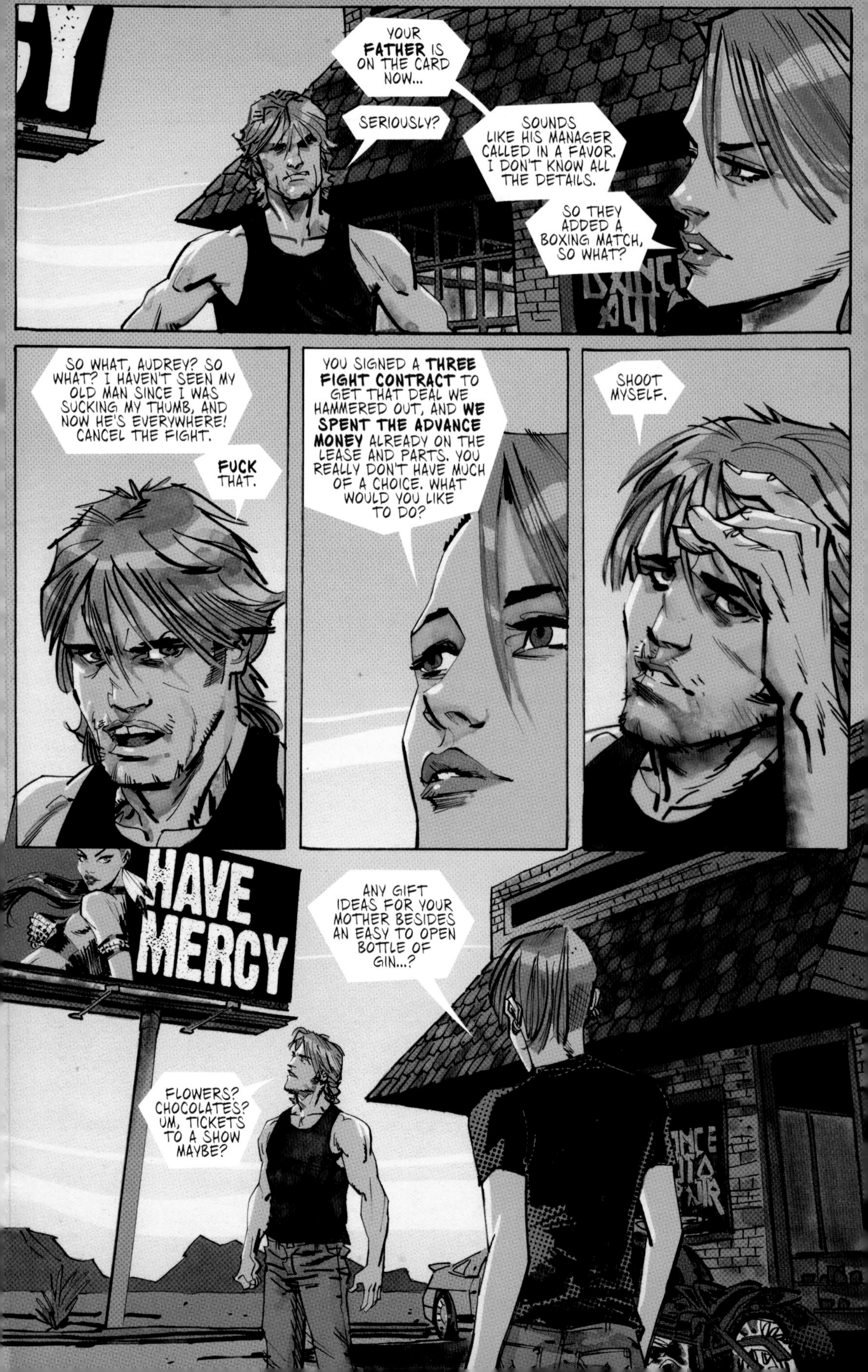
YOUR FATHER IS ON THE CARD NOW...
SERIOUSLY?
SOUNDS LIKE HIS MANAGER CALLED IN A FAVOR. I DON'T KNOW ALL THE DETAILS.
SO THEY ADDED A BOXING MATCH, SO WHAT?
SO WHAT, AUDREY? SO WHAT? I HAVEN'T SEEN MY OLD MAN SINCE I WAS SUCKING MY THUMB, AND NOW HE'S EVERYWHERE! CANCEL THE FIGHT.
FUCK THAT.
YOU SIGNED A THREE FIGHT CONTRACT TO GET THAT DEAL WE HAMMERED OUT, AND WE SPENT THE ADVANCE MONEY ALREADY ON THE LEASE AND PARTS. YOU REALLY DON'T HAVE MUCH OF A CHOICE. WHAT WOULD YOU LIKE TO DO?
SHOOT MYSELF.
HAVE MERCY
ANY GIFT IDEAS FOR YOUR MOTHER BESIDES AN EASY TO OPEN BOTTLE OF GIN...?
FLOWERS? CHOCOLATES? UM, TICKETS TO A SHOW MAYBE?

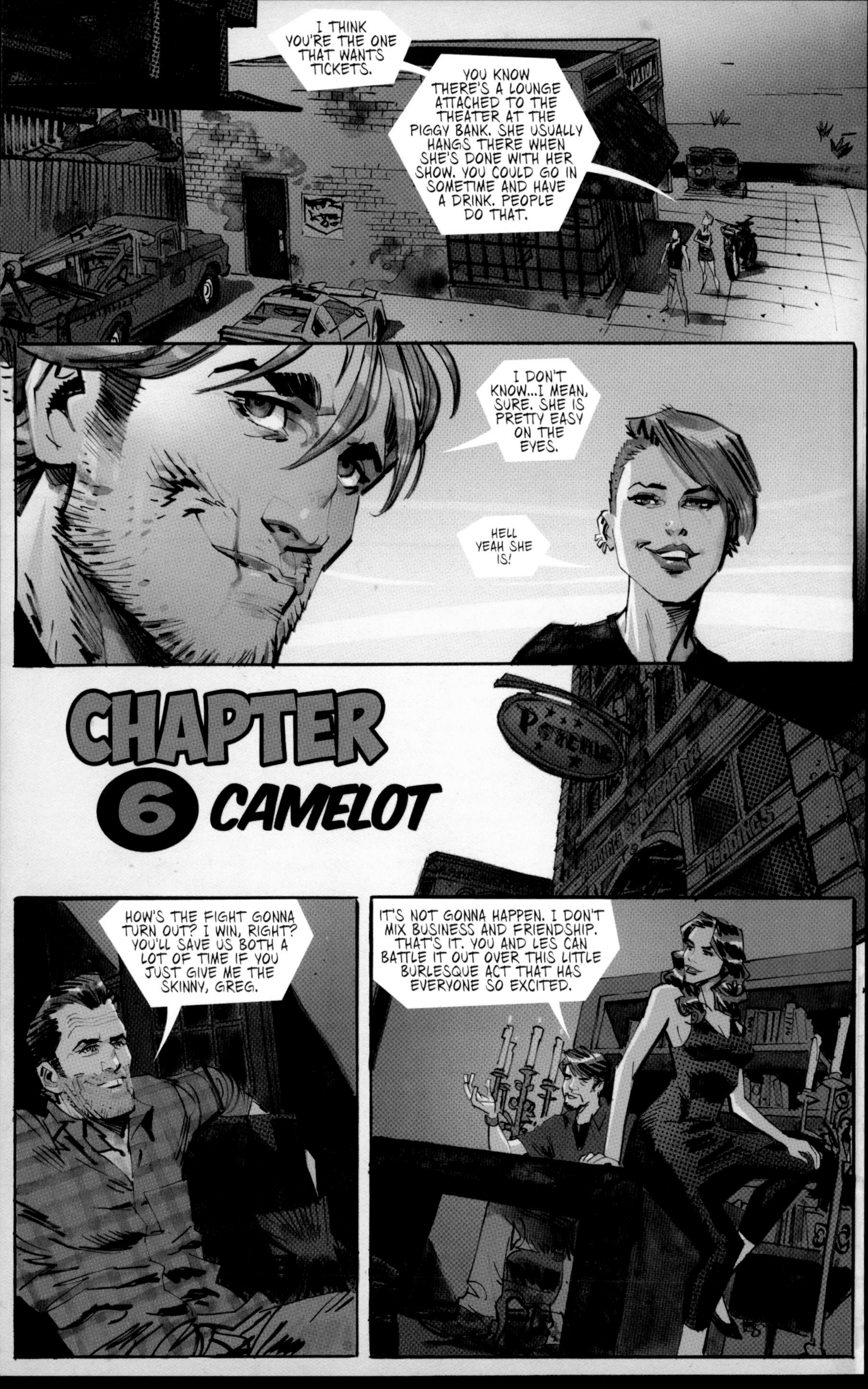
I THINK YOU'RE THE ONE THAT WANTS TICKETS.
YOU KNOW THERE'S A LOUNGE ATTACHED TO THE THEATER AT THE PIGGY BANK. SHE USUALLY HANGS THERE WHEN SHE'S DONE WITH HER SHOW. YOU COULD GO IN SOMETIME AND HAVE A DRINK. PEOPLE DO THAT.
I DON'T KNOW...I MEAN, SURE. SHE IS PRETTY EASY ON THE EYES.
HELL YEAH SHE IS!
CHAPTER
6 CAMELOT
HOW'S THE FIGHT GONNA TURN OUT? I WIN, RIGHT? YOU'LL SAVE US BOTH A LOT OF TIME IF YOU JUST GIVE ME THE SKINNY, GREG.
IT'S NOT GONNA HAPPEN. I DON'T MIX BUSINESS AND FRIENDSHIP. THAT'S IT. YOU AND LES CAN BATTLE IT OUT OVER THIS LITTLE BURLESQUE ACT THAT HAS EVERYONE SO EXCITED.

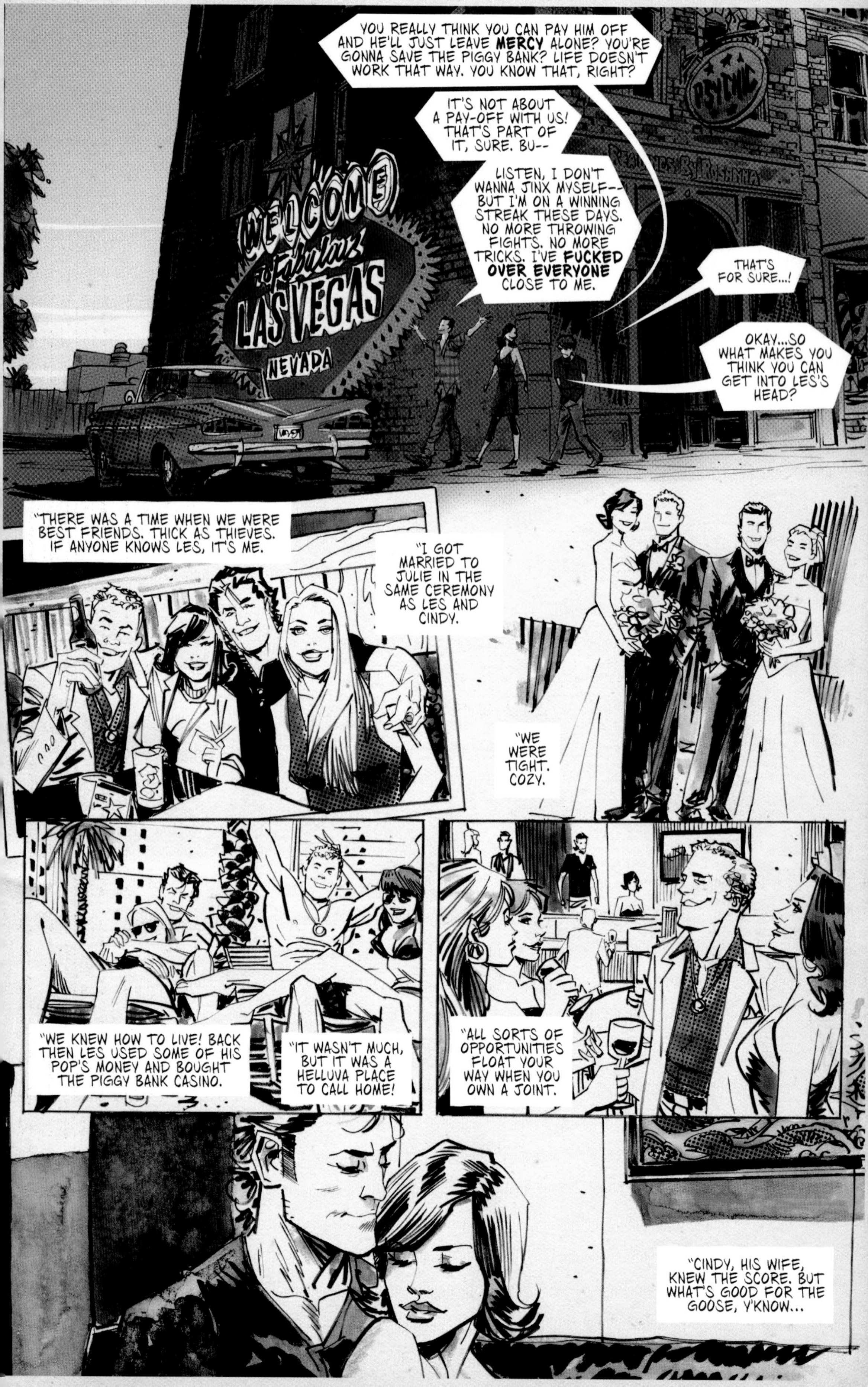

YOU REALLY THINK YOU CAN PAY HIM OFF AND HE'LL JUST LEAVE **MERCY** ALONE? YOU'RE GONNA SAVE THE PIGGY BANK? LIFE DOESN'T WORK THAT WAY. YOU KNOW THAT, RIGHT?
IT'S NOT ABOUT A PAY-OFF WITH US! THAT'S PART OF IT, SURE. BU--
LISTEN, I DON'T WANNA JINX MYSELF-- BUT I'M ON A WINNING STREAK THESE DAYS. NO MORE THROWING FIGHTS. NO MORE TRICKS. I'VE **FUCKED OVER EVERYONE** CLOSE TO ME.
THAT'S FOR SURE...!
OKAY...SO WHAT MAKES YOU THINK YOU CAN GET INTO LES'S HEAD?
PSYCHIC
WELCOME to Fabulous LAS VEGAS NEVADA
"THERE WAS A TIME WHEN WE WERE BEST FRIENDS. THICK AS THIEVES. IF ANYONE KNOWS LES, IT'S ME.
"I GOT MARRIED TO JULIE IN THE SAME CEREMONY AS LES AND CINDY.
"WE WERE TIGHT. COZY.
"WE KNEW HOW TO LIVE! BACK THEN LES USED SOME OF HIS POP'S MONEY AND BOUGHT THE PIGGY BANK CASINO.
"IT WASN'T MUCH, BUT IT WAS A HELLUVA PLACE TO CALL HOME!
"ALL SORTS OF OPPORTUNITIES FLOAT YOUR WAY WHEN YOU OWN A JOINT.
"CINDY, HIS WIFE, KNEW THE SCORE. BUT WHAT'S GOOD FOR THE GOOSE, Y'KNOW...

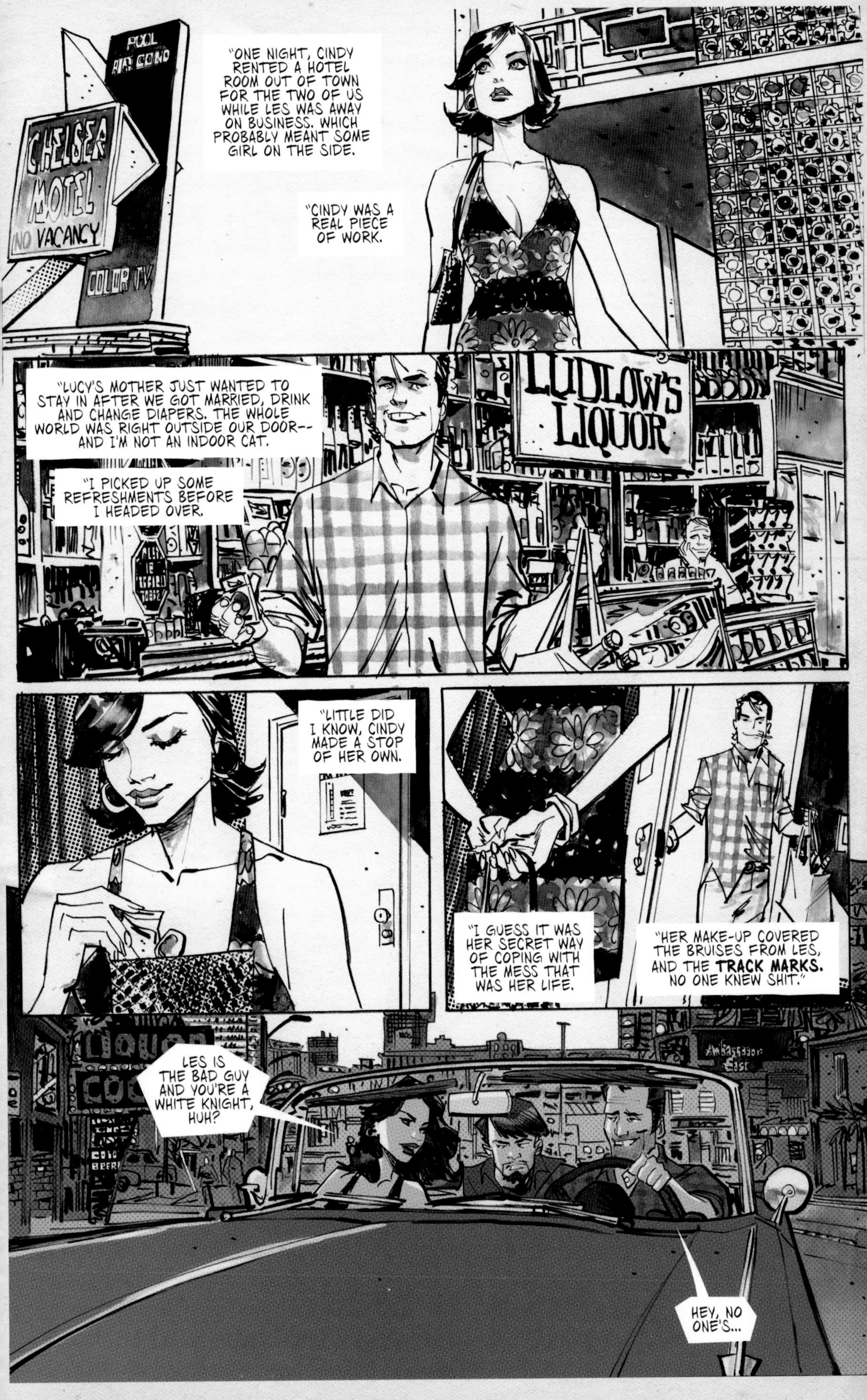

"ONE NIGHT, CINDY RENTED A HOTEL ROOM OUT OF TOWN FOR THE TWO OF US WHILE LES WAS AWAY ON BUSINESS. WHICH PROBABLY MEANT SOME GIRL ON THE SIDE.
"CINDY WAS A REAL PIECE OF WORK.
POOL
AIR COND
CHELSEA MOTEL
NO VACANCY
COLOR TV
"LUCY'S MOTHER JUST WANTED TO STAY IN AFTER WE GOT MARRIED, DRINK AND CHANGE DIAPERS. THE WHOLE WORLD WAS RIGHT OUTSIDE OUR DOOR--AND I'M NOT AN INDOOR CAT.
"I PICKED UP SOME REFRESHMENTS BEFORE I HEADED OVER.
LUDLOW'S LIQUOR
"LITTLE DID I KNOW, CINDY MADE A STOP OF HER OWN.
"I GUESS IT WAS HER SECRET WAY OF COPING WITH THE MESS THAT WAS HER LIFE.
"HER MAKE-UP COVERED THE BRUISES FROM LES, AND THE **TRACK MARKS.** NO ONE KNEW SHIT."
LES IS THE BAD GUY AND YOU'RE A WHITE KNIGHT, HUH?
HEY, NO ONE'S...

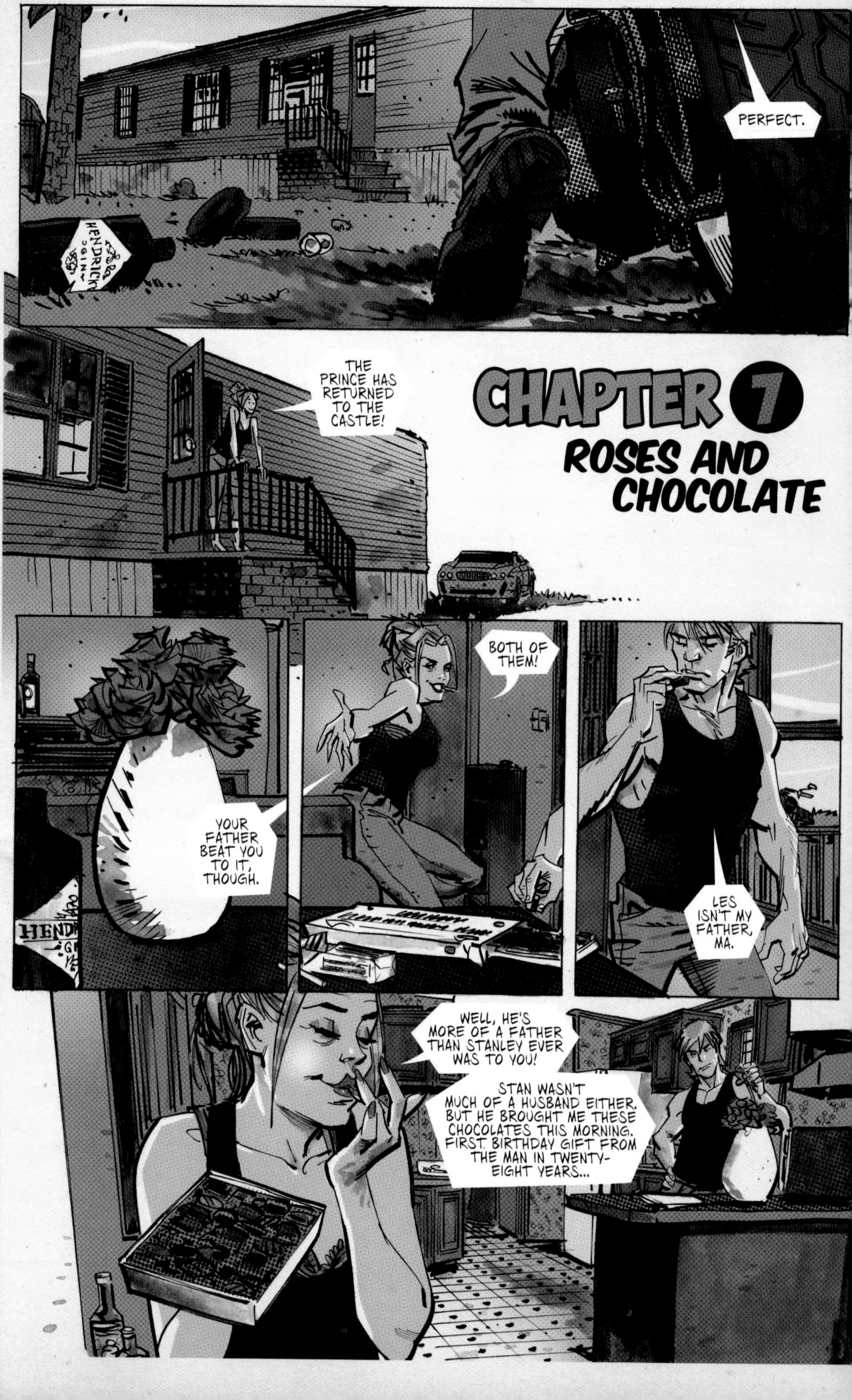
PERFECT.
HENDRICK'S GIN
THE PRINCE HAS RETURNED TO THE CASTLE!
CHAPTER 7
ROSES AND CHOCOLATE
YOUR FATHER BEAT YOU TO IT, THOUGH.
BOTH OF THEM!
LES ISN'T MY FATHER, MA.
WELL, HE'S MORE OF A FATHER THAN STANLEY EVER WAS TO YOU!
STAN WASN'T MUCH OF A HUSBAND EITHER. BUT HE BROUGHT ME THESE CHOCOLATES THIS MORNING. FIRST BIRTHDAY GIFT FROM THE MAN IN TWENTY-EIGHT YEARS...

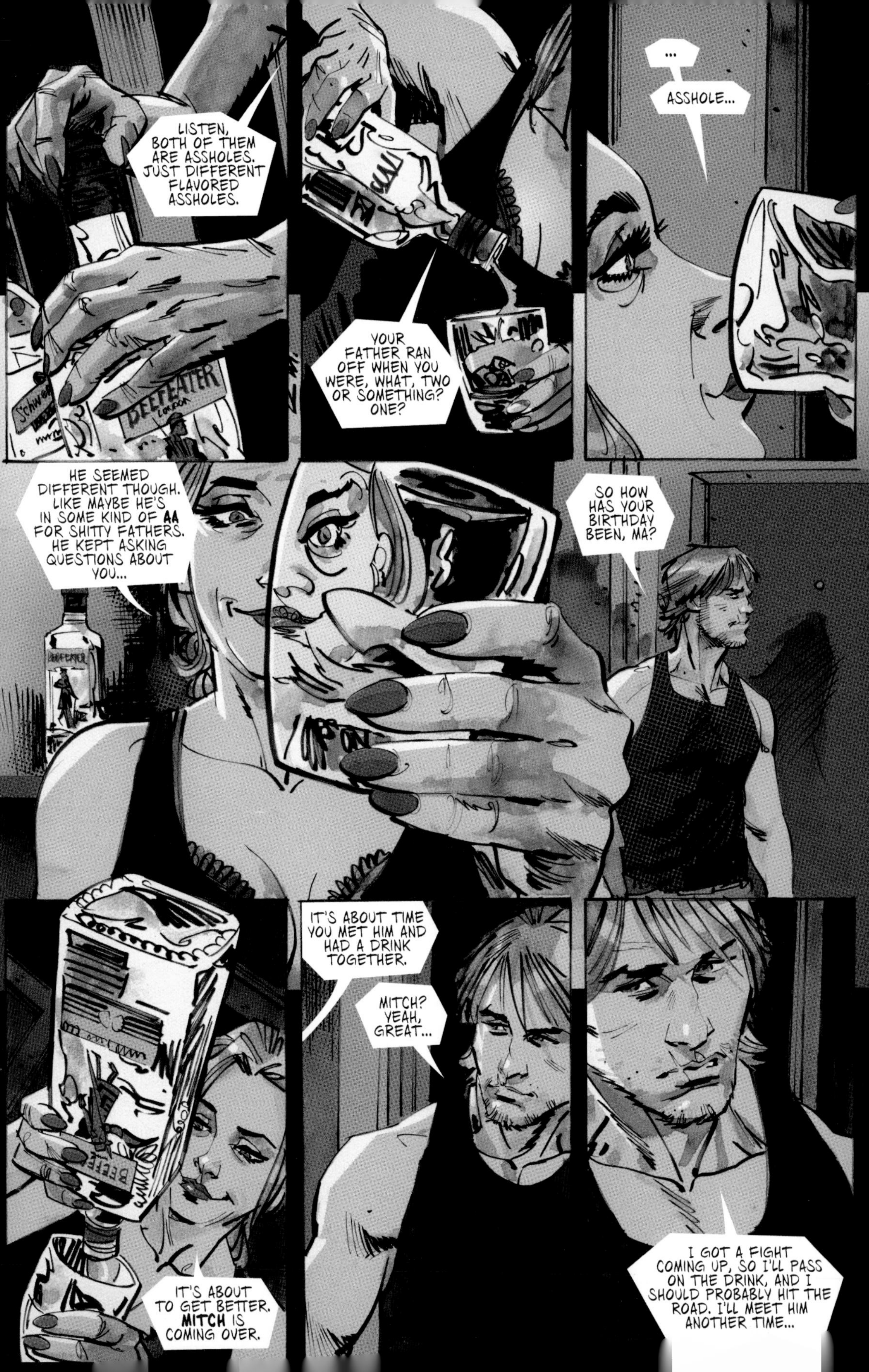
LISTEN, BOTH OF THEM ARE ASSHOLES. JUST DIFFERENT FLAVORED ASSHOLES.
BEEFEATER
YOUR FATHER RAN OFF WHEN YOU WERE, WHAT, TWO OR SOMETHING? ONE?
...
ASSHOLE...
HE SEEMED DIFFERENT THOUGH. LIKE MAYBE HE'S IN SOME KIND OF **AA** FOR SHITTY FATHERS. HE KEPT ASKING QUESTIONS ABOUT YOU...
SO HOW HAS YOUR BIRTHDAY BEEN, MA?
IT'S ABOUT TO GET BETTER. **MITCH** IS COMING OVER.
IT'S ABOUT TIME YOU MET HIM AND HAD A DRINK TOGETHER.
MITCH? YEAH, GREAT...
I GOT A FIGHT COMING UP, SO I'LL PASS ON THE DRINK, AND I SHOULD PROBABLY HIT THE ROAD. I'LL MEET HIM ANOTHER TIME...

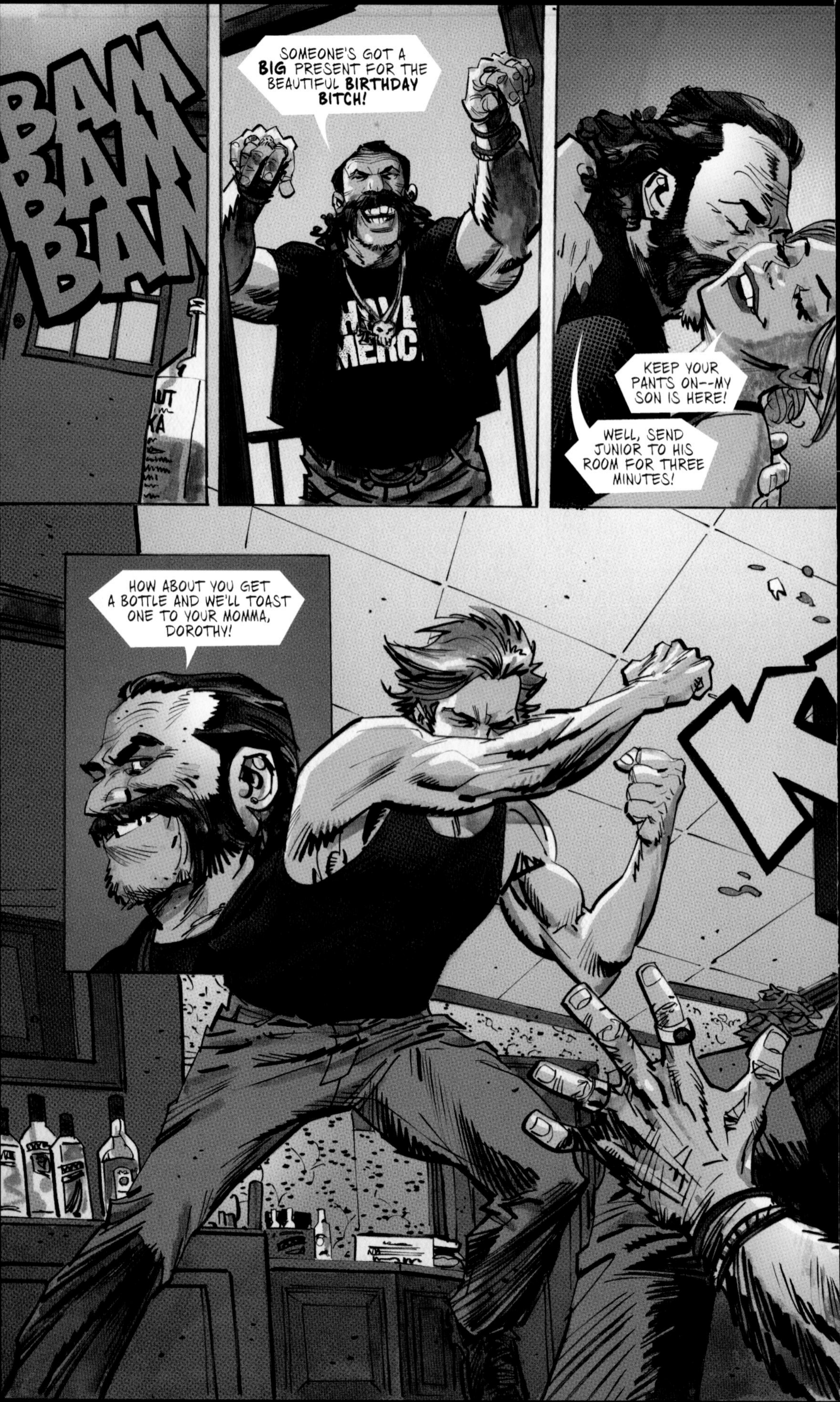
BAM BAM
SOMEONE'S GOT A **BIG** PRESENT FOR THE BEAUTIFUL **BIRTHDAY BITCH!**
KEEP YOUR PANTS ON--MY SON IS HERE!
WELL, SEND JUNIOR TO HIS ROOM FOR THREE MINUTES!
HOW ABOUT YOU GET A BOTTLE AND WE'LL TOAST ONE TO YOUR MOMMA, DOROTHY!

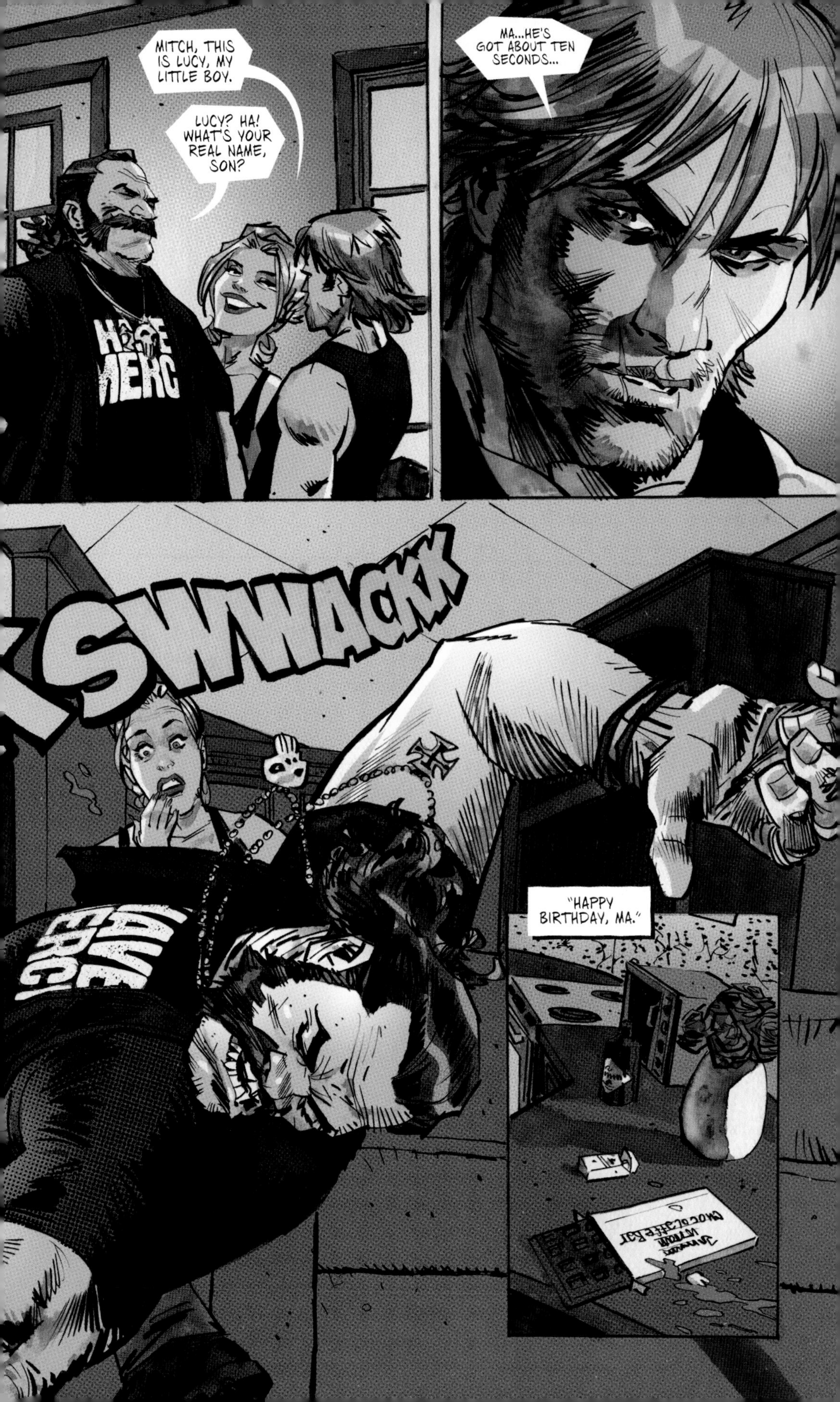
MITCH, THIS IS LUCY, MY LITTLE BOY.
LUCY? HA! WHAT'S YOUR REAL NAME, SON?
MA...HE'S GOT ABOUT TEN SECONDS...
SWWACKK
"HAPPY BIRTHDAY, MA."

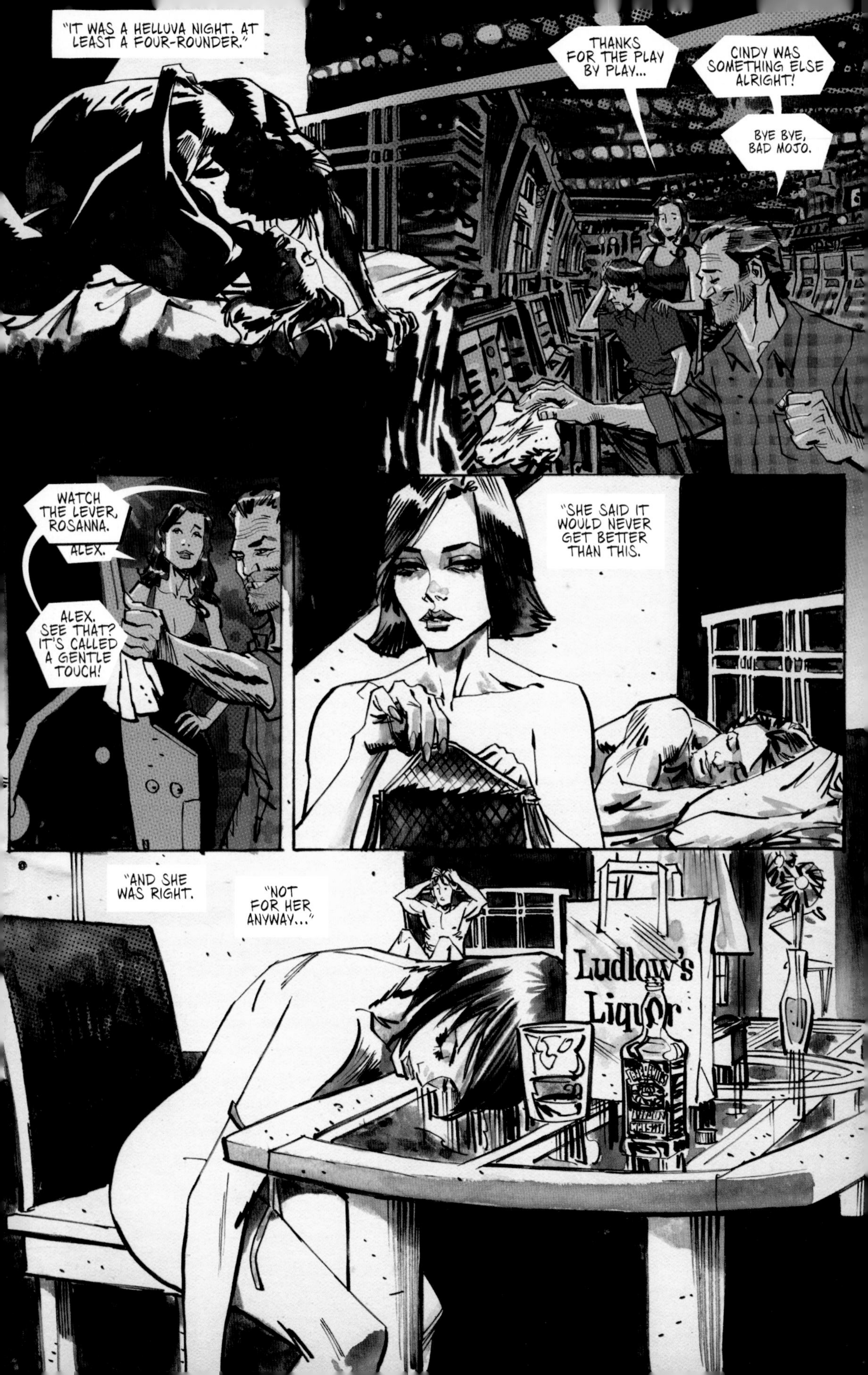
"IT WAS A HELLUVA NIGHT. AT LEAST A FOUR-ROUNDER."
THANKS FOR THE PLAY BY PLAY...
CINDY WAS SOMETHING ELSE ALRIGHT!
BYE BYE, BAD MOJO.
WATCH THE LEVER, ROSANNA.
ALEX.
ALEX. SEE THAT? IT'S CALLED A GENTLE TOUCH!
"SHE SAID IT WOULD NEVER GET BETTER THAN THIS.
"AND SHE WAS RIGHT.
"NOT FOR HER ANYWAY..."
Ludlow's Liquor

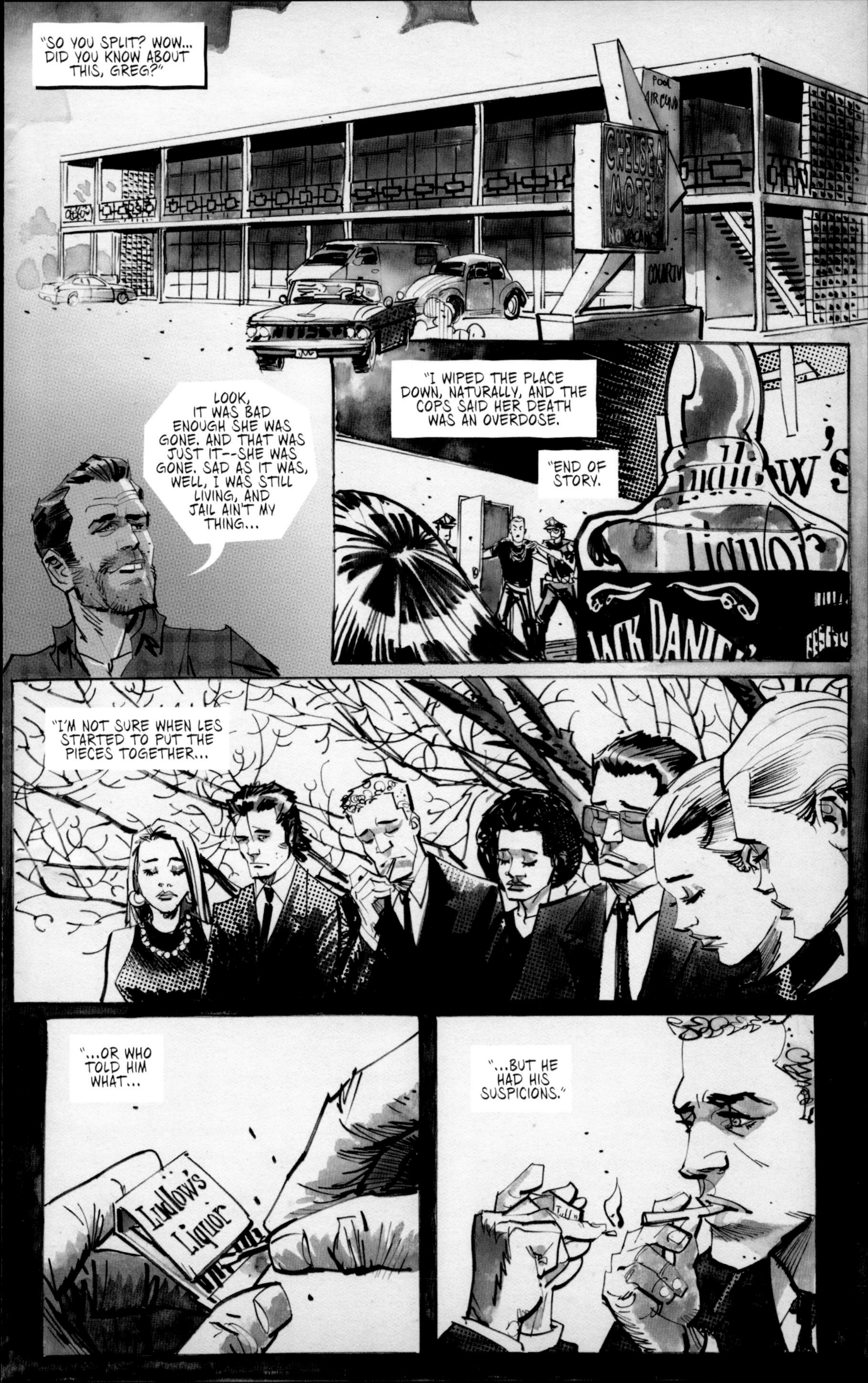
"SO YOU SPLIT? WOW... DID YOU KNOW ABOUT THIS, GREG?"
CHELSEA MOTEL
NO VACANCY
LOOK, IT WAS BAD ENOUGH SHE WAS GONE. AND THAT WAS JUST IT--SHE WAS GONE. SAD AS IT WAS, WELL, I WAS STILL LIVING, AND JAIL AIN'T MY THING...
"I WIPED THE PLACE DOWN, NATURALLY, AND THE COPS SAID HER DEATH WAS AN OVERDOSE.
"END OF STORY.
JACK DANIEL'S
"I'M NOT SURE WHEN LES STARTED TO PUT THE PIECES TOGETHER...
"...OR WHO TOLD HIM WHAT...
Ludlow's Liquor
"...BUT HE HAD HIS SUSPICIONS."

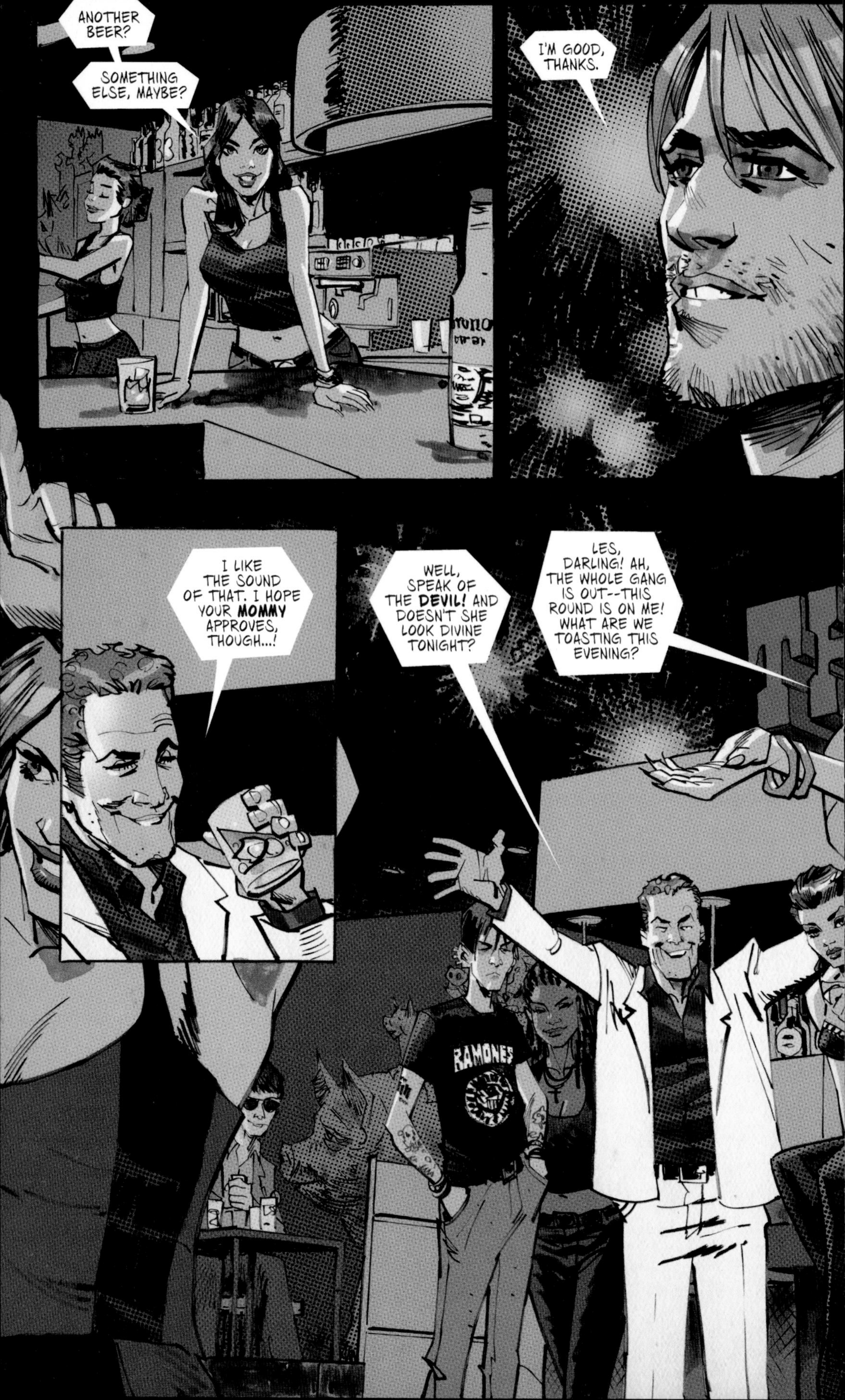
ANOTHER BEER?
SOMETHING ELSE, MAYBE?
I'M GOOD, THANKS.
I LIKE THE SOUND OF THAT. I HOPE YOUR **MOMMY** APPROVES, THOUGH...!
WELL, SPEAK OF THE **DEVIL!** AND DOESN'T SHE LOOK DIVINE TONIGHT?
LES, DARLING! AH, THE WHOLE GANG IS OUT--THIS ROUND IS ON ME! WHAT ARE WE TOASTING THIS EVENING?
RAMONES

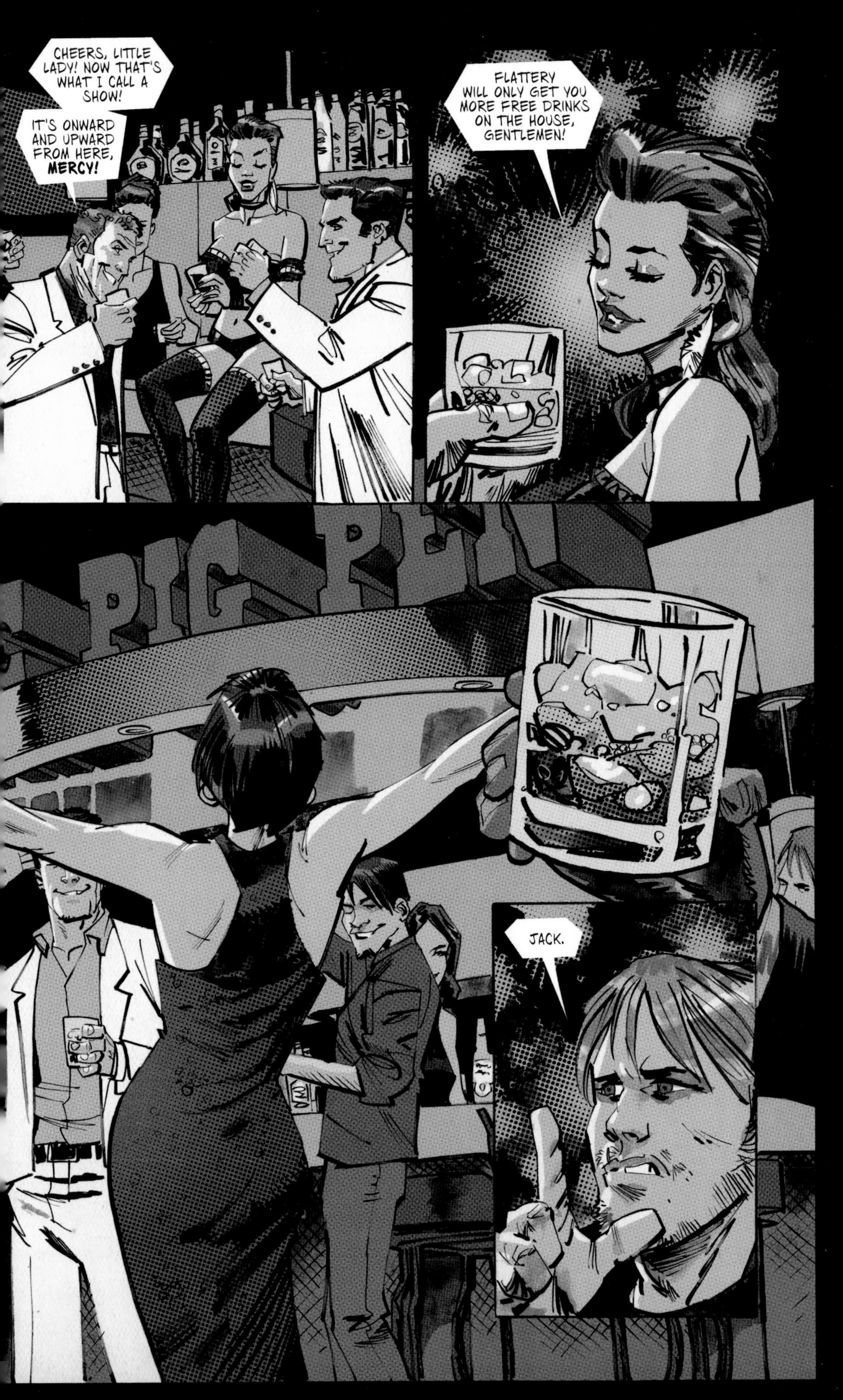
CHEERS, LITTLE LADY! NOW THAT'S WHAT I CALL A SHOW!
IT'S ONWARD AND UPWARD FROM HERE, **MERCY!**
FLATTERY WILL ONLY GET YOU MORE FREE DRINKS ON THE HOUSE, GENTLEMEN!
JACK.

TO ANOTHER GREAT SHOW, WHAT CAN I SAY?

PLENTY, I BET!

HAVE MERCY

THREE SLAVES NIGHT

THIS MAKES **THREE NIGHTS** IN A ROW! WHAT'S LEFT TO TOAST?

NEW HORIZONS.

SO THE SAME OLD SONG AND DANCE THEN, EH, LES?

THAT'S THE PROBLEM. THE SINGER AND DANCER HAS SOME CHANGES IN MIND.

THE SINGER AND DANCER CAN DISCUSS NEW HORIZONS WITH MOMMY DEAREST ANYTIME SHE WANTS!

BOOORRINGG! LET'S BOUNCE, MERCY.

GOOD IDEA, **ZILLS**. G'NIGHT, BETSY!

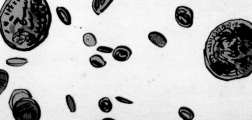

CHAPTER
8 FAMILY & FRIENDS

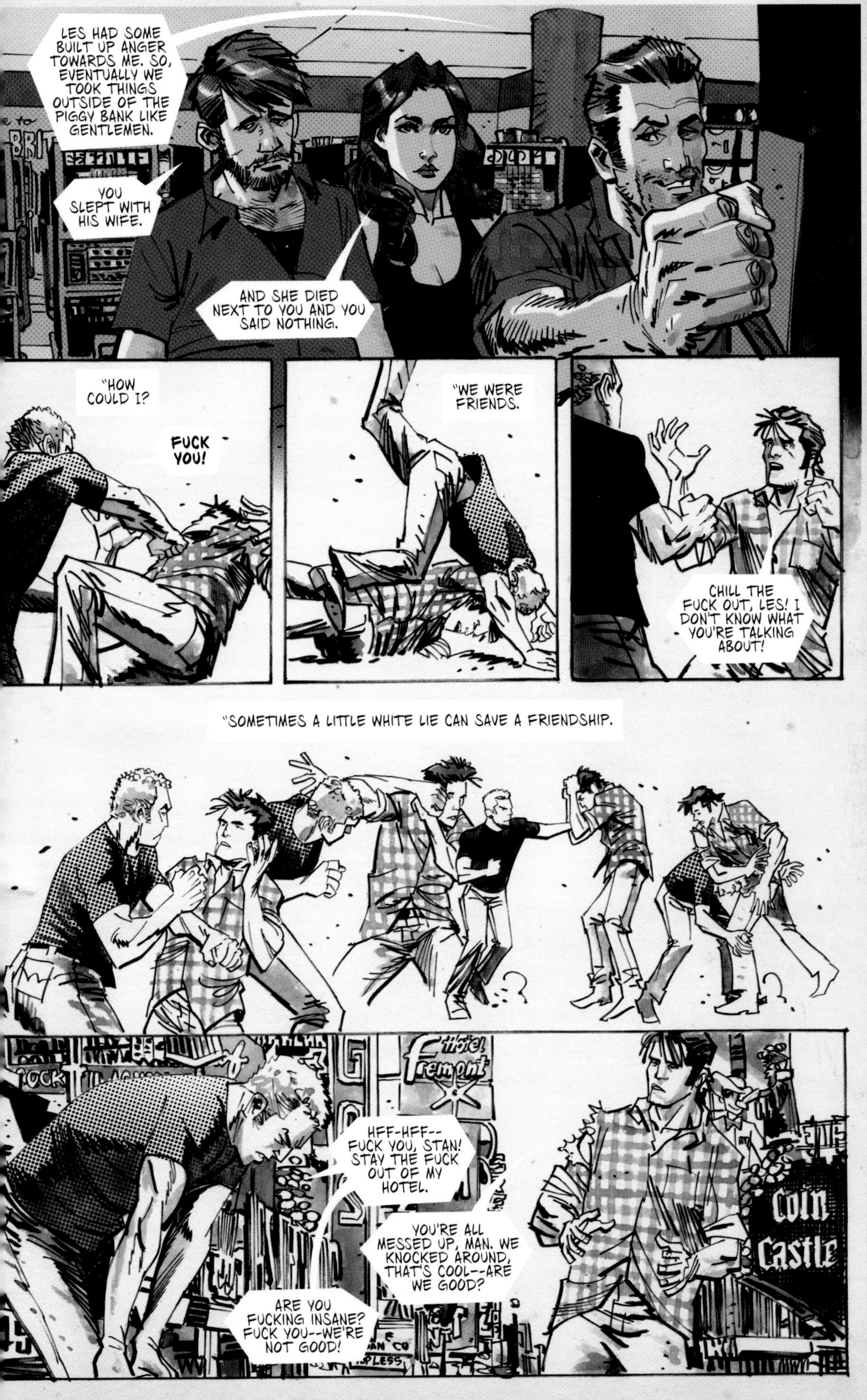
LES HAD SOME BUILT UP ANGER TOWARDS ME. SO, EVENTUALLY WE TOOK THINGS OUTSIDE OF THE PIGGY BANK LIKE GENTLEMEN.
YOU SLEPT WITH HIS WIFE.
AND SHE DIED NEXT TO YOU AND YOU SAID NOTHING.
"HOW COULD I?
FUCK YOU!
"WE WERE FRIENDS.
CHILL THE FUCK OUT, LES! I DON'T KNOW WHAT YOU'RE TALKING ABOUT!
"SOMETIMES A LITTLE WHITE LIE CAN SAVE A FRIENDSHIP.
Hotel Fremont
HFF-HFF-- FUCK YOU, STAN! STAY THE FUCK OUT OF MY HOTEL.
YOU'RE ALL MESSED UP, MAN. WE KNOCKED AROUND, THAT'S COOL--ARE WE GOOD?
ARE YOU FUCKING INSANE? FUCK YOU--WE'RE NOT GOOD!
coin castle

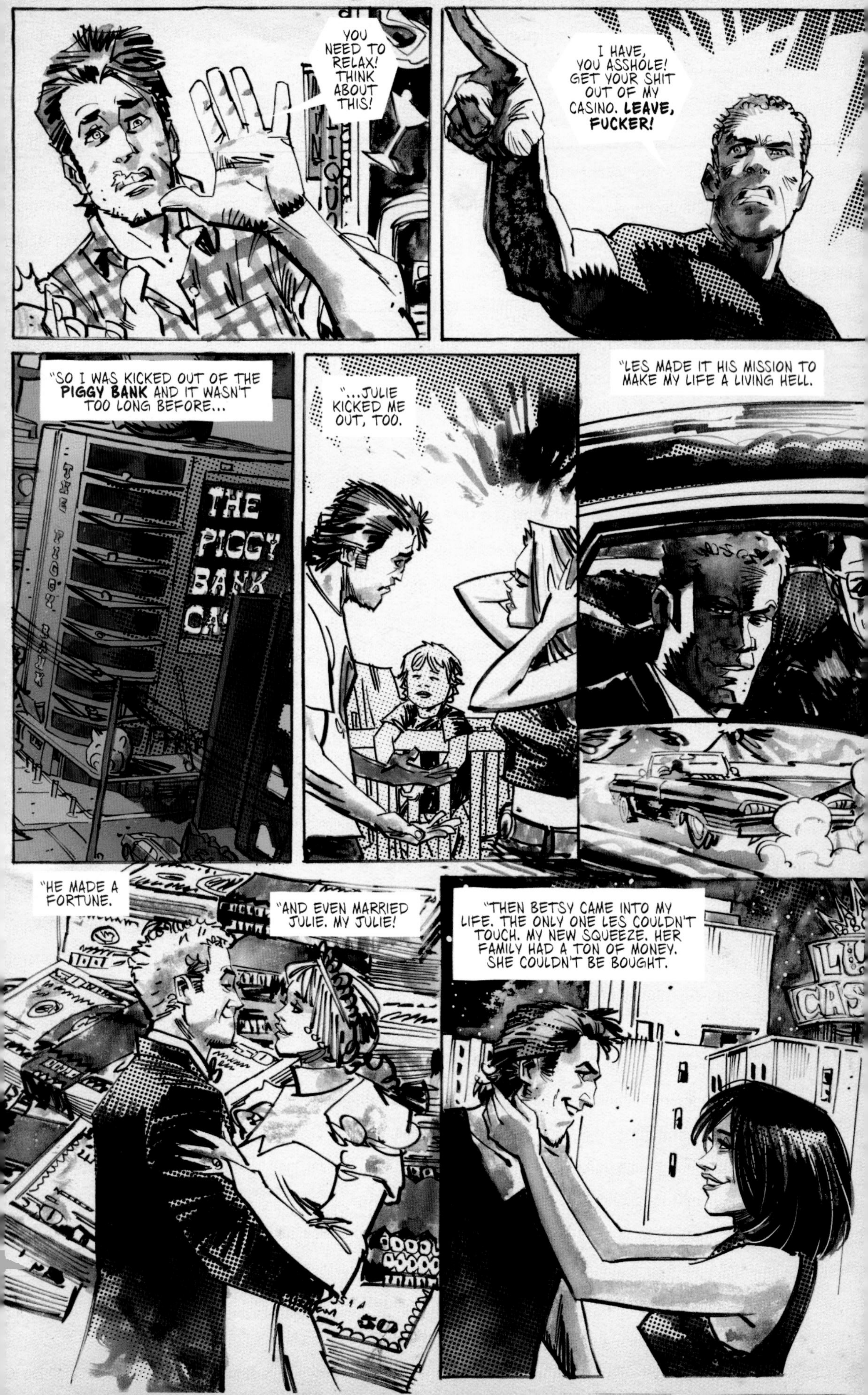
YOU NEED TO RELAX! THINK ABOUT THIS!
I HAVE, YOU ASSHOLE! GET YOUR SHIT OUT OF MY CASINO. **LEAVE, FUCKER!**
"SO I WAS KICKED OUT OF THE **PIGGY BANK** AND IT WASN'T TOO LONG BEFORE...
THE PIGGY BANK
"...JULIE KICKED ME OUT, TOO.
"LES MADE IT HIS MISSION TO MAKE MY LIFE A LIVING HELL.
"HE MADE A FORTUNE.
"AND EVEN MARRIED JULIE. MY JULIE!
"THEN BETSY CAME INTO MY LIFE. THE ONLY ONE LES COULDN'T TOUCH. MY NEW SQUEEZE. HER FAMILY HAD A TON OF MONEY. SHE COULDN'T BE BOUGHT.

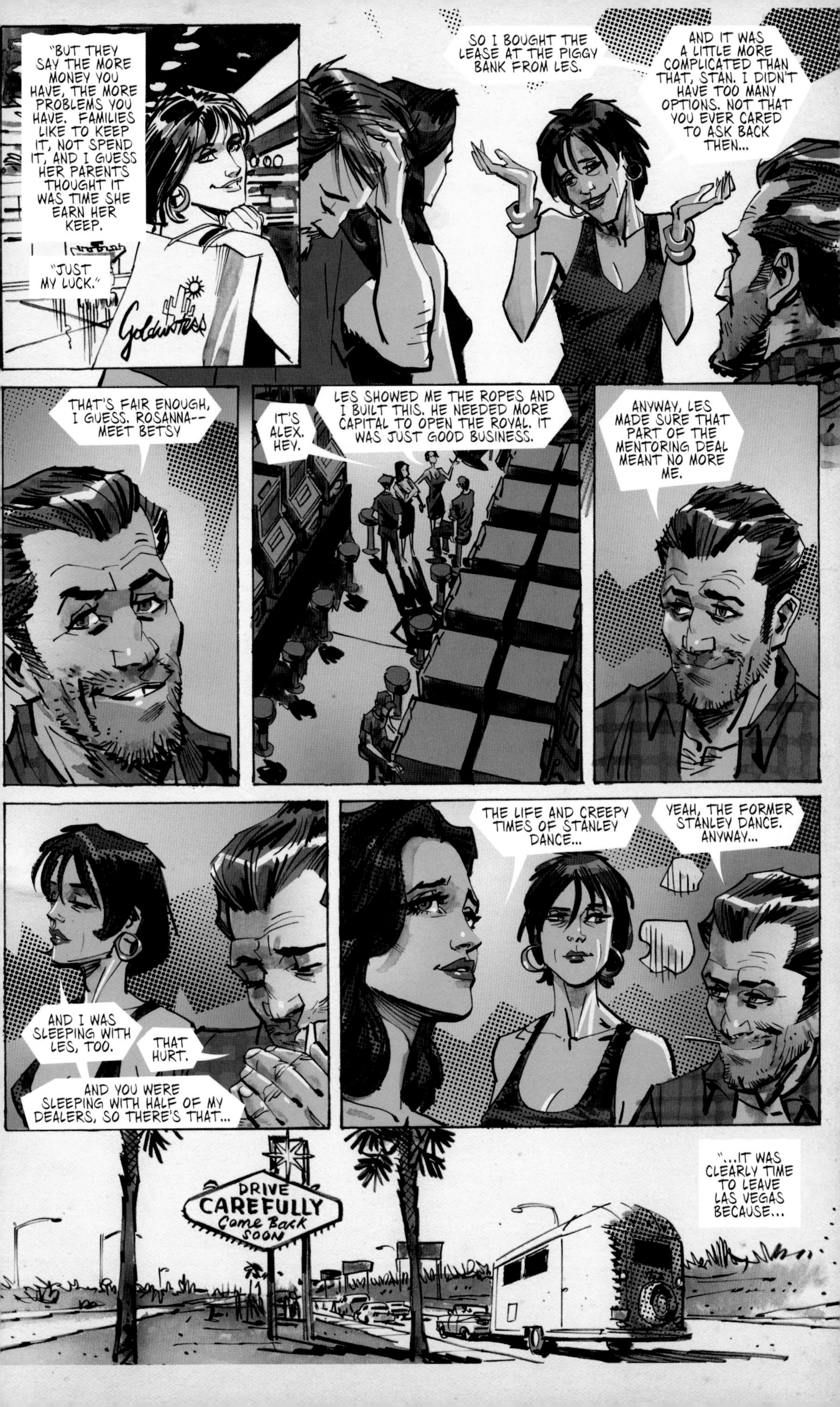
"BUT THEY SAY THE MORE MONEY YOU HAVE, THE MORE PROBLEMS YOU HAVE. FAMILIES LIKE TO KEEP IT, NOT SPEND IT, AND I GUESS HER PARENTS THOUGHT IT WAS TIME SHE EARN HER KEEP.
"JUST MY LUCK."
Goldwater's
SO I BOUGHT THE LEASE AT THE PIGGY BANK FROM LES.
AND IT WAS A LITTLE MORE COMPLICATED THAN THAT, STAN. I DIDN'T HAVE TOO MANY OPTIONS. NOT THAT YOU EVER CARED TO ASK BACK THEN...
THAT'S FAIR ENOUGH, I GUESS. ROSANNA-- MEET BETSY
IT'S ALEX. HEY.
LES SHOWED ME THE ROPES AND I BUILT THIS. HE NEEDED MORE CAPITAL TO OPEN THE ROYAL. IT WAS JUST GOOD BUSINESS.
ANYWAY, LES MADE SURE THAT PART OF THE MENTORING DEAL MEANT NO MORE ME.
AND I WAS SLEEPING WITH LES, TOO.
THAT HURT.
AND YOU WERE SLEEPING WITH HALF OF MY DEALERS, SO THERE'S THAT...
THE LIFE AND CREEPY TIMES OF STANLEY DANCE...
YEAH, THE FORMER STANLEY DANCE. ANYWAY...
DRIVE CAREFULLY Come Back SOON
"...IT WAS CLEARLY TIME TO LEAVE LAS VEGAS BECAUSE...

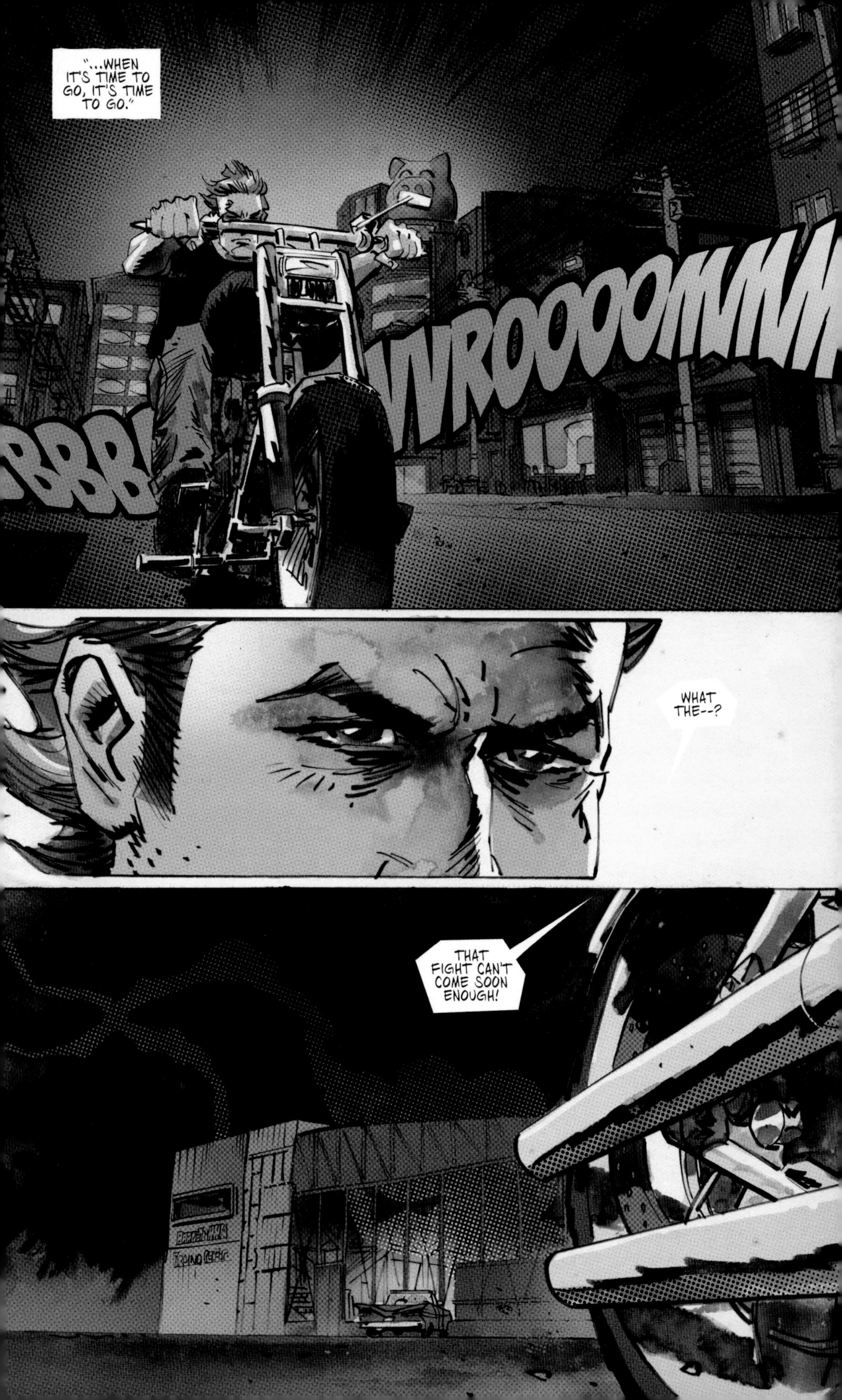
"...WHEN IT'S TIME TO GO, IT'S TIME TO GO."
BBB
VVROOOOOMMM
WHAT THE--?
THAT FIGHT CAN'T COME SOON ENOUGH!

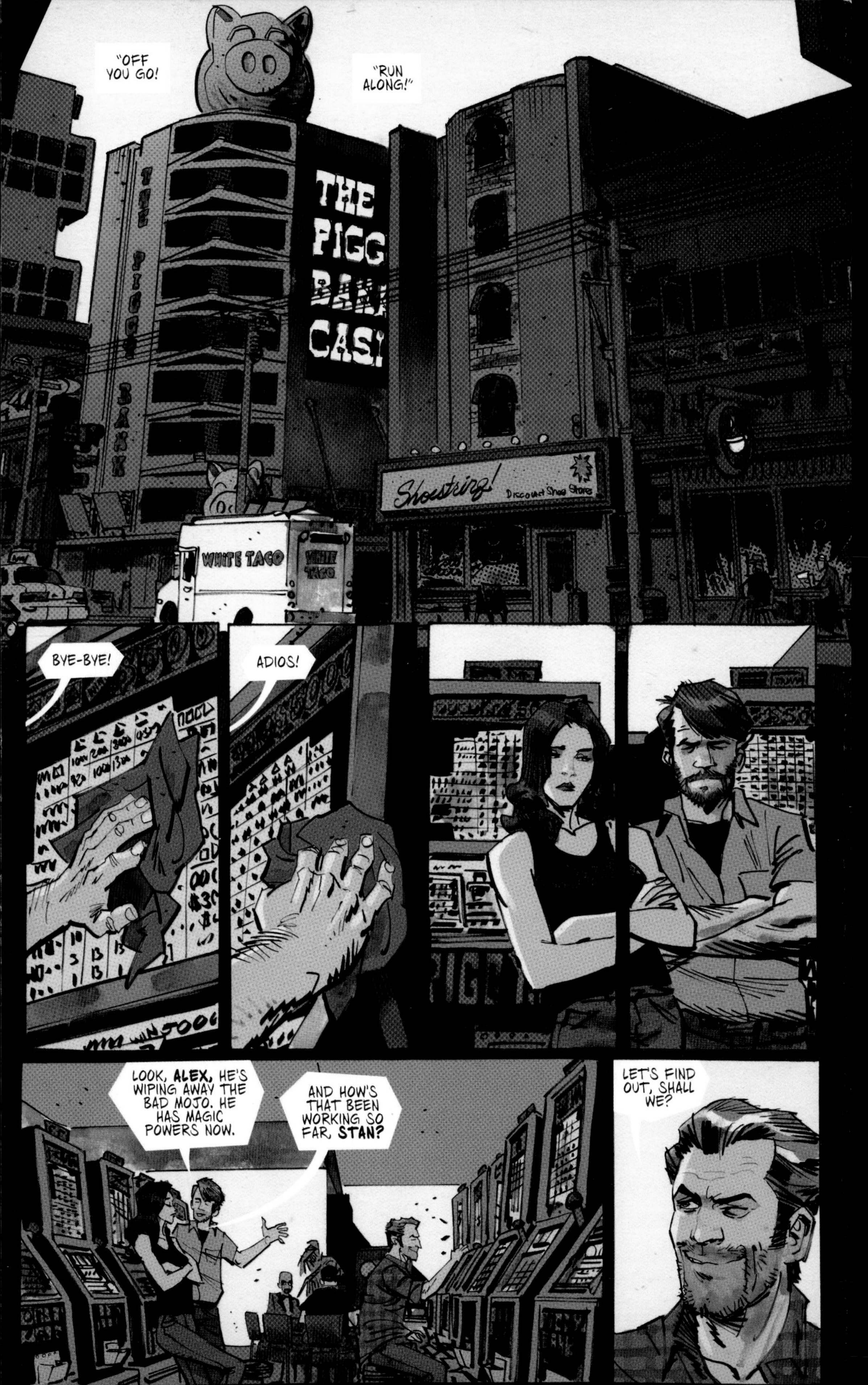
"OFF YOU GO!
"RUN ALONG!"
THE PIGG BAN CASI
Shoestring! Discount Shoe Store
WHITE TACO
BYE-BYE!
ADIOS!
LOOK, ALEX, HE'S WIPING AWAY THE BAD MOJO. HE HAS MAGIC POWERS NOW.
AND HOW'S THAT BEEN WORKING SO FAR, STAN?
LET'S FIND OUT, SHALL WE?

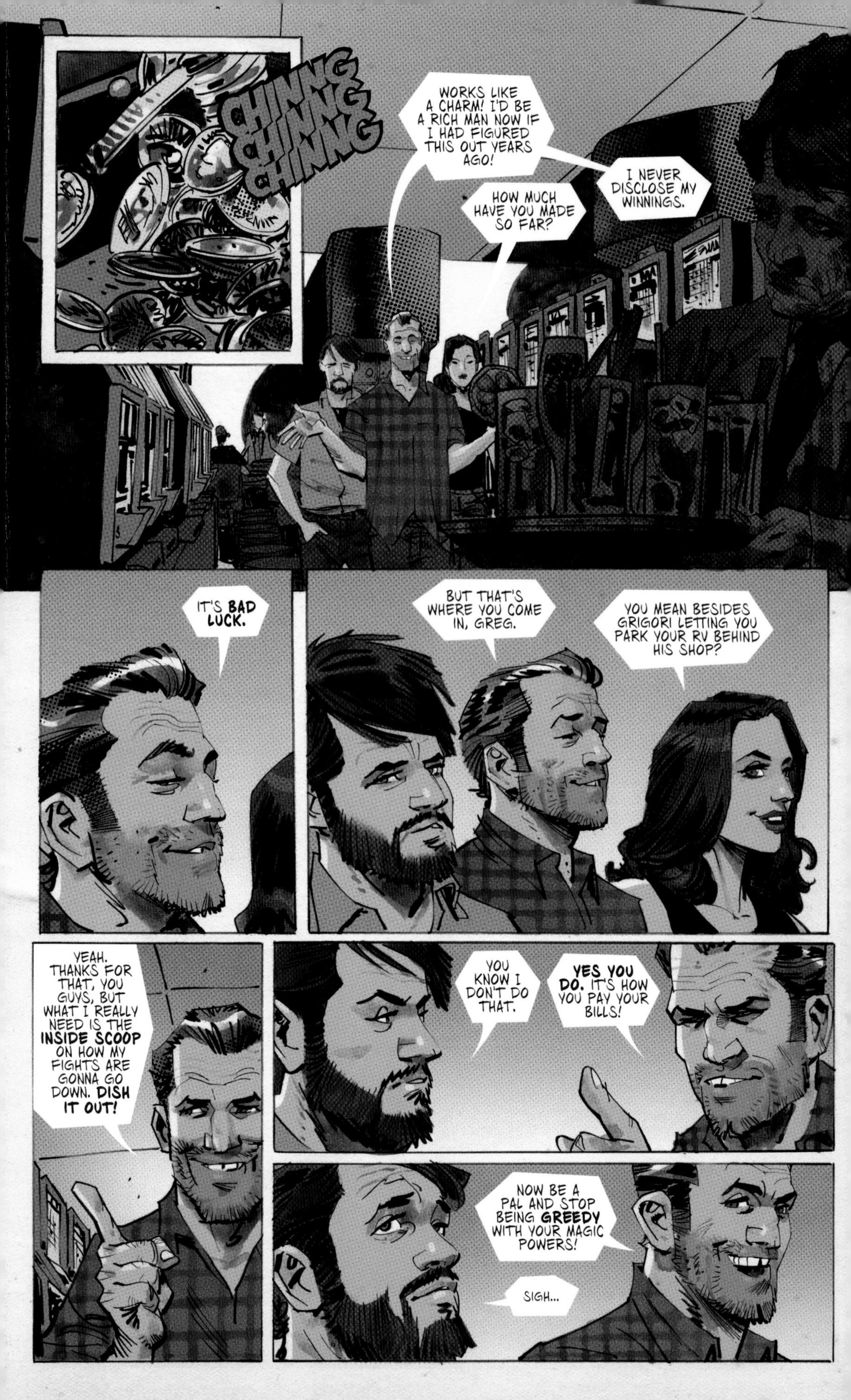
CHINNG CHINNG CHINNG
WORKS LIKE A CHARM! I'D BE A RICH MAN NOW IF I HAD FIGURED THIS OUT YEARS AGO!
HOW MUCH HAVE YOU MADE SO FAR?
I NEVER DISCLOSE MY WINNINGS.
IT'S BAD LUCK.
BUT THAT'S WHERE YOU COME IN, GREG.
YOU MEAN BESIDES GRIGORI LETTING YOU PARK YOUR RV BEHIND HIS SHOP?
YEAH. THANKS FOR THAT, YOU GUYS, BUT WHAT I REALLY NEED IS THE INSIDE SCOOP ON HOW MY FIGHTS ARE GONNA GO DOWN. DISH IT OUT!
YOU KNOW I DON'T DO THAT.
YES YOU DO. IT'S HOW YOU PAY YOUR BILLS!
NOW BE A PAL AND STOP BEING GREEDY WITH YOUR MAGIC POWERS!
SIGH...

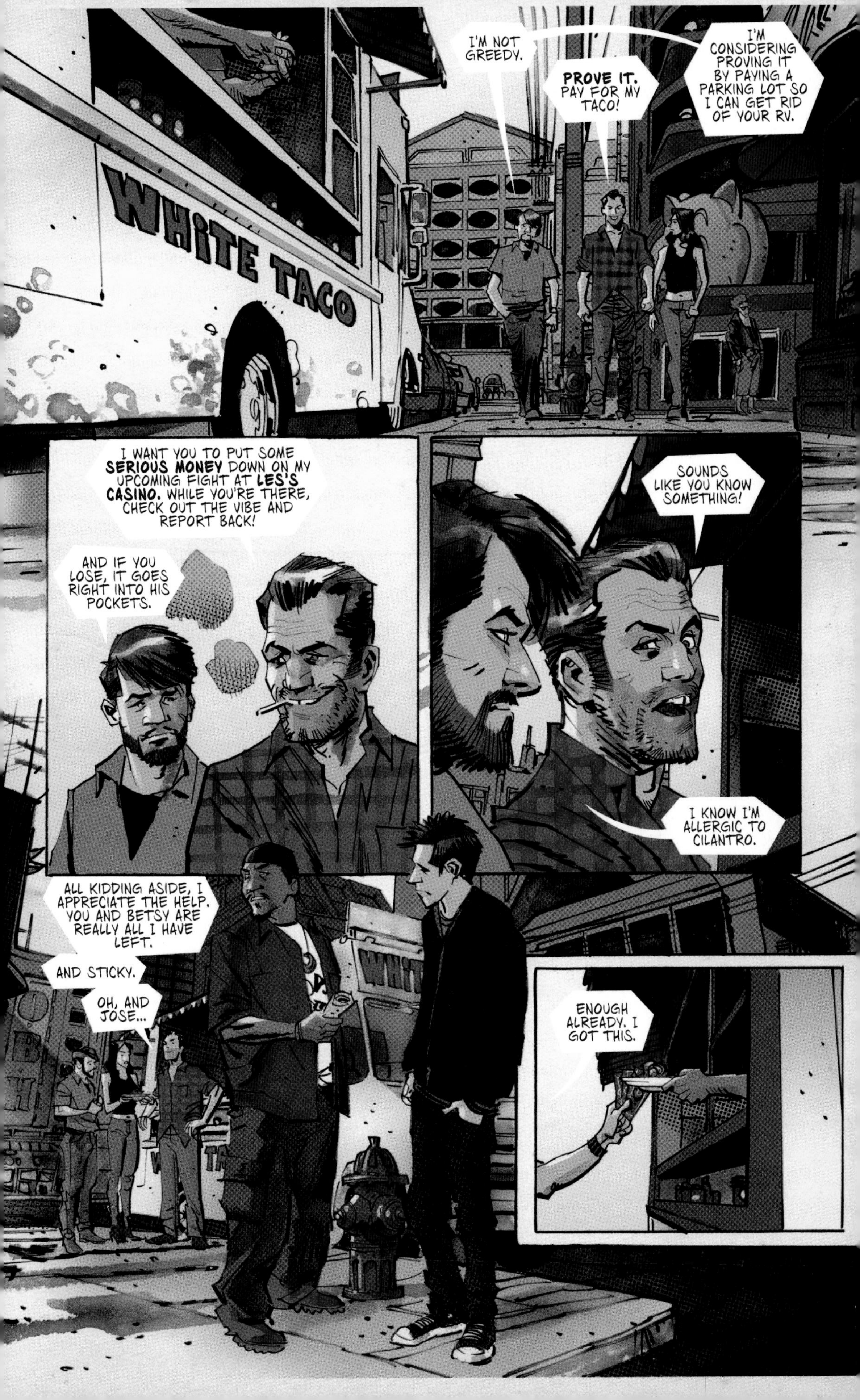

I'M NOT GREEDY.
PROVE IT. PAY FOR MY TACO!
I'M CONSIDERING PROVING IT BY PAYING A PARKING LOT SO I CAN GET RID OF YOUR RV.
WHITE TACO
I WANT YOU TO PUT SOME SERIOUS MONEY DOWN ON MY UPCOMING FIGHT AT LES'S CASINO. WHILE YOU'RE THERE, CHECK OUT THE VIBE AND REPORT BACK!
AND IF YOU LOSE, IT GOES RIGHT INTO HIS POCKETS.
SOUNDS LIKE YOU KNOW SOMETHING!
I KNOW I'M ALLERGIC TO CILANTRO.
ALL KIDDING ASIDE, I APPRECIATE THE HELP. YOU AND BETSY ARE REALLY ALL I HAVE LEFT.
AND STICKY.
OH, AND JOSE...
ENOUGH ALREADY. I GOT THIS.

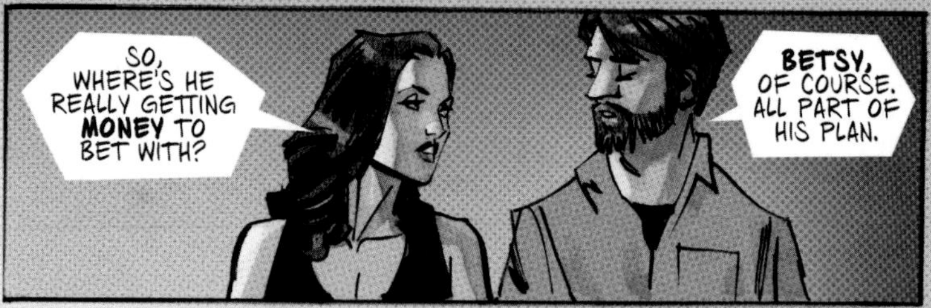
SO, WHERE'S HE REALLY GETTING MONEY TO BET WITH?
BETSY, OF COURSE. ALL PART OF HIS PLAN.

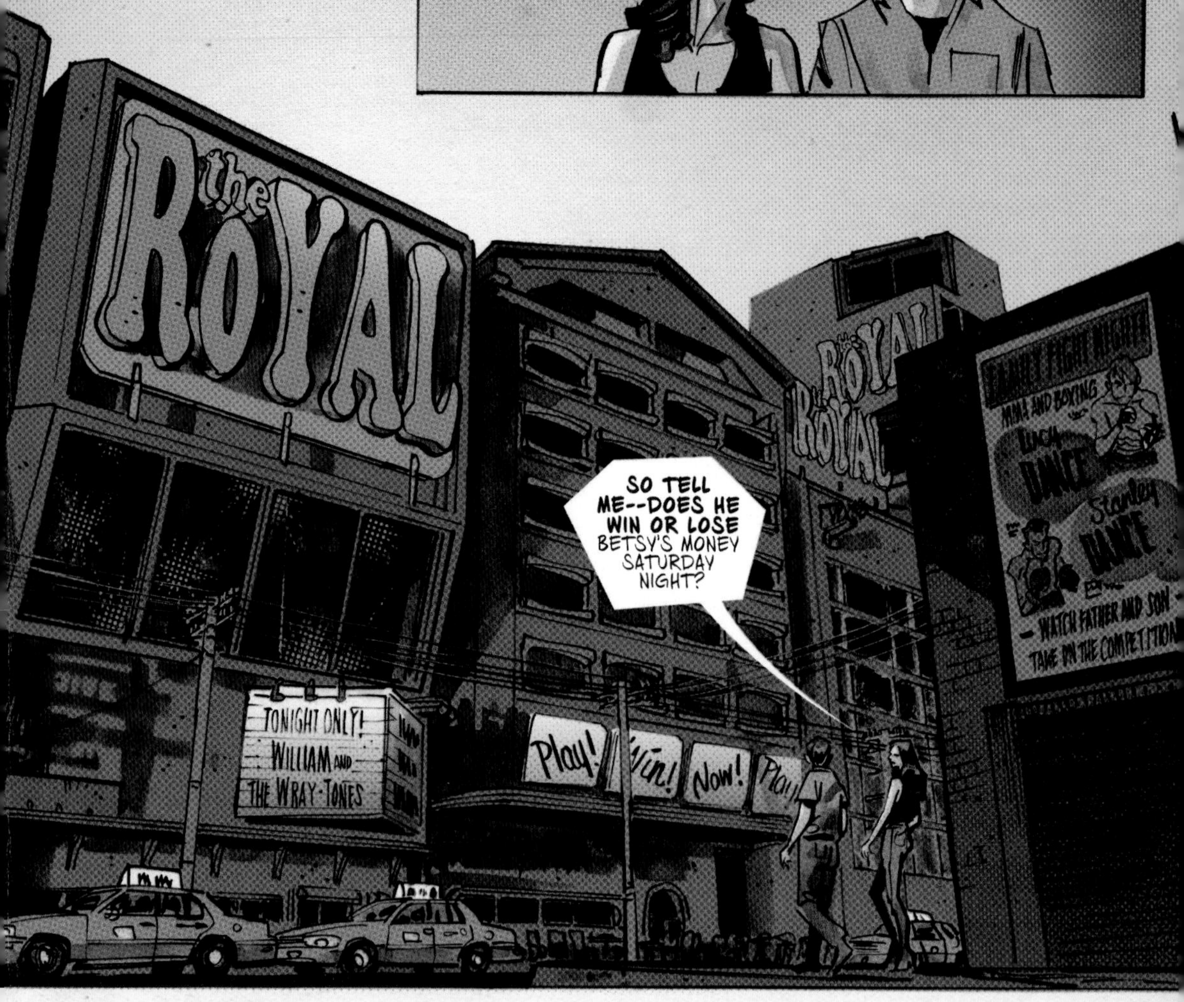
the ROYAL
SO TELL ME--DOES HE WIN OR LOSE BETSY'S MONEY SATURDAY NIGHT?
TONIGHT ONLY! WILLIAM AND THE WRAY-TONES
Play! Win! Now!
MMA AND BOXING

CHAPTER 9 HIT ME

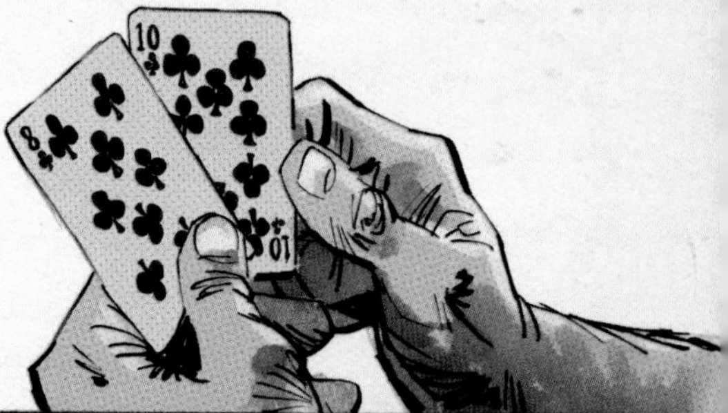

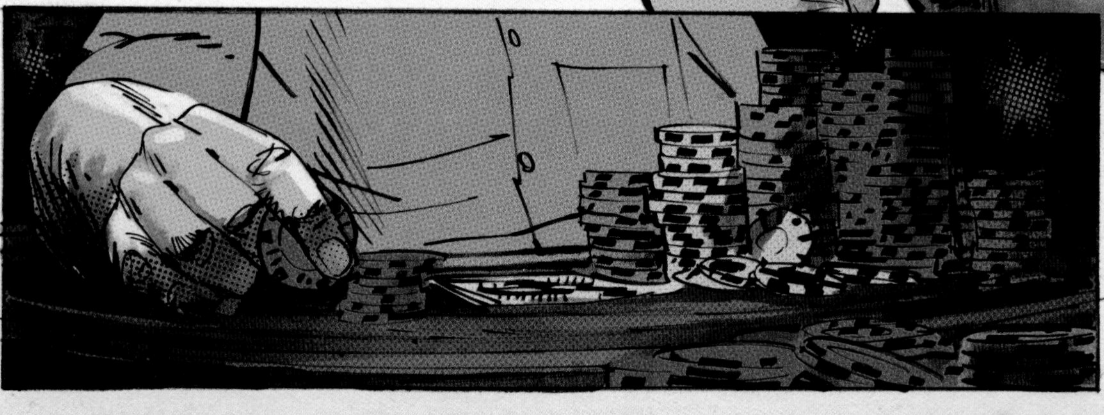

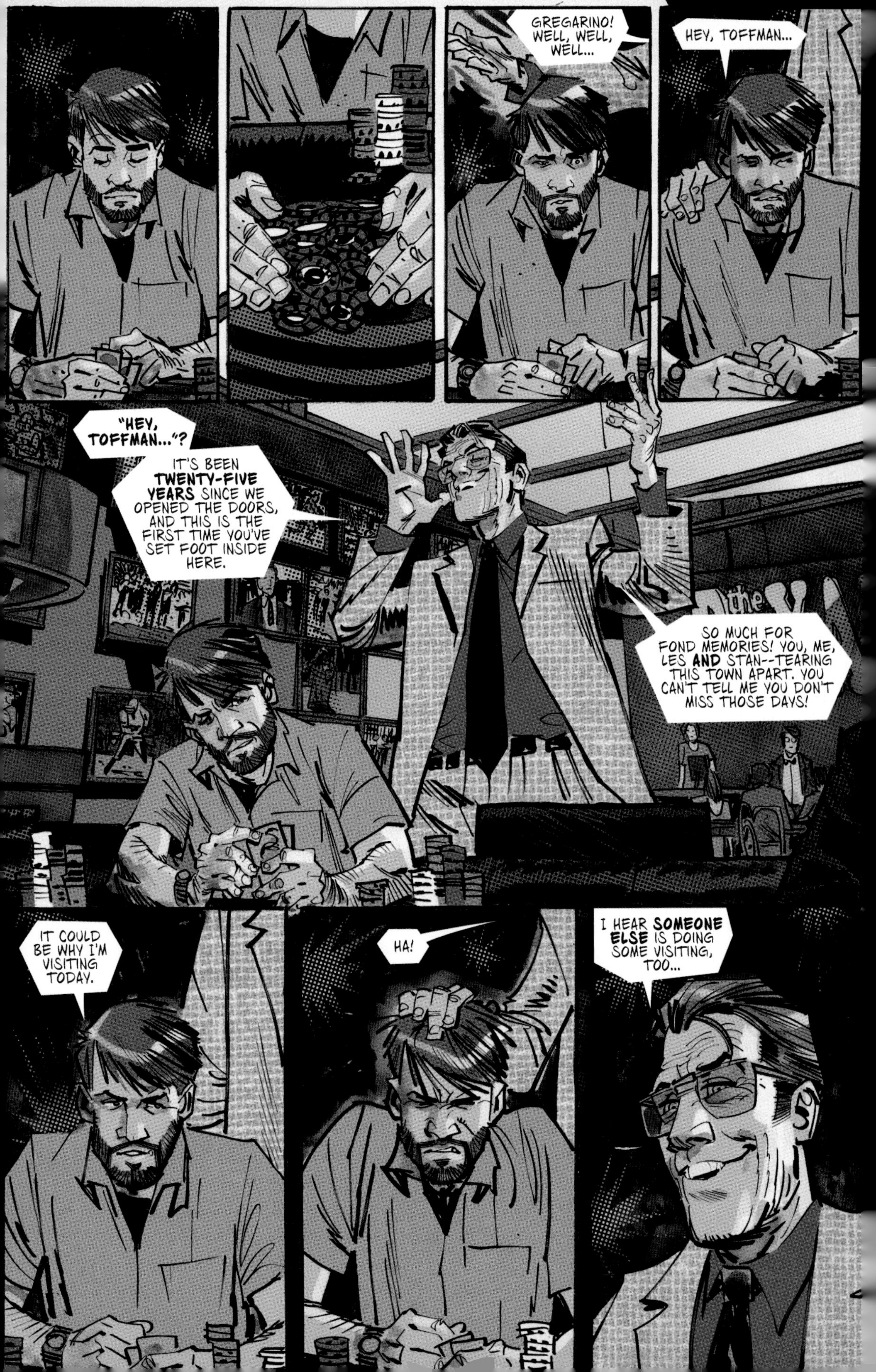
GREGARINO! WELL, WELL, WELL...
HEY, TOFFMAN...
"HEY, TOFFMAN..."?
IT'S BEEN **TWENTY-FIVE YEARS** SINCE WE OPENED THE DOORS, AND THIS IS THE FIRST TIME YOU'VE SET FOOT INSIDE HERE.
SO MUCH FOR FOND MEMORIES! YOU, ME, LES **AND** STAN--TEARING THIS TOWN APART. YOU CAN'T TELL ME YOU DON'T MISS THOSE DAYS!
IT COULD BE WHY I'M VISITING TODAY.
HA!
I HEAR **SOMEONE ELSE** IS DOING SOME VISITING, TOO...

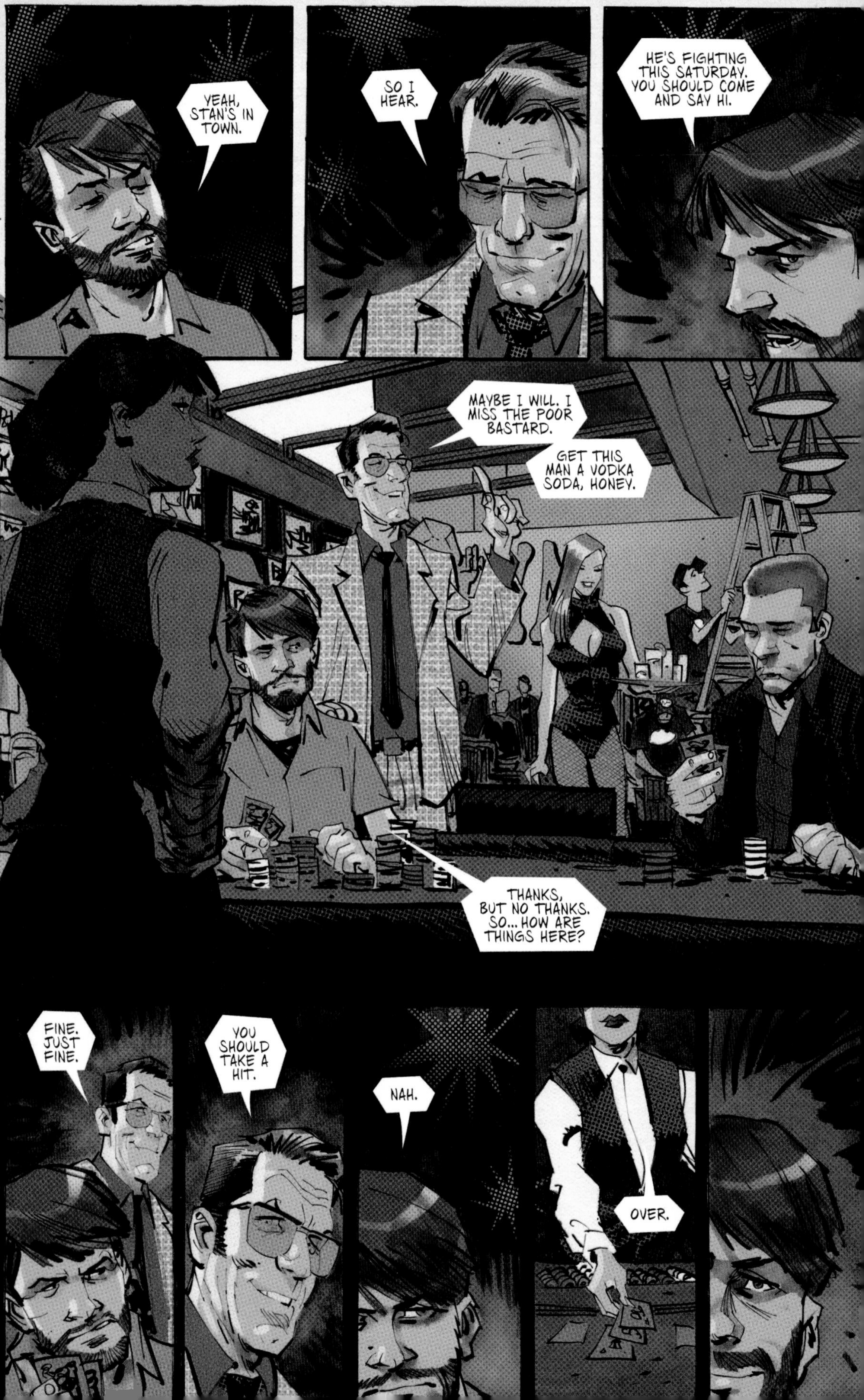
YEAH, STAN'S IN TOWN.
SO I HEAR.
HE'S FIGHTING THIS SATURDAY. YOU SHOULD COME AND SAY HI.
MAYBE I WILL. I MISS THE POOR BASTARD.
GET THIS MAN A VODKA SODA, HONEY.
THANKS, BUT NO THANKS. SO... HOW ARE THINGS HERE?
FINE. JUST FINE.
YOU SHOULD TAKE A HIT.
NAH.
OVER.

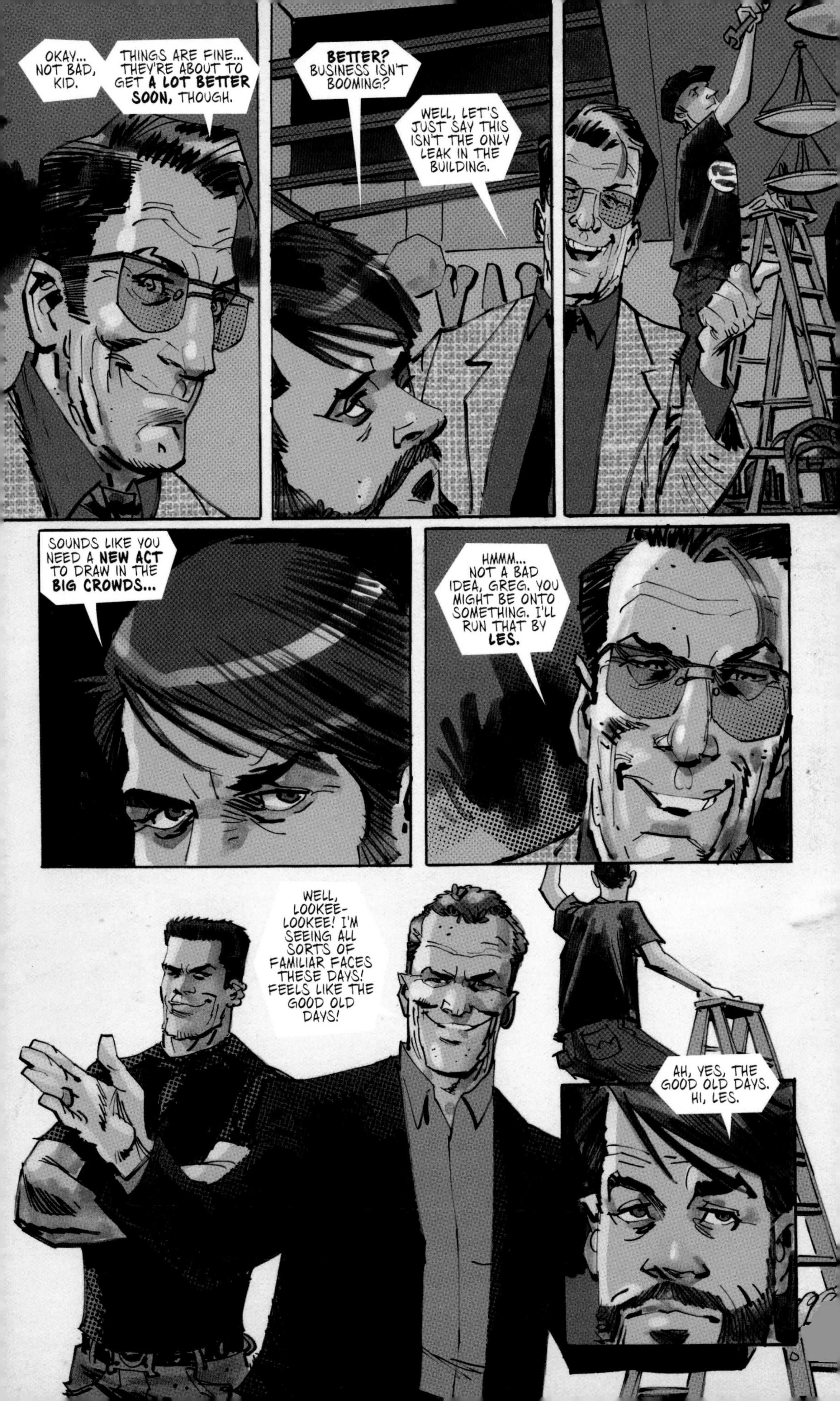
OKAY... NOT BAD, KID.
THINGS ARE FINE... THEY'RE ABOUT TO GET A LOT BETTER SOON, THOUGH.
BETTER? BUSINESS ISN'T BOOMING?
WELL, LET'S JUST SAY THIS ISN'T THE ONLY LEAK IN THE BUILDING.
SOUNDS LIKE YOU NEED A NEW ACT TO DRAW IN THE BIG CROWDS...
HMMM... NOT A BAD IDEA, GREG. YOU MIGHT BE ONTO SOMETHING. I'LL RUN THAT BY LES.
WELL, LOOKEE-LOOKEE! I'M SEEING ALL SORTS OF FAMILIAR FACES THESE DAYS! FEELS LIKE THE GOOD OLD DAYS!
AH, YES, THE GOOD OLD DAYS. HI, LES.

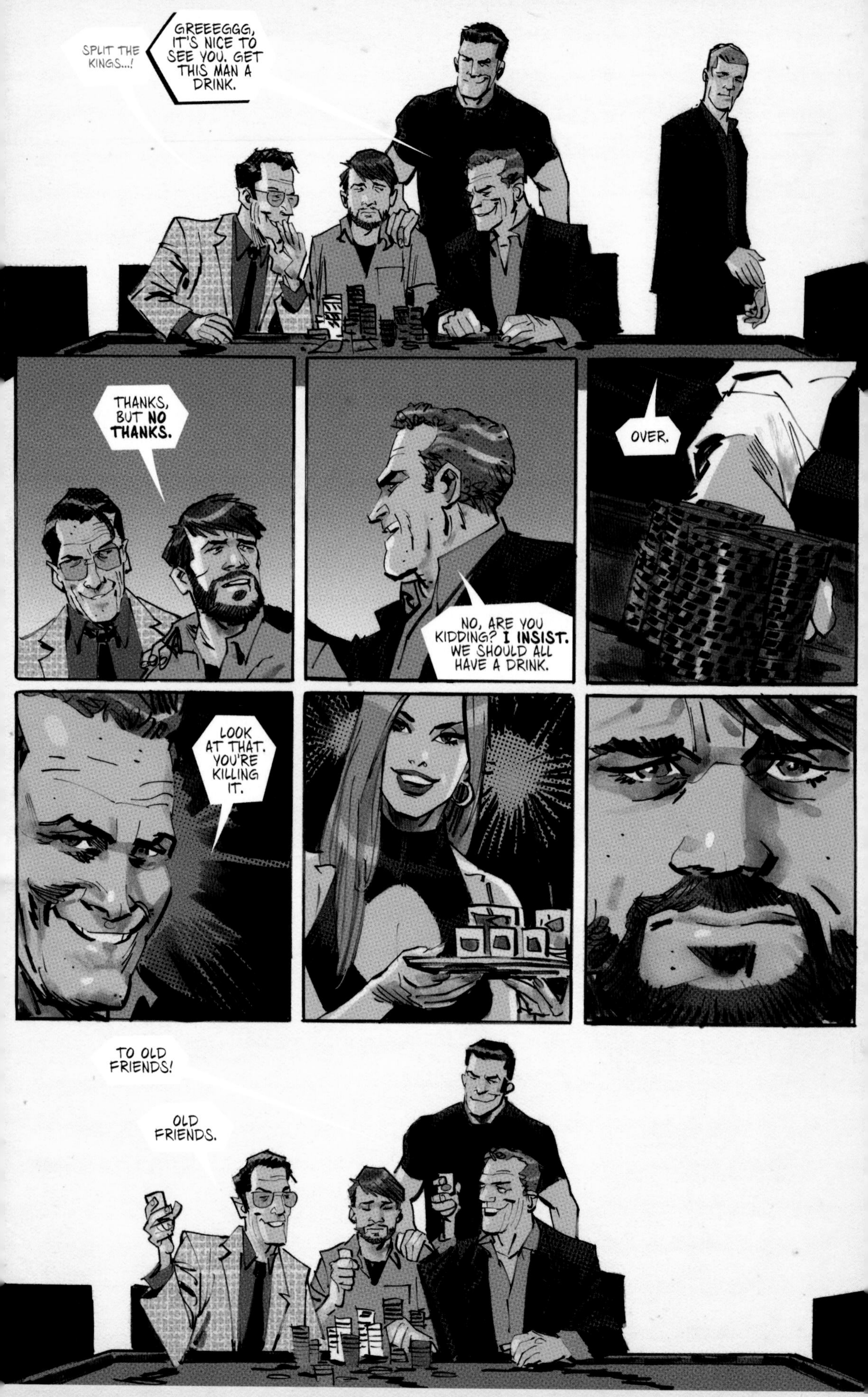
SPLIT THE KINGS...!
GREEEGGG, IT'S NICE TO SEE YOU. GET THIS MAN A DRINK.
THANKS, BUT NO THANKS.
NO, ARE YOU KIDDING? I INSIST. WE SHOULD ALL HAVE A DRINK.
OVER.
LOOK AT THAT. YOU'RE KILLING IT.
TO OLD FRIENDS!
OLD FRIENDS.

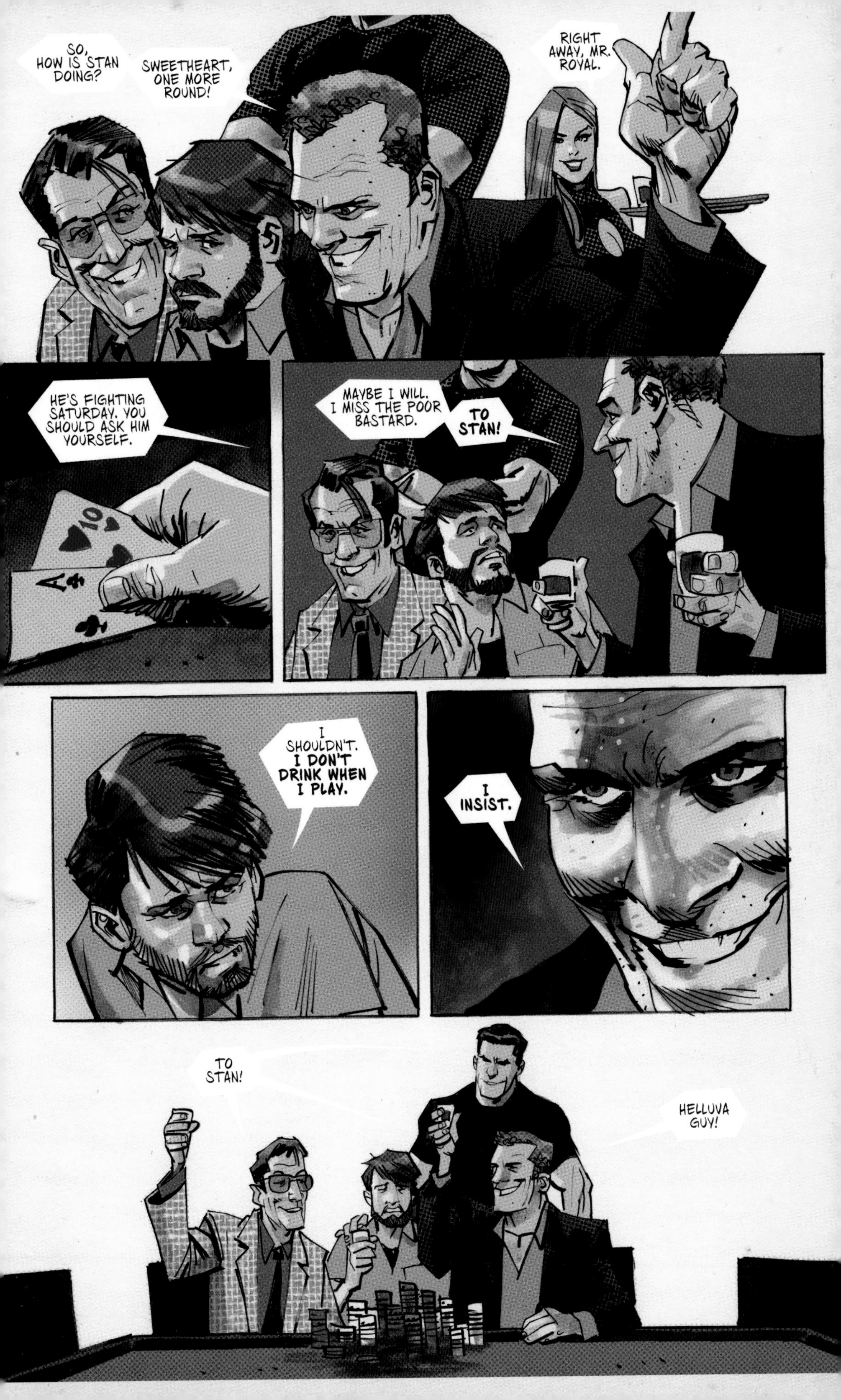
SO, HOW IS STAN DOING?
SWEETHEART, ONE MORE ROUND!
RIGHT AWAY, MR. ROYAL.
HE'S FIGHTING SATURDAY. YOU SHOULD ASK HIM YOURSELF.
MAYBE I WILL. I MISS THE POOR BASTARD.
TO STAN!
I SHOULDN'T. I DON'T DRINK WHEN I PLAY.
I INSIST.
TO STAN!
HELLUVA GUY!

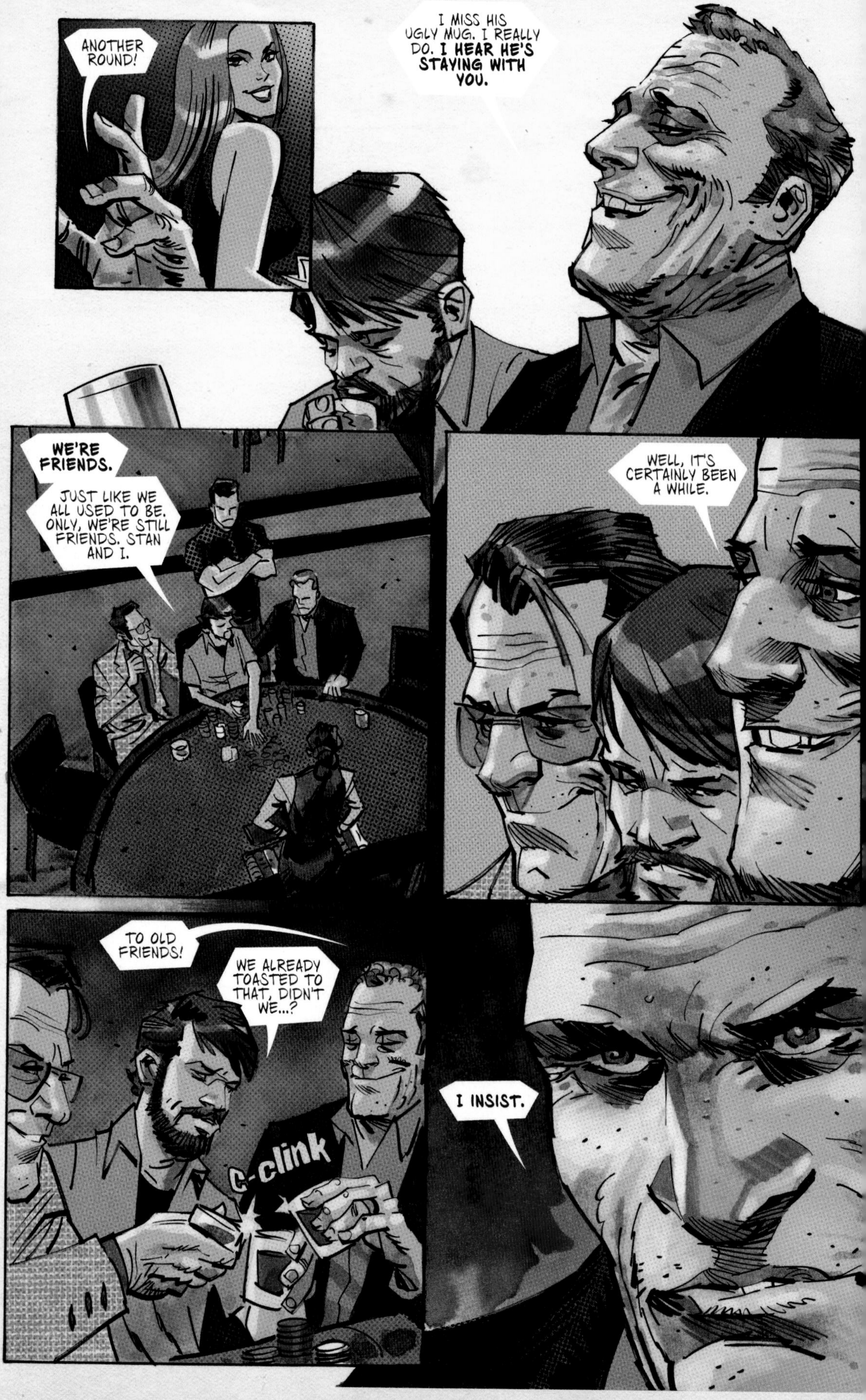

ANOTHER ROUND!
I MISS HIS UGLY MUG. I REALLY DO. I HEAR HE'S STAYING WITH YOU.
WE'RE FRIENDS.
JUST LIKE WE ALL USED TO BE. ONLY, WE'RE STILL FRIENDS. STAN AND I.
WELL, IT'S CERTAINLY BEEN A WHILE.
TO OLD FRIENDS!
WE ALREADY TOASTED TO THAT, DIDN'T WE...?
C-clink
I INSIST.

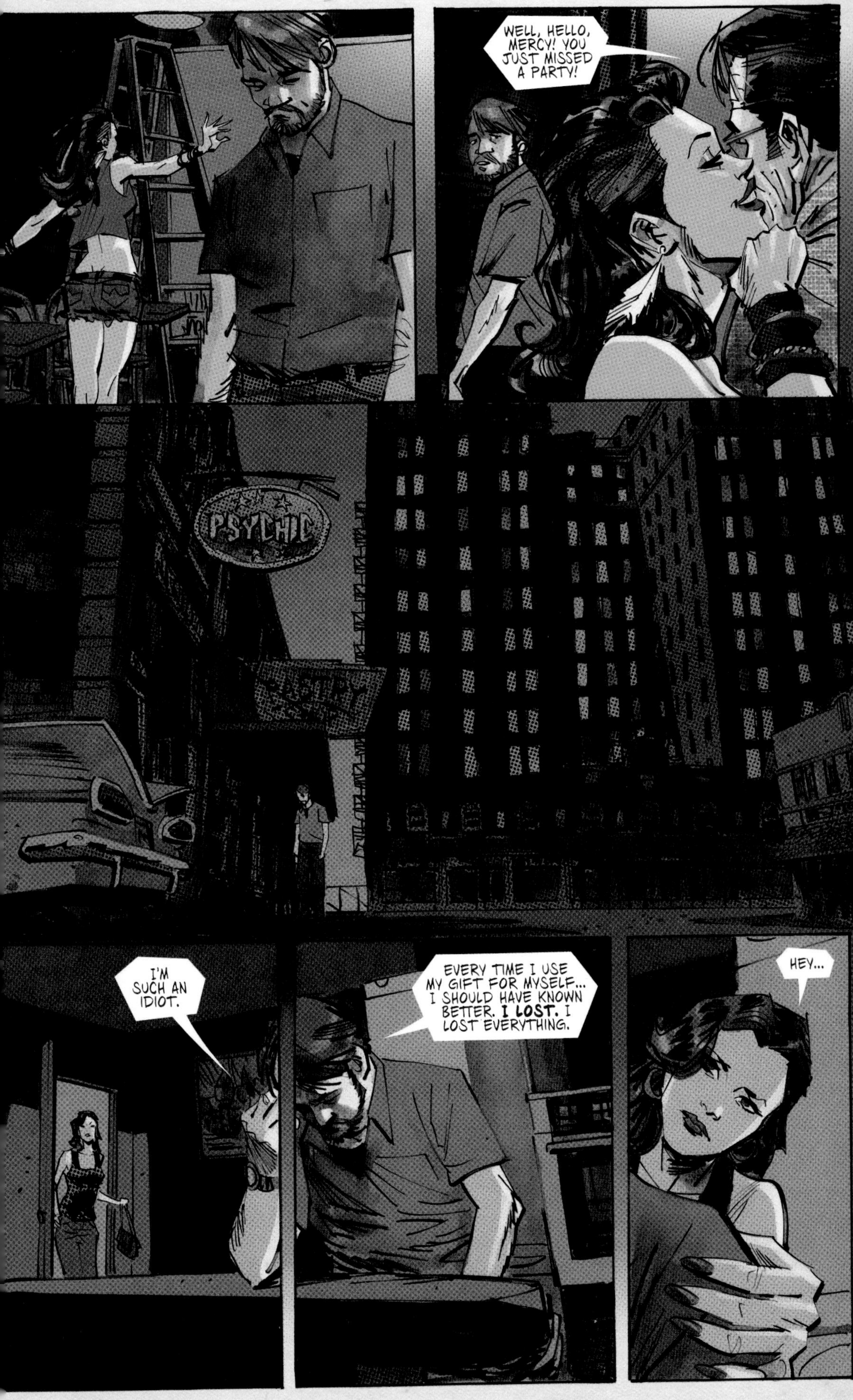
WELL, HELLO, MERCY! YOU JUST MISSED A PARTY!
PSYCHIC
I'M SUCH AN IDIOT.
EVERY TIME I USE MY GIFT FOR MYSELF... I SHOULD HAVE KNOWN BETTER. **I LOST.** I LOST EVERYTHING.
HEY...

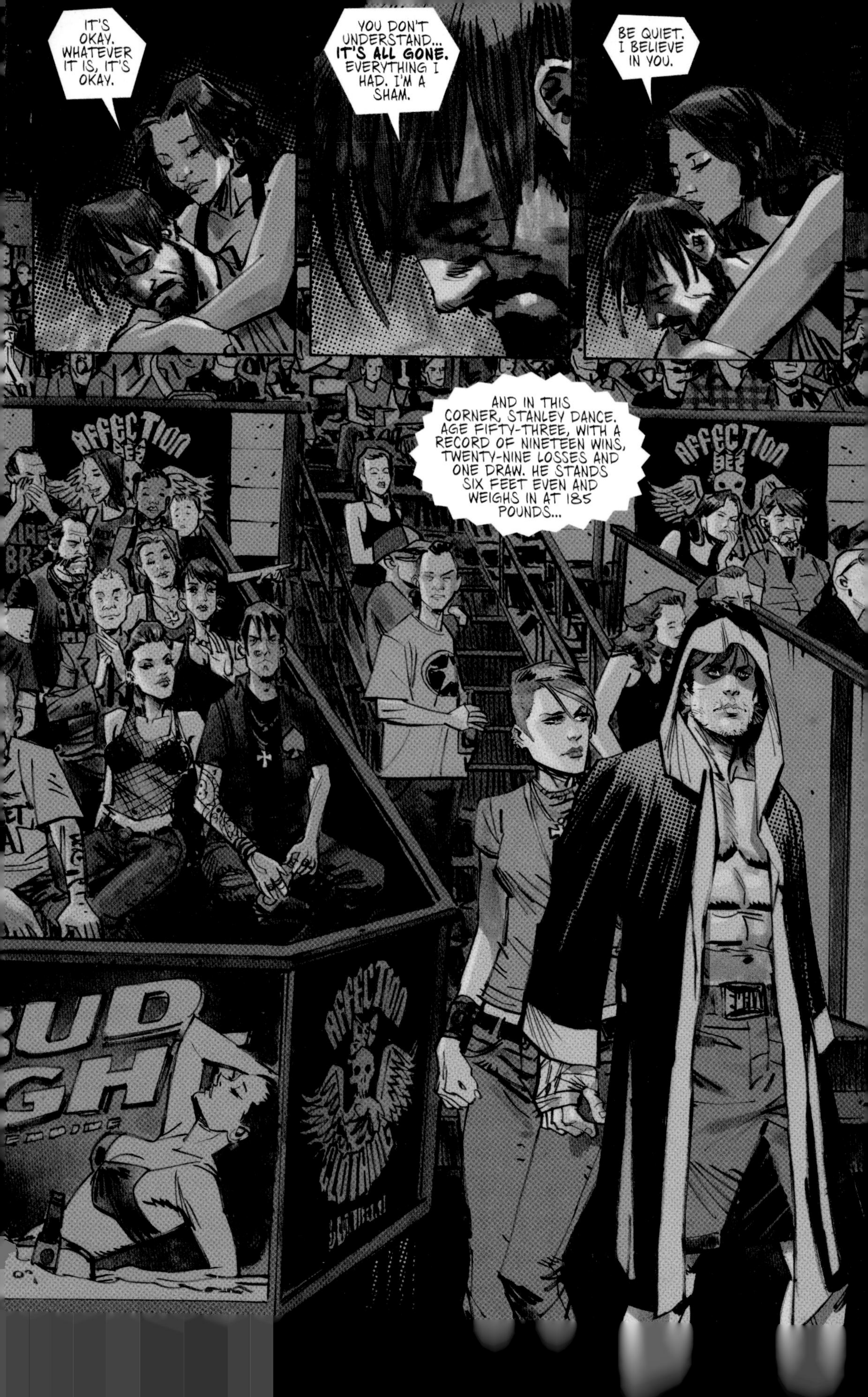
IT'S OKAY. WHATEVER IT IS, IT'S OKAY.
YOU DON'T UNDERSTAND... **IT'S ALL GONE.** EVERYTHING I HAD. I'M A SHAM.
BE QUIET. I BELIEVE IN YOU.
AFFECTION
AND IN THIS CORNER, STANLEY DANCE. AGE FIFTY-THREE, WITH A RECORD OF NINETEEN WINS, TWENTY-NINE LOSSES AND ONE DRAW. HE STANDS SIX FEET EVEN AND WEIGHS IN AT 185 POUNDS...
AFFECTION
AFFECTION

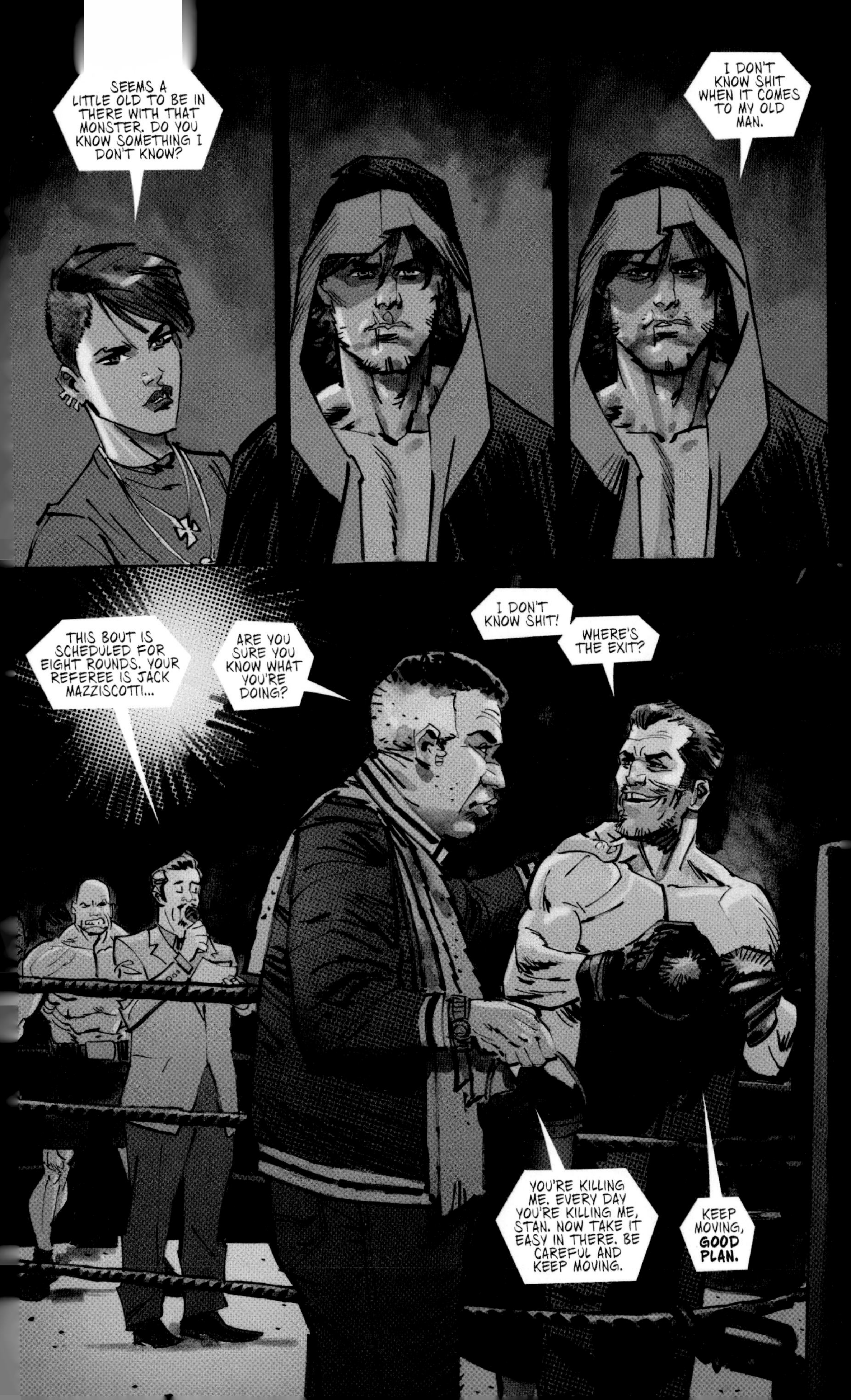
SEEMS A LITTLE OLD TO BE IN THERE WITH THAT MONSTER. DO YOU KNOW SOMETHING I DON'T KNOW?
I DON'T KNOW SHIT WHEN IT COMES TO MY OLD MAN.
THIS BOUT IS SCHEDULED FOR EIGHT ROUNDS. YOUR REFEREE IS JACK MAZZISCOTTI...
ARE YOU SURE YOU KNOW WHAT YOU'RE DOING?
I DON'T KNOW SHIT!
WHERE'S THE EXIT?
YOU'RE KILLING ME. EVERY DAY YOU'RE KILLING ME, STAN. NOW TAKE IT EASY IN THERE. BE CAREFUL AND KEEP MOVING.
KEEP MOVING, GOOD PLAN.

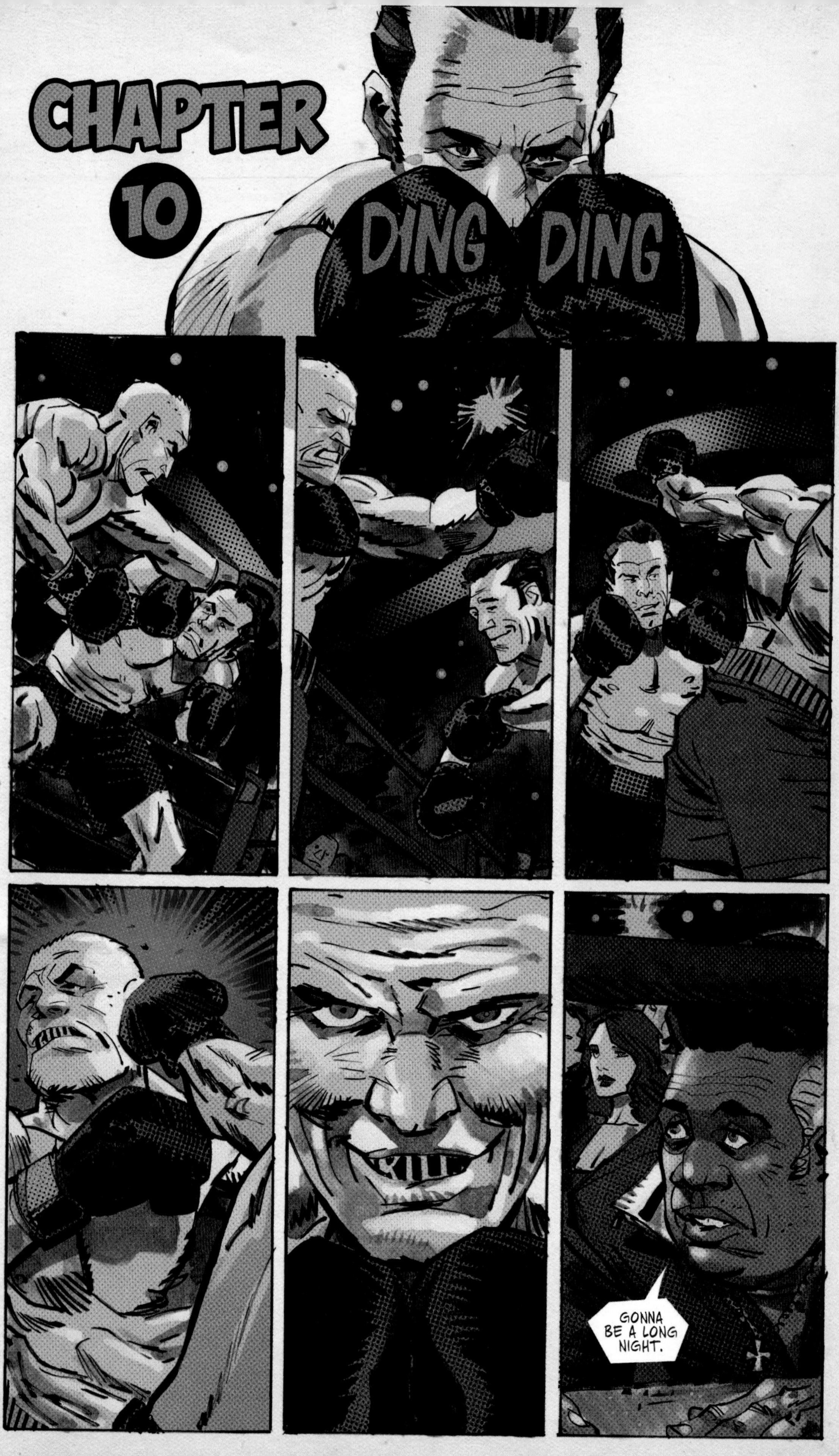
CHAPTER
10
DING DING
GONNA BE A LONG NIGHT.

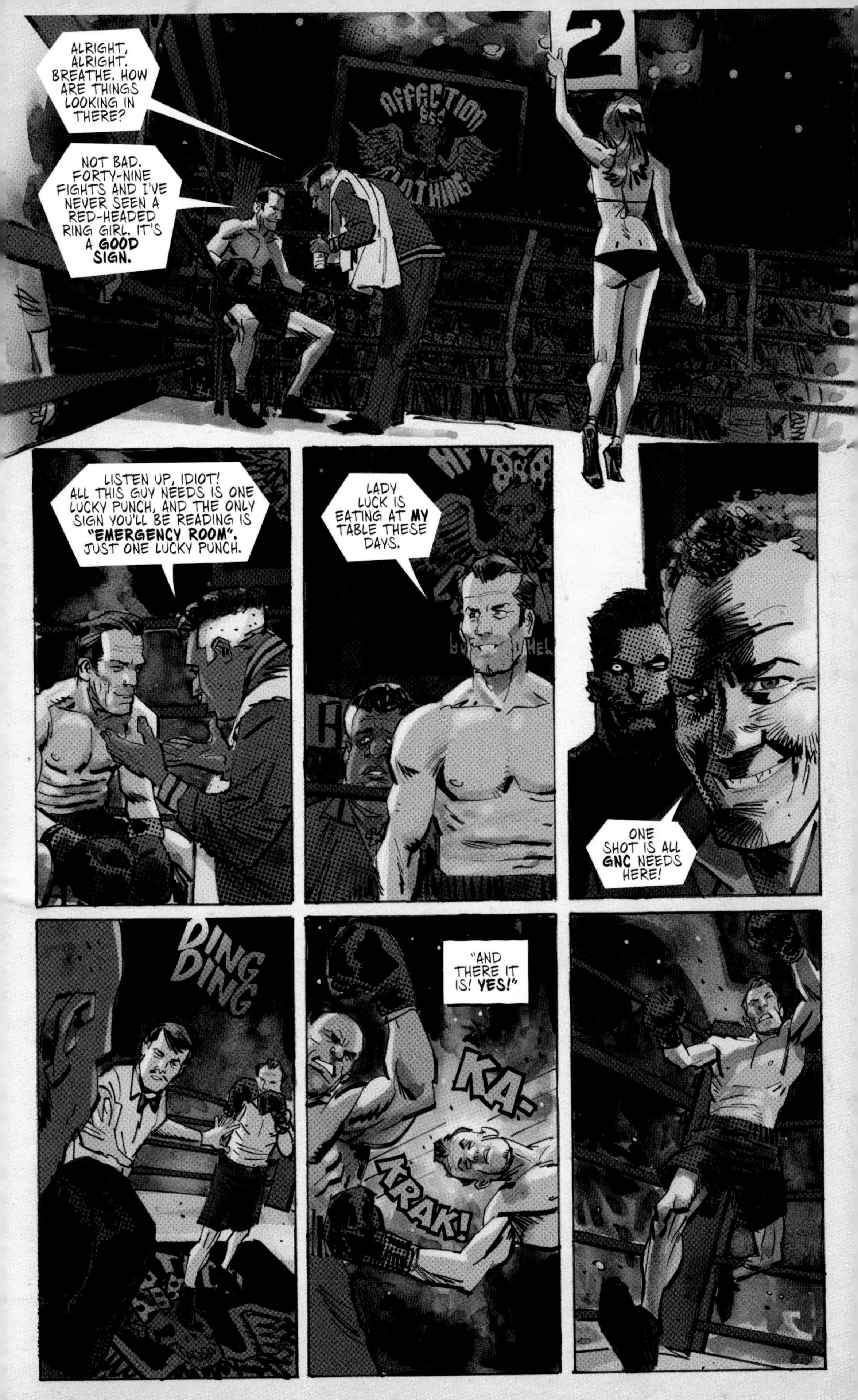
2
ALRIGHT, ALRIGHT. BREATHE. HOW ARE THINGS LOOKING IN THERE?
NOT BAD. FORTY-NINE FIGHTS AND I'VE NEVER SEEN A RED-HEADED RING GIRL. IT'S A GOOD SIGN.
AFFECTION
LISTEN UP, IDIOT! ALL THIS GUY NEEDS IS ONE LUCKY PUNCH, AND THE ONLY SIGN YOU'LL BE READING IS "EMERGENCY ROOM". JUST ONE LUCKY PUNCH.
LADY LUCK IS EATING AT MY TABLE THESE DAYS.
ONE SHOT IS ALL GNC NEEDS HERE!
DING DING
"AND THERE IT IS! YES!"
KA-TRAK!

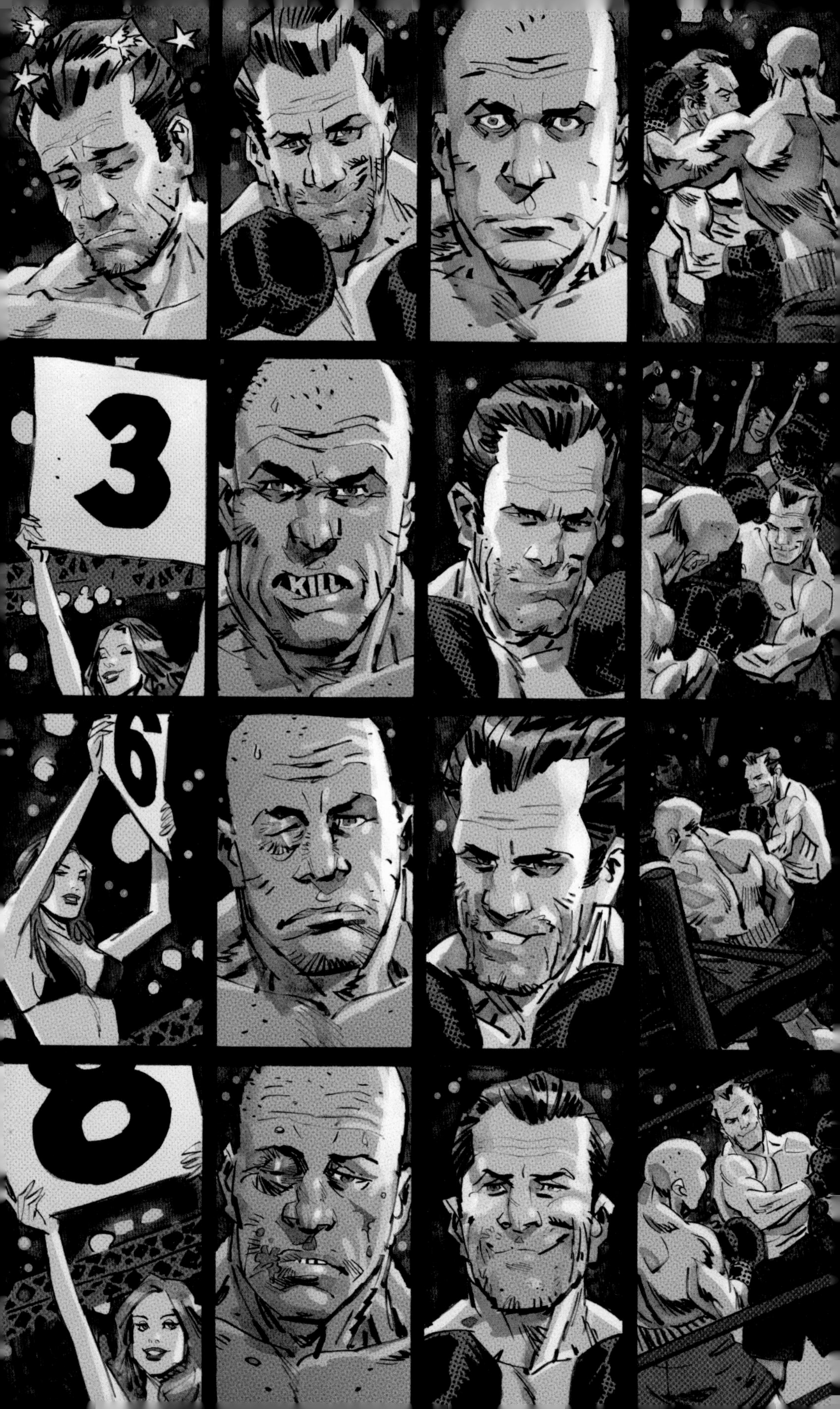
3
KILL
6
8

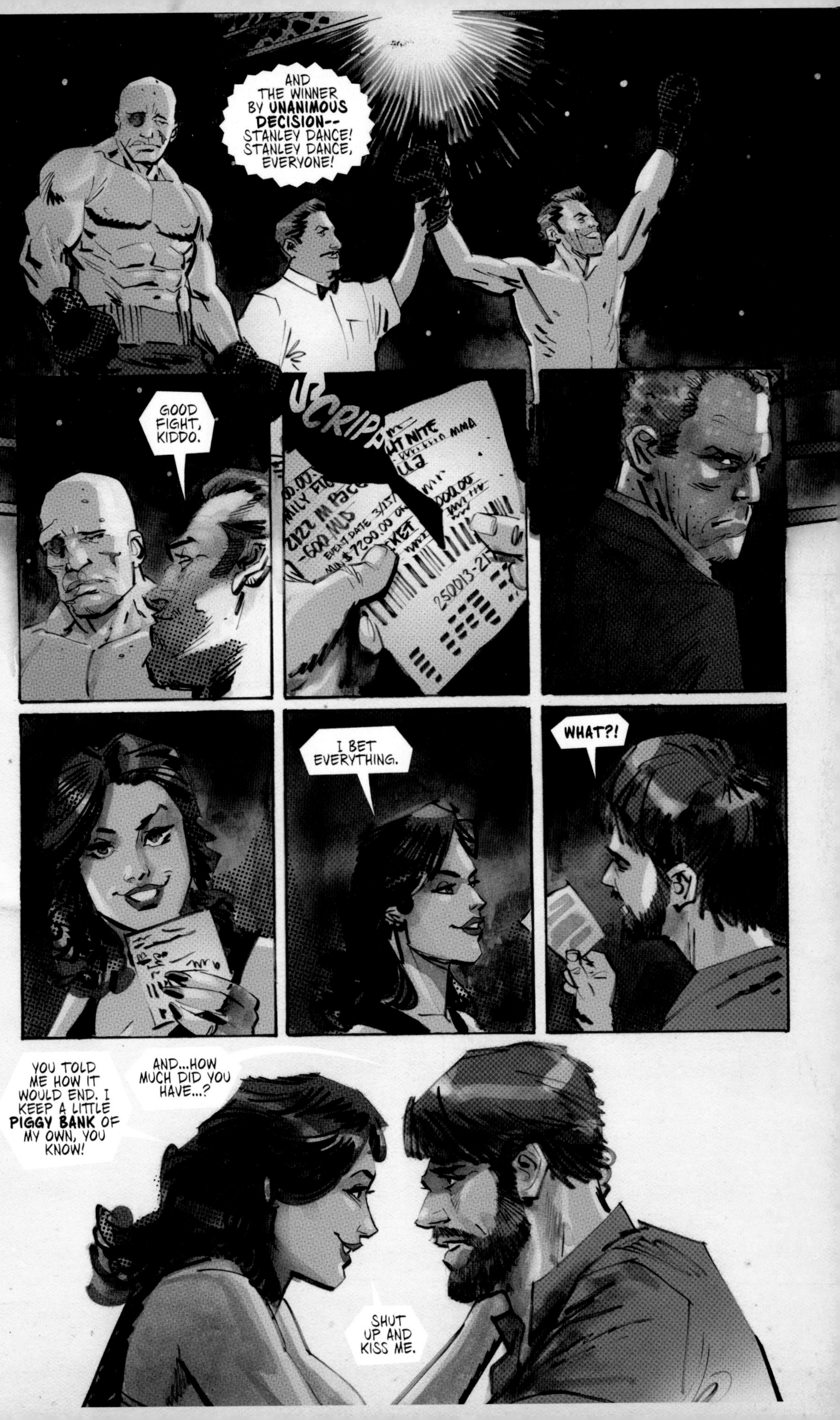
AND THE WINNER BY UNANIMOUS DECISION-- STANLEY DANCE! STANLEY DANCE, EVERYONE!
GOOD FIGHT, KIDDO.
SCRIPP
WHAT?!
I BET EVERYTHING.
YOU TOLD ME HOW IT WOULD END. I KEEP A LITTLE PIGGY BANK OF MY OWN, YOU KNOW!
AND...HOW MUCH DID YOU HAVE...?
SHUT UP AND KISS ME.

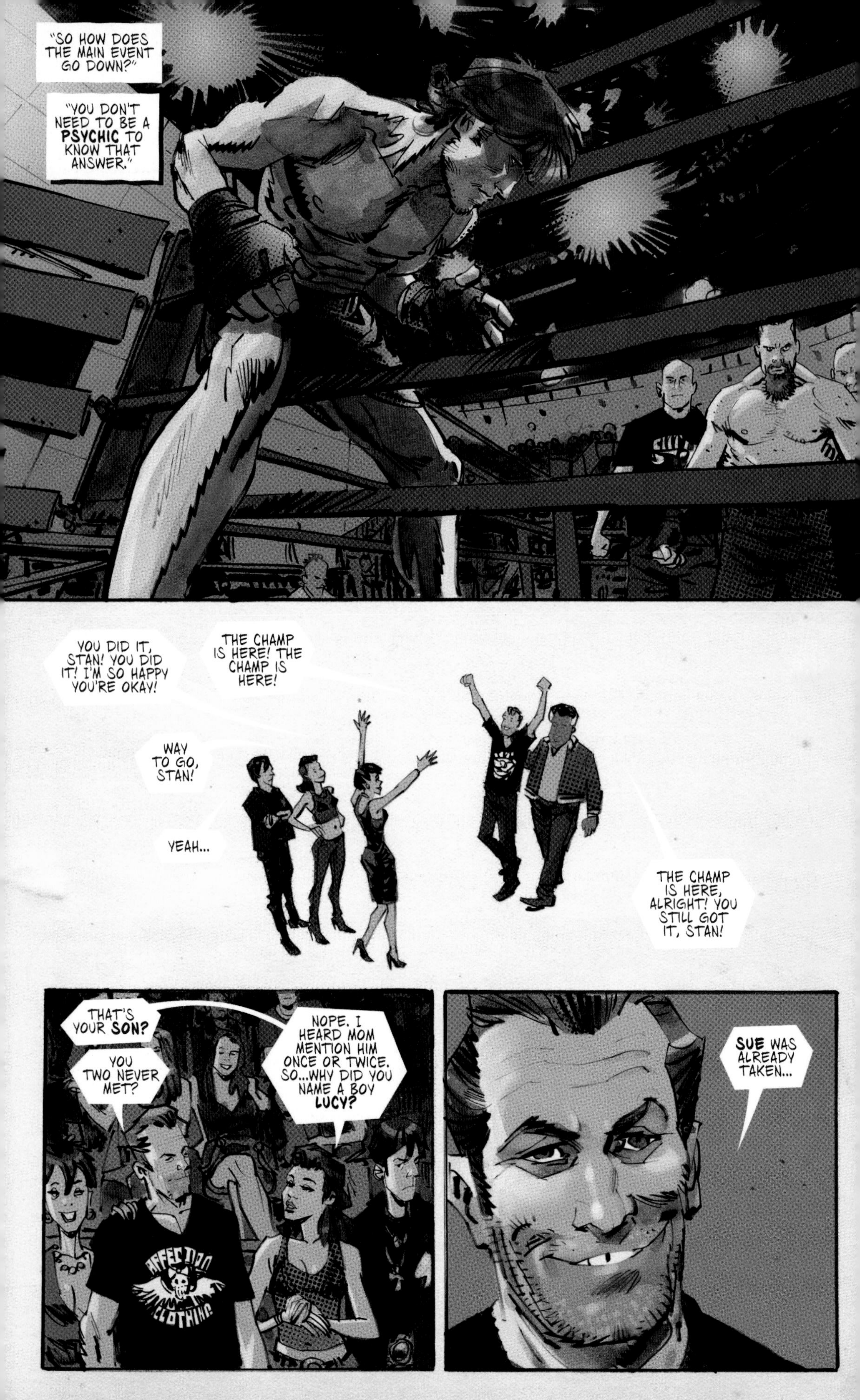
"SO HOW DOES THE MAIN EVENT GO DOWN?"
"YOU DON'T NEED TO BE A PSYCHIC TO KNOW THAT ANSWER."
YOU DID IT, STAN! YOU DID IT! I'M SO HAPPY YOU'RE OKAY!
THE CHAMP IS HERE! THE CHAMP IS HERE!
WAY TO GO, STAN!
YEAH...
THE CHAMP IS HERE, ALRIGHT! YOU STILL GOT IT, STAN!
THAT'S YOUR SON?
YOU TWO NEVER MET?
NOPE. I HEARD MOM MENTION HIM ONCE OR TWICE. SO...WHY DID YOU NAME A BOY LUCY?
SUE WAS ALREADY TAKEN...

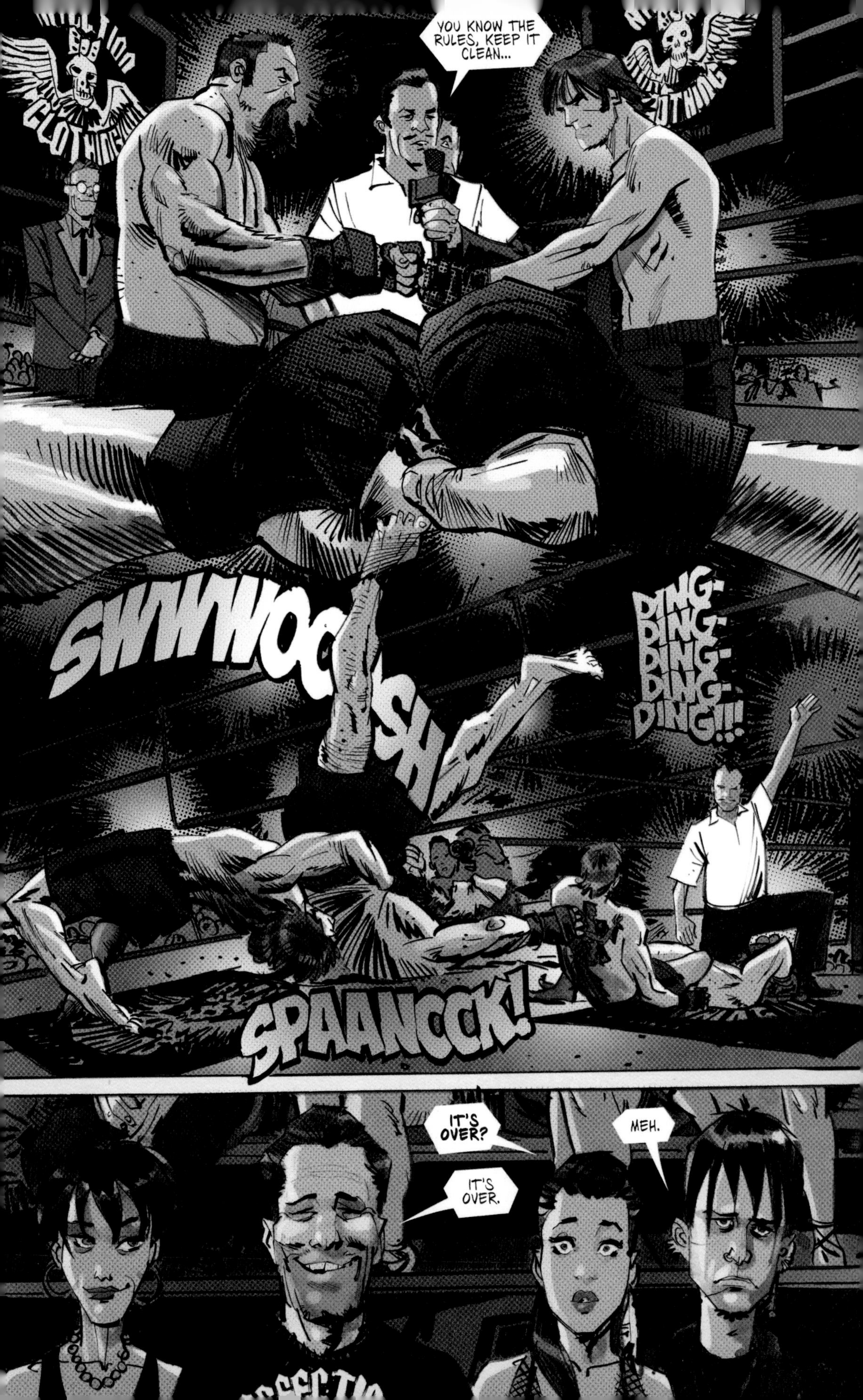
YOU KNOW THE RULES, KEEP IT CLEAN...
SWWOOOSH
DING-DING-DING-DING-DING!!!
SPAANCCK!
IT'S OVER?
IT'S OVER.
MEH.

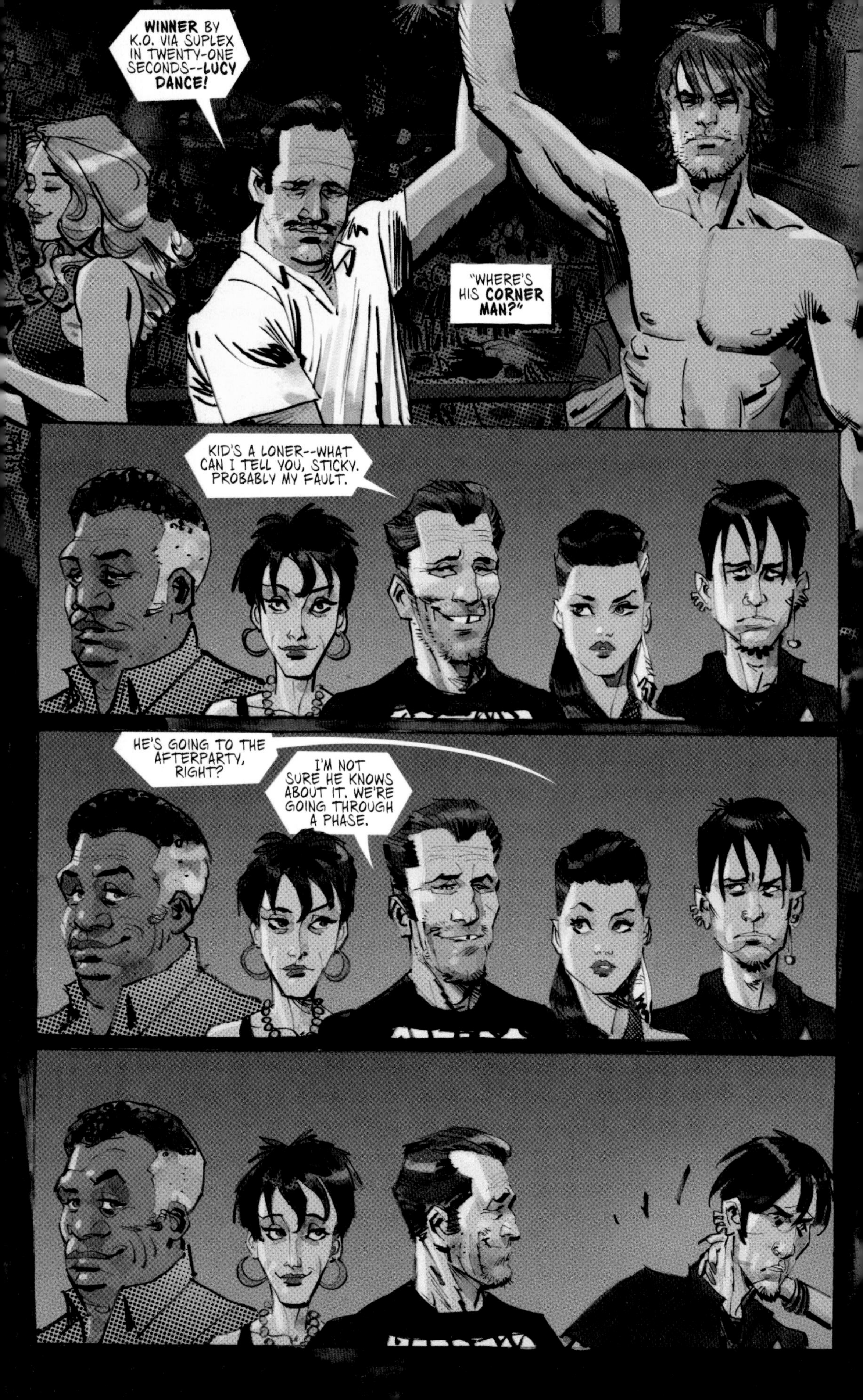
WINNER BY K.O. VIA SUPLEX IN TWENTY-ONE SECONDS--LUCY DANCE!
"WHERE'S HIS CORNER MAN?"
KID'S A LONER--WHAT CAN I TELL YOU, STICKY. PROBABLY MY FAULT.
HE'S GOING TO THE AFTERPARTY, RIGHT?
I'M NOT SURE HE KNOWS ABOUT IT. WE'RE GOING THROUGH A PHASE.

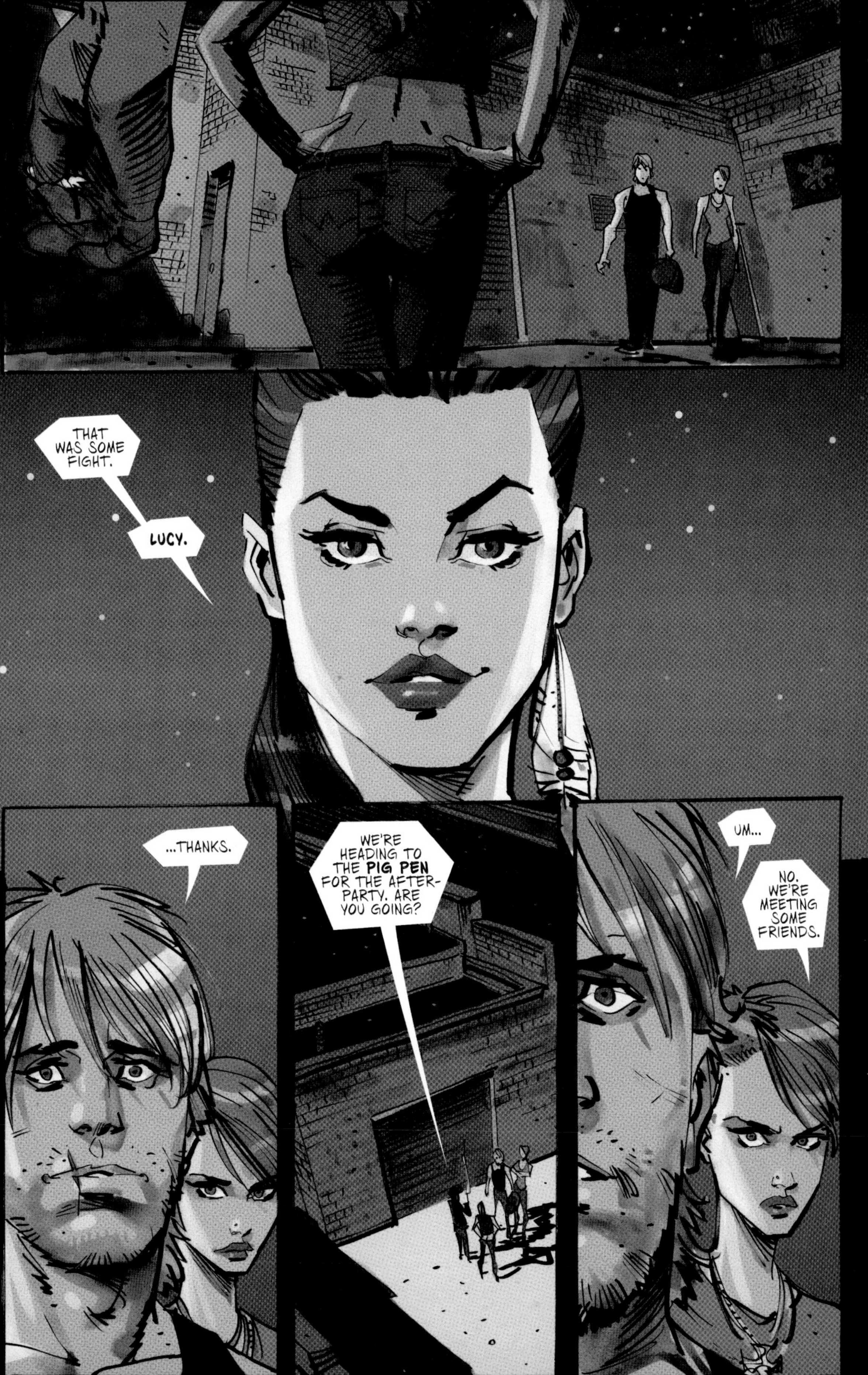
THAT WAS SOME FIGHT.
LUCY.
...THANKS.
WE'RE HEADING TO THE **PIG PEN** FOR THE AFTER-PARTY. ARE YOU GOING?
UM...
NO. WE'RE MEETING SOME FRIENDS.

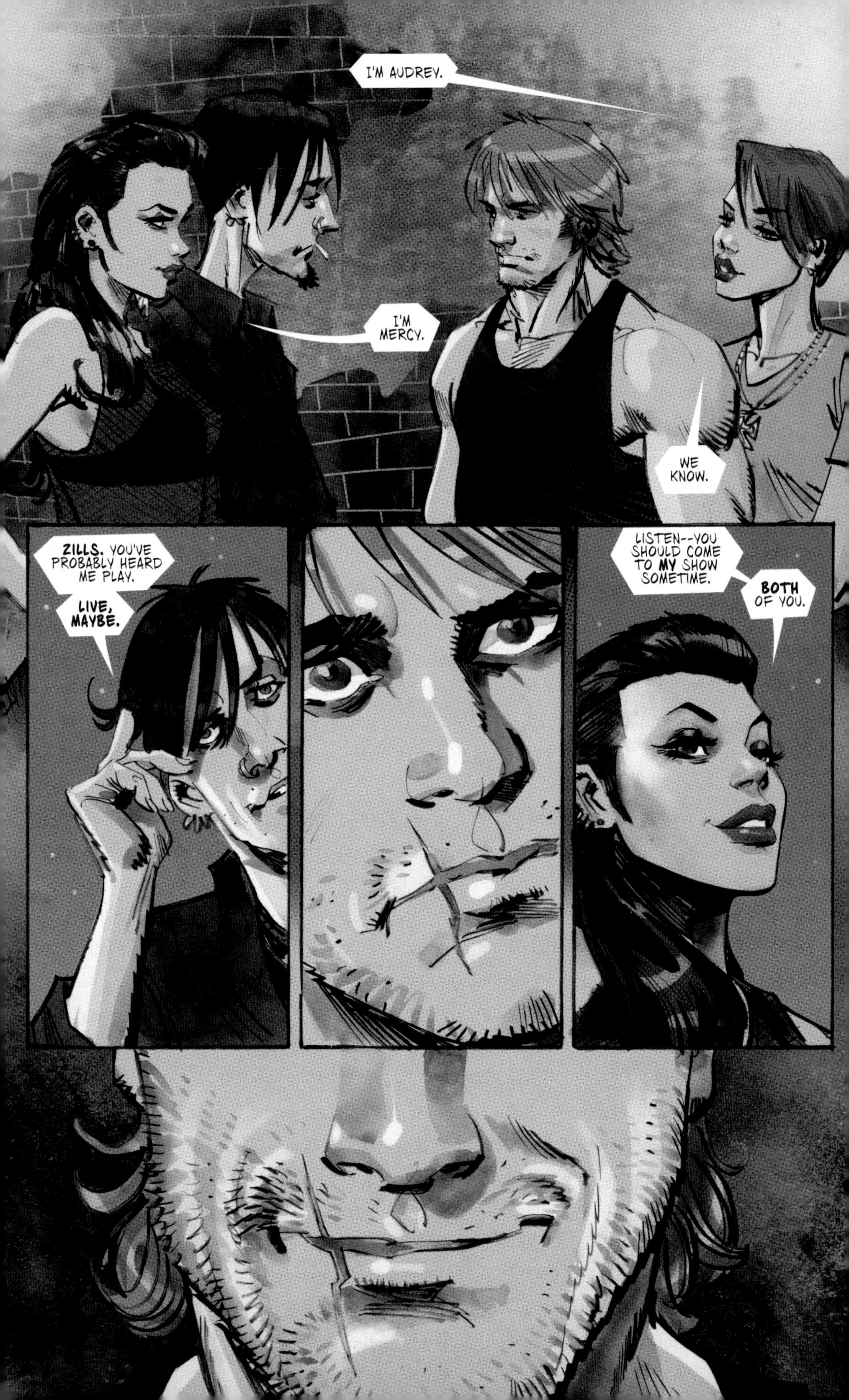
I'M AUDREY.
I'M MERCY.
WE KNOW.
ZILLS. YOU'VE PROBABLY HEARD ME PLAY.
LIVE, MAYBE.
LISTEN--YOU SHOULD COME TO MY SHOW SOMETIME.
BOTH OF YOU.

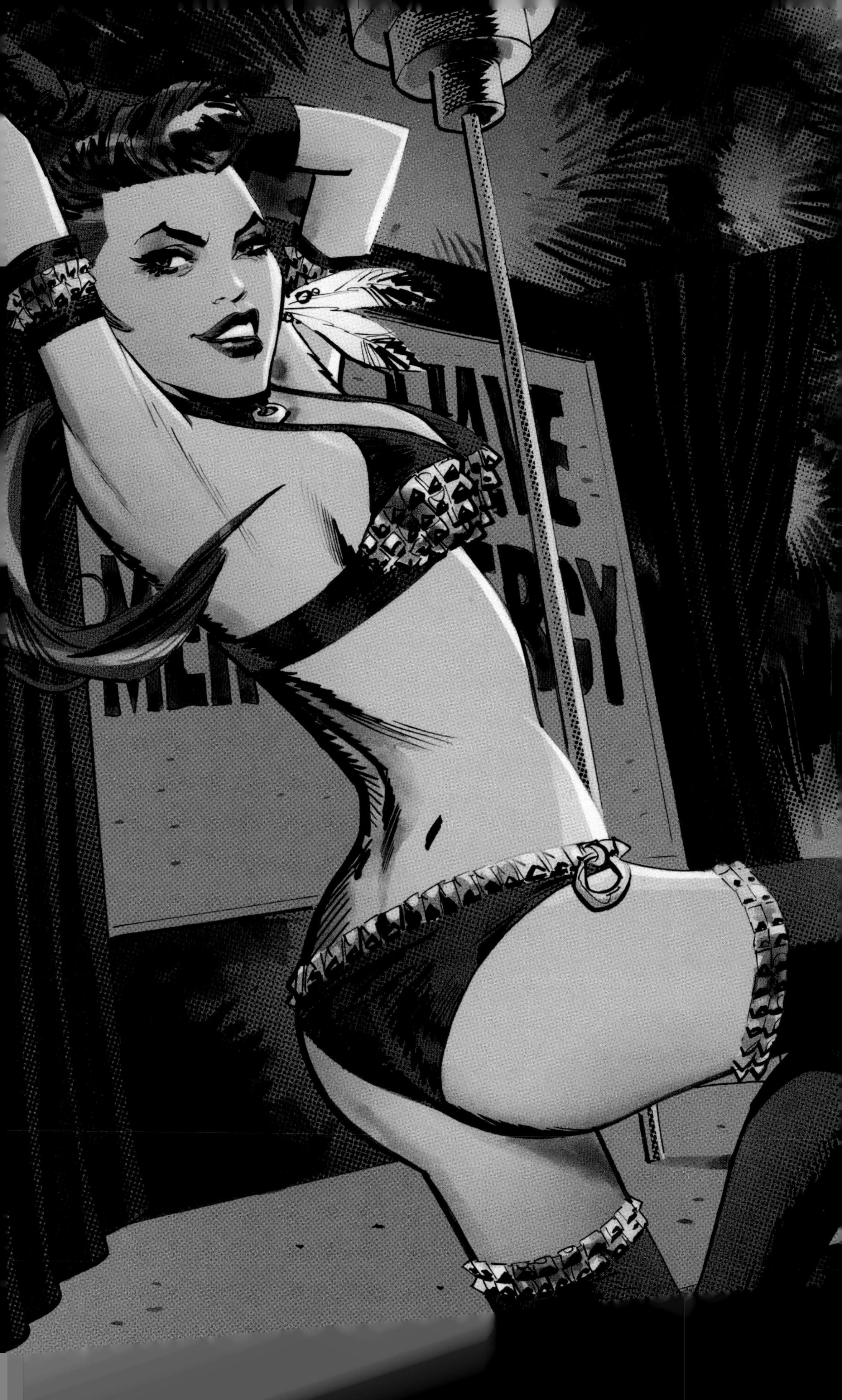

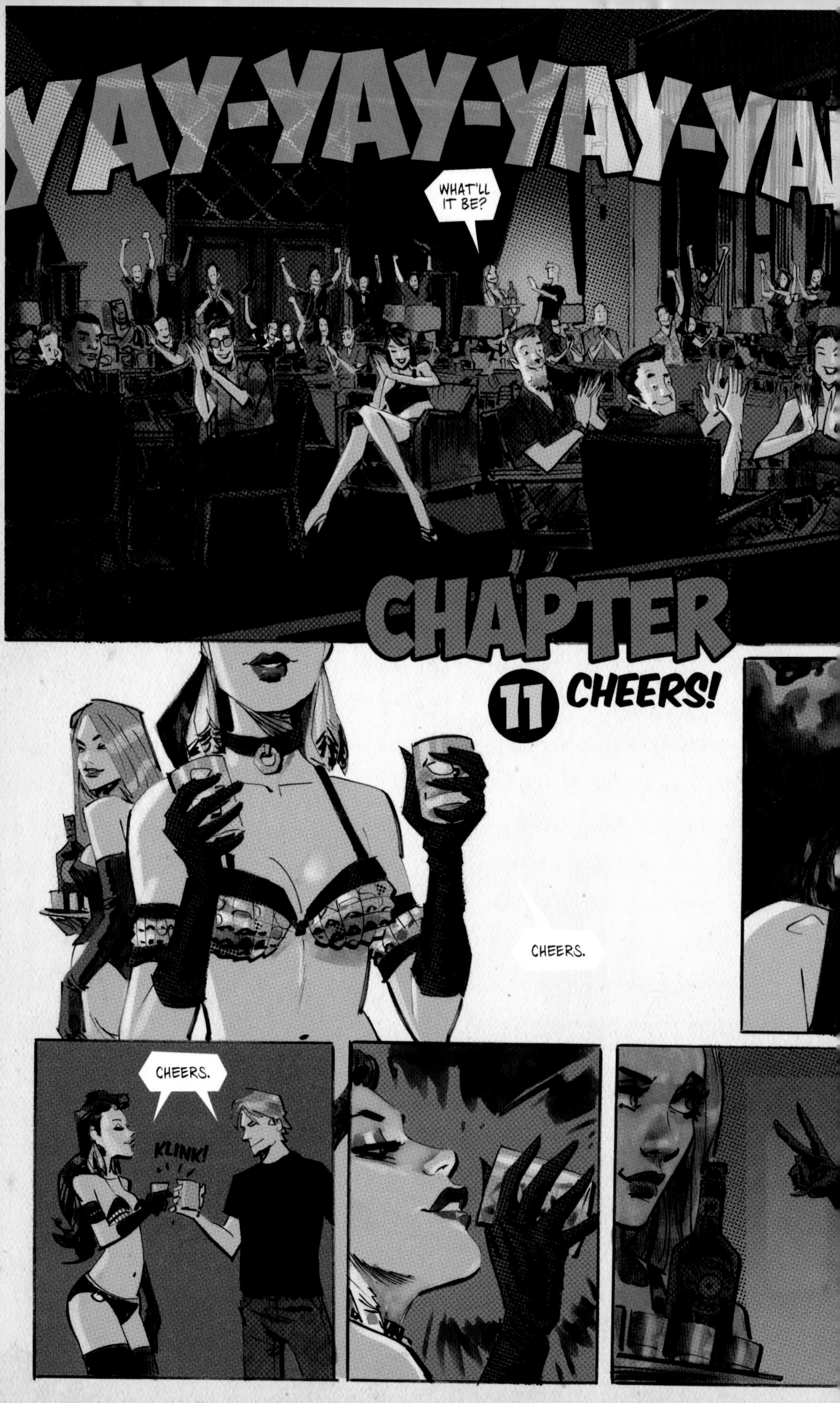

YAY-YAY-YAY-YA
WHAT'LL IT BE?
CHAPTER
11 CHEERS!
CHEERS.
CHEERS.
KLINK!

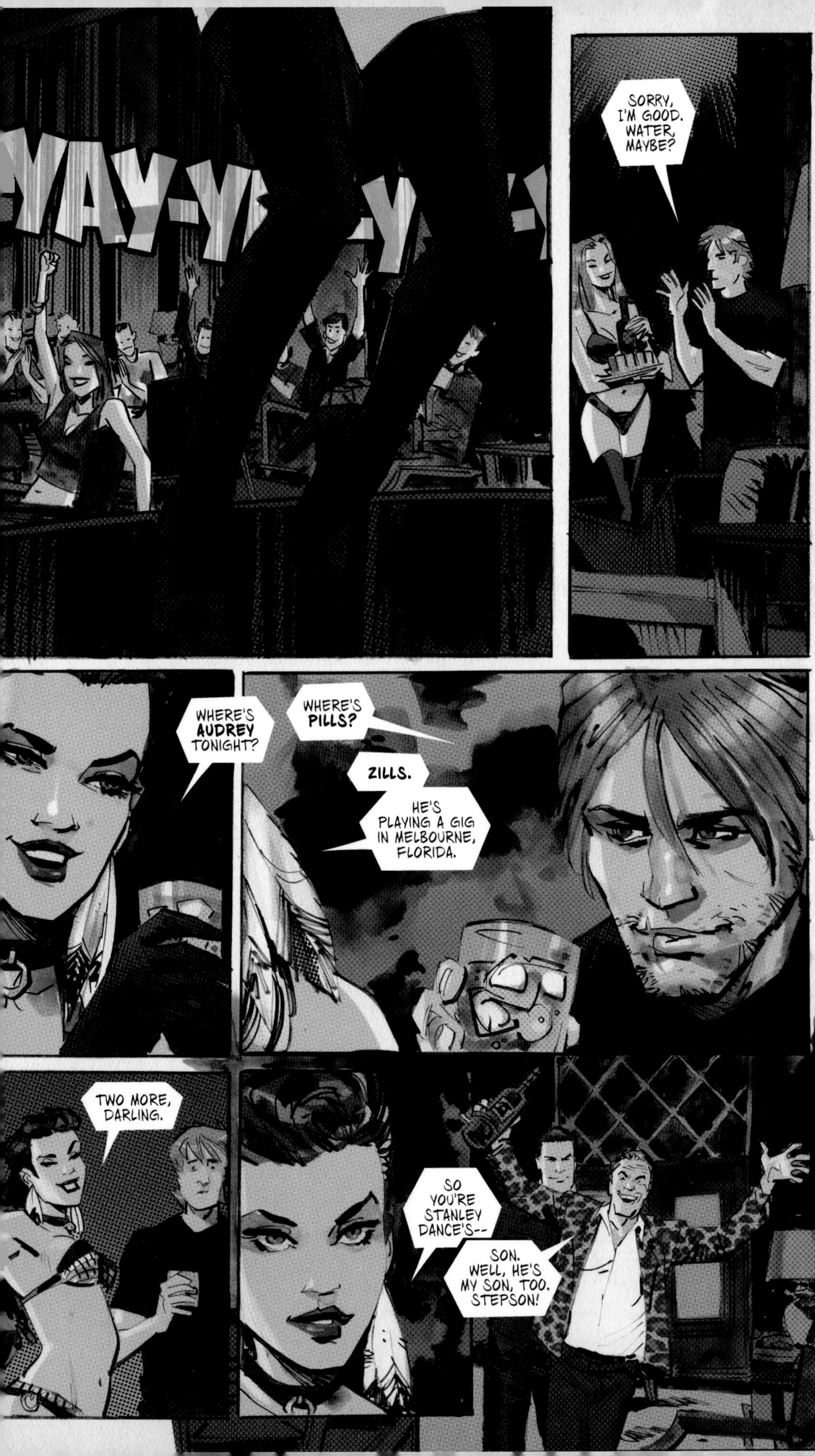
YAY-Y Y-Y
SORRY, I'M GOOD. WATER, MAYBE?
WHERE'S AUDREY TONIGHT?
WHERE'S PILLS?
ZILLS.
HE'S PLAYING A GIG IN MELBOURNE, FLORIDA.
TWO MORE, DARLING.
SO YOU'RE STANLEY DANCE'S--
SON. WELL, HE'S MY SON, TOO. STEPSON!

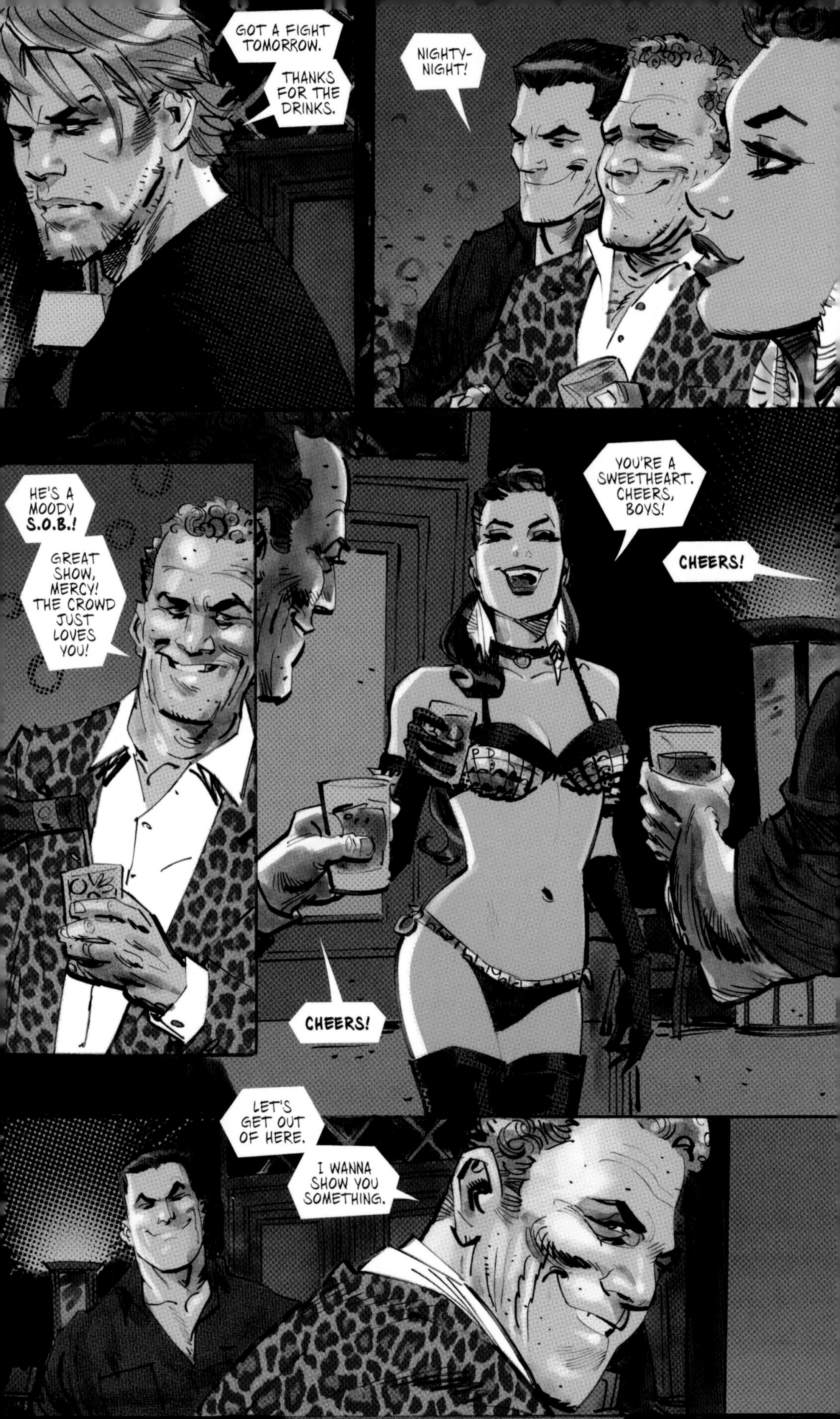
GOT A FIGHT TOMORROW.
THANKS FOR THE DRINKS.
NIGHTY-NIGHT!
HE'S A MOODY **S.O.B.!**
GREAT SHOW, MERCY! THE CROWD JUST LOVES YOU!
YOU'RE A SWEETHEART. CHEERS, BOYS!
CHEERS!
CHEERS!
LET'S GET OUT OF HERE.
I WANNA SHOW YOU SOMETHING.

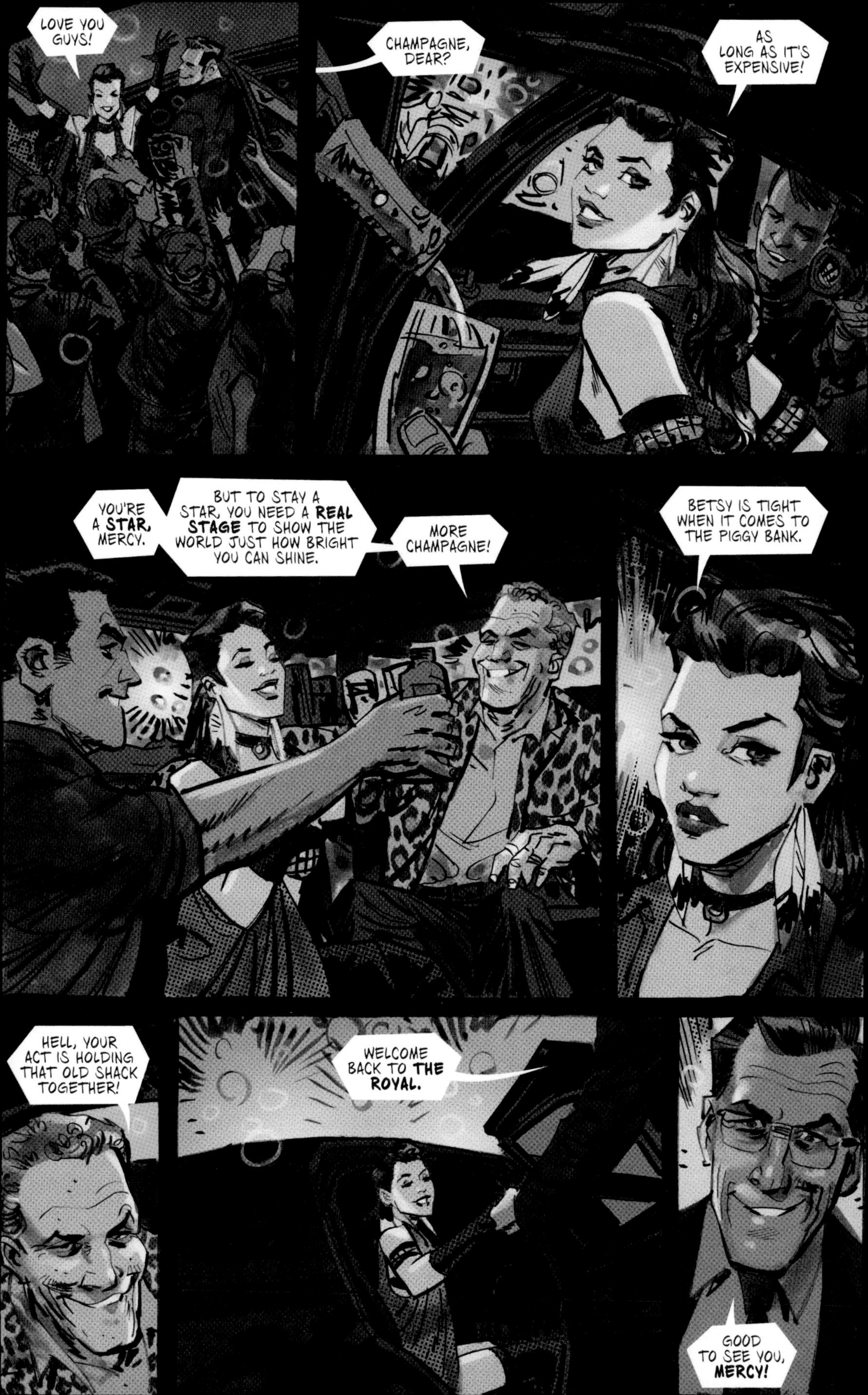
LOVE YOU GUYS!
CHAMPAGNE, DEAR?
AS LONG AS IT'S EXPENSIVE!
YOU'RE A **STAR,** MERCY.
BUT TO STAY A STAR, YOU NEED A **REAL STAGE** TO SHOW THE WORLD JUST HOW BRIGHT YOU CAN SHINE.
MORE CHAMPAGNE!
BETSY IS TIGHT WHEN IT COMES TO THE PIGGY BANK.
HELL, YOUR ACT IS HOLDING THAT OLD SHACK TOGETHER!
WELCOME BACK TO **THE ROYAL.**
GOOD TO SEE YOU, **MERCY!**

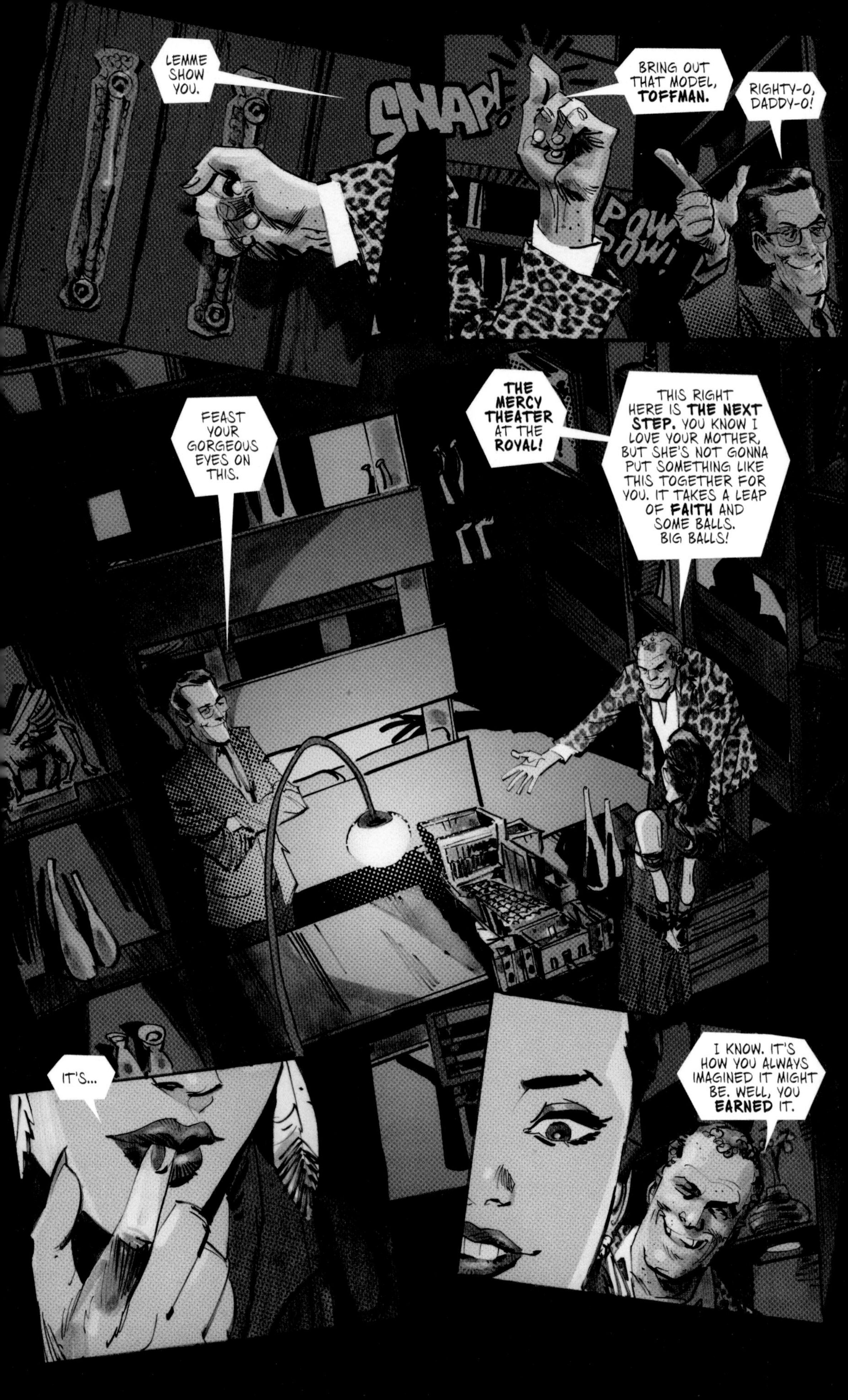

LEMME SHOW YOU.
SNAP!
BRING OUT THAT MODEL, TOFFMAN.
RIGHTY-O, DADDY-O!
POW POW!
FEAST YOUR GORGEOUS EYES ON THIS.
THE MERCY THEATER AT THE ROYAL!
THIS RIGHT HERE IS THE NEXT STEP. YOU KNOW I LOVE YOUR MOTHER, BUT SHE'S NOT GONNA PUT SOMETHING LIKE THIS TOGETHER FOR YOU. IT TAKES A LEAP OF FAITH AND SOME BALLS. BIG BALLS!
IT'S...
I KNOW. IT'S HOW YOU ALWAYS IMAGINED IT MIGHT BE. WELL, YOU EARNED IT.

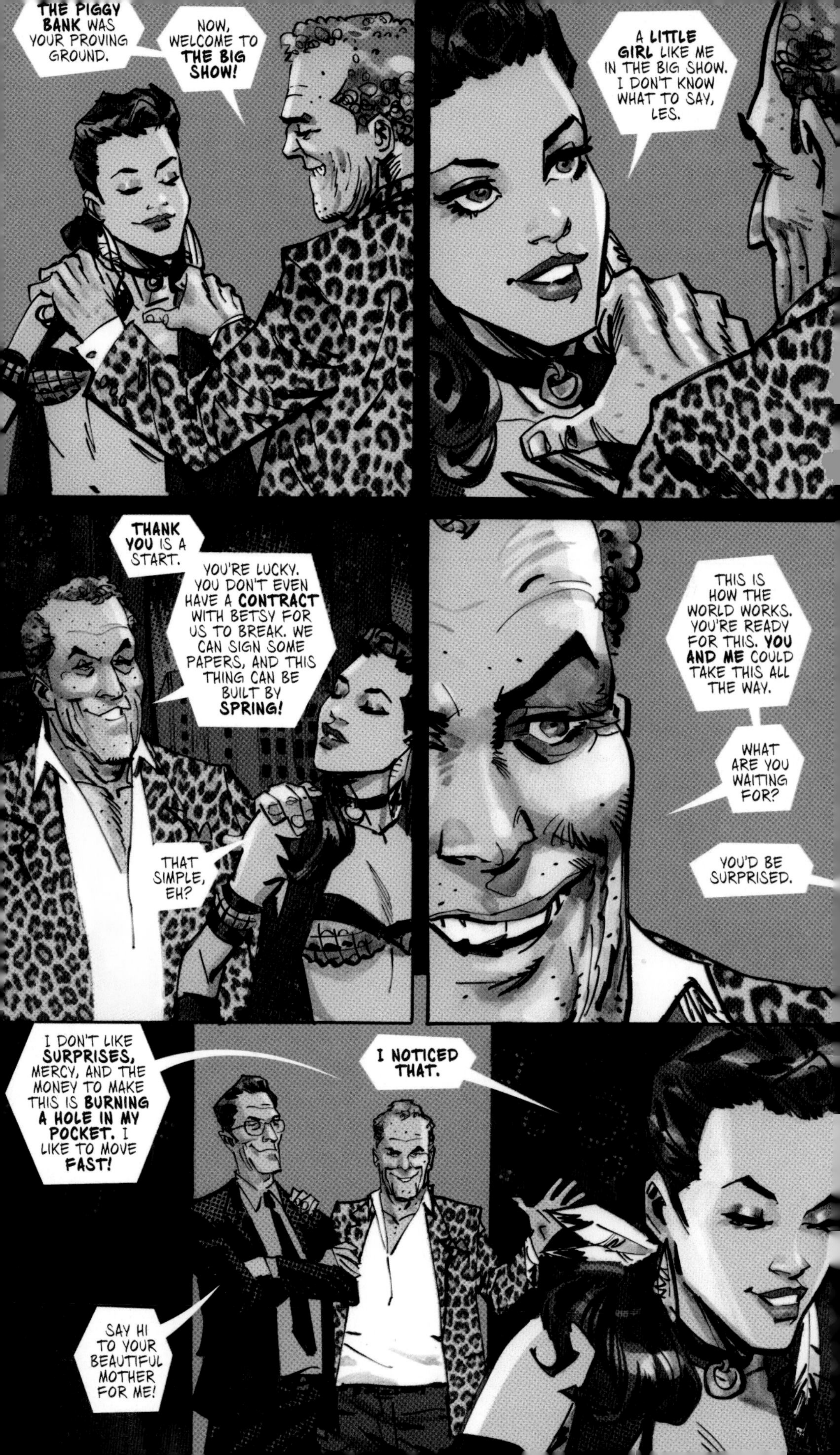

THE PIGGY BANK WAS YOUR PROVING GROUND.
NOW, WELCOME TO THE BIG SHOW!
A LITTLE GIRL LIKE ME IN THE BIG SHOW. I DON'T KNOW WHAT TO SAY, LES.
THANK YOU IS A START.
YOU'RE LUCKY. YOU DON'T EVEN HAVE A CONTRACT WITH BETSY FOR US TO BREAK. WE CAN SIGN SOME PAPERS, AND THIS THING CAN BE BUILT BY SPRING!
THAT SIMPLE, EH?
THIS IS HOW THE WORLD WORKS. YOU'RE READY FOR THIS. YOU AND ME COULD TAKE THIS ALL THE WAY.
WHAT ARE YOU WAITING FOR?
YOU'D BE SURPRISED.
I DON'T LIKE SURPRISES, MERCY, AND THE MONEY TO MAKE THIS IS BURNING A HOLE IN MY POCKET. I LIKE TO MOVE FAST!
I NOTICED THAT.
SAY HI TO YOUR BEAUTIFUL MOTHER FOR ME!

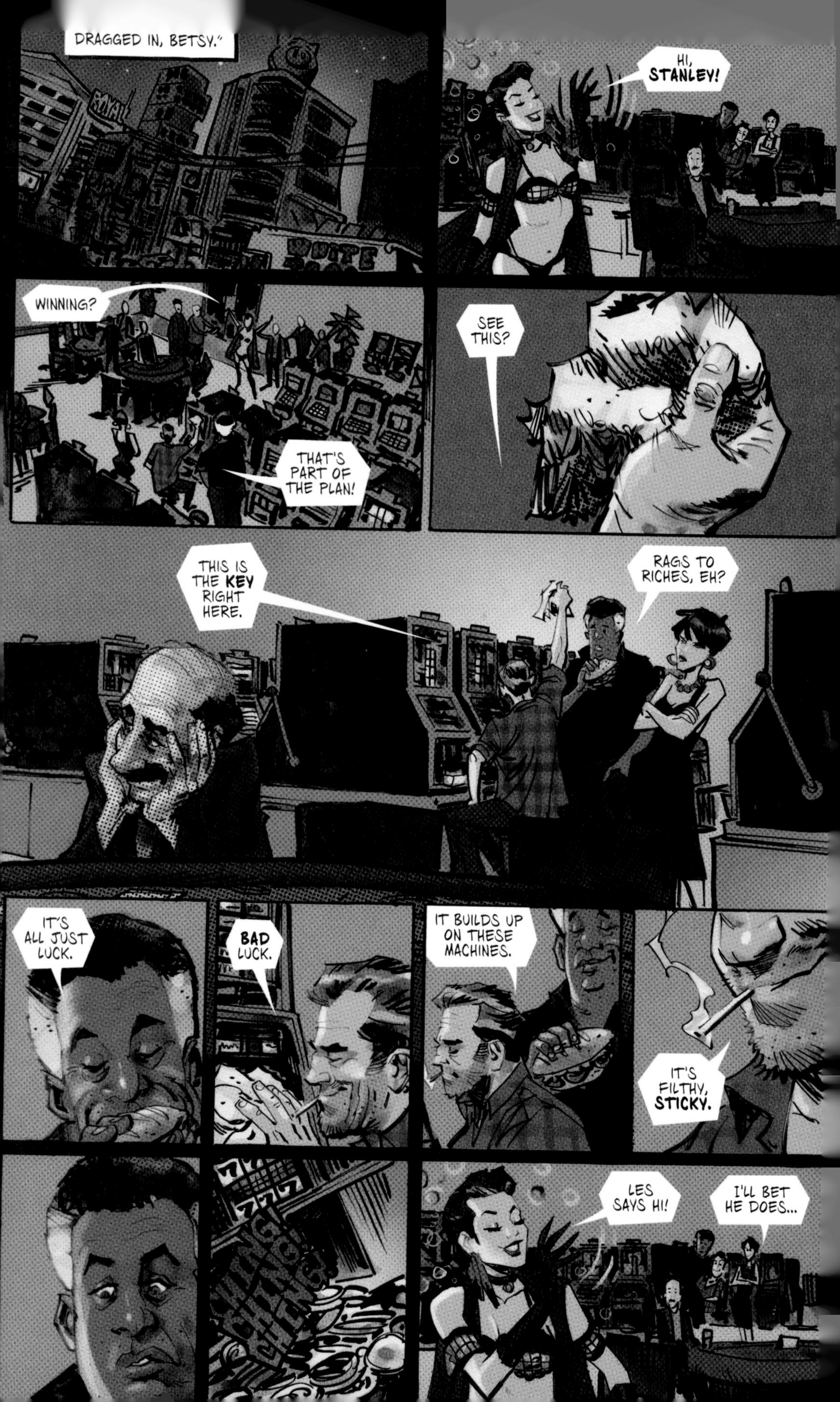
DRAGGED IN, BETSY."
HI, STANLEY!
WINNING?
THAT'S PART OF THE PLAN!
SEE THIS?
THIS IS THE KEY RIGHT HERE.
RAGS TO RICHES, EH?
IT'S ALL JUST LUCK.
BAD LUCK.
IT BUILDS UP ON THESE MACHINES.
IT'S FILTHY, STICKY.
LES SAYS HI!
I'LL BET HE DOES...

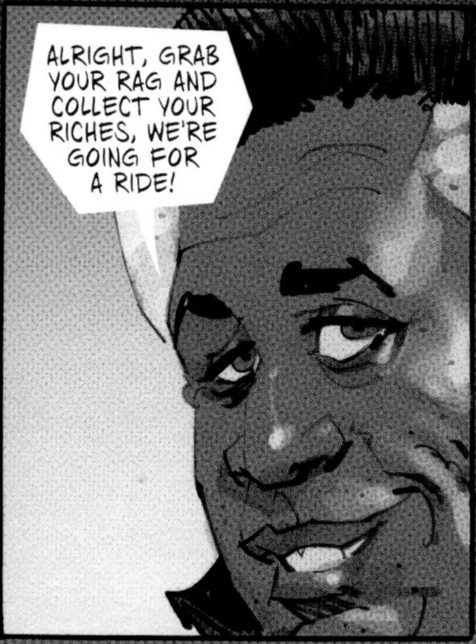
ALRIGHT, GRAB YOUR RAG AND COLLECT YOUR RICHES, WE'RE GOING FOR A RIDE!

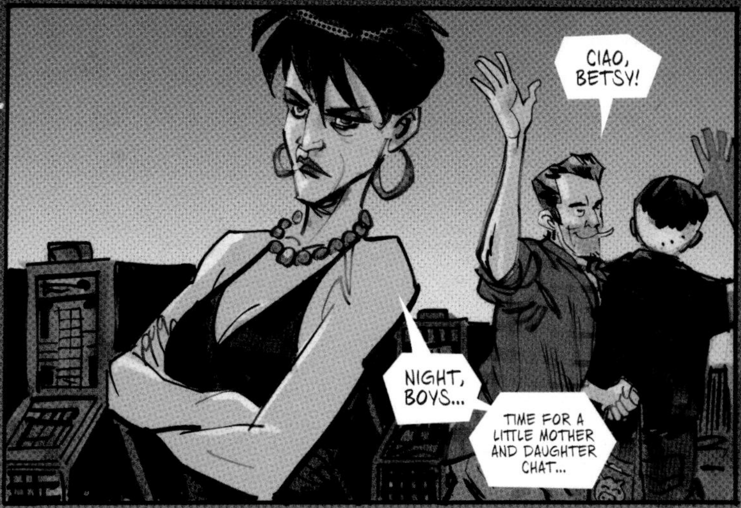
CIAO, BETSY!
NIGHT, BOYS...
TIME FOR A LITTLE MOTHER AND DAUGHTER CHAT...

CHAPTER 12
HOLY ROLLERS

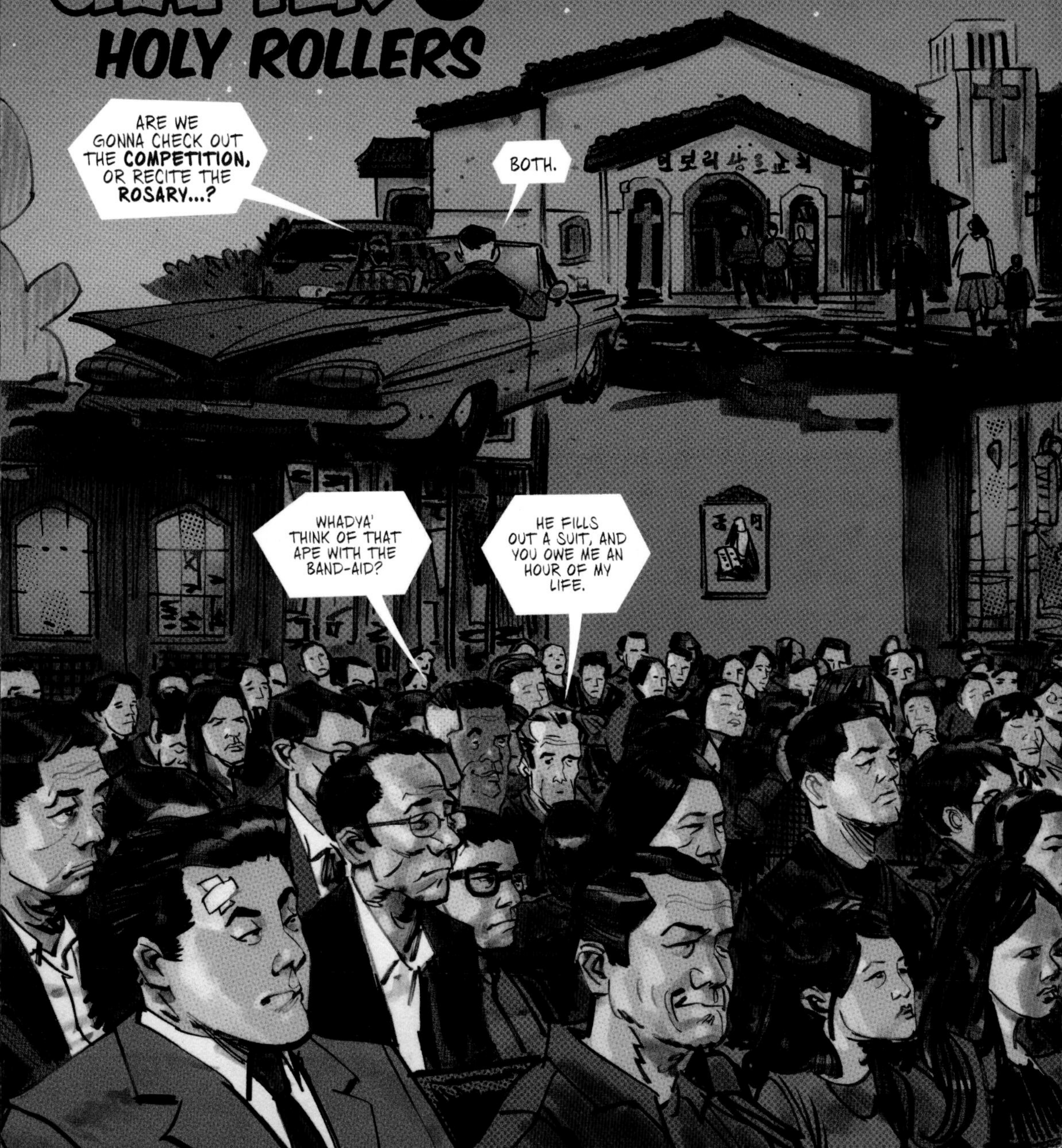
ARE WE GONNA CHECK OUT THE **COMPETITION**, OR RECITE THE **ROSARY...?**
BOTH.
WHADYA' THINK OF THAT APE WITH THE BAND-AID?
HE FILLS OUT A SUIT, AND YOU OWE ME AN HOUR OF MY LIFE.

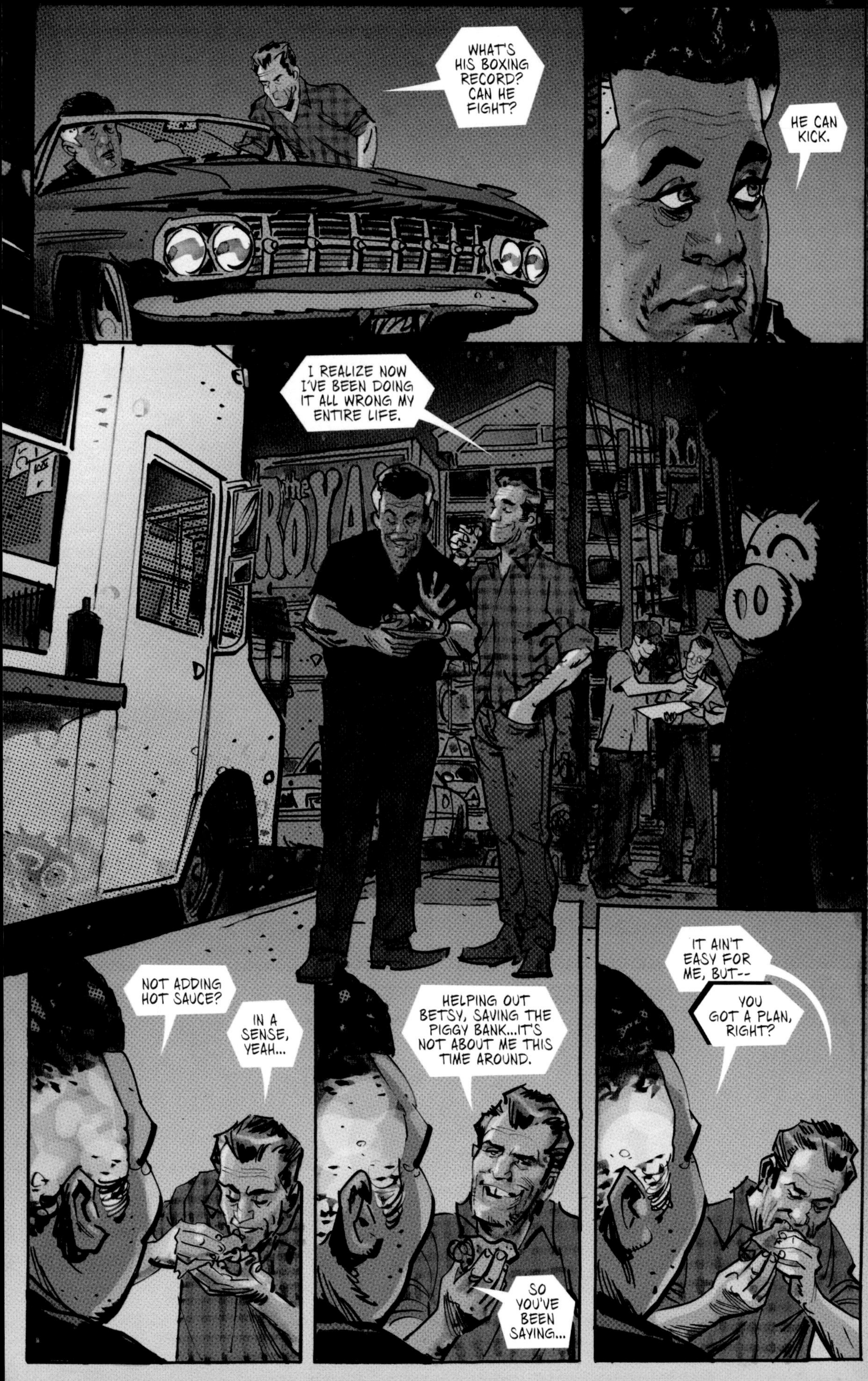
WHAT'S HIS BOXING RECORD? CAN HE FIGHT?
HE CAN KICK.
I REALIZE NOW I'VE BEEN DOING IT ALL WRONG MY ENTIRE LIFE.
NOT ADDING HOT SAUCE?
IN A SENSE, YEAH...
HELPING OUT BETSY, SAVING THE PIGGY BANK...IT'S NOT ABOUT ME THIS TIME AROUND.
SO YOU'VE BEEN SAYING...
IT AIN'T EASY FOR ME, BUT--
YOU GOT A PLAN, RIGHT?

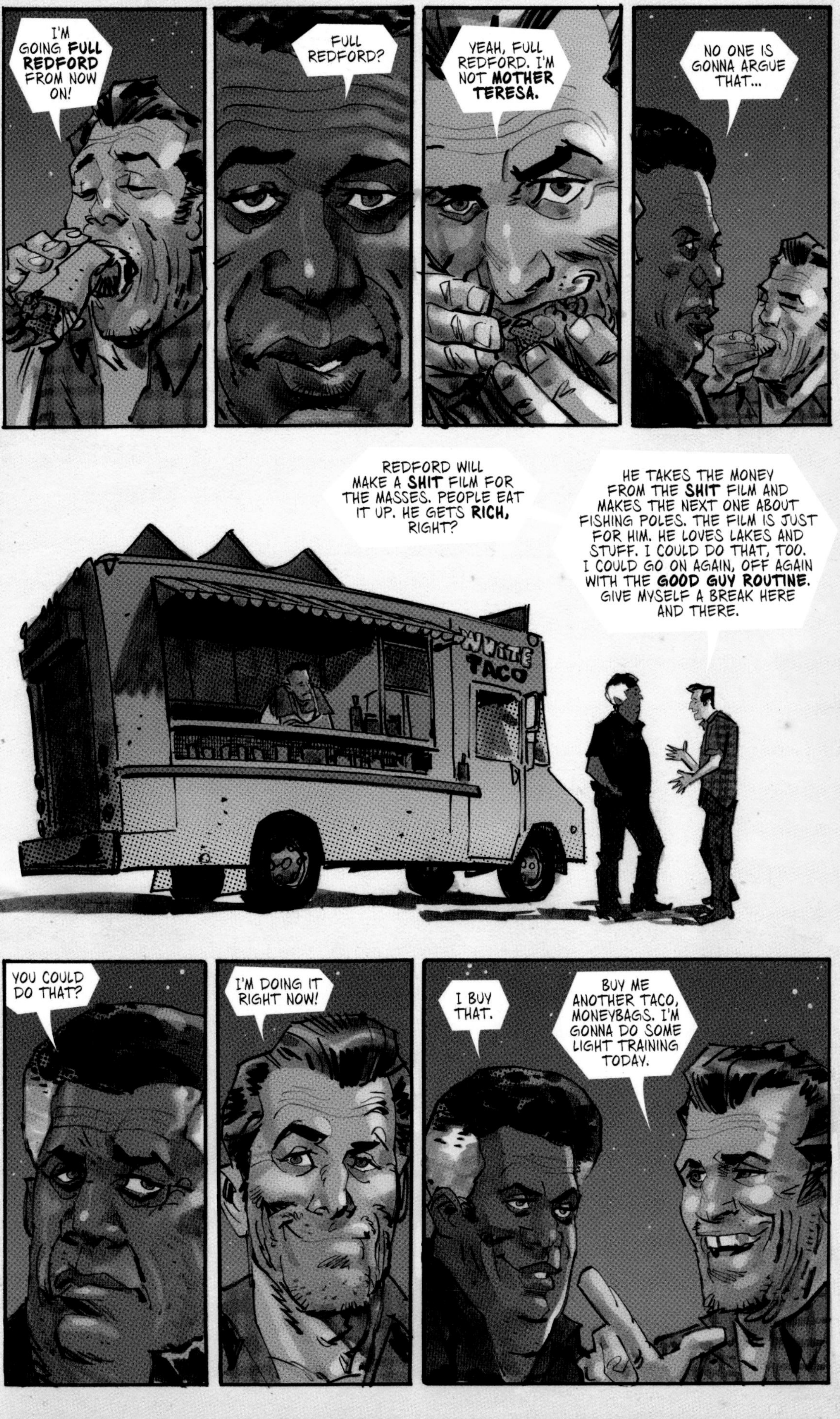

I'M GOING **FULL REDFORD** FROM NOW ON!
FULL REDFORD?
YEAH, FULL REDFORD. I'M NOT **MOTHER TERESA.**
NO ONE IS GONNA ARGUE THAT...
REDFORD WILL MAKE A **SHIT** FILM FOR THE MASSES. PEOPLE EAT IT UP. HE GETS **RICH,** RIGHT?
HE TAKES THE MONEY FROM THE **SHIT** FILM AND MAKES THE NEXT ONE ABOUT FISHING POLES. THE FILM IS JUST FOR HIM. HE LOVES LAKES AND STUFF. I COULD DO THAT, TOO. I COULD GO ON AGAIN, OFF AGAIN WITH THE **GOOD GUY ROUTINE.** GIVE MYSELF A BREAK HERE AND THERE.
WHITE TACO
YOU COULD DO THAT?
I'M DOING IT RIGHT NOW!
I BUY THAT.
BUY ME ANOTHER TACO, MONEYBAGS. I'M GONNA DO SOME LIGHT TRAINING TODAY.

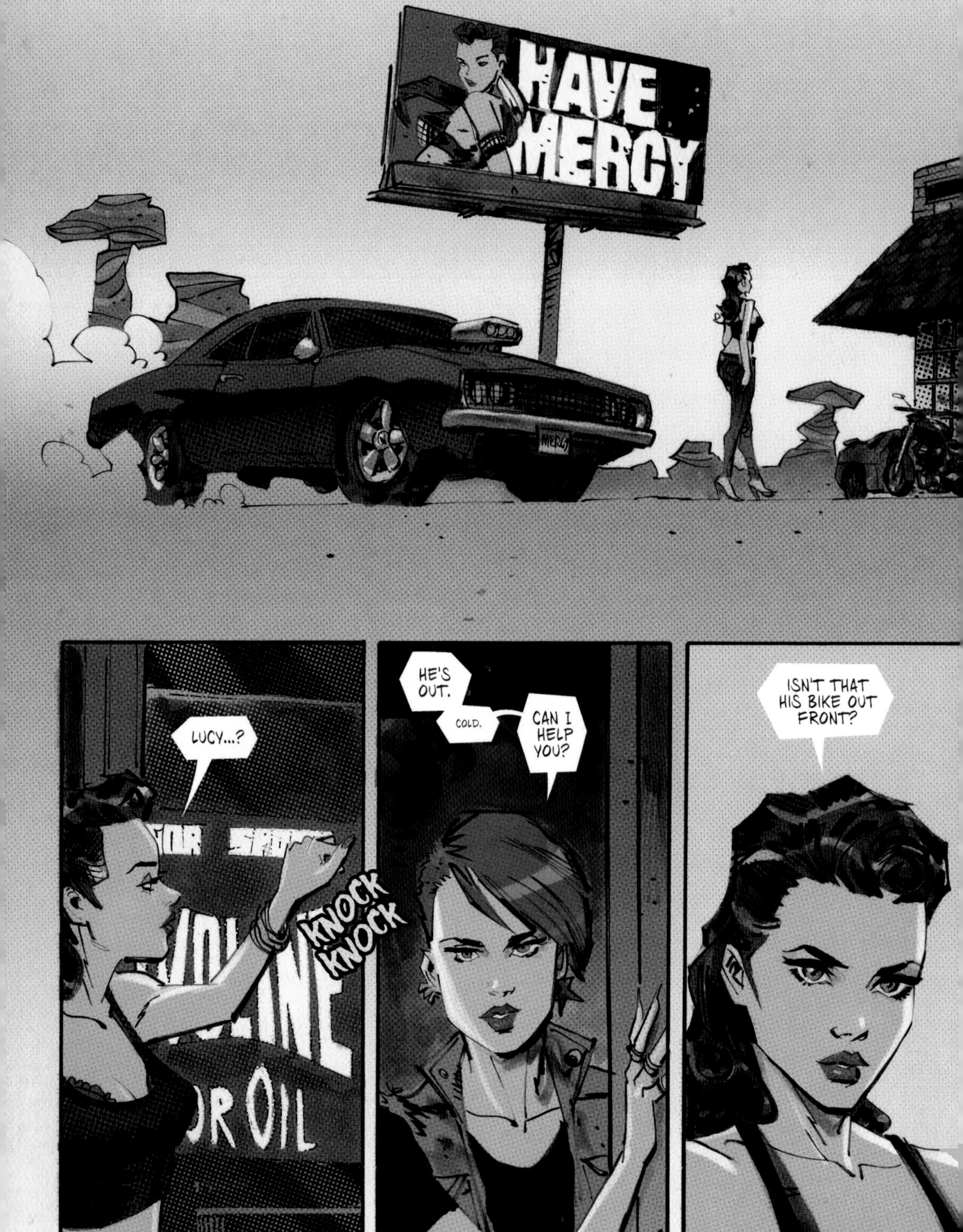
HAVE MERCY
LUCY...?
KNOCK KNOCK
HE'S OUT.
COLD.
CAN I HELP YOU?
ISN'T THAT HIS BIKE OUT FRONT?

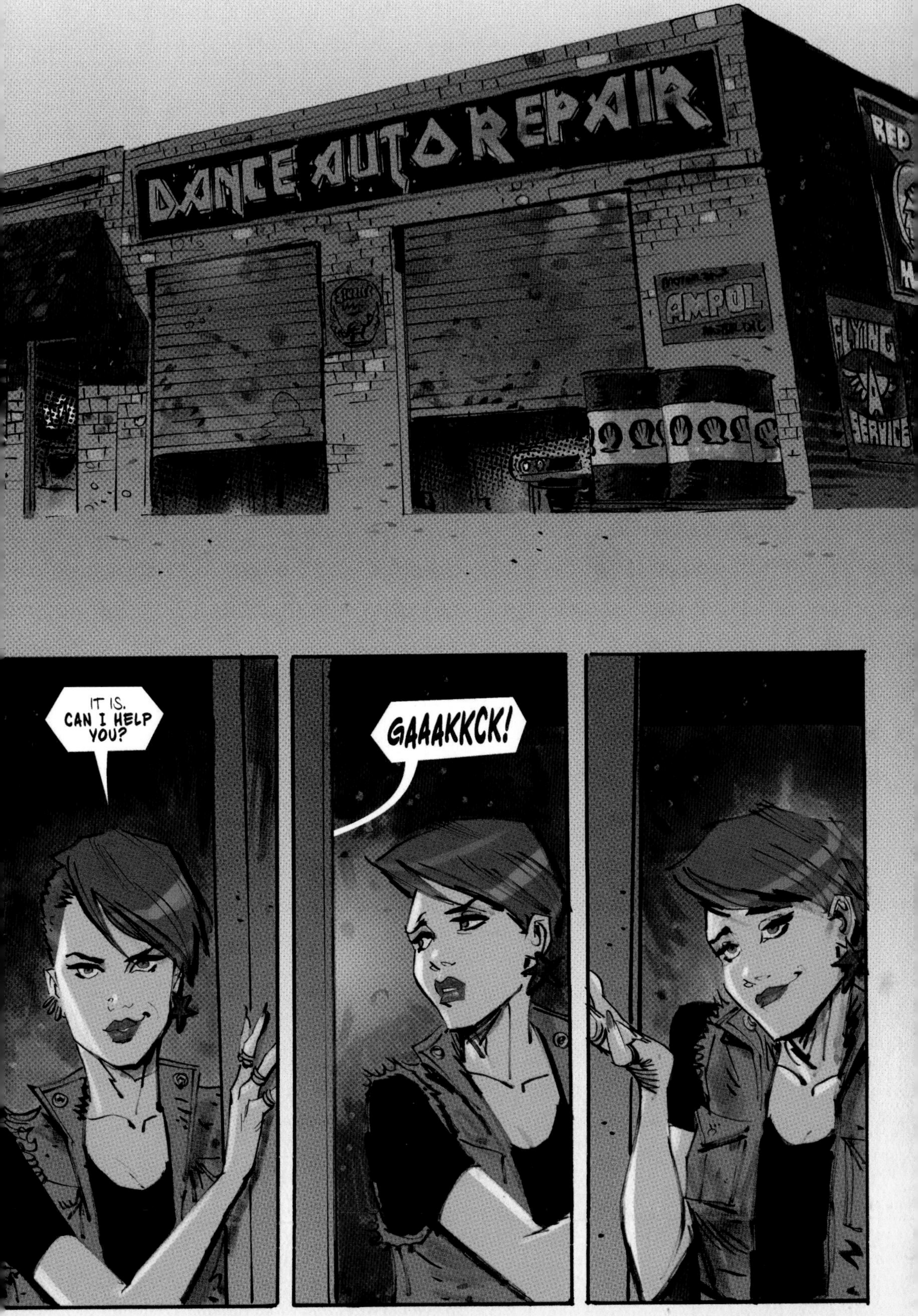
DANCE AUTO REPAIR
AMPOL
IT IS. CAN I HELP YOU?
GAAAKKCK!

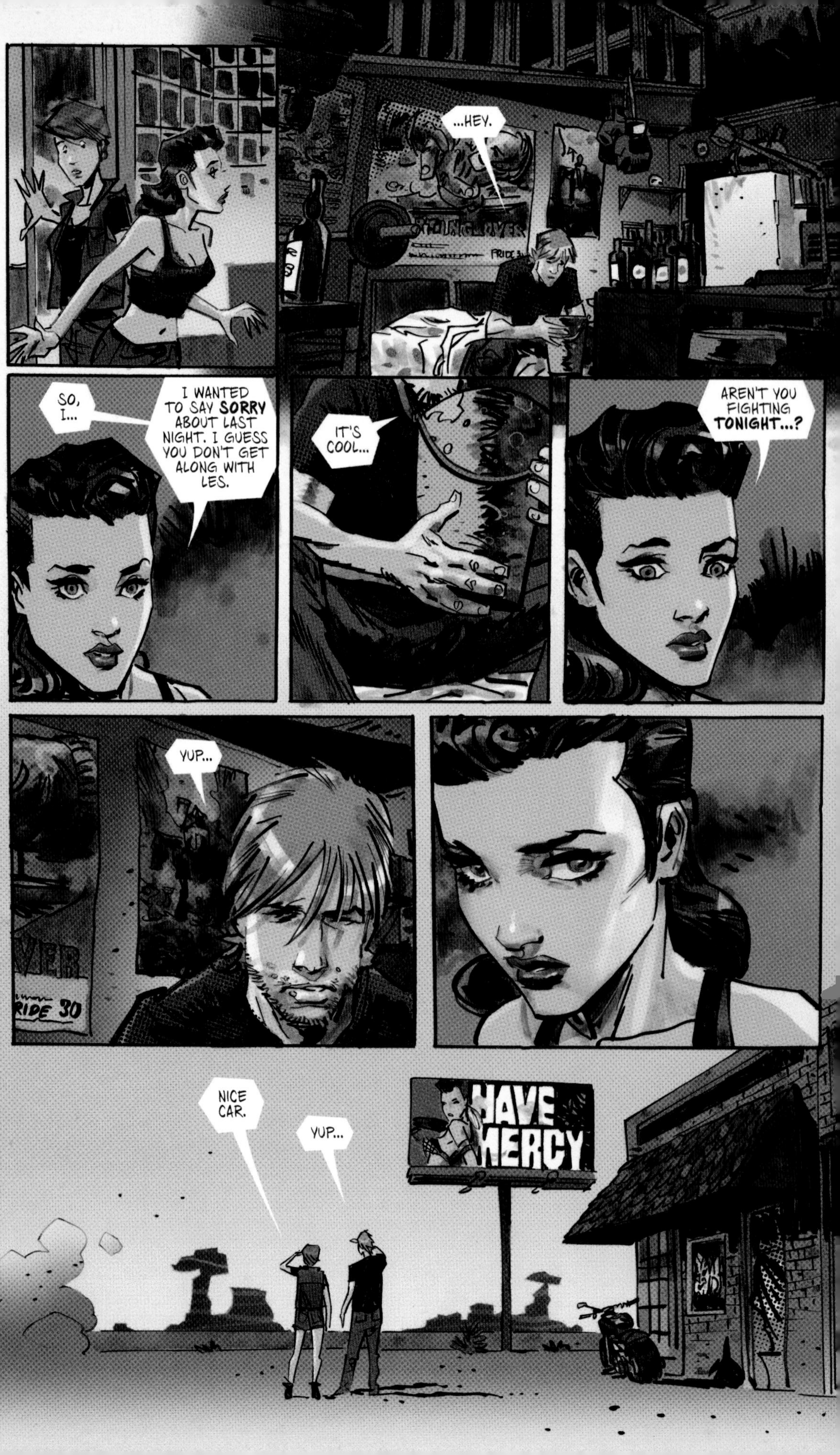

...HEY.
SO, I...
I WANTED TO SAY SORRY ABOUT LAST NIGHT. I GUESS YOU DON'T GET ALONG WITH LES.
IT'S COOL...
AREN'T YOU FIGHTING TONIGHT...?
YUP...
NICE CAR.
YUP...
HAVE MERCY

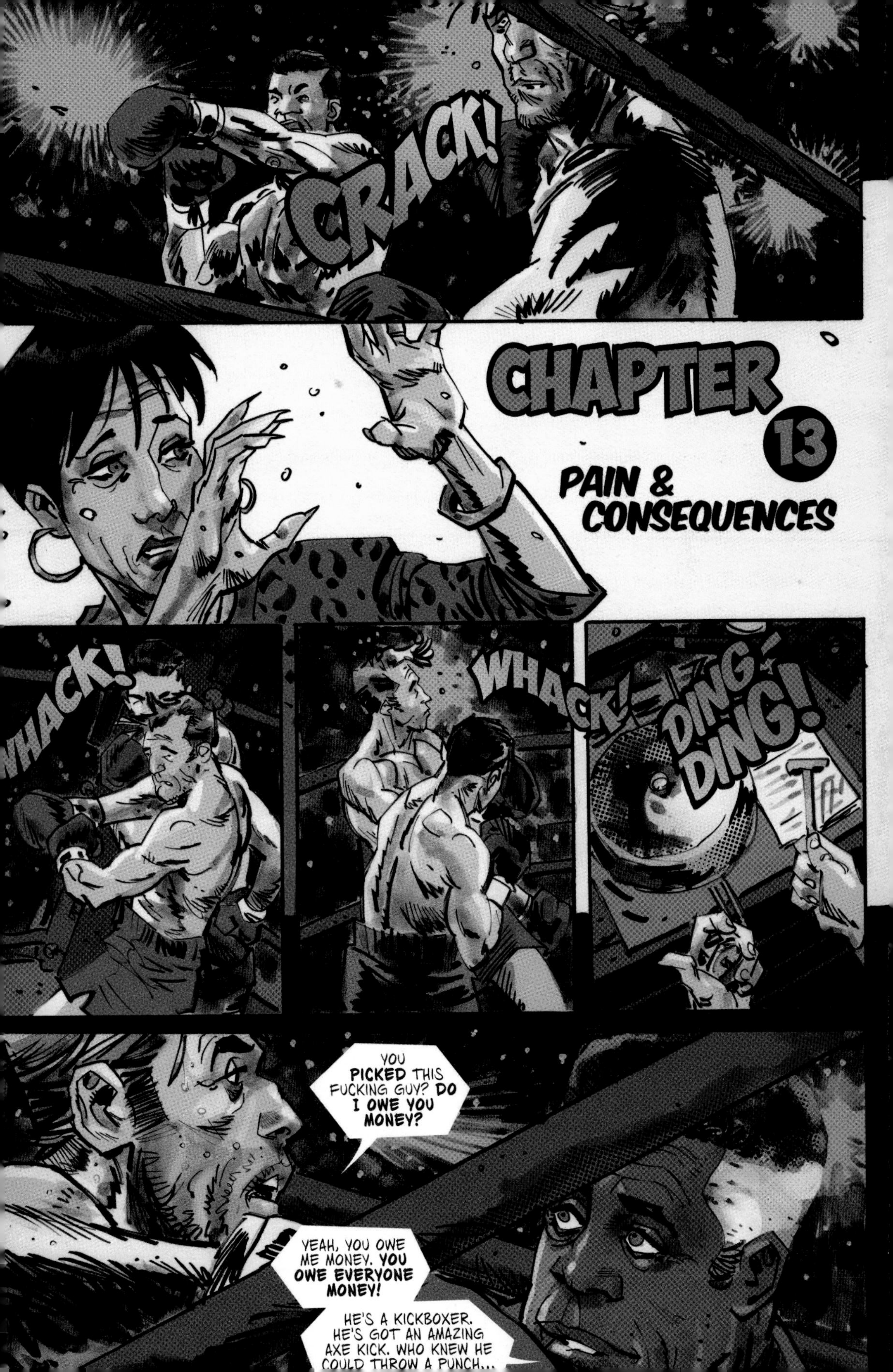
CRACK!
CHAPTER
13
PAIN & CONSEQUENCES
WHACK!
WHACK!
DING-DING!
YOU PICKED THIS FUCKING GUY? DO I OWE YOU MONEY?
YEAH, YOU OWE ME MONEY. YOU OWE EVERYONE MONEY!
HE'S A KICKBOXER. HE'S GOT AN AMAZING AXE KICK. WHO KNEW HE COULD THROW A PUNCH...

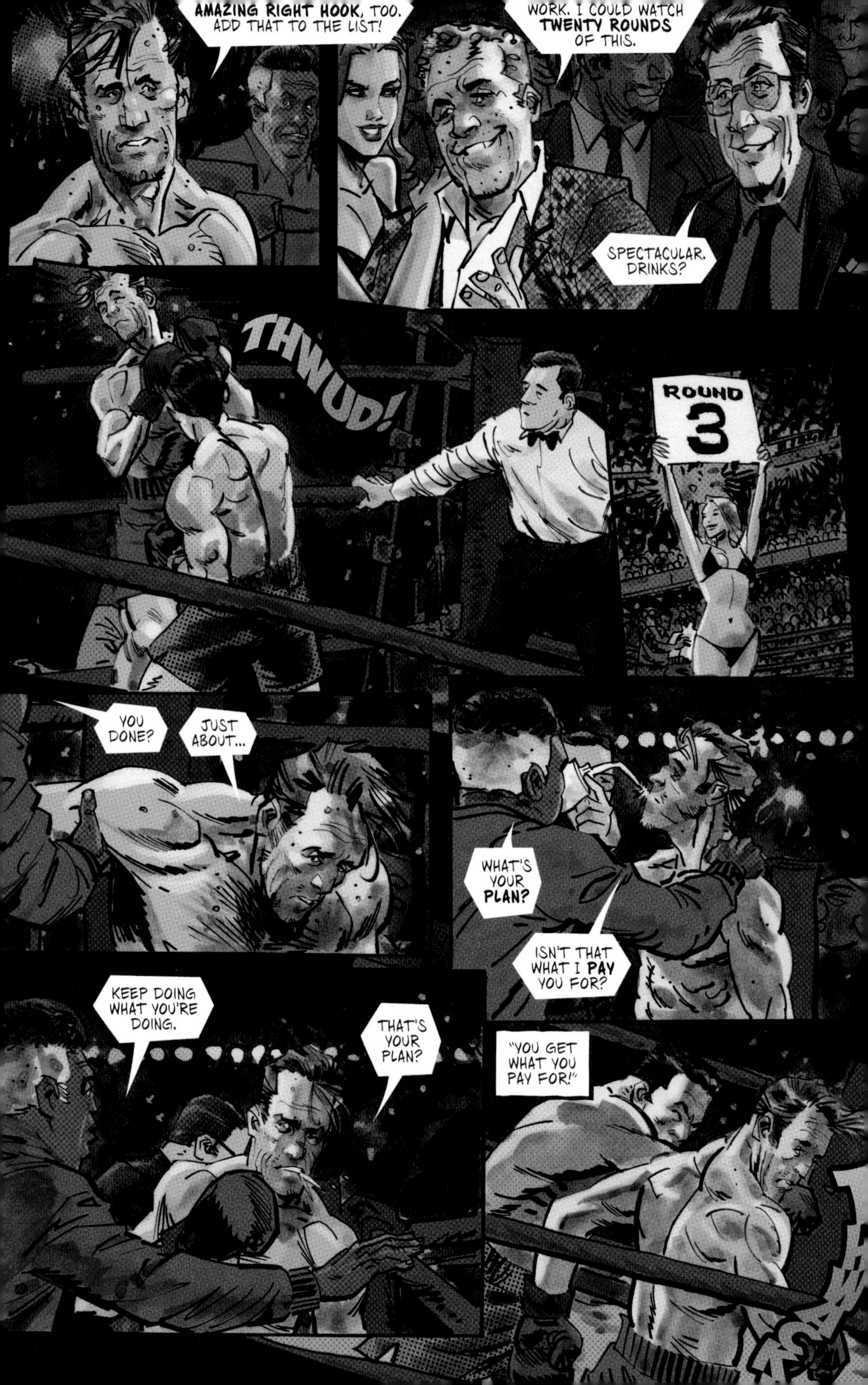
AMAZING RIGHT HOOK, TOO. ADD THAT TO THE LIST!
WORK. I COULD WATCH TWENTY ROUNDS OF THIS.
SPECTACULAR. DRINKS?
THWUD!
ROUND 3
YOU DONE?
JUST ABOUT...
WHAT'S YOUR PLAN?
ISN'T THAT WHAT I PAY YOU FOR?
KEEP DOING WHAT YOU'RE DOING.
THAT'S YOUR PLAN?
"YOU GET WHAT YOU PAY FOR!"

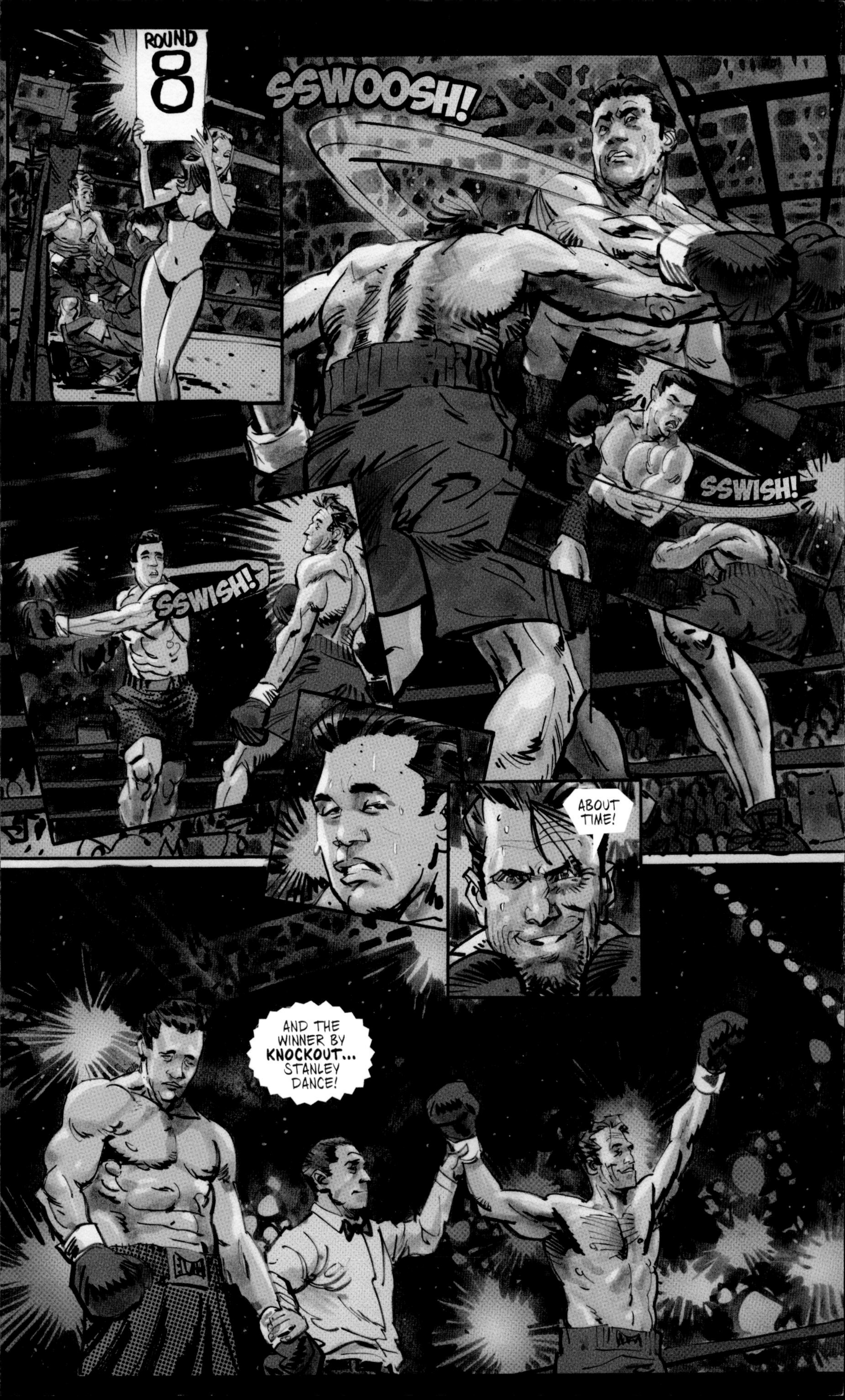
ROUND 8
SSWOOSH!
SSWISH!
SSWISH!
ABOUT TIME!
AND THE WINNER BY KNOCKOUT... STANLEY DANCE!

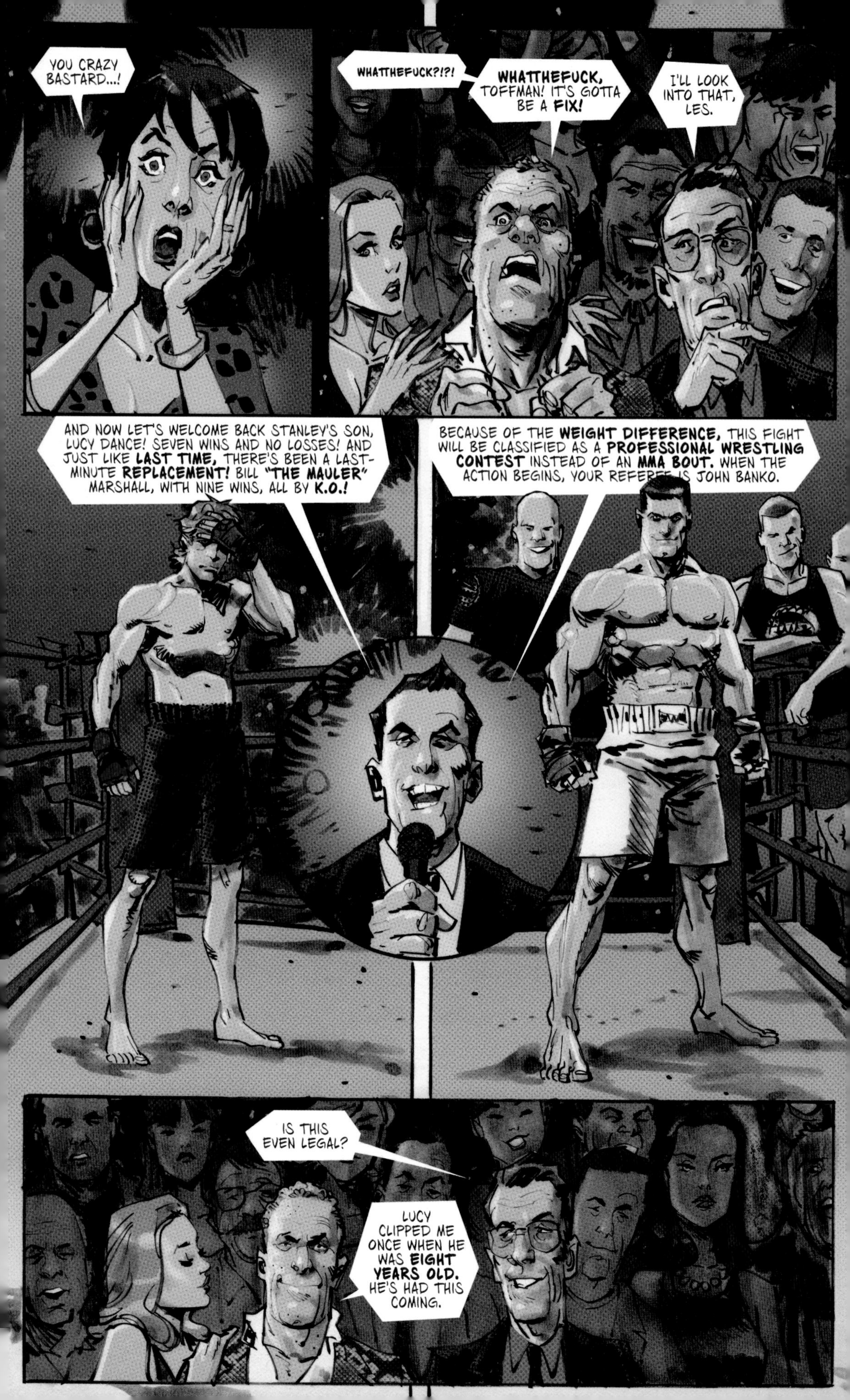
YOU CRAZY BASTARD...!
WHATTHEFUCK?!?!
WHATTHEFUCK, TOFFMAN! IT'S GOTTA BE A FIX!
I'LL LOOK INTO THAT, LES.
AND NOW LET'S WELCOME BACK STANLEY'S SON, LUCY DANCE! SEVEN WINS AND NO LOSSES! AND JUST LIKE LAST TIME, THERE'S BEEN A LAST-MINUTE REPLACEMENT! BILL "THE MAULER" MARSHALL, WITH NINE WINS, ALL BY K.O.!
BECAUSE OF THE WEIGHT DIFFERENCE, THIS FIGHT WILL BE CLASSIFIED AS A PROFESSIONAL WRESTLING CONTEST INSTEAD OF AN MMA BOUT. WHEN THE ACTION BEGINS, YOUR REFEREE IS JOHN BANKO.
IS THIS EVEN LEGAL?
LUCY CLIPPED ME ONCE WHEN HE WAS EIGHT YEARS OLD. HE'S HAD THIS COMING.

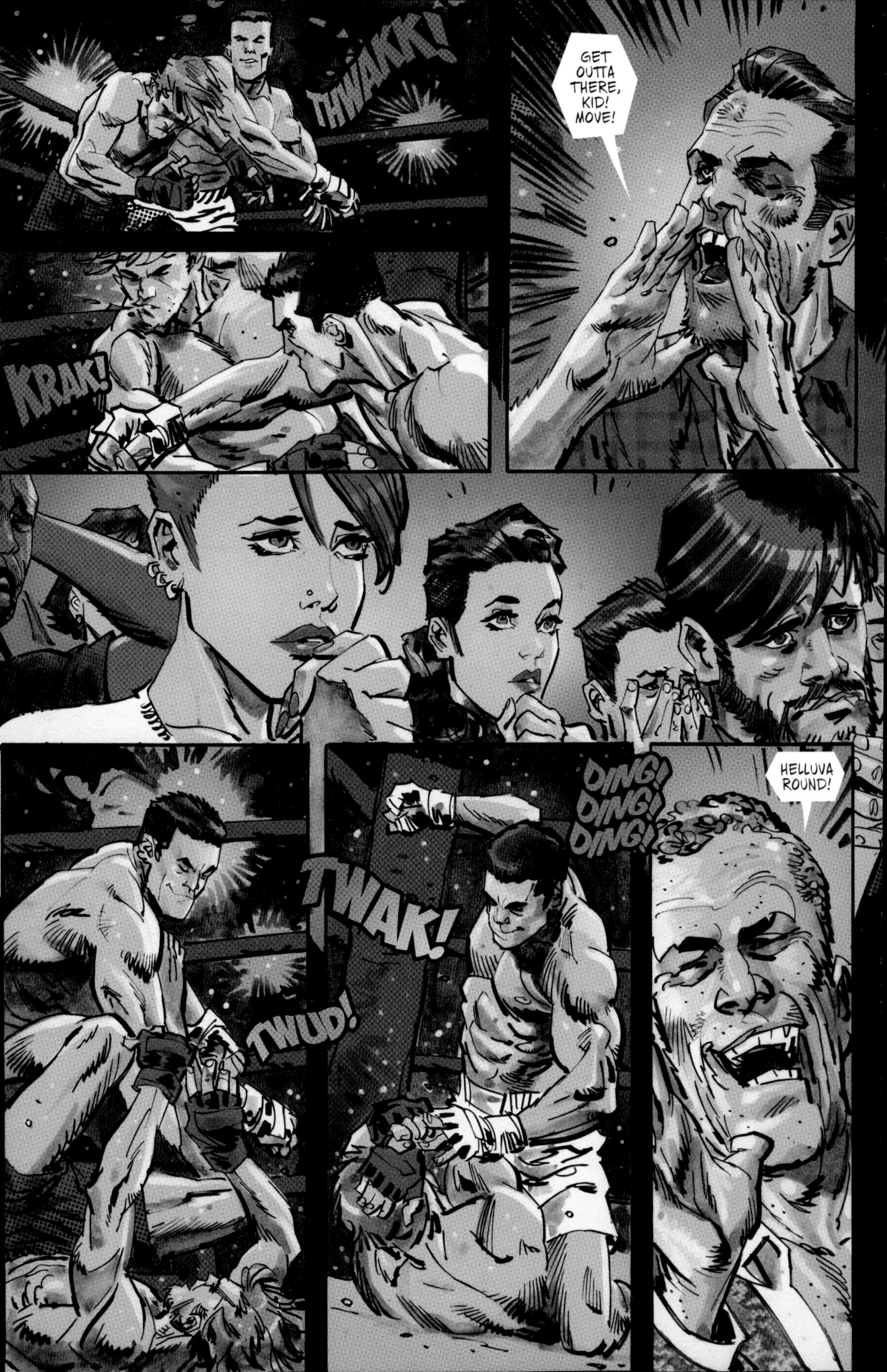
THWAKK!
GET OUTTA THERE, KID! MOVE!
KRAK!
TWAK!
DING! DING! DING!
TWUD!
HELLUVA ROUND!

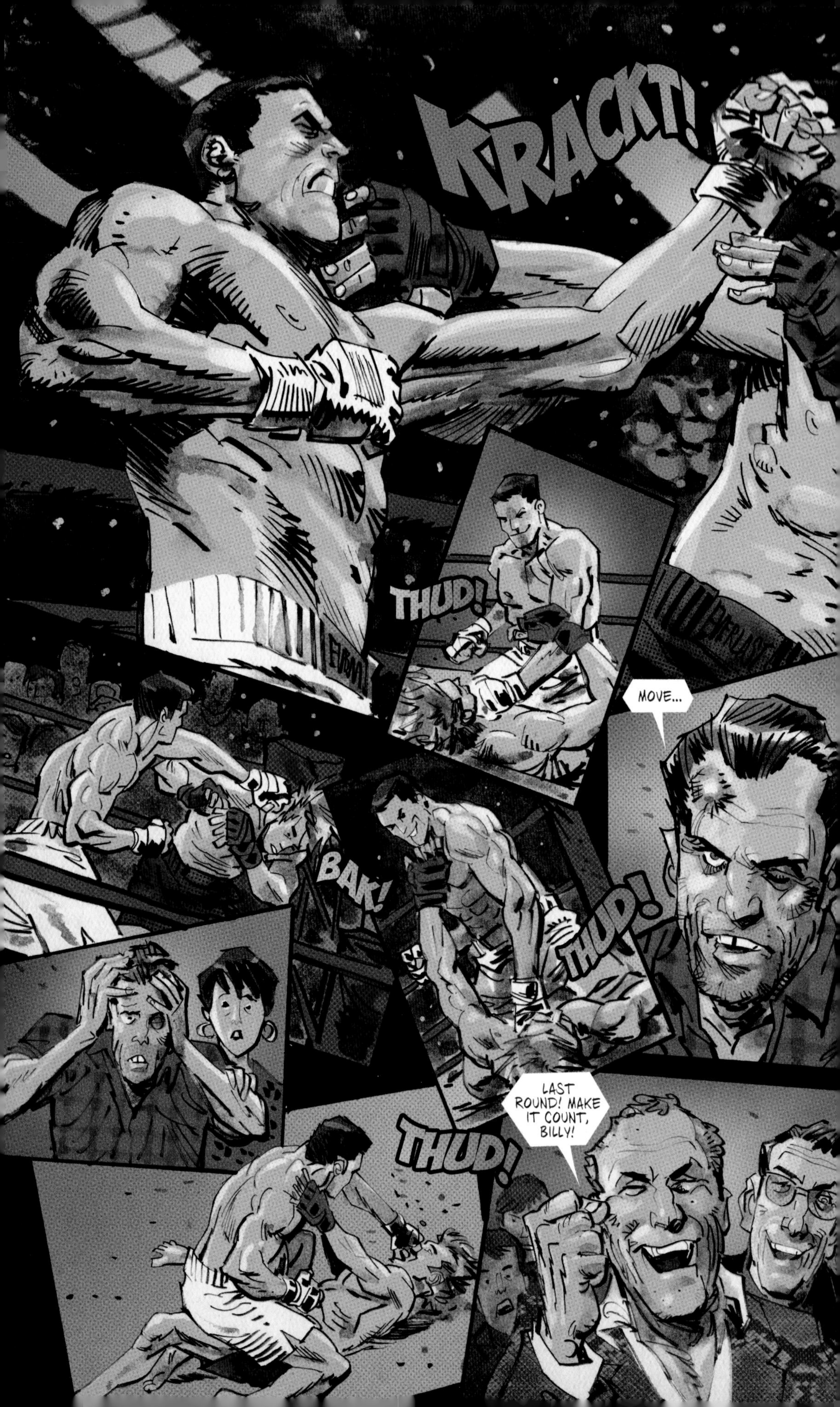
KRACKT!
THUD!
MOVE...
BAK!
THUD!
THUD!
LAST ROUND! MAKE IT COUNT, BILLY!

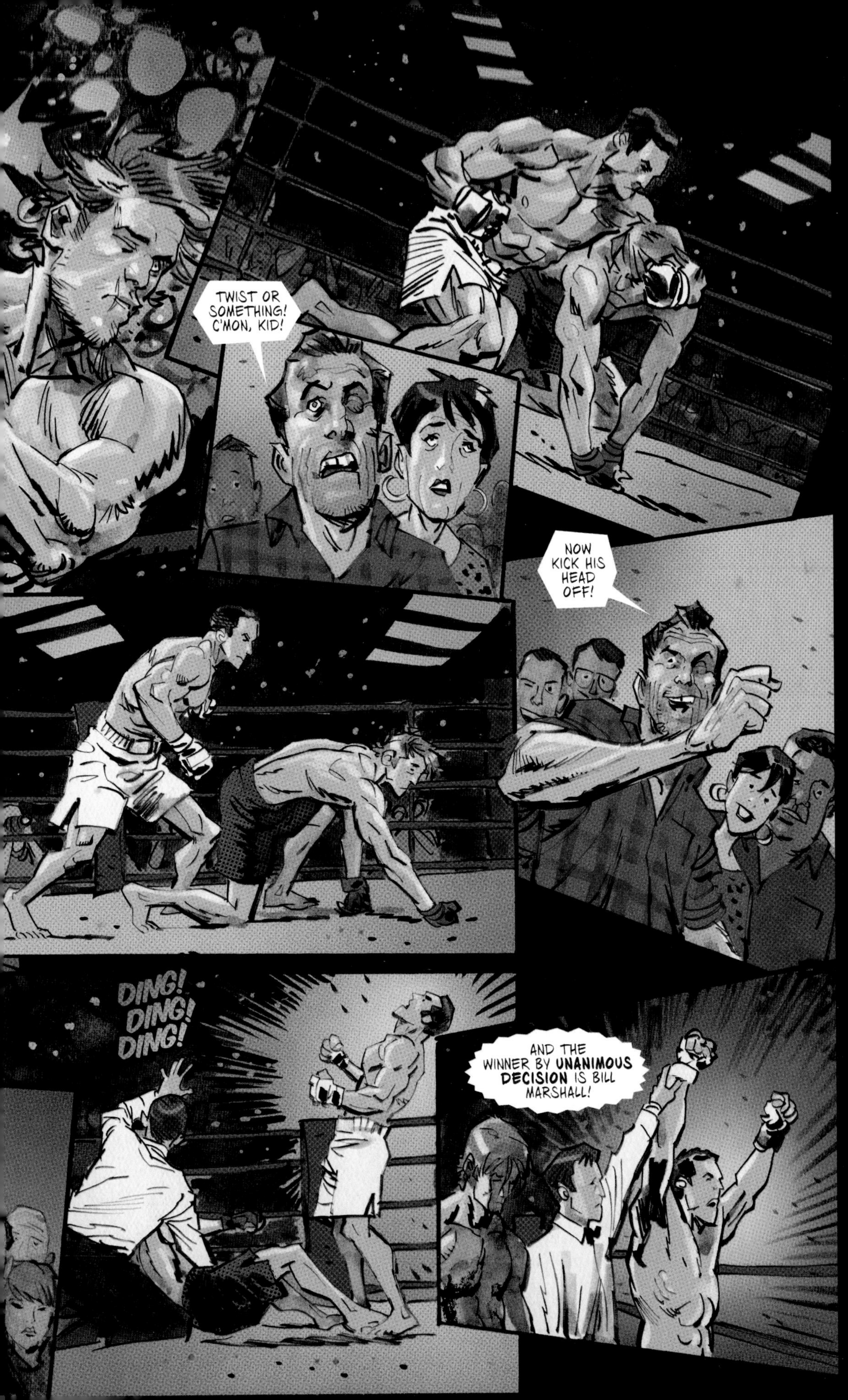

TWIST OR SOMETHING! C'MON, KID!
NOW KICK HIS HEAD OFF!
DING! DING! DING!
AND THE WINNER BY **UNANIMOUS DECISION** IS BILL MARSHALL!

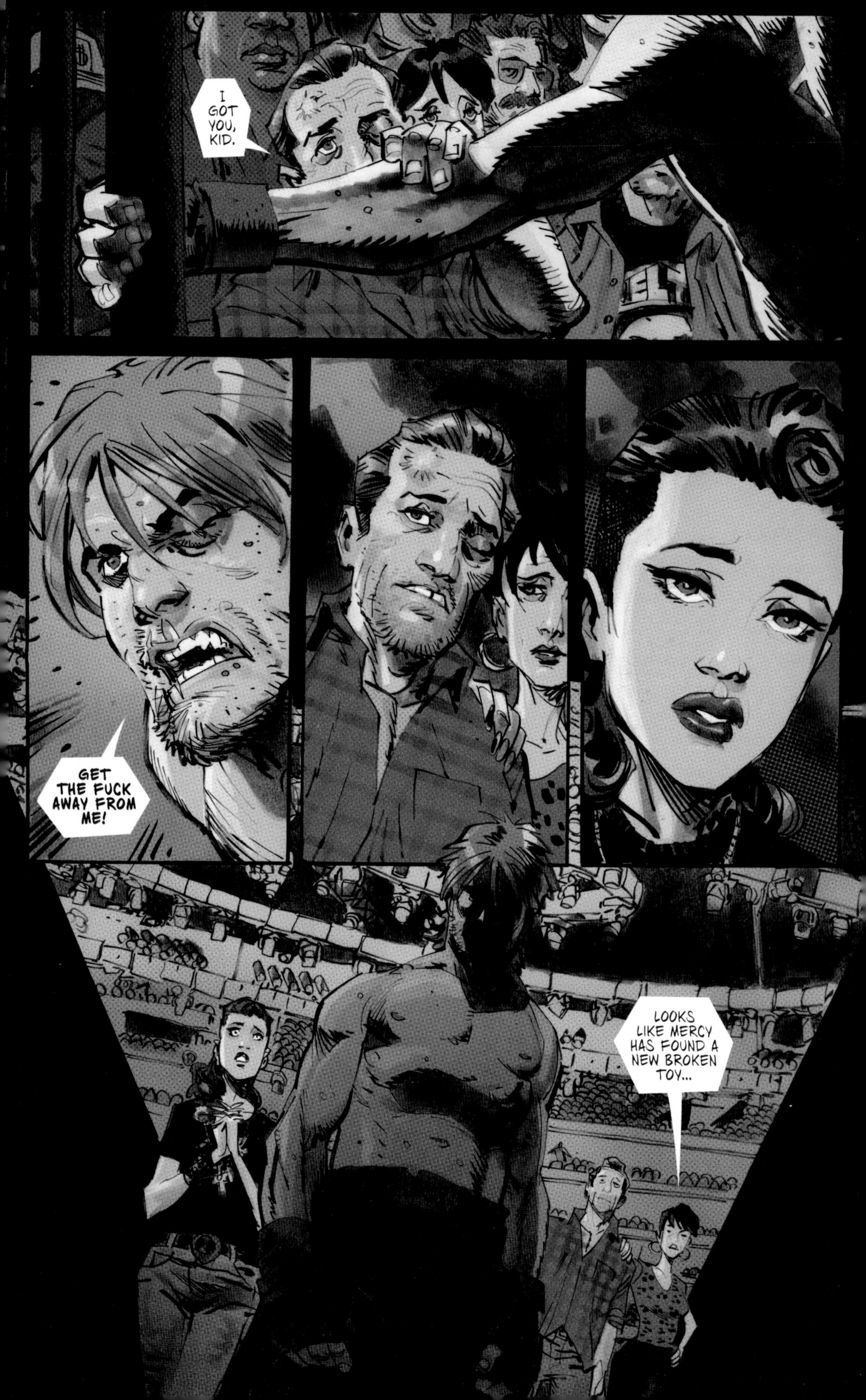
I GOT YOU, KID.
GET THE FUCK AWAY FROM ME!
LOOKS LIKE MERCY HAS FOUND A NEW BROKEN TOY...

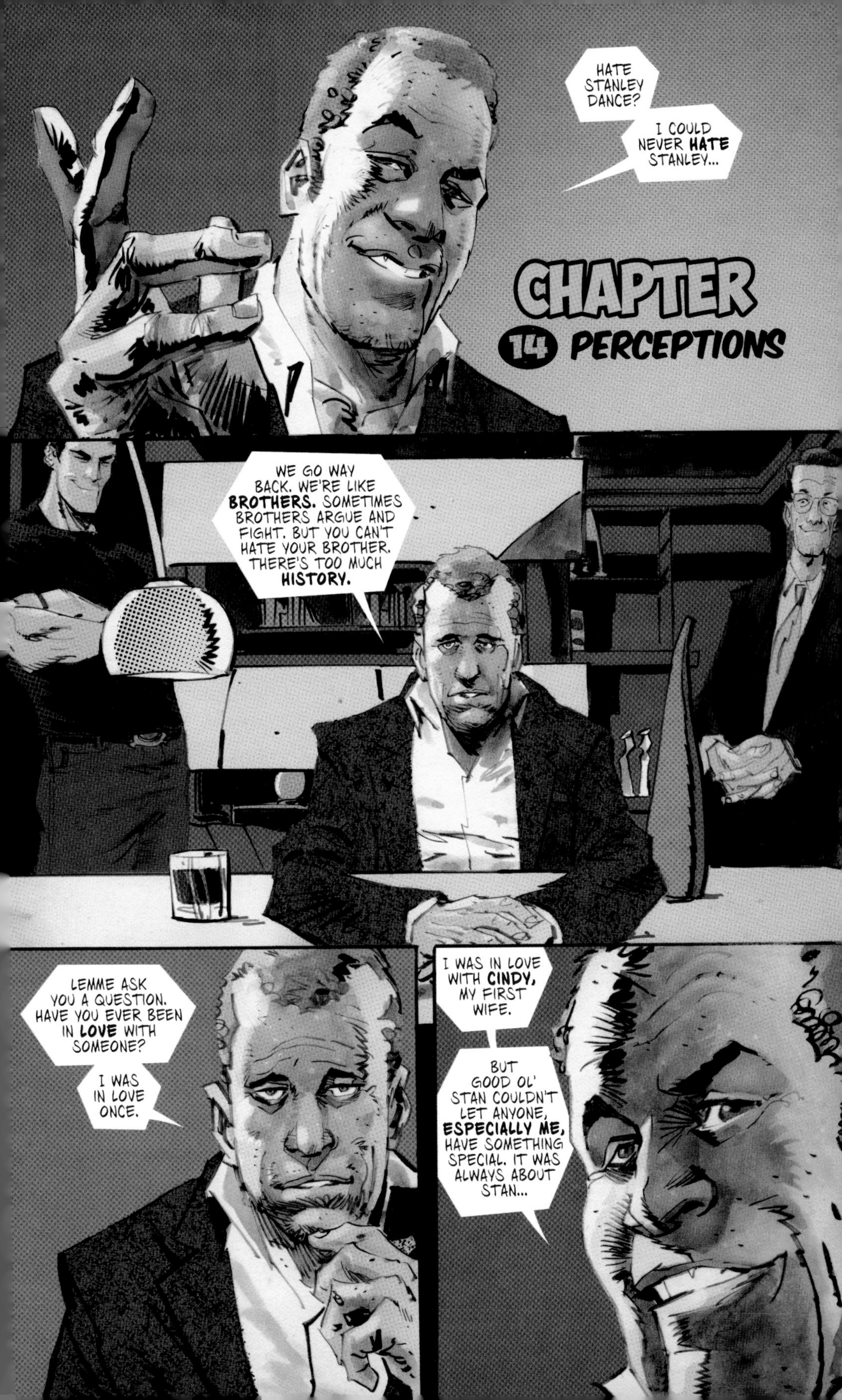
HATE STANLEY DANCE?
I COULD NEVER HATE STANLEY...
CHAPTER
14 PERCEPTIONS
WE GO WAY BACK. WE'RE LIKE BROTHERS. SOMETIMES BROTHERS ARGUE AND FIGHT. BUT YOU CAN'T HATE YOUR BROTHER. THERE'S TOO MUCH HISTORY.
LEMME ASK YOU A QUESTION. HAVE YOU EVER BEEN IN LOVE WITH SOMEONE?
I WAS IN LOVE ONCE.
I WAS IN LOVE WITH CINDY, MY FIRST WIFE.
BUT GOOD OL' STAN COULDN'T LET ANYONE, ESPECIALLY ME, HAVE SOMETHING SPECIAL. IT WAS ALWAYS ABOUT STAN...

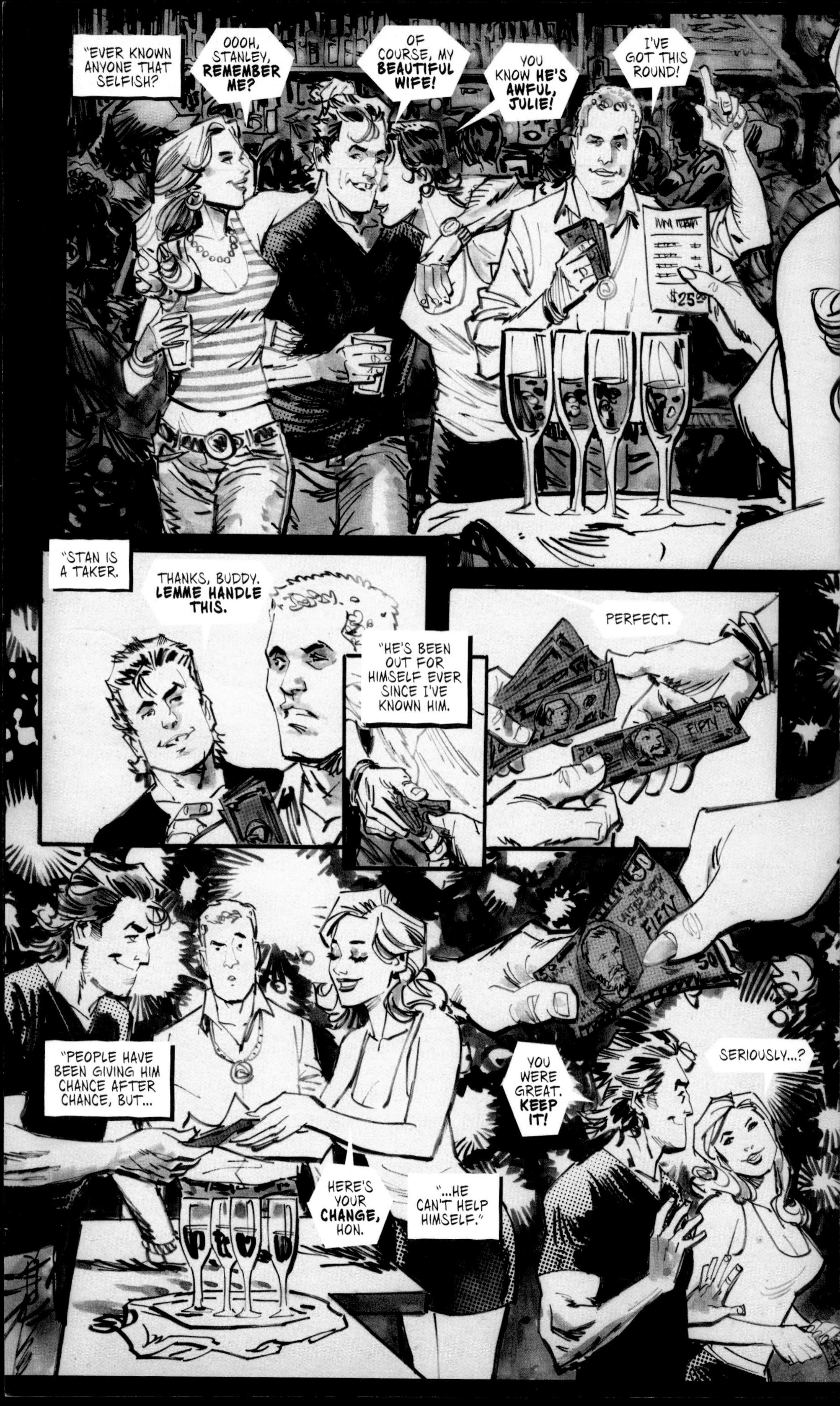
"EVER KNOWN ANYONE THAT SELFISH?
OOOH, STANLEY, REMEMBER ME?
OF COURSE, MY BEAUTIFUL WIFE!
YOU KNOW HE'S AWFUL, JULIE!
I'VE GOT THIS ROUND!
$25.00
"STAN IS A TAKER.
THANKS, BUDDY. LEMME HANDLE THIS.
"HE'S BEEN OUT FOR HIMSELF EVER SINCE I'VE KNOWN HIM.
PERFECT.
"PEOPLE HAVE BEEN GIVING HIM CHANCE AFTER CHANCE, BUT...
HERE'S YOUR CHANGE, HON.
"...HE CAN'T HELP HIMSELF."
YOU WERE GREAT. KEEP IT!
SERIOUSLY...?

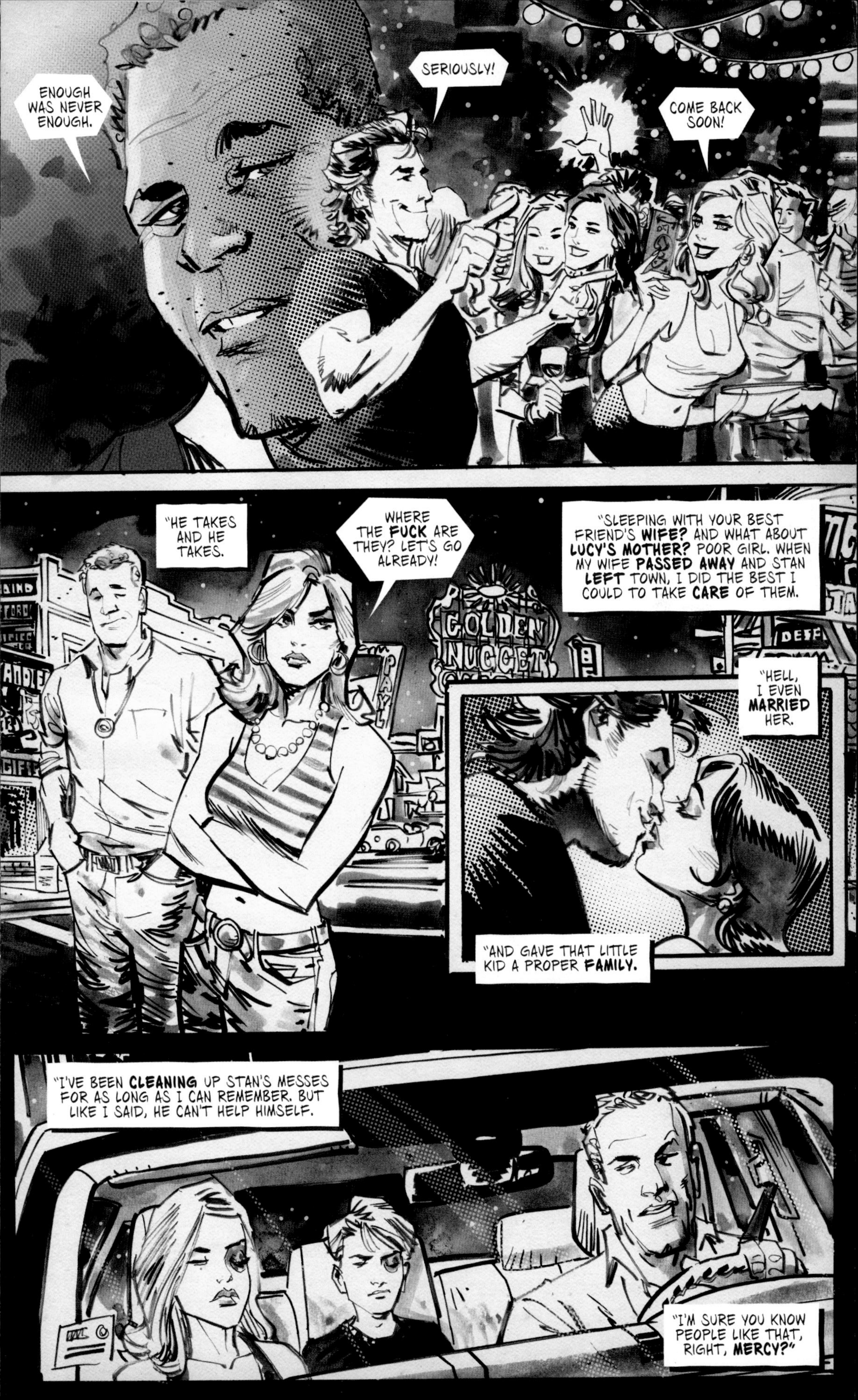
ENOUGH WAS NEVER ENOUGH.
SERIOUSLY!
COME BACK SOON!
"HE TAKES AND HE TAKES.
WHERE THE FUCK ARE THEY? LET'S GO ALREADY!
"SLEEPING WITH YOUR BEST FRIEND'S WIFE? AND WHAT ABOUT LUCY'S MOTHER? POOR GIRL. WHEN MY WIFE PASSED AWAY AND STAN LEFT TOWN, I DID THE BEST I COULD TO TAKE CARE OF THEM.
GOLDEN NUGGET
"HELL, I EVEN MARRIED HER.
"AND GAVE THAT LITTLE KID A PROPER FAMILY.
"I'VE BEEN CLEANING UP STAN'S MESSES FOR AS LONG AS I CAN REMEMBER. BUT LIKE I SAID, HE CAN'T HELP HIMSELF.
"I'M SURE YOU KNOW PEOPLE LIKE THAT, RIGHT, MERCY?"

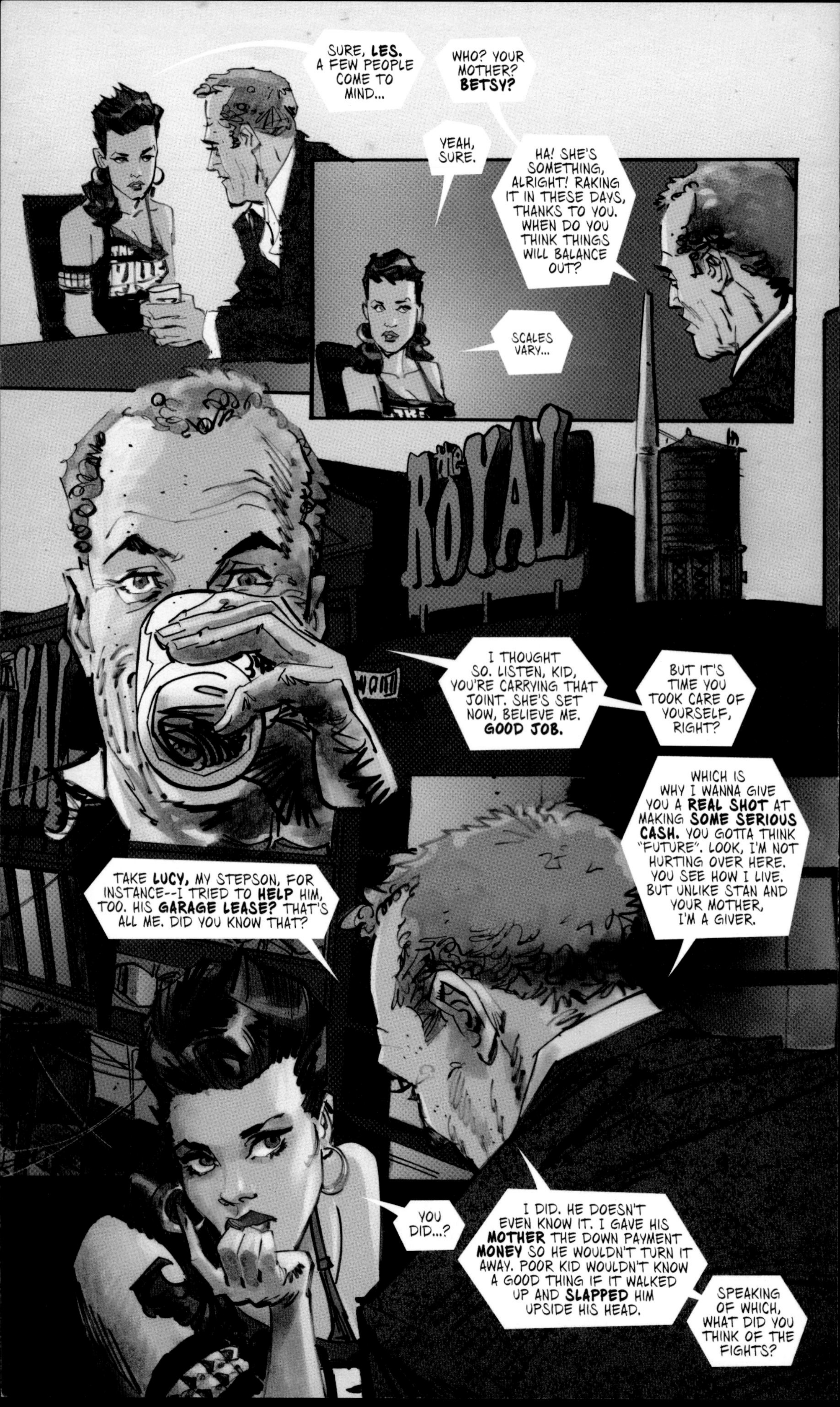
SURE, LES. A FEW PEOPLE COME TO MIND...
WHO? YOUR MOTHER? BETSY?
YEAH, SURE.
HA! SHE'S SOMETHING, ALRIGHT! RAKING IT IN THESE DAYS, THANKS TO YOU. WHEN DO YOU THINK THINGS WILL BALANCE OUT?
SCALES VARY...
THE ROYAL
I THOUGHT SO. LISTEN, KID, YOU'RE CARRYING THAT JOINT. SHE'S SET NOW, BELIEVE ME. GOOD JOB.
BUT IT'S TIME YOU TOOK CARE OF YOURSELF, RIGHT?
WHICH IS WHY I WANNA GIVE YOU A REAL SHOT AT MAKING SOME SERIOUS CASH. YOU GOTTA THINK "FUTURE". LOOK, I'M NOT HURTING OVER HERE. YOU SEE HOW I LIVE. BUT UNLIKE STAN AND YOUR MOTHER, I'M A GIVER.
TAKE LUCY, MY STEPSON, FOR INSTANCE--I TRIED TO HELP HIM, TOO. HIS GARAGE LEASE? THAT'S ALL ME. DID YOU KNOW THAT?
YOU DID...?
I DID. HE DOESN'T EVEN KNOW IT. I GAVE HIS MOTHER THE DOWN PAYMENT MONEY SO HE WOULDN'T TURN IT AWAY. POOR KID WOULDN'T KNOW A GOOD THING IF IT WALKED UP AND SLAPPED HIM UPSIDE HIS HEAD.
SPEAKING OF WHICH, WHAT DID YOU THINK OF THE FIGHTS?

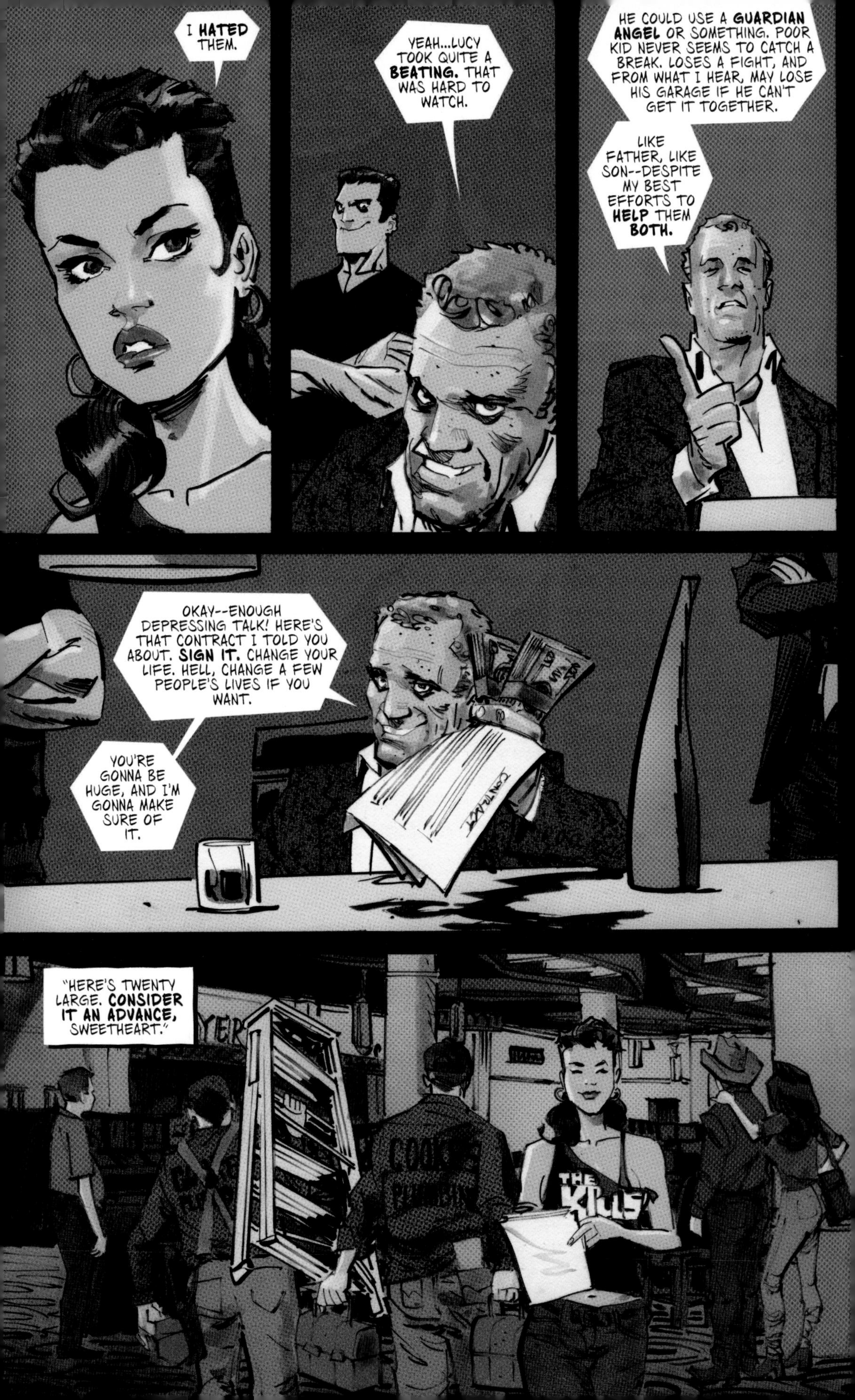
I HATED THEM.
YEAH...LUCY TOOK QUITE A BEATING. THAT WAS HARD TO WATCH.
HE COULD USE A GUARDIAN ANGEL OR SOMETHING. POOR KID NEVER SEEMS TO CATCH A BREAK. LOSES A FIGHT, AND FROM WHAT I HEAR, MAY LOSE HIS GARAGE IF HE CAN'T GET IT TOGETHER.
LIKE FATHER, LIKE SON--DESPITE MY BEST EFFORTS TO HELP THEM BOTH.
OKAY--ENOUGH DEPRESSING TALK! HERE'S THAT CONTRACT I TOLD YOU ABOUT. SIGN IT. CHANGE YOUR LIFE. HELL, CHANGE A FEW PEOPLE'S LIVES IF YOU WANT.
YOU'RE GONNA BE HUGE, AND I'M GONNA MAKE SURE OF IT.
CONTRACT
"HERE'S TWENTY LARGE. CONSIDER IT AN ADVANCE, SWEETHEART."
THE KILLS

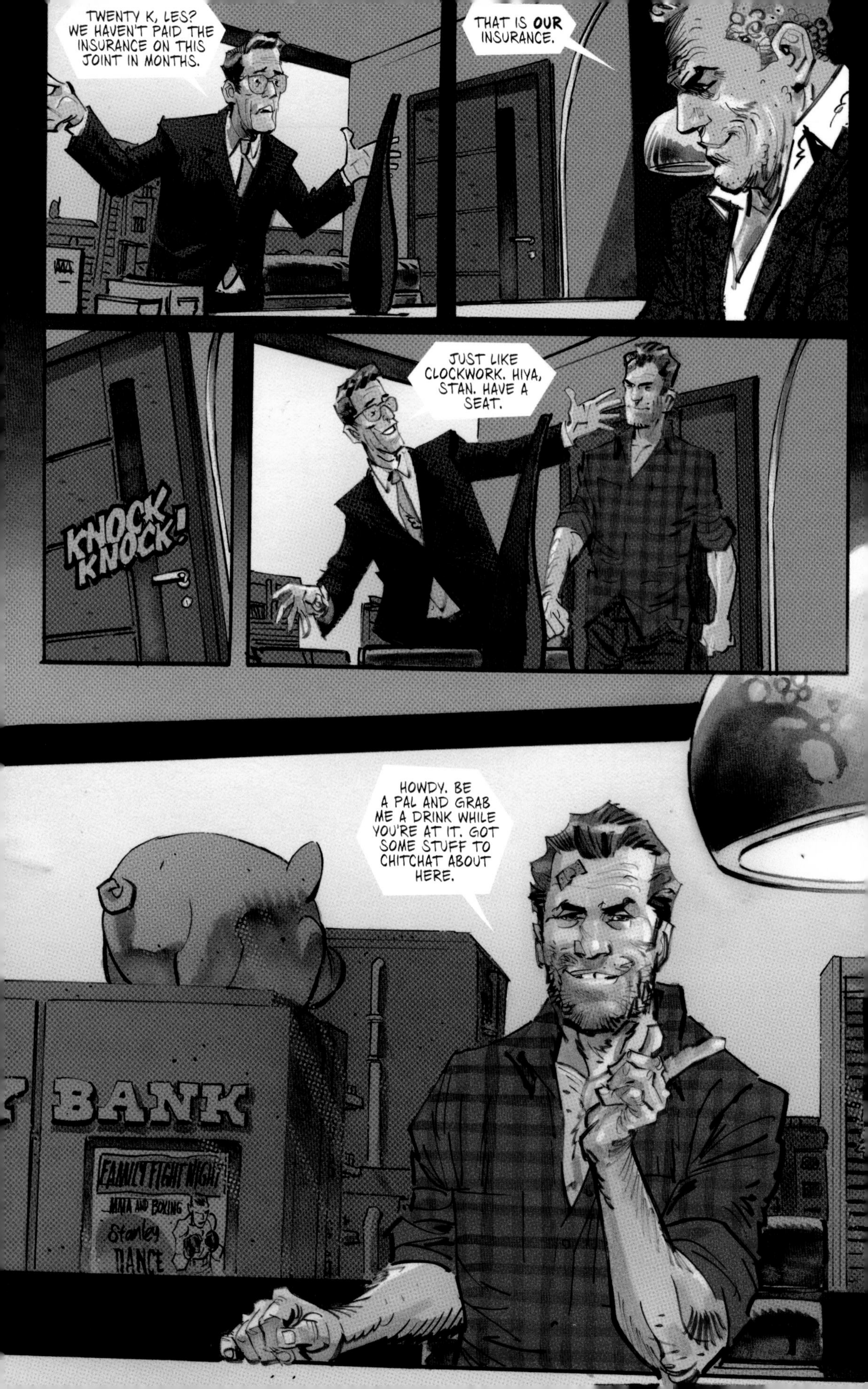
TWENTY K, LES? WE HAVEN'T PAID THE INSURANCE ON THIS JOINT IN MONTHS.
THAT IS OUR INSURANCE.
KNOCK KNOCK!
JUST LIKE CLOCKWORK. HIYA, STAN. HAVE A SEAT.
HOWDY. BE A PAL AND GRAB ME A DRINK WHILE YOU'RE AT IT. GOT SOME STUFF TO CHITCHAT ABOUT HERE.
BANK
FAMILY FIGHT NIGHT
MMA AND BOXING
Stanley
DANCE

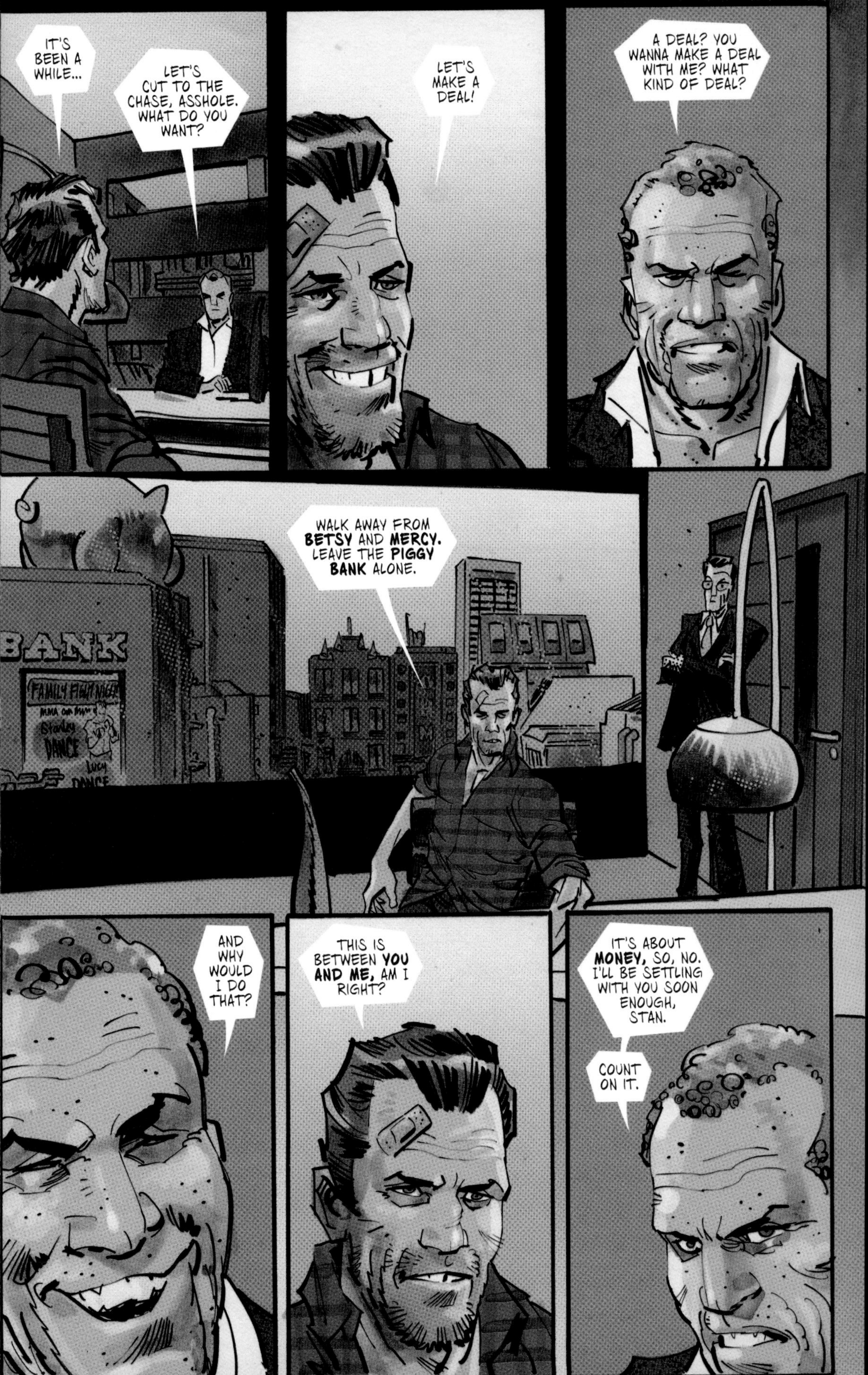
IT'S BEEN A WHILE...
LET'S CUT TO THE CHASE, ASSHOLE. WHAT DO YOU WANT?
LET'S MAKE A DEAL!
A DEAL? YOU WANNA MAKE A DEAL WITH ME? WHAT KIND OF DEAL?
BANK
WALK AWAY FROM BETSY AND MERCY. LEAVE THE PIGGY BANK ALONE.
AND WHY WOULD I DO THAT?
THIS IS BETWEEN YOU AND ME, AM I RIGHT?
IT'S ABOUT MONEY, SO, NO. I'LL BE SETTLING WITH YOU SOON ENOUGH, STAN.
COUNT ON IT.

I'M SURPRISED YOU HAVE THE BALLS TO EVEN WALK IN HERE. BUT YOU'VE NEVER BEEN TOO BRIGHT. SO SPIT IT OUT. JUST TRY NOT TO LEAVE ANY TEETH ON MY DESK WHEN YOU DO.

YOU LOOK LIKE SHIT.

A CABLE STATION HAS TAKEN AN INTEREST IN THE WHOLE FATHER AND SON THING. WHAT CAN I SAY-- PEOPLE LIKE ME.

SO THEY SET ME UP WITH AN EASY OPPONENT. SOME WASHED-UP BOXER NO ONE HAS EVER HEARD OF.

SOUNDS LIKE THEY FOUND YOUR LONG-LOST TWIN...

THE ODDS ARE ACTUALLY IN MY FAVOR THIS TIME. I'LL THROW IT, AND YOU CAN CASH IN IF YOU LEAVE MERCY AND BETSY ALONE. YOU CAN MAKE A FORTUNE. EVERYONE KNOWS YOU HATE ME. OF COURSE YOU WOULD BET AGAINST ME. IT MAKES SENSE.

AND NO ONE WOULD EVER GUESS I WOULD WALK AWAY FROM AN EASY WIN AND A CABLE DEAL LIKE THIS.

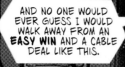

YOU WIN. I LOSE. HOW CAN YOU BEAT THAT?

THAT DOES HAVE A NICE RING TO IT...

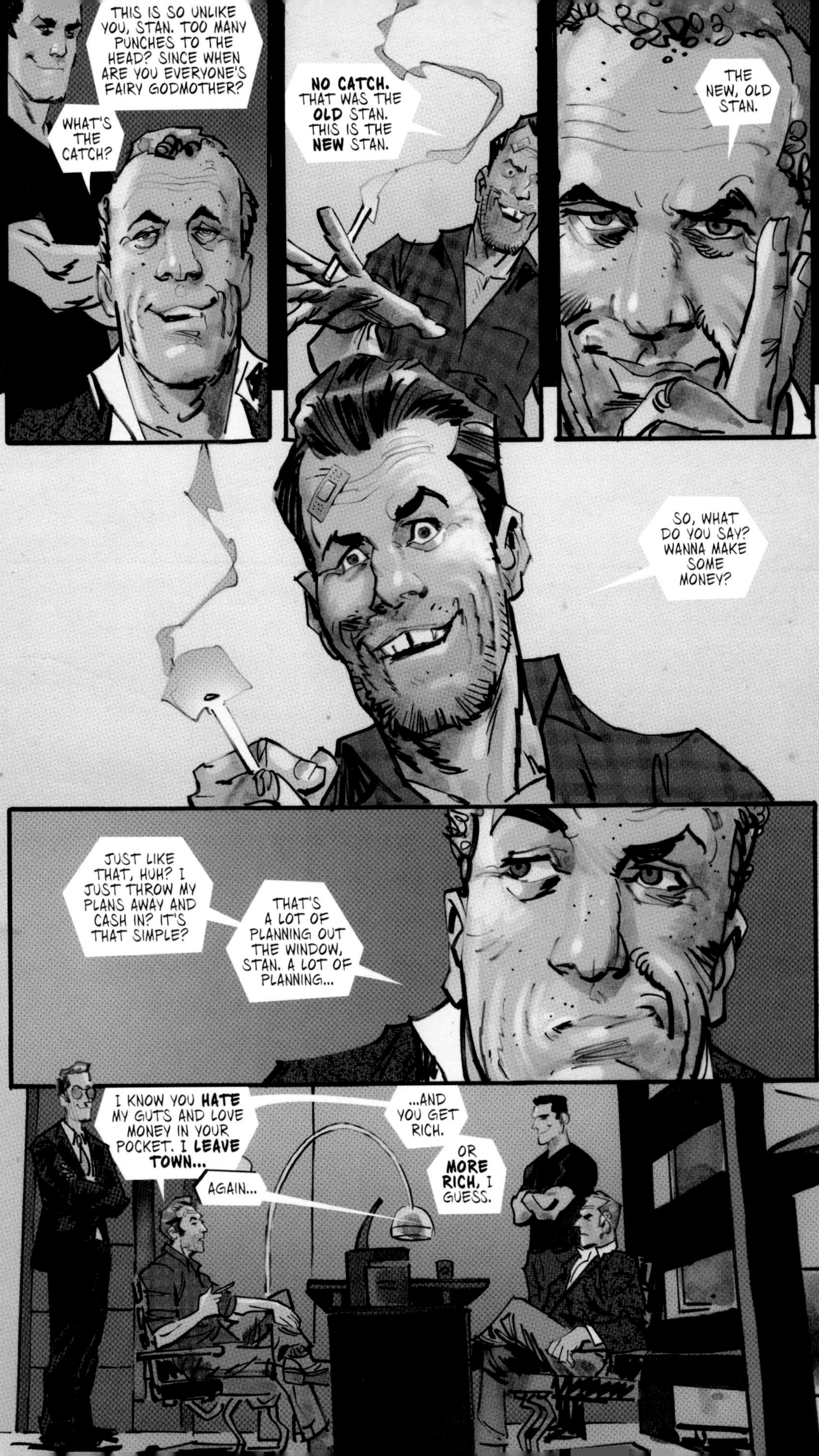
THIS IS SO UNLIKE YOU, STAN. TOO MANY PUNCHES TO THE HEAD? SINCE WHEN ARE YOU EVERYONE'S FAIRY GODMOTHER?
WHAT'S THE CATCH?
NO CATCH. THAT WAS THE OLD STAN. THIS IS THE NEW STAN.
THE NEW, OLD STAN.
SO, WHAT DO YOU SAY? WANNA MAKE SOME MONEY?
JUST LIKE THAT, HUH? I JUST THROW MY PLANS AWAY AND CASH IN? IT'S THAT SIMPLE?
THAT'S A LOT OF PLANNING OUT THE WINDOW, STAN. A LOT OF PLANNING...
I KNOW YOU HATE MY GUTS AND LOVE MONEY IN YOUR POCKET. I LEAVE TOWN...
AGAIN...
...AND YOU GET RICH.
OR MORE RICH, I GUESS.

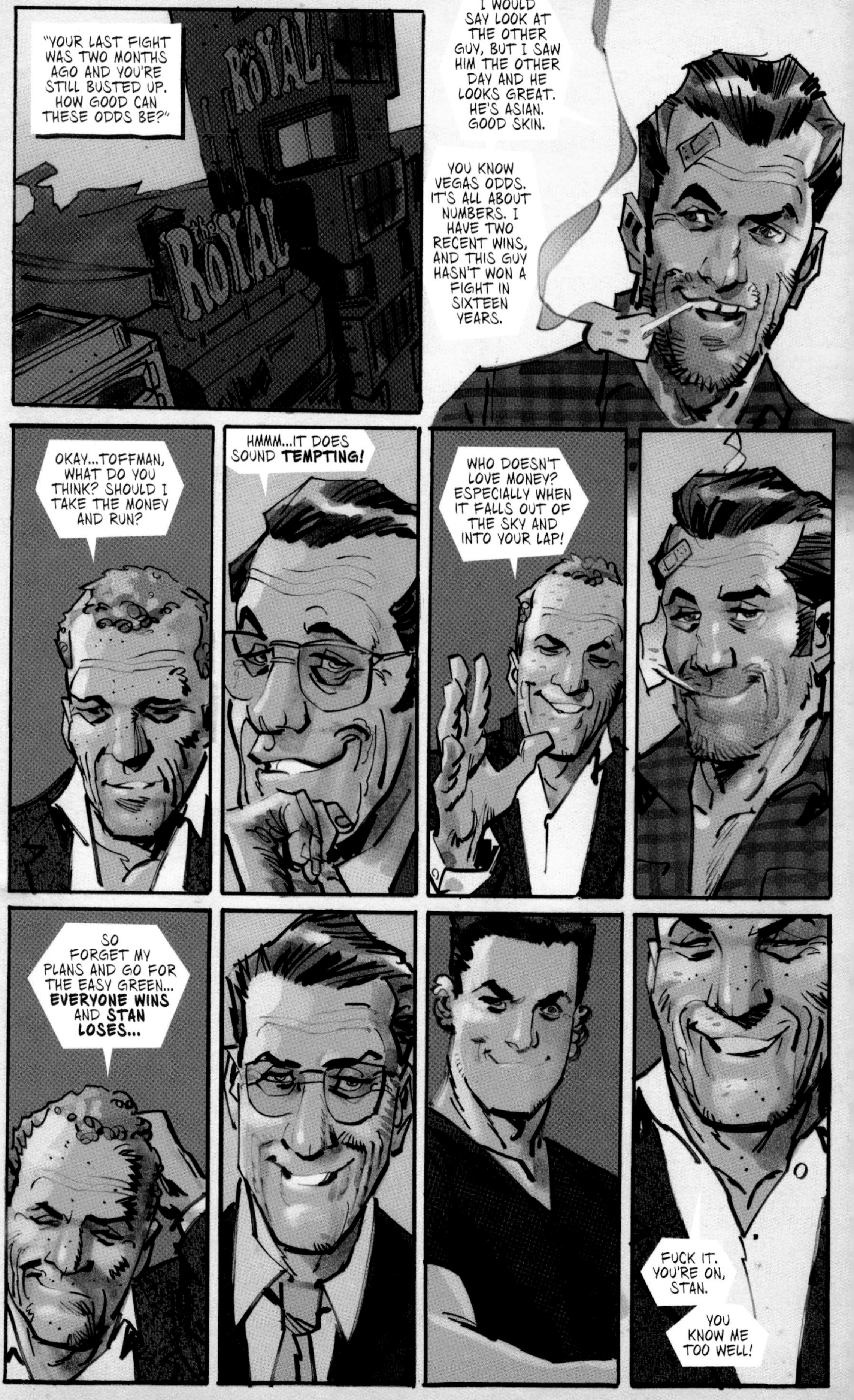

"YOUR LAST FIGHT WAS TWO MONTHS AGO AND YOU'RE STILL BUSTED UP. HOW GOOD CAN THESE ODDS BE?"
I WOULD SAY LOOK AT THE OTHER GUY, BUT I SAW HIM THE OTHER DAY AND HE LOOKS GREAT. HE'S ASIAN. GOOD SKIN.
YOU KNOW VEGAS ODDS. IT'S ALL ABOUT NUMBERS. I HAVE TWO RECENT WINS, AND THIS GUY HASN'T WON A FIGHT IN SIXTEEN YEARS.
OKAY...TOFFMAN, WHAT DO YOU THINK? SHOULD I TAKE THE MONEY AND RUN?
HMMM...IT DOES SOUND **TEMPTING!**
WHO DOESN'T LOVE MONEY? ESPECIALLY WHEN IT FALLS OUT OF THE SKY AND INTO YOUR LAP!
SO FORGET MY PLANS AND GO FOR THE EASY GREEN... **EVERYONE WINS** AND **STAN LOSES...**
FUCK IT. YOU'RE ON, STAN.
YOU KNOW ME TOO WELL!

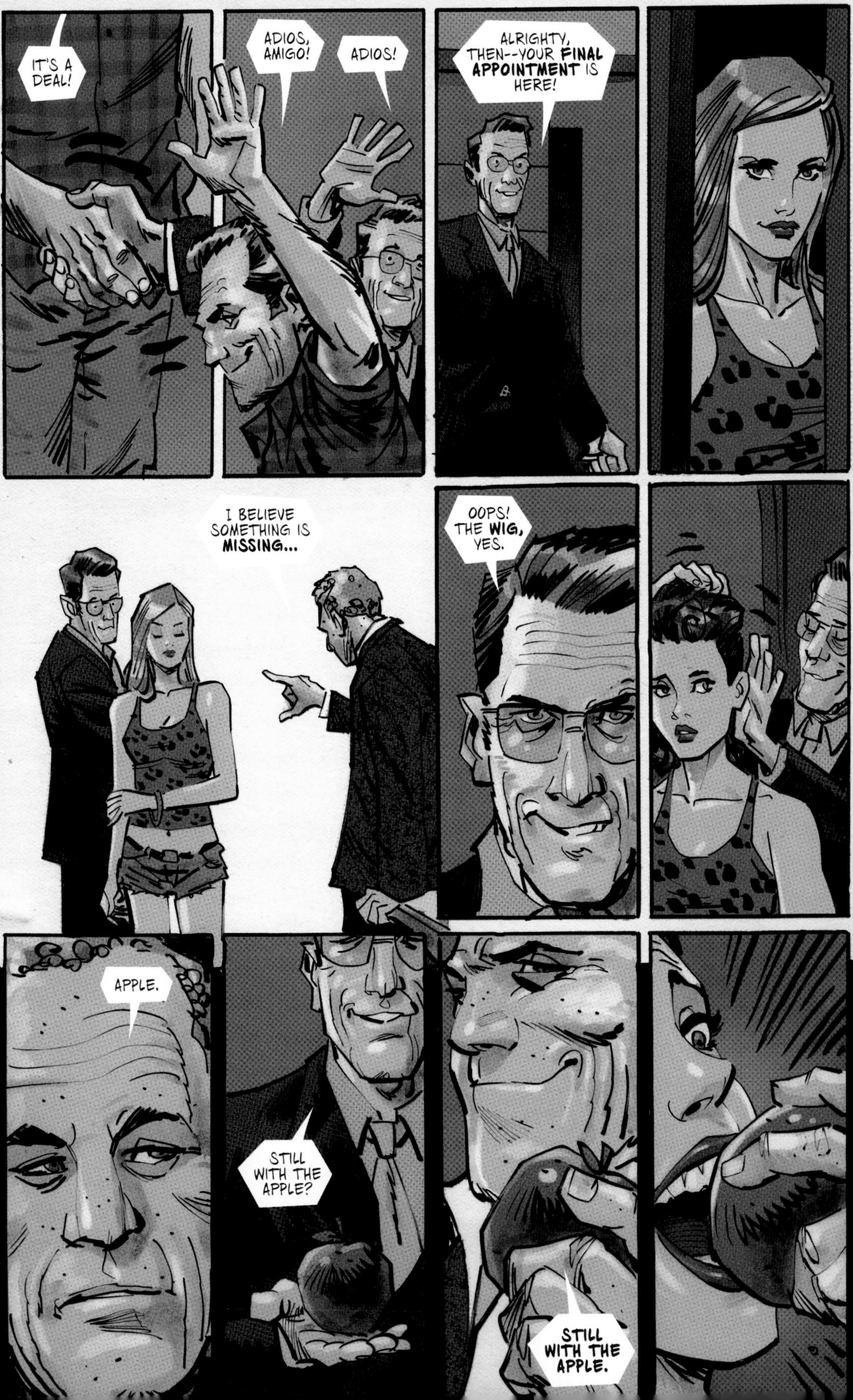

IT'S A DEAL!
ADIOS, AMIGO!
ADIOS!
ALRIGHTY, THEN--YOUR FINAL APPOINTMENT IS HERE!
I BELIEVE SOMETHING IS MISSING...
OOPS! THE WIG, YES.
APPLE.
STILL WITH THE APPLE?
STILL WITH THE APPLE.

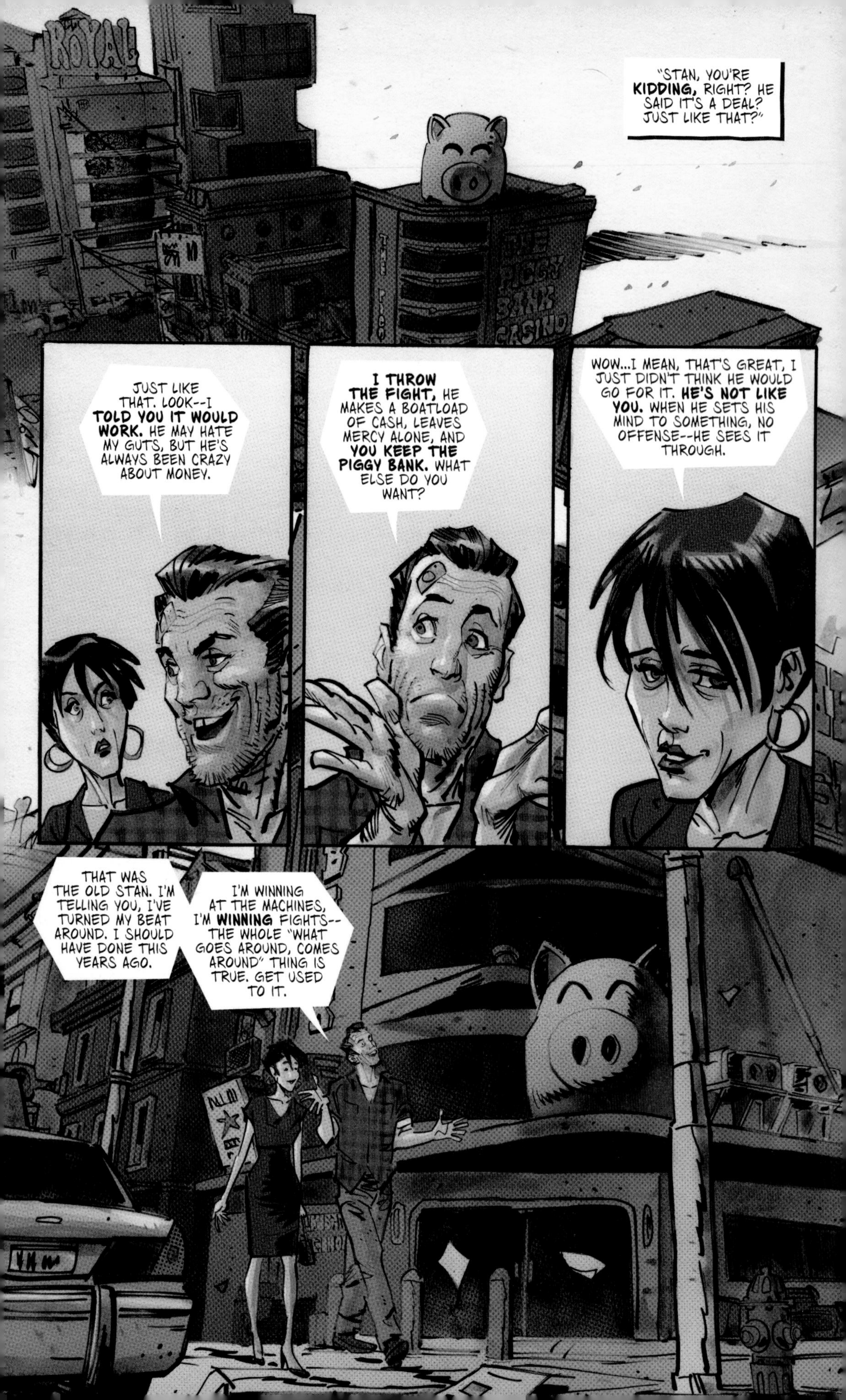
"STAN, YOU'RE KIDDING, RIGHT? HE SAID IT'S A DEAL? JUST LIKE THAT?"
JUST LIKE THAT. LOOK--I TOLD YOU IT WOULD WORK. HE MAY HATE MY GUTS, BUT HE'S ALWAYS BEEN CRAZY ABOUT MONEY.
I THROW THE FIGHT, HE MAKES A BOATLOAD OF CASH, LEAVES MERCY ALONE, AND YOU KEEP THE PIGGY BANK. WHAT ELSE DO YOU WANT?
WOW...I MEAN, THAT'S GREAT, I JUST DIDN'T THINK HE WOULD GO FOR IT. HE'S NOT LIKE YOU. WHEN HE SETS HIS MIND TO SOMETHING, NO OFFENSE--HE SEES IT THROUGH.
THAT WAS THE OLD STAN. I'M TELLING YOU, I'VE TURNED MY BEAT AROUND. I SHOULD HAVE DONE THIS YEARS AGO.
I'M WINNING AT THE MACHINES, I'M WINNING FIGHTS-- THE WHOLE "WHAT GOES AROUND, COMES AROUND" THING IS TRUE. GET USED TO IT.
THE PIGGY BANK CASINO
ROYAL

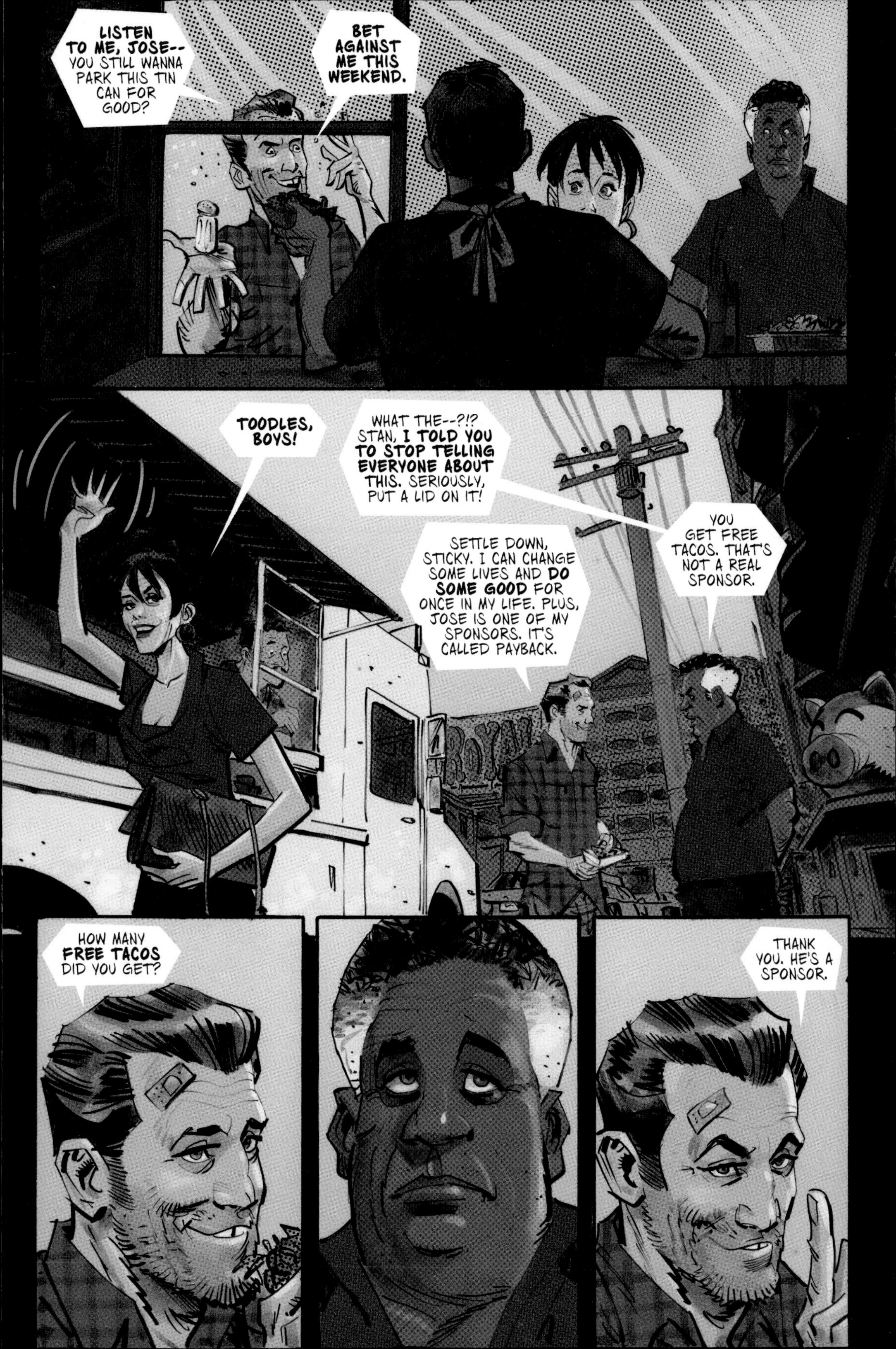
LISTEN TO ME, JOSE-- YOU STILL WANNA PARK THIS TIN CAN FOR GOOD?
BET AGAINST ME THIS WEEKEND.
TOODLES, BOYS!
WHAT THE--?!? STAN, I TOLD YOU TO STOP TELLING EVERYONE ABOUT THIS. SERIOUSLY, PUT A LID ON IT!
SETTLE DOWN, STICKY. I CAN CHANGE SOME LIVES AND DO SOME GOOD FOR ONCE IN MY LIFE. PLUS, JOSE IS ONE OF MY SPONSORS. IT'S CALLED PAYBACK.
YOU GET FREE TACOS. THAT'S NOT A REAL SPONSOR.
HOW MANY FREE TACOS DID YOU GET?
THANK YOU. HE'S A SPONSOR.

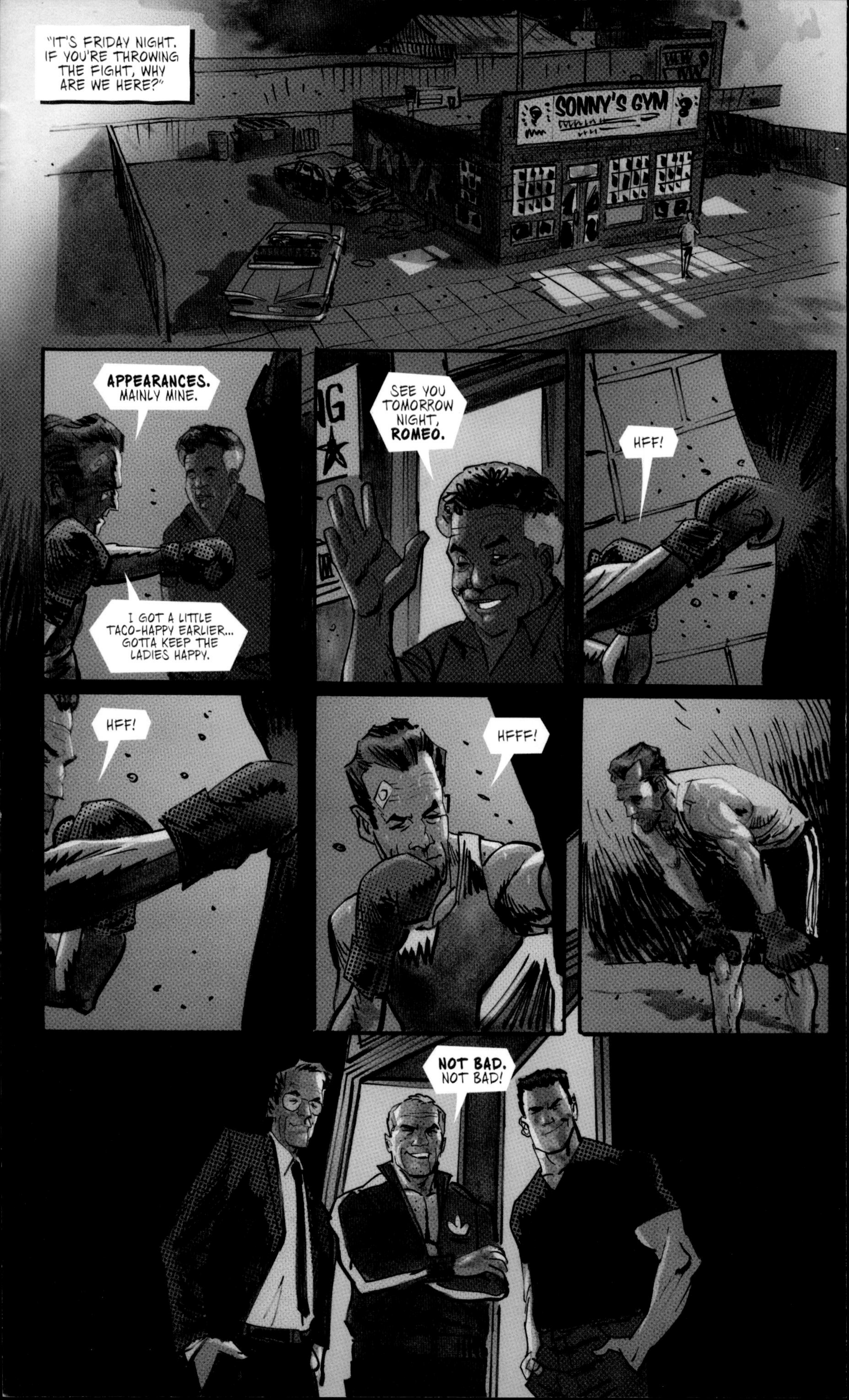
"IT'S FRIDAY NIGHT. IF YOU'RE THROWING THE FIGHT, WHY ARE WE HERE?"
SONNY'S GYM
APPEARANCES. MAINLY MINE.
I GOT A LITTLE TACO-HAPPY EARLIER... GOTTA KEEP THE LADIES HAPPY.
SEE YOU TOMORROW NIGHT, ROMEO.
HFF!
HFF!
HFFF!
NOT BAD. NOT BAD!

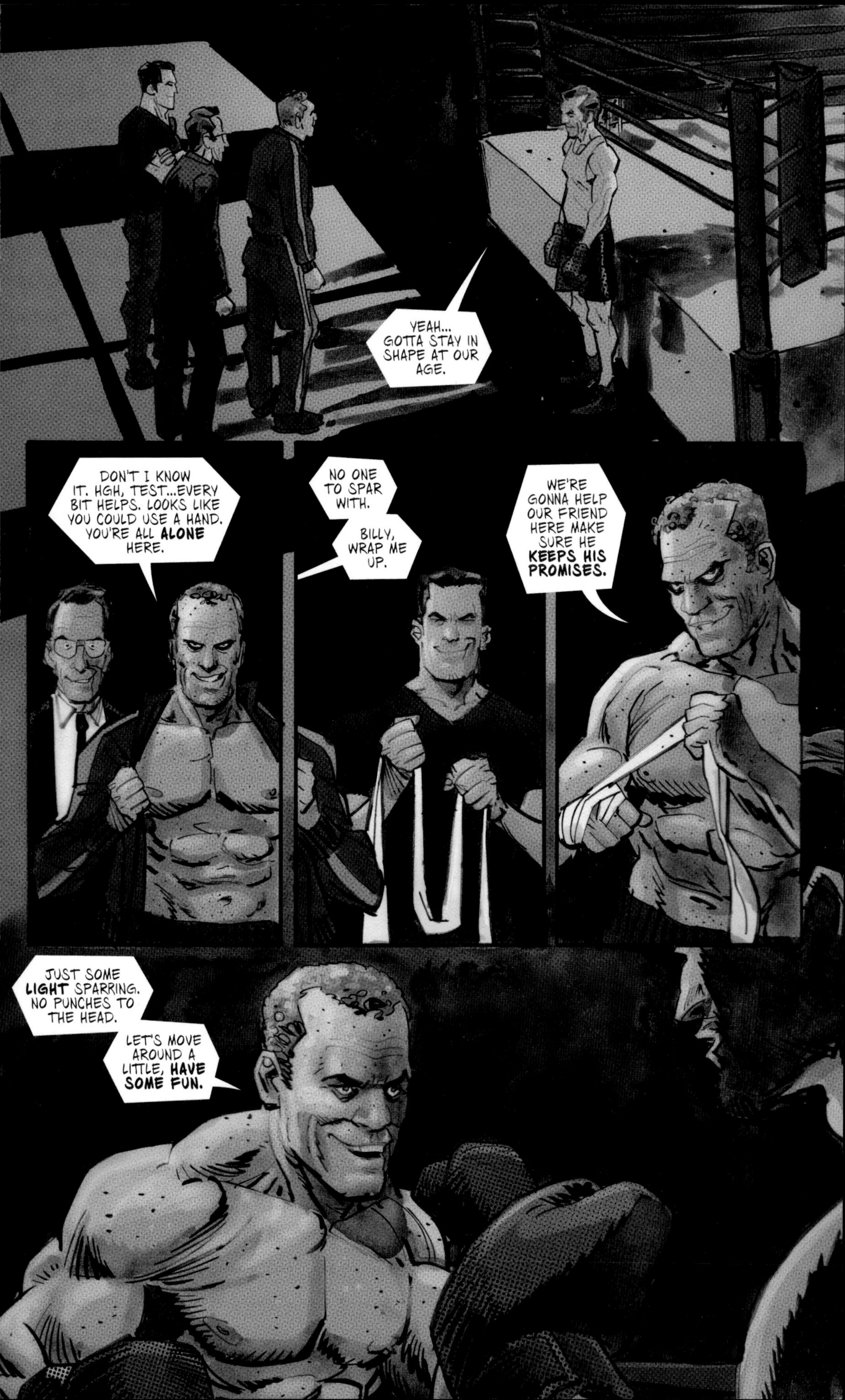
YEAH... GOTTA STAY IN SHAPE AT OUR AGE.
DON'T I KNOW IT. HGH, TEST...EVERY BIT HELPS. LOOKS LIKE YOU COULD USE A HAND. YOU'RE ALL **ALONE** HERE.
NO ONE TO SPAR WITH.
BILLY, WRAP ME UP.
WE'RE GONNA HELP OUR FRIEND HERE MAKE SURE HE **KEEPS HIS PROMISES.**
JUST SOME **LIGHT** SPARRING. NO PUNCHES TO THE HEAD.
LET'S MOVE AROUND A LITTLE, **HAVE SOME FUN.**

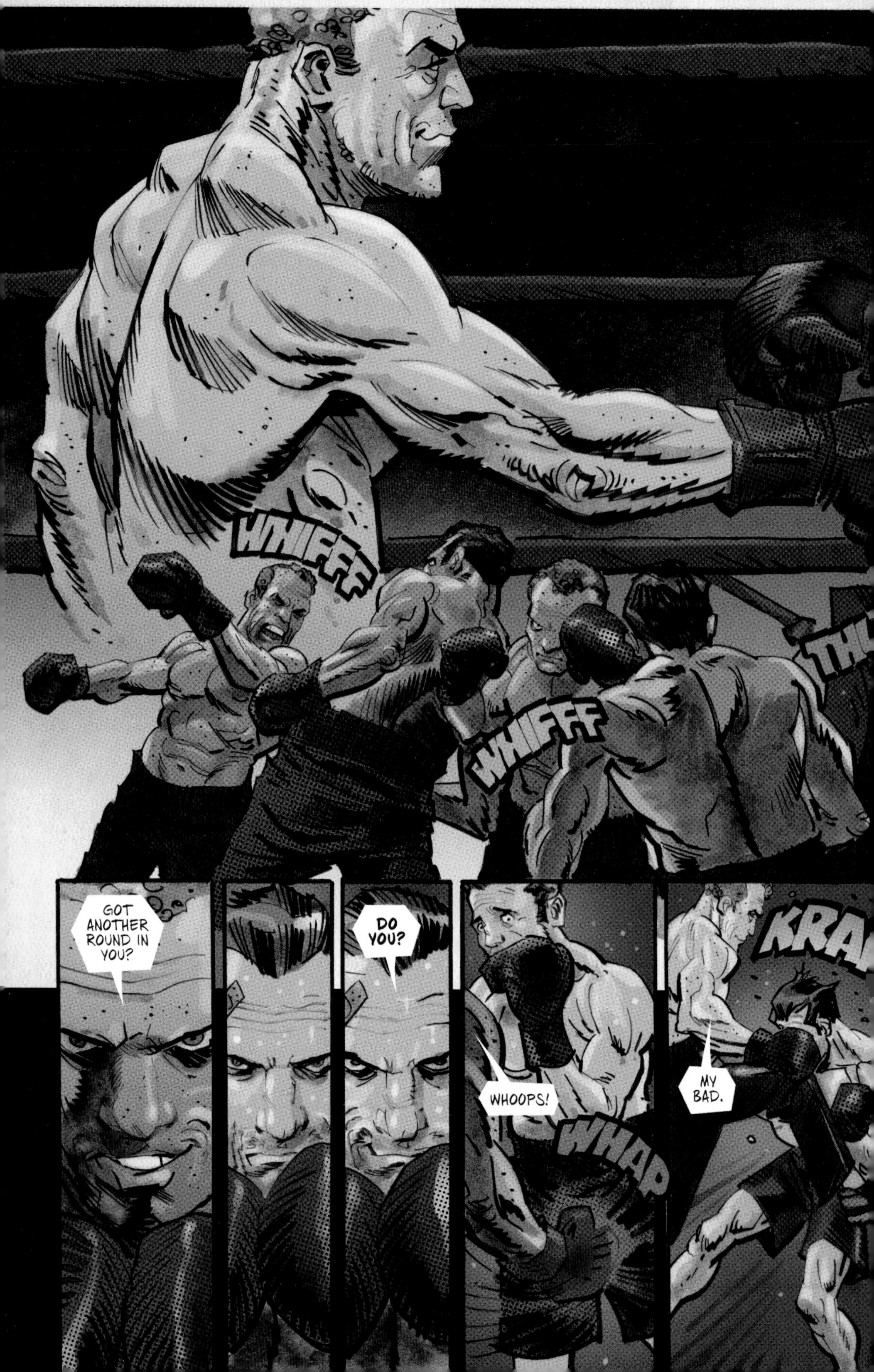
WHIFFF
WHIFFF
GOT ANOTHER ROUND IN YOU?
DO YOU?
WHOOPS!
WHAP
MY BAD.

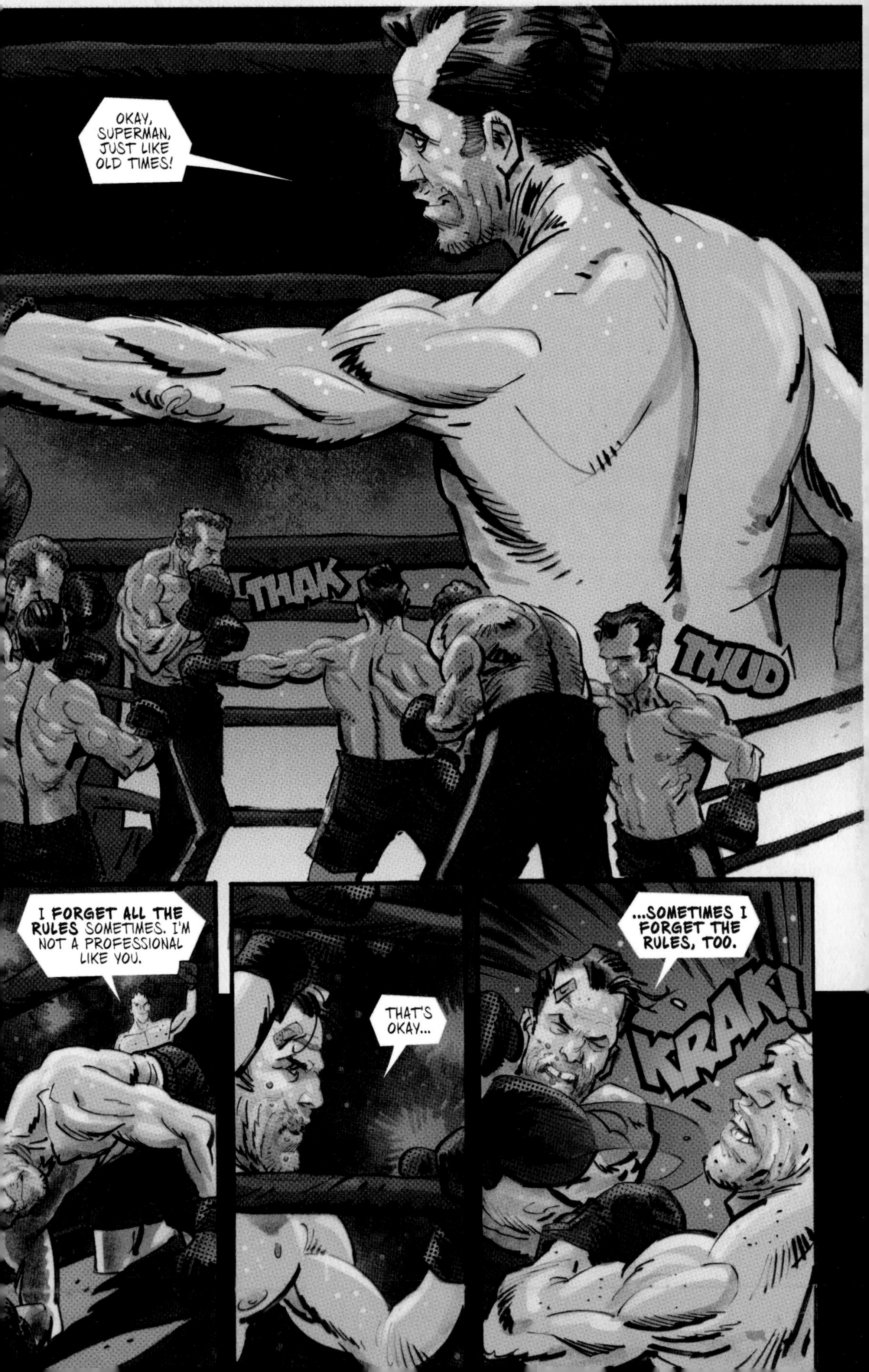
OKAY, SUPERMAN, JUST LIKE OLD TIMES!
THAK
THUD
I FORGET ALL THE RULES SOMETIMES. I'M NOT A PROFESSIONAL LIKE YOU.
THAT'S OKAY...
...SOMETIMES I FORGET THE RULES, TOO.
KRAK!

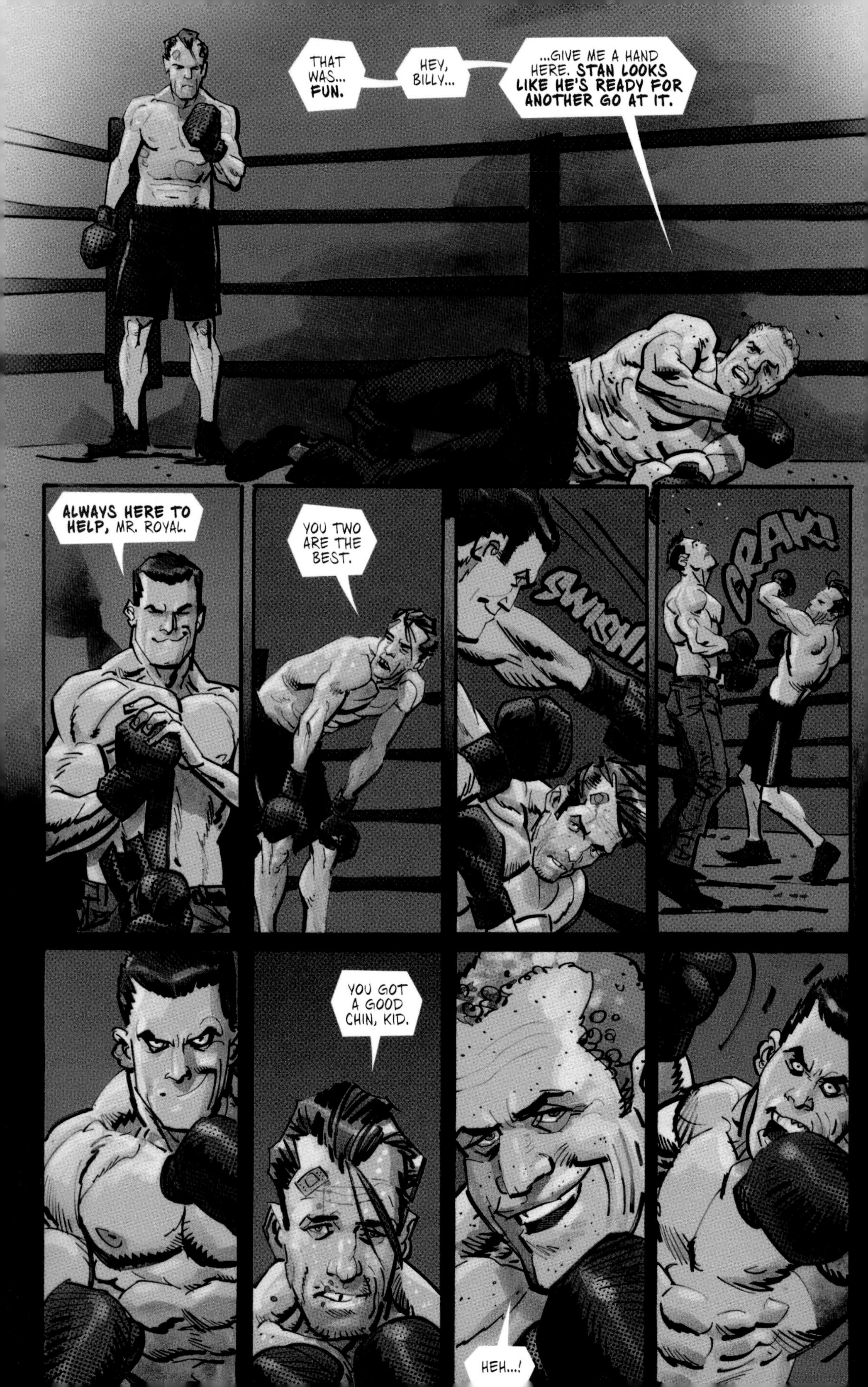
THAT WAS... FUN.
HEY, BILLY...
...GIVE ME A HAND HERE. STAN LOOKS LIKE HE'S READY FOR ANOTHER GO AT IT.
ALWAYS HERE TO HELP, MR. ROYAL.
YOU TWO ARE THE BEST.
SWISH
CRAK!
YOU GOT A GOOD CHIN, KID.
HEH...!

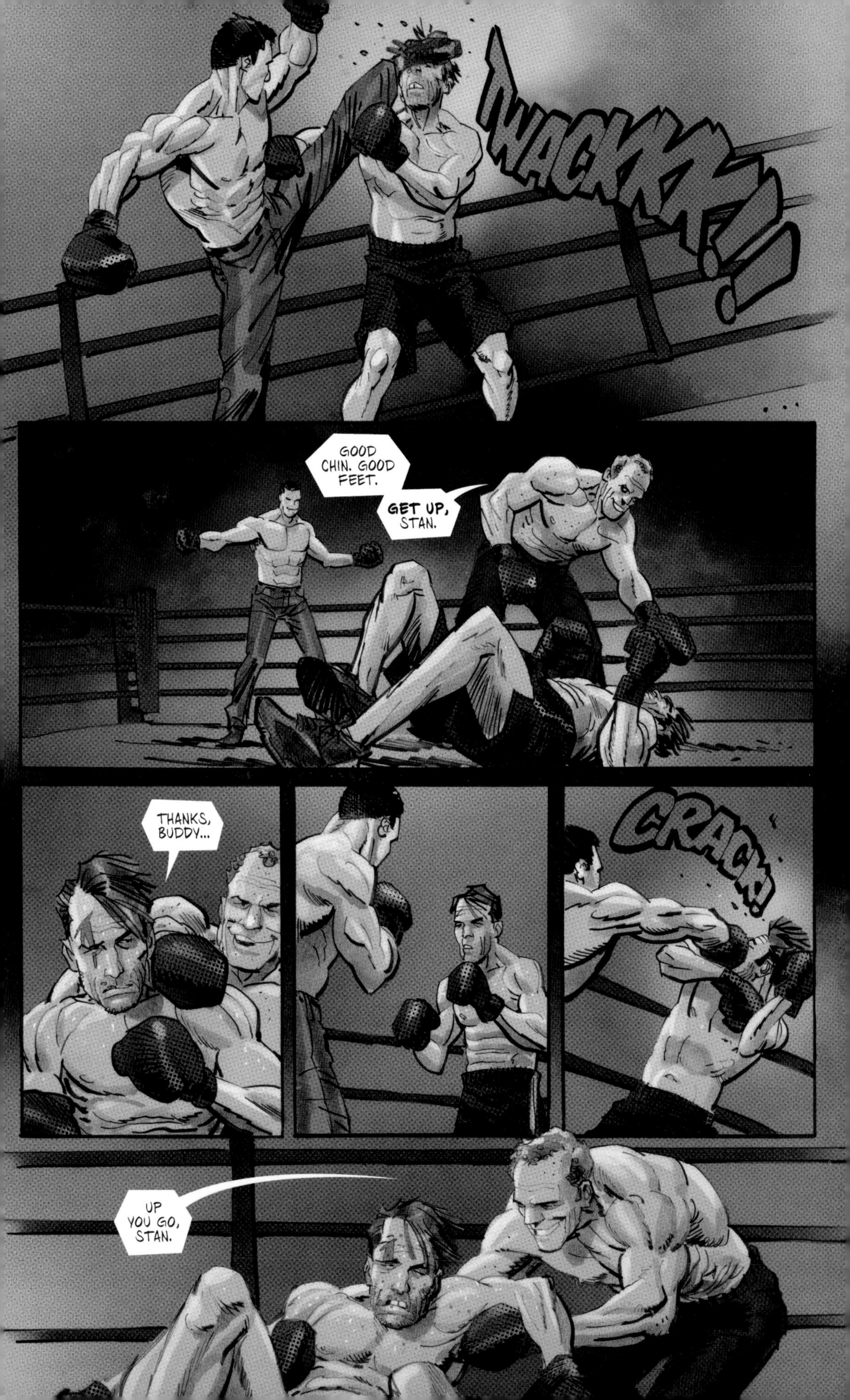
WHACKKK!!
GOOD CHIN. GOOD FEET.
GET UP, STAN.
THANKS, BUDDY...
CRACK!
UP YOU GO, STAN.

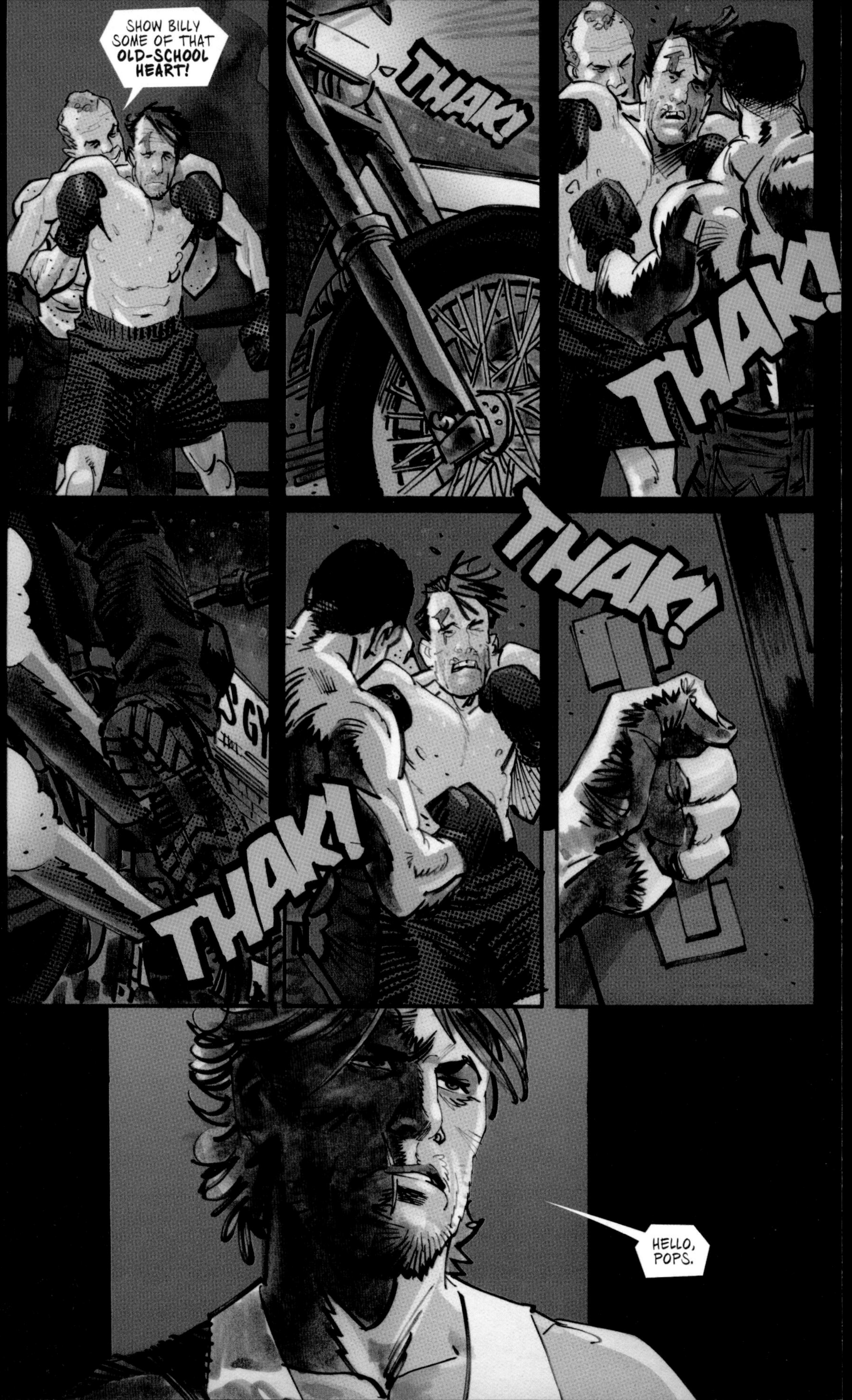
SHOW BILLY SOME OF THAT OLD-SCHOOL HEART!
THAK!
THAK!
THAK!
THAK!
HELLO, POPS.

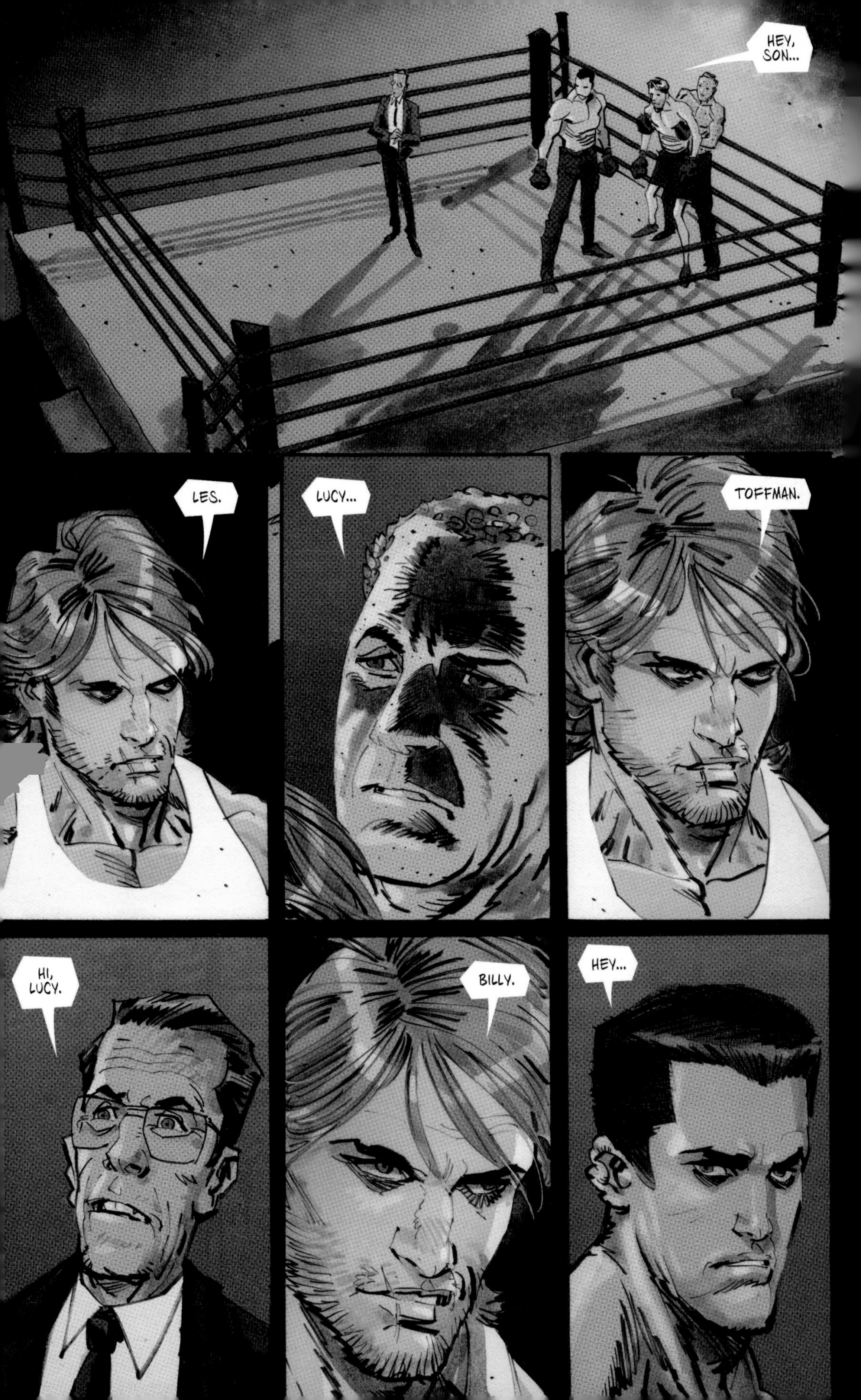
HEY, SON...
LES.
LUCY...
TOFFMAN.
HI, LUCY.
BILLY.
HEY...

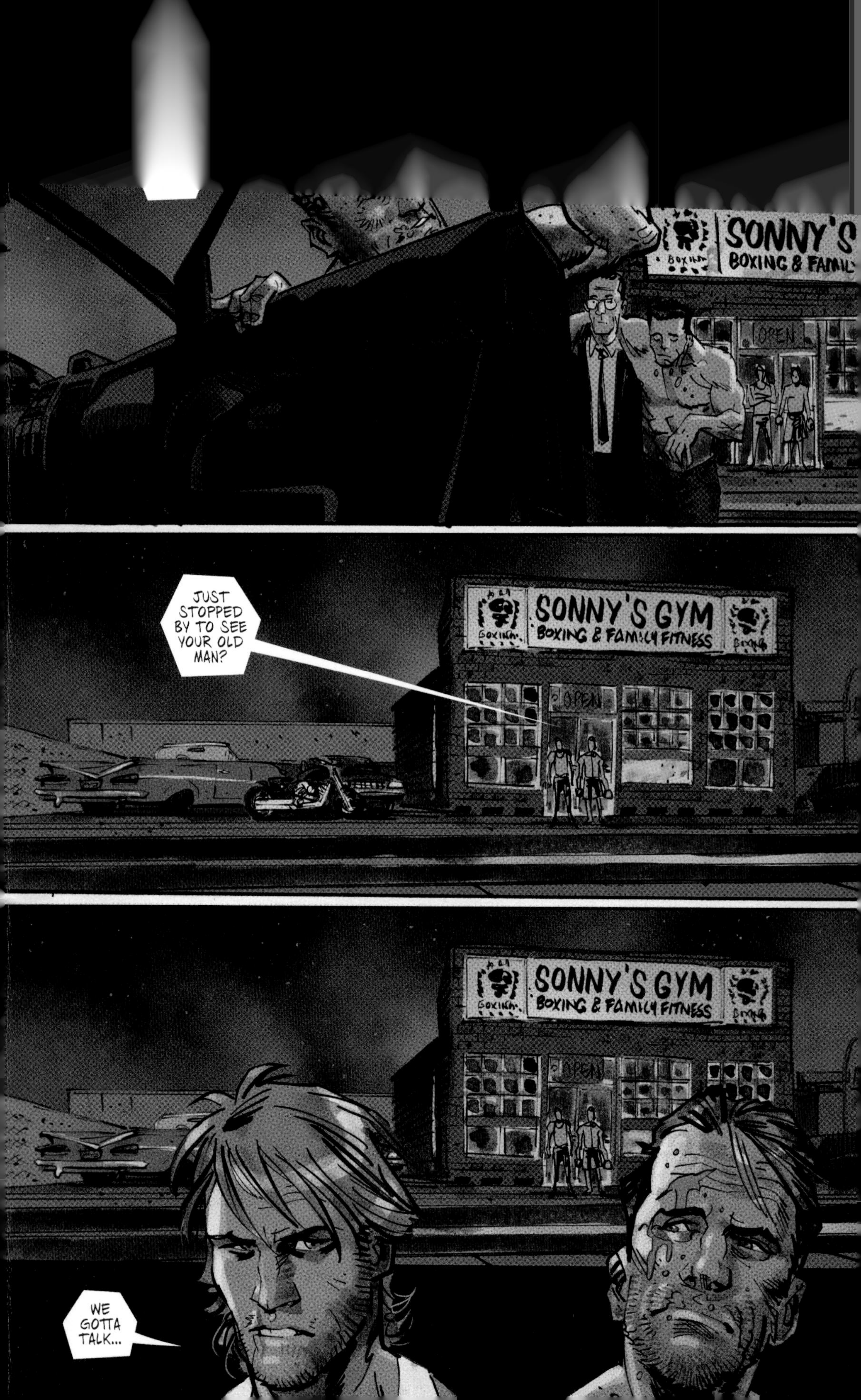
SONNY'S
BOXING & FAMIL
OPEN
SONNY'S GYM
BOXING & FAMILY FITNESS
JUST STOPPED BY TO SEE YOUR OLD MAN?
SONNY'S GYM
BOXING & FAMILY FITNESS
WE GOTTA TALK...

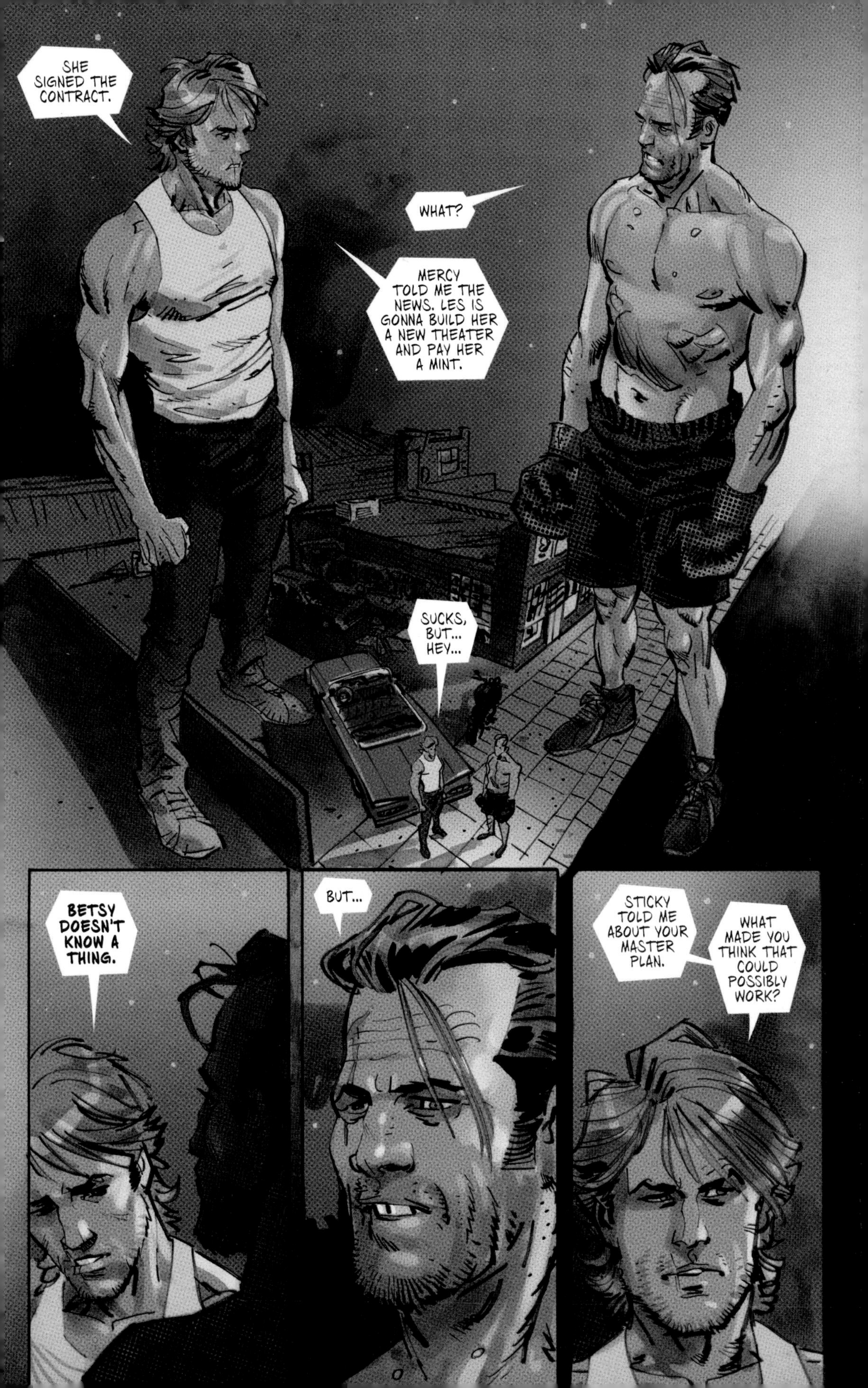
SHE SIGNED THE CONTRACT.
WHAT?
MERCY TOLD ME THE NEWS. LES IS GONNA BUILD HER A NEW THEATER AND PAY HER A MINT.
SUCKS, BUT... HEY...
BETSY DOESN'T KNOW A THING.
BUT...
STICKY TOLD ME ABOUT YOUR MASTER PLAN.
WHAT MADE YOU THINK THAT COULD POSSIBLY WORK?

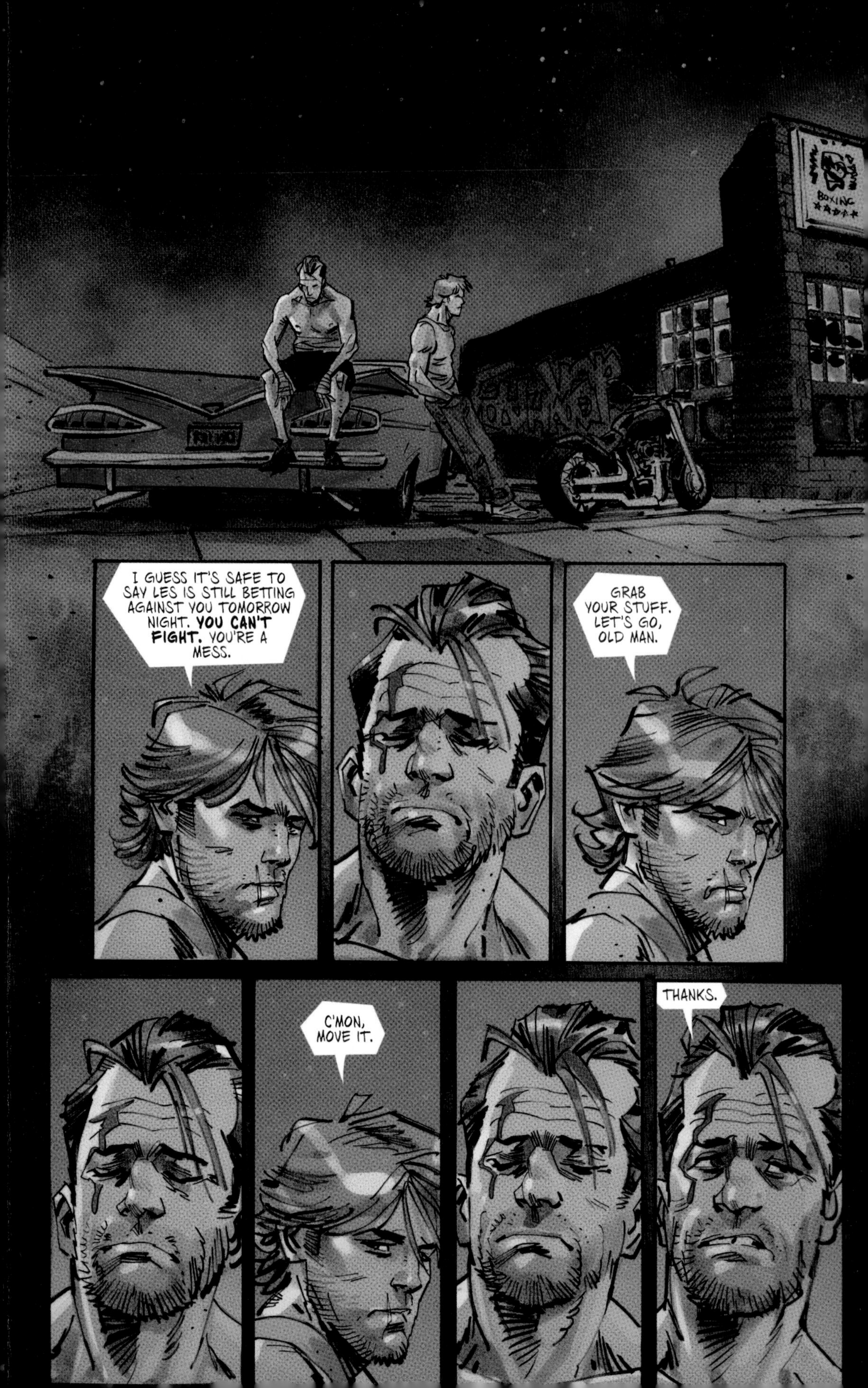
BOXING
I GUESS IT'S SAFE TO SAY LES IS STILL BETTING AGAINST YOU TOMORROW NIGHT. **YOU CAN'T FIGHT.** YOU'RE A MESS.
GRAB YOUR STUFF. LET'S GO, OLD MAN.
C'MON, MOVE IT.
THANKS.

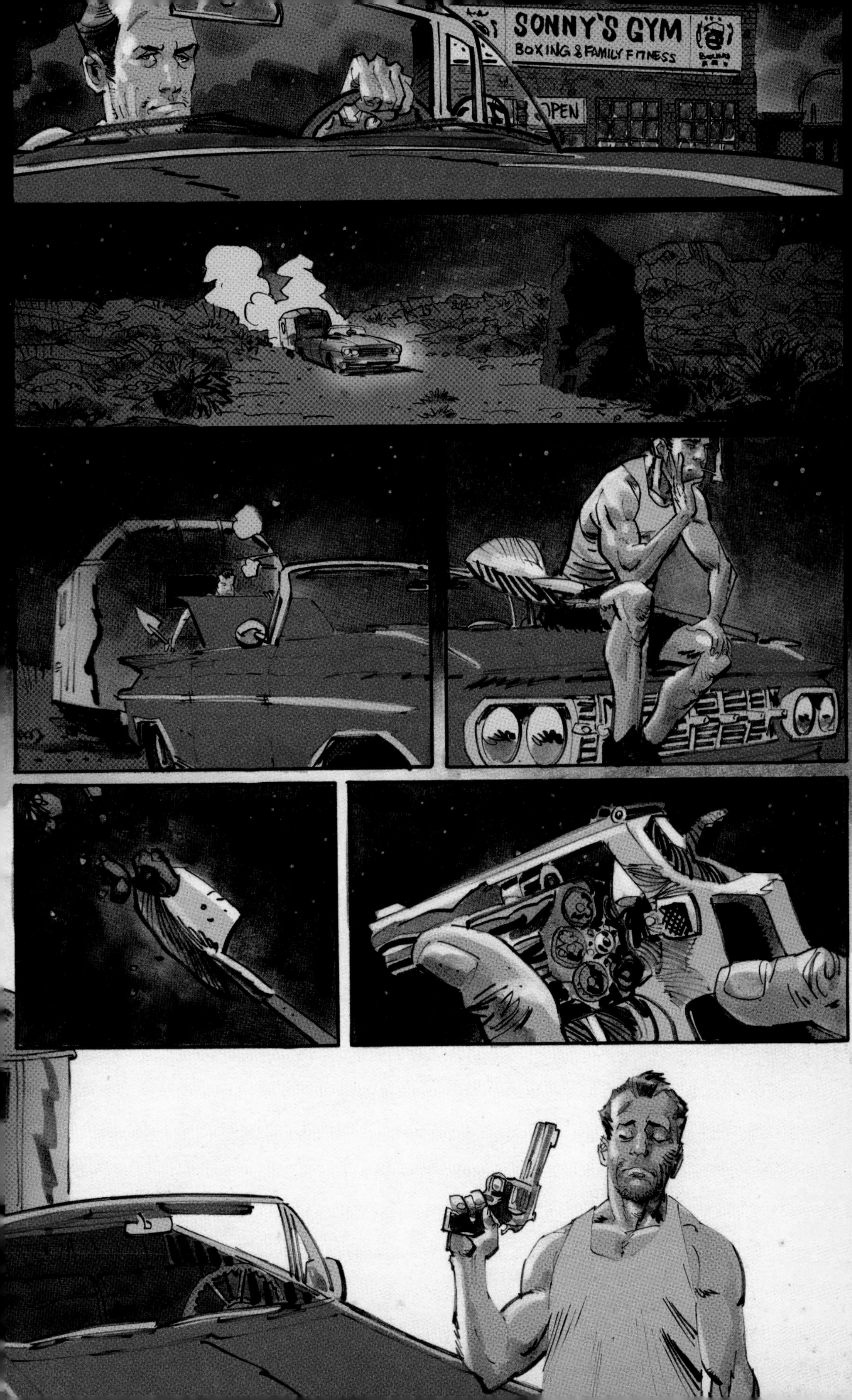
SONNY'S GYM
BOXING & FAMILY FITNESS
OPEN

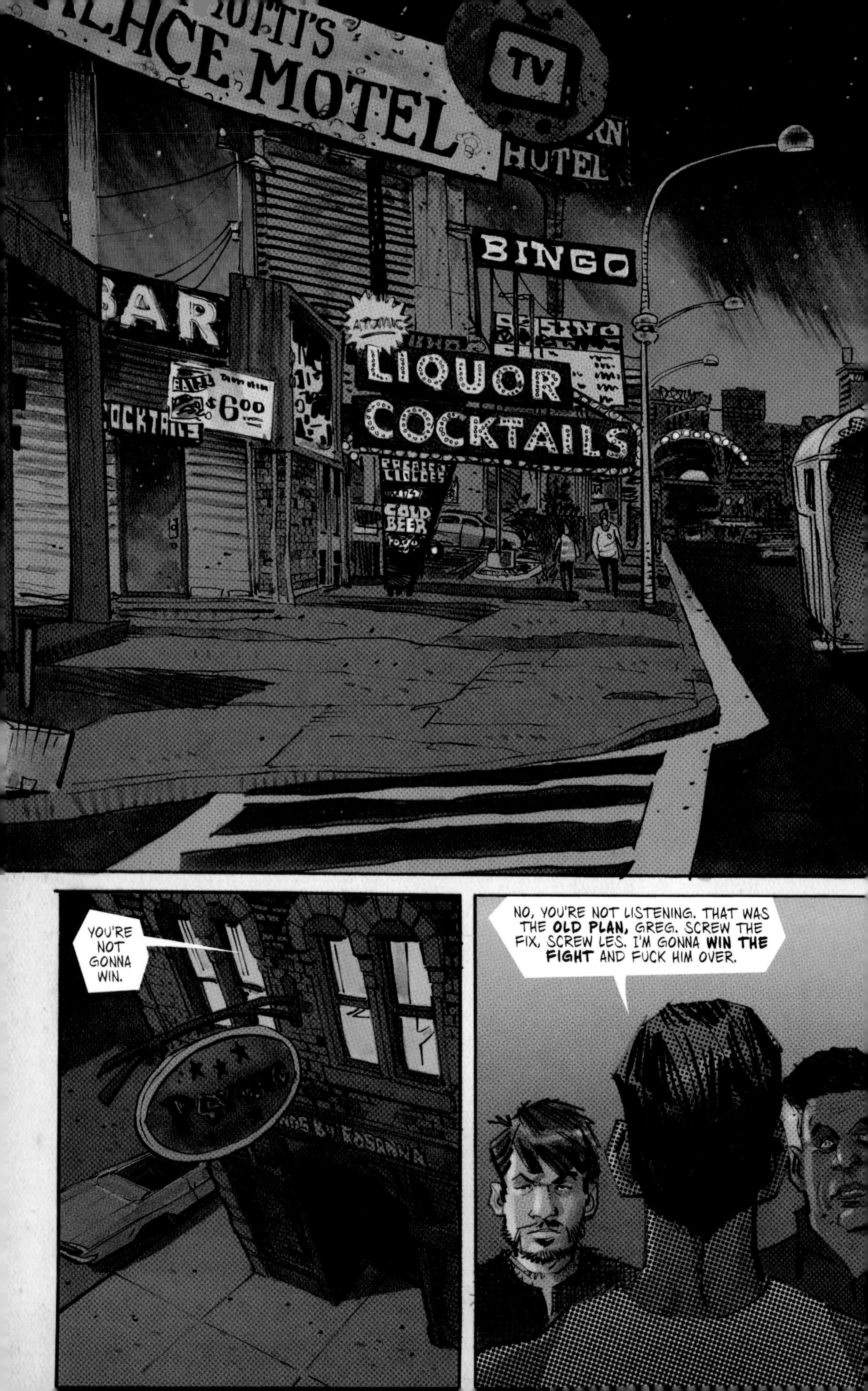
MOTEL
TV
HOTEL
BINGO
BAR
$6.00
ATOMIC
LIQUOR
COCKTAILS
COLD BEER
YOU'RE NOT GONNA WIN.
NO, YOU'RE NOT LISTENING. THAT WAS THE **OLD PLAN**, GREG. SCREW THE FIX, SCREW LES. I'M GONNA **WIN THE FIGHT** AND FUCK HIM OVER.

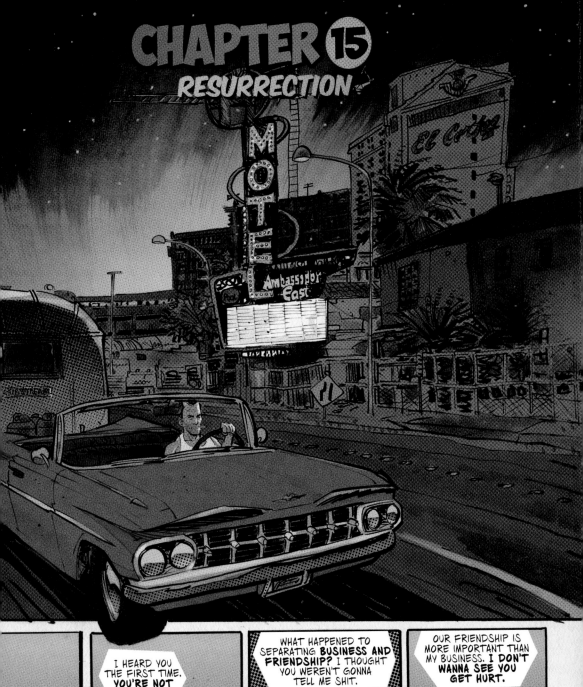

CHAPTER 15
RESURRECTION

I HEARD YOU THE FIRST TIME. **YOU'RE NOT GONNA WIN,** STAN.

WHAT HAPPENED TO SEPARATING **BUSINESS AND FRIENDSHIP?** I THOUGHT YOU WEREN'T GONNA TELL ME SHIT.

OUR FRIENDSHIP IS MORE IMPORTANT THAN MY BUSINESS. **I DON'T WANNA SEE YOU GET HURT.**

FUCK YOUR **MAGICAL POWERS!** YOU SAID IT YOURSELF, HE'S HURTING FOR CASH.

IF LES LOSES, HE LOSES BIG AND HE CAN'T FINANCE THE THEATER, AND THAT MEANS HIS CONTRACT WITH MERCY IS SHIT.

ACCORDING TO **TOFFMAN**, BUT THAT GUY IS A BIGGER SNAKE THAN LES IS. I WAS PRETTY DRUNK THAT NIGHT, AND WHO KNOWS WHAT GAME HE'S PLAYING.

SO NOW YOUR POWERS **DON'T WORK?** FOR ME THEY **WORK**, BUT FOR TOFFMAN THEY DON'T WORK. **WHICH IS IT?**

MY POWERS--**FUCK**-- LISTEN, I KNOW WHAT I KNOW. YES, I BELIEVE HIM. LES IS HURTING. **WORD IS HE'S LATE ON ALL OF HIS ACCOUNTS.** BUT WHO ISN'T IN THIS TOWN?

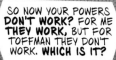

WELL, FUCK YOU, I'M **WINNING THE FIGHT!**

YOU **HOBBLED** IN HERE. **TELL ME HOW YOU WIN.**

THERE ARE WAYS.

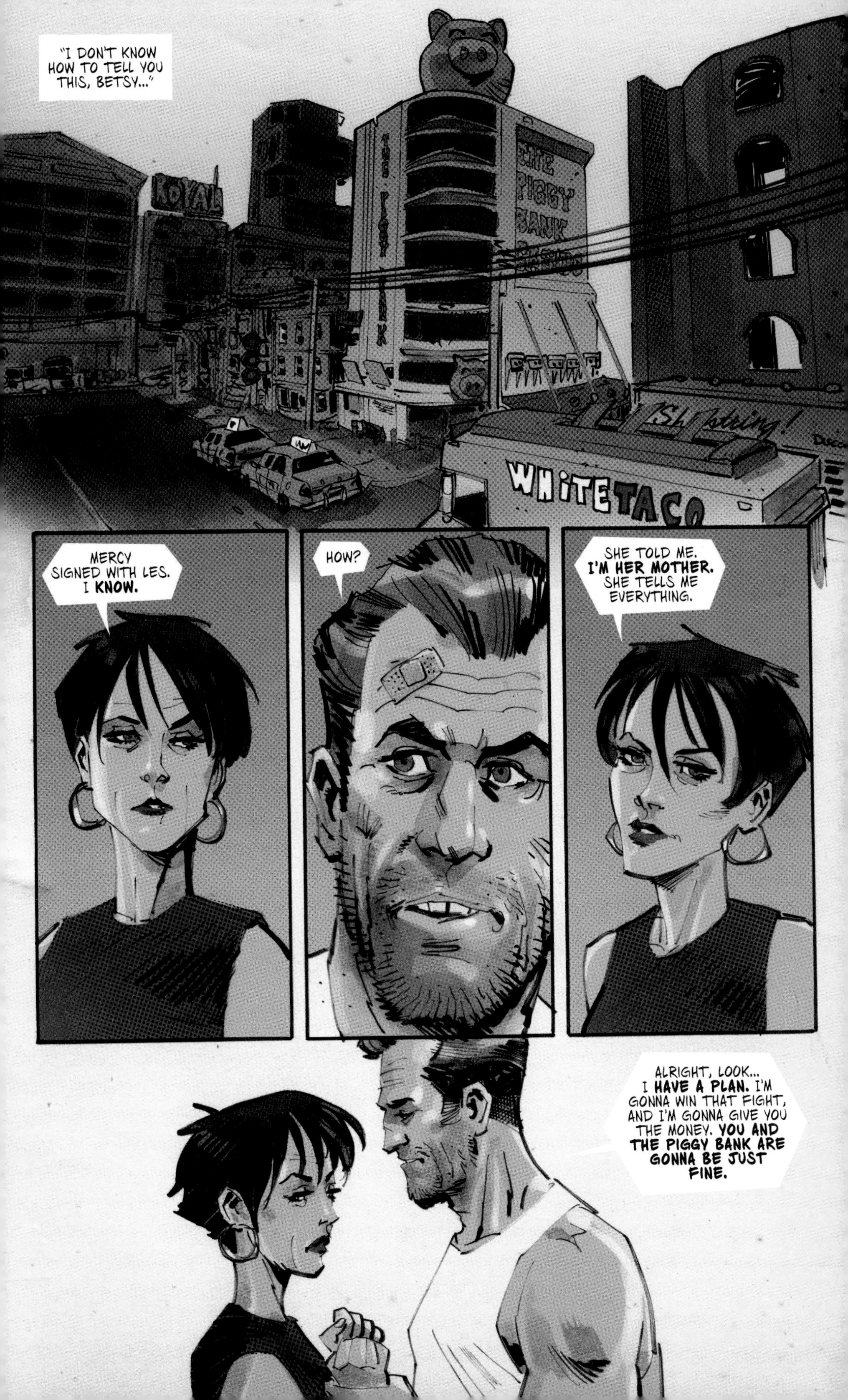
"I DON'T KNOW HOW TO TELL YOU THIS, BETSY..."
THE PIGGY BANK
THE PIGGY BANK
ROYAL
WHITE TACO
MERCY SIGNED WITH LES. I **KNOW.**
HOW?
SHE TOLD ME. **I'M HER MOTHER.** SHE TELLS ME EVERYTHING.
ALRIGHT, LOOK... I **HAVE A PLAN.** I'M GONNA WIN THAT FIGHT, AND I'M GONNA GIVE YOU THE MONEY. **YOU AND THE PIGGY BANK ARE GONNA BE JUST FINE.**

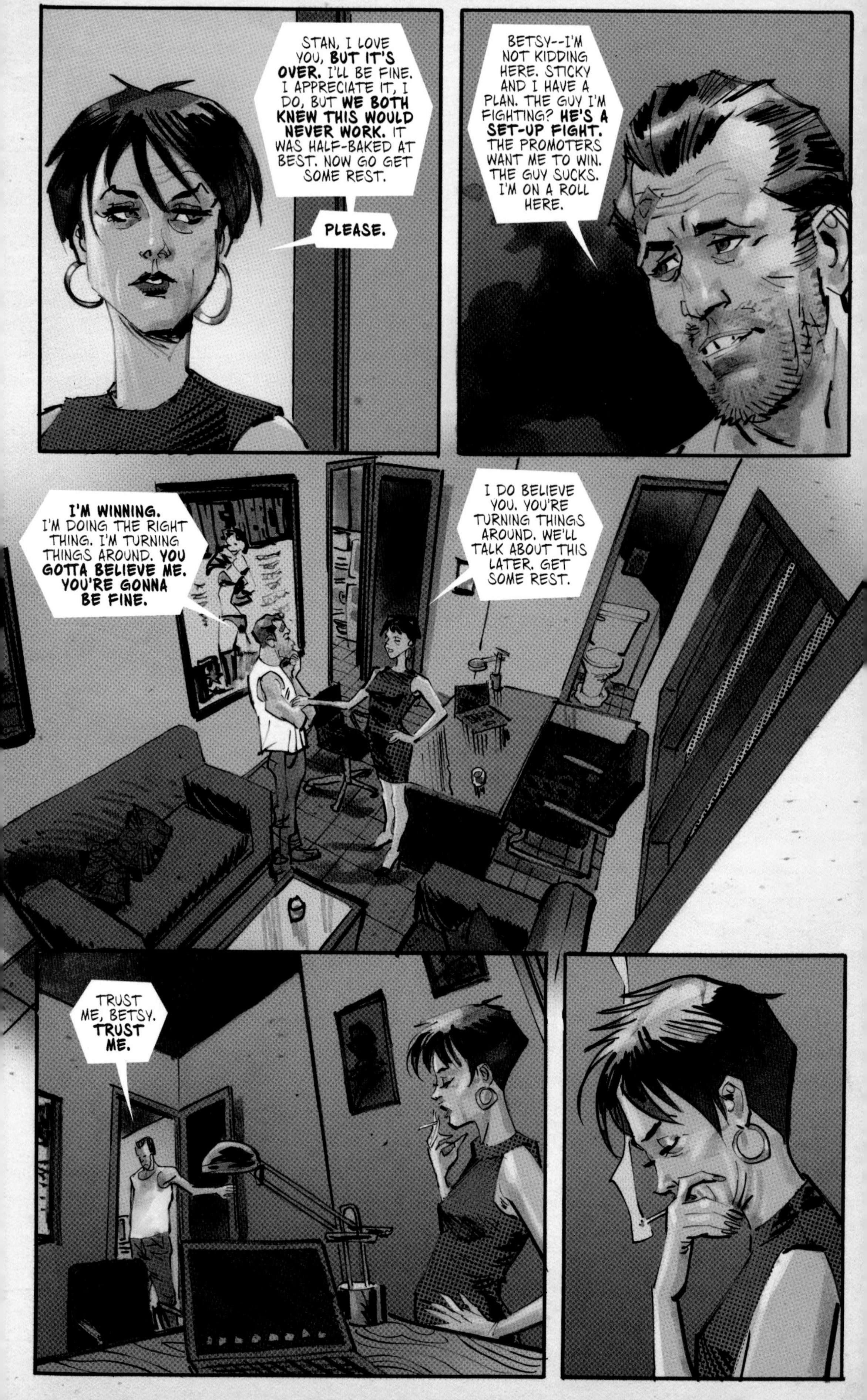
STAN, I LOVE YOU, BUT IT'S OVER. I'LL BE FINE. I APPRECIATE IT, I DO, BUT WE BOTH KNEW THIS WOULD NEVER WORK. IT WAS HALF-BAKED AT BEST. NOW GO GET SOME REST.
PLEASE.
BETSY--I'M NOT KIDDING HERE. STICKY AND I HAVE A PLAN. THE GUY I'M FIGHTING? HE'S A SET-UP FIGHT. THE PROMOTERS WANT ME TO WIN. THE GUY SUCKS. I'M ON A ROLL HERE.
I'M WINNING. I'M DOING THE RIGHT THING. I'M TURNING THINGS AROUND. YOU GOTTA BELIEVE ME. YOU'RE GONNA BE FINE.
I DO BELIEVE YOU. YOU'RE TURNING THINGS AROUND. WE'LL TALK ABOUT THIS LATER. GET SOME REST.
TRUST ME, BETSY. TRUST ME.

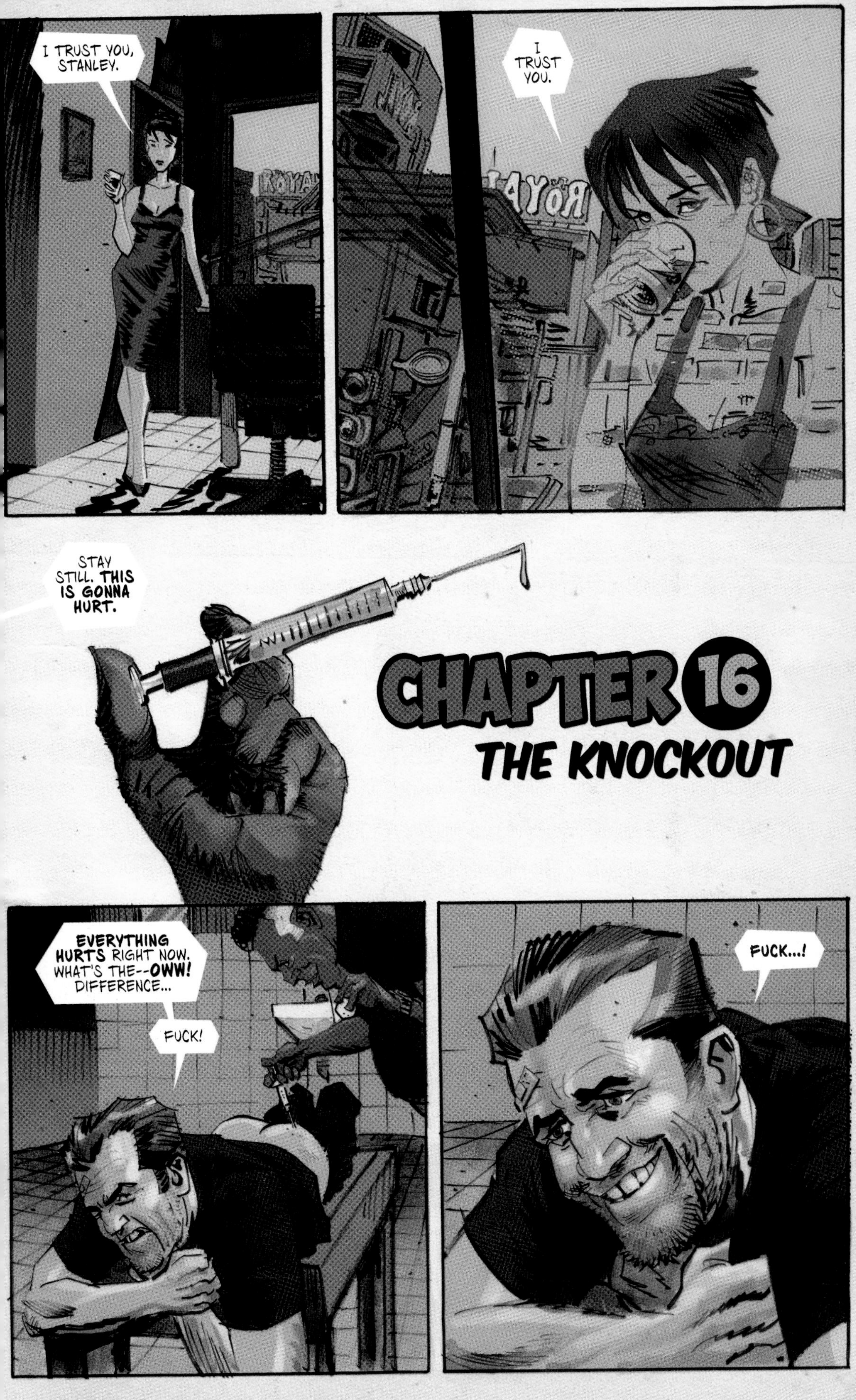
I TRUST YOU, STANLEY.
I TRUST YOU.
STAY STILL. THIS IS GONNA HURT.
CHAPTER 16
THE KNOCKOUT
EVERYTHING HURTS RIGHT NOW. WHAT'S THE--OWW! DIFFERENCE...
FUCK!
FUCK...!

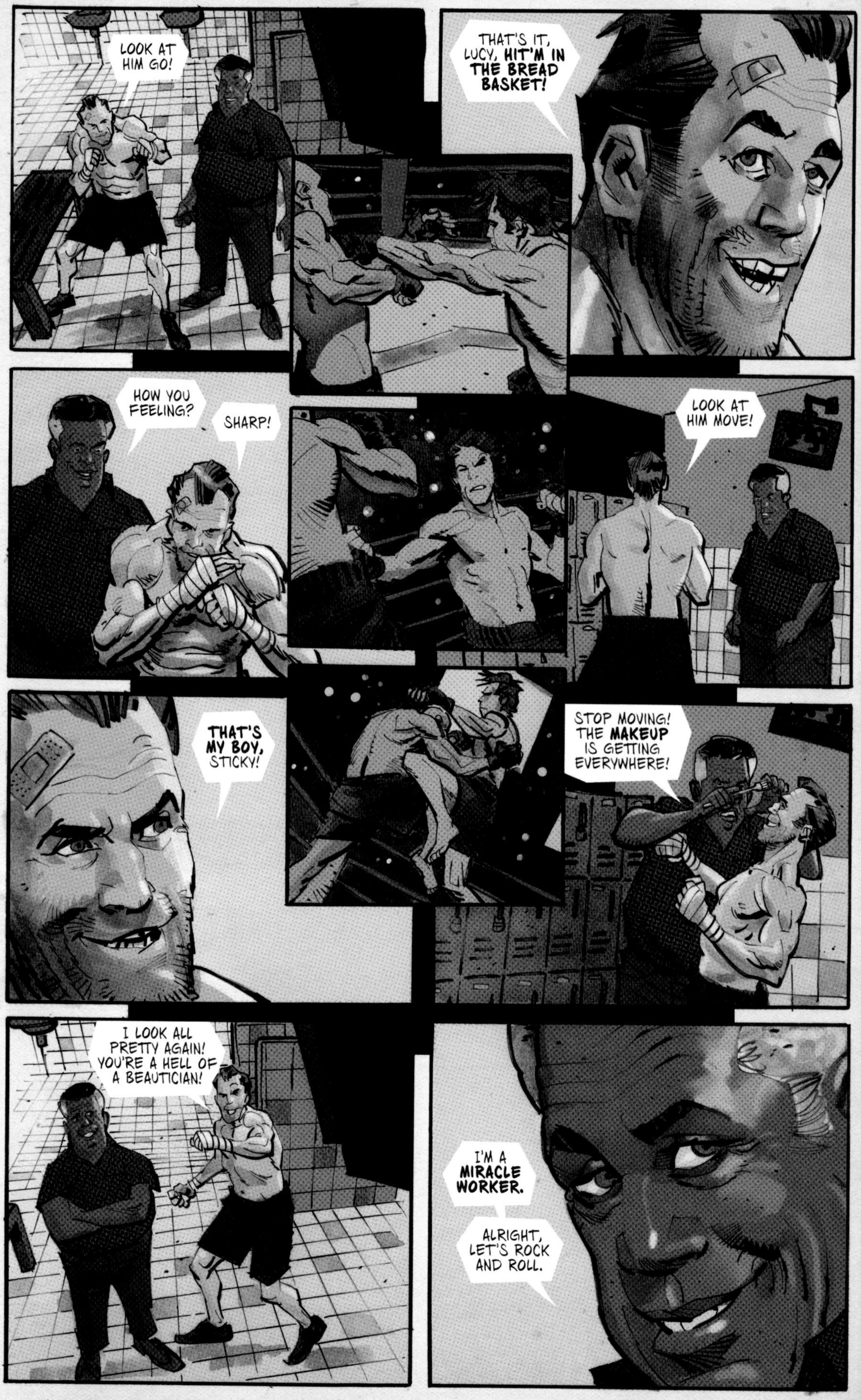
LOOK AT HIM GO!
THAT'S IT, LUCY, HIT'M IN THE BREAD BASKET!
HOW YOU FEELING?
SHARP!
LOOK AT HIM MOVE!
THAT'S MY BOY, STICKY!
STOP MOVING! THE MAKEUP IS GETTING EVERYWHERE!
I LOOK ALL PRETTY AGAIN! YOU'RE A HELL OF A BEAUTICIAN!
I'M A MIRACLE WORKER.
ALRIGHT, LET'S ROCK AND ROLL.

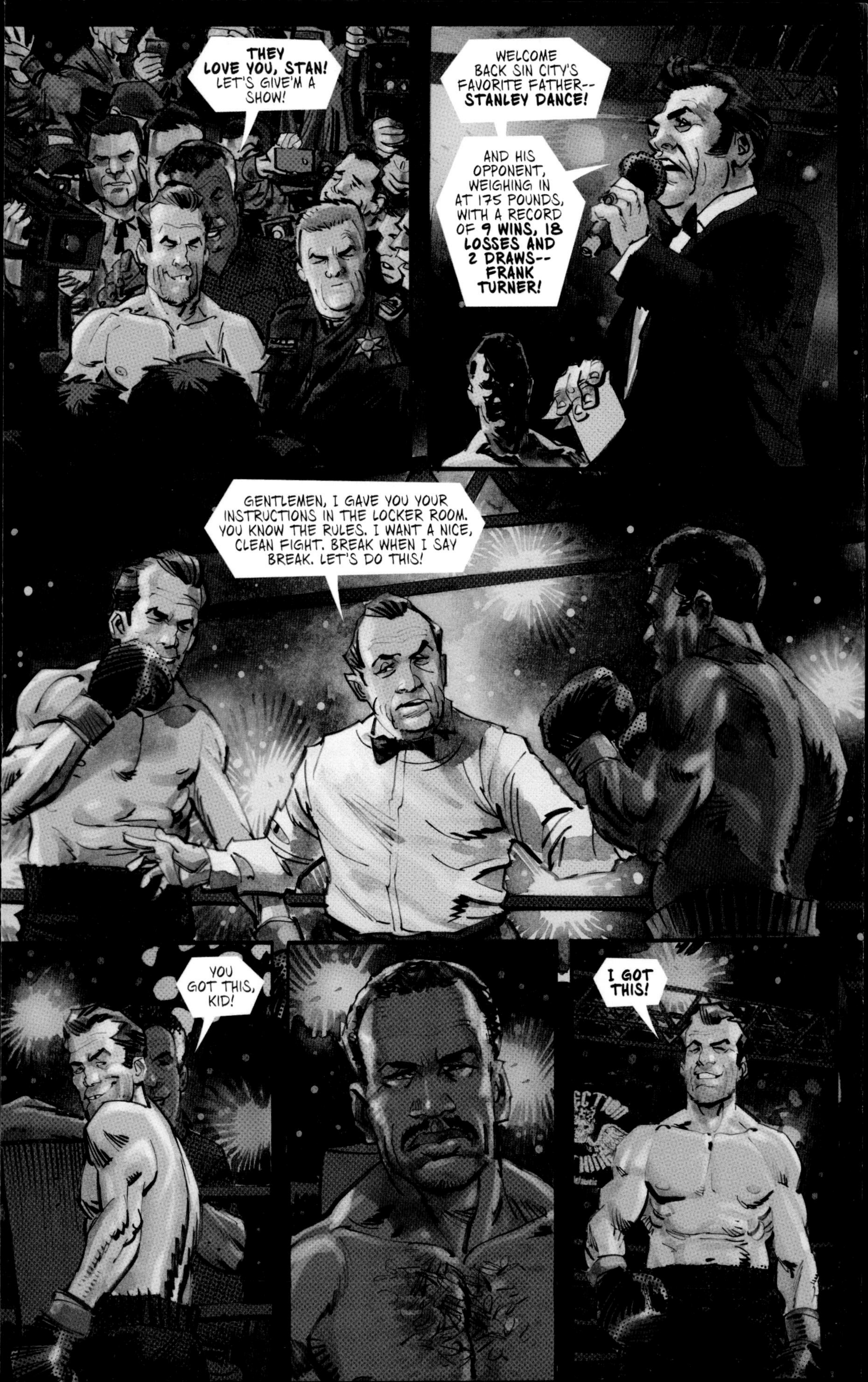
THEY LOVE YOU, STAN! LET'S GIVE'M A SHOW!
WELCOME BACK SIN CITY'S FAVORITE FATHER-- STANLEY DANCE!
AND HIS OPPONENT, WEIGHING IN AT 175 POUNDS, WITH A RECORD OF 9 WINS, 18 LOSSES AND 2 DRAWS-- FRANK TURNER!
GENTLEMEN, I GAVE YOU YOUR INSTRUCTIONS IN THE LOCKER ROOM. YOU KNOW THE RULES. I WANT A NICE, CLEAN FIGHT. BREAK WHEN I SAY BREAK. LET'S DO THIS!
YOU GOT THIS, KID!
I GOT THIS!

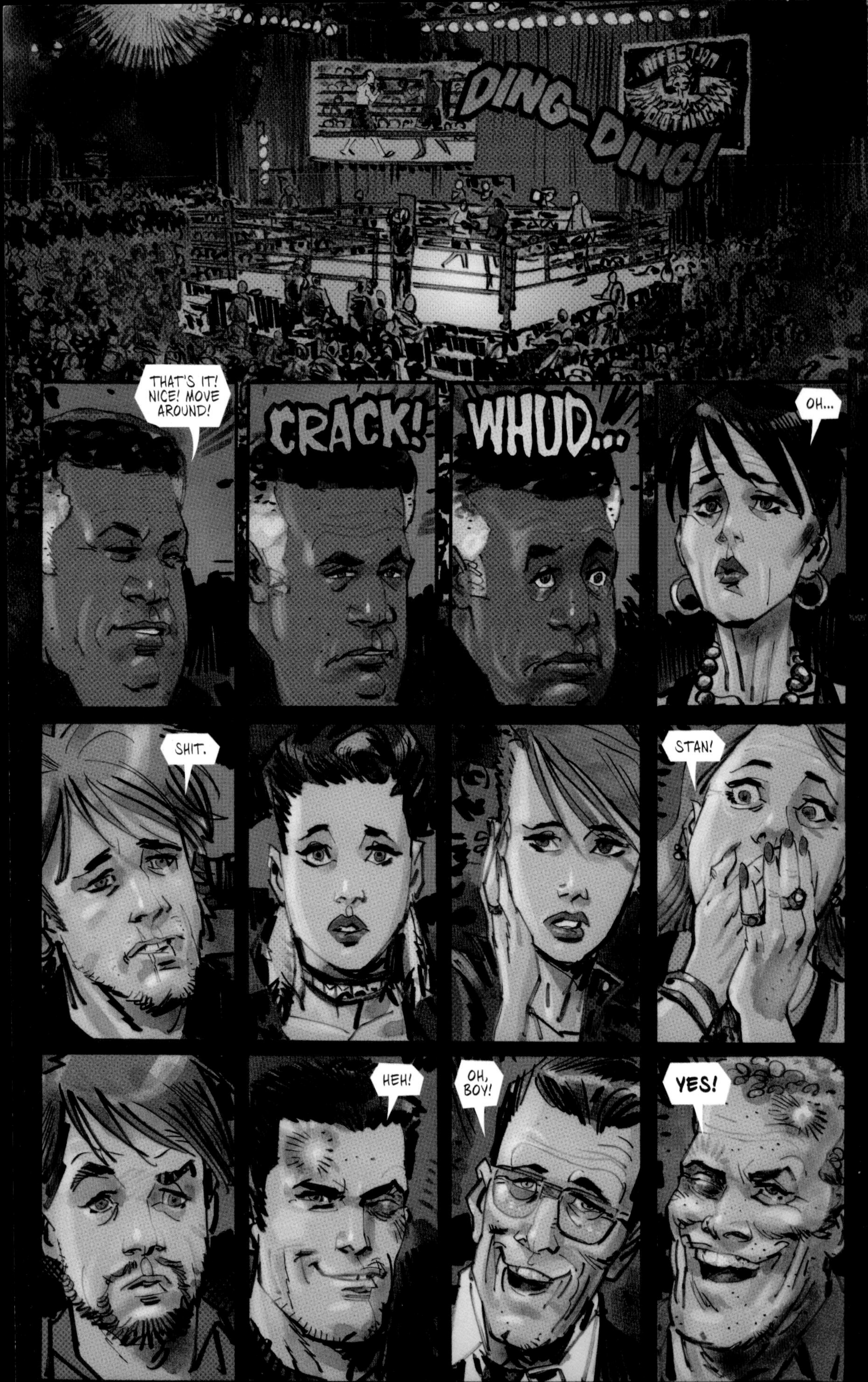
DING-DING!
THAT'S IT! NICE! MOVE AROUND!
CRACK!
WHUD...
OH...
SHIT.
STAN!
HEH!
OH, BOY!
YES!

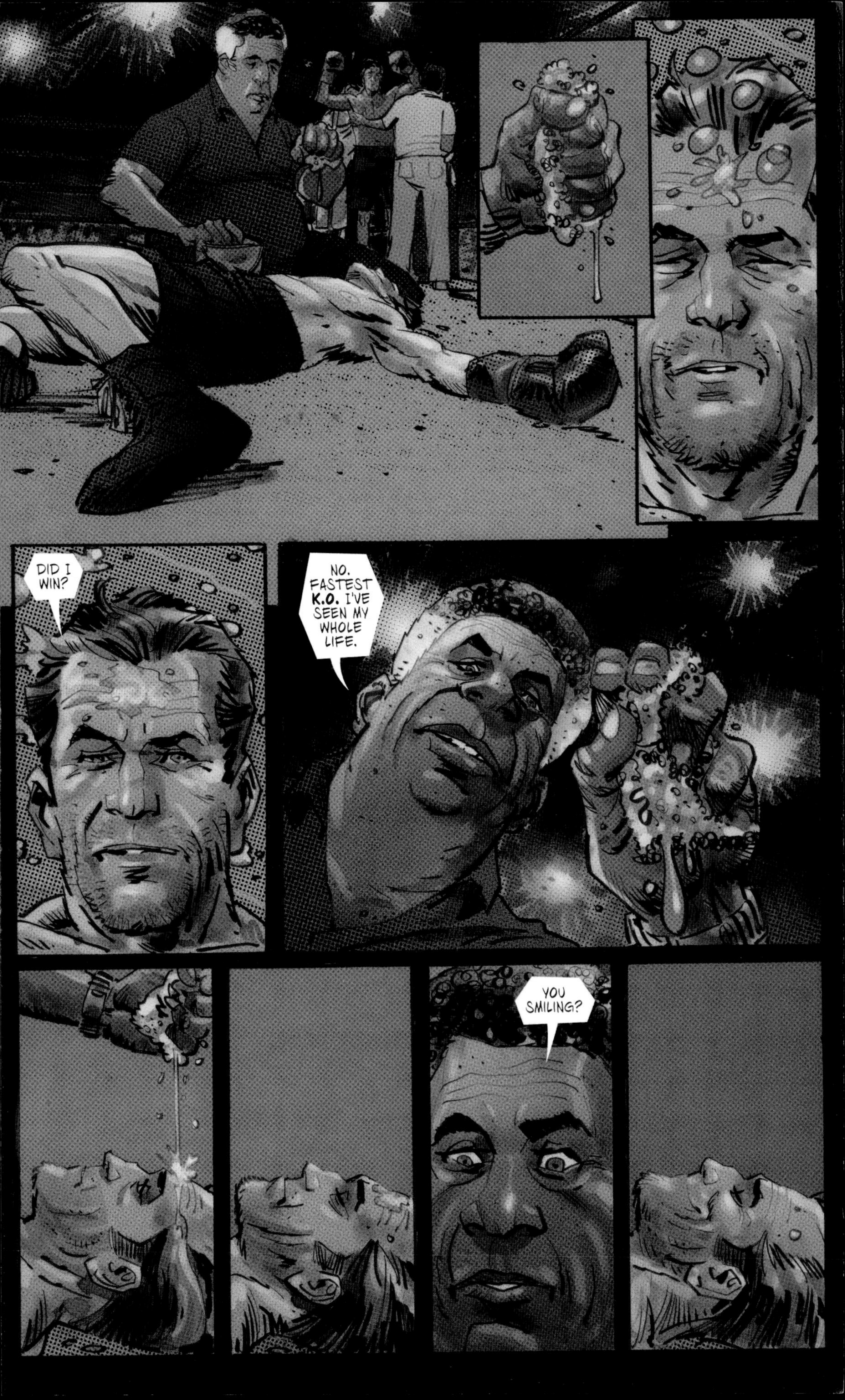
DID I WIN?
NO. FASTEST K.O. I'VE SEEN MY WHOLE LIFE.
YOU SMILING?

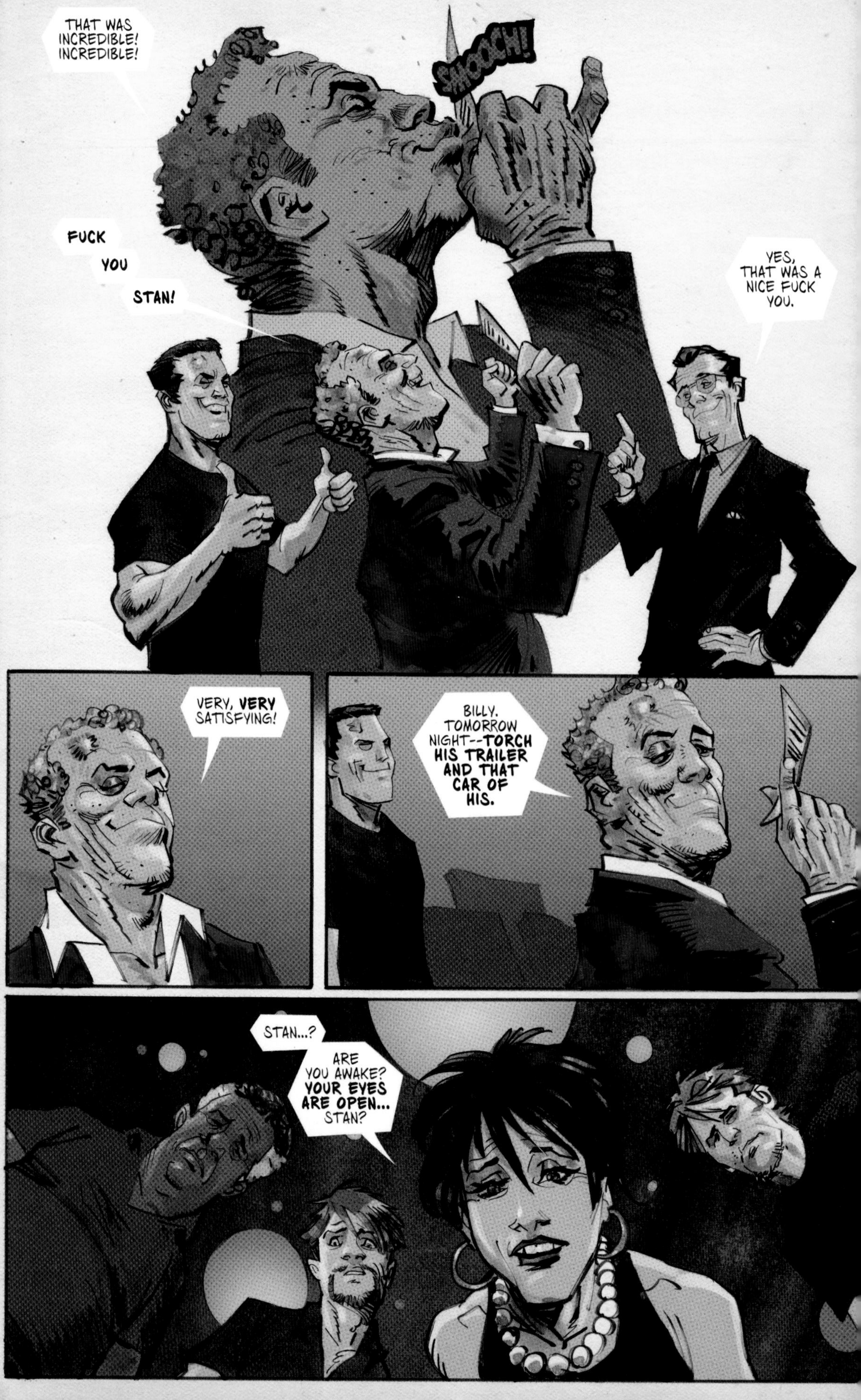
THAT WAS INCREDIBLE! INCREDIBLE!
SHOOCH!
FUCK YOU STAN!
YES, THAT WAS A NICE FUCK YOU.
VERY, VERY SATISFYING!
BILLY. TOMORROW NIGHT--TORCH HIS TRAILER AND THAT CAR OF HIS.
STAN...?
ARE YOU AWAKE? YOUR EYES ARE OPEN... STAN?

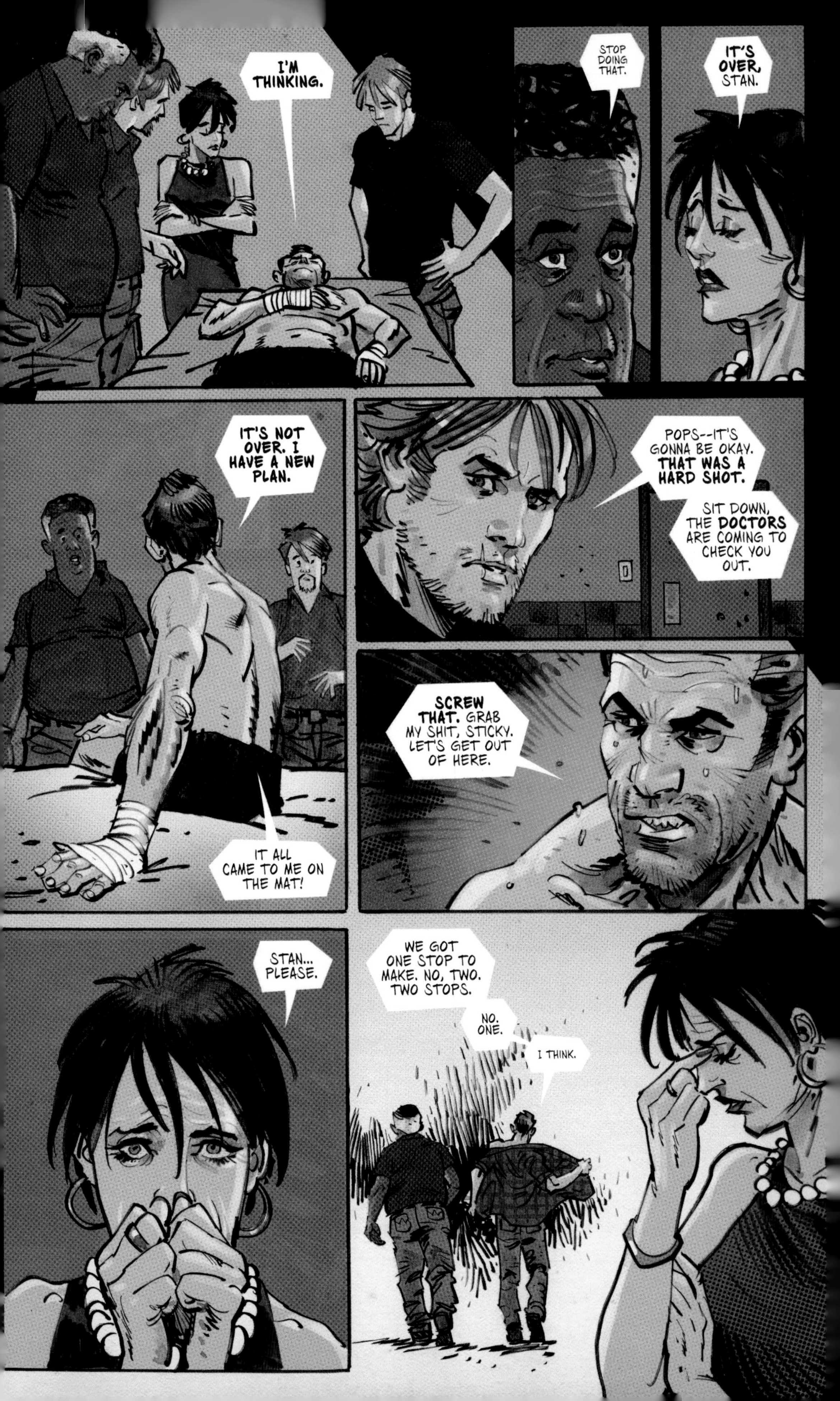
I'M THINKING.
STOP DOING THAT.
IT'S OVER, STAN.
IT'S NOT OVER. I HAVE A NEW PLAN.
IT ALL CAME TO ME ON THE MAT!
POPS--IT'S GONNA BE OKAY. THAT WAS A HARD SHOT.
SIT DOWN, THE DOCTORS ARE COMING TO CHECK YOU OUT.
SCREW THAT. GRAB MY SHIT, STICKY. LET'S GET OUT OF HERE.
STAN... PLEASE.
WE GOT ONE STOP TO MAKE. NO, TWO. TWO STOPS.
NO. ONE.
I THINK.

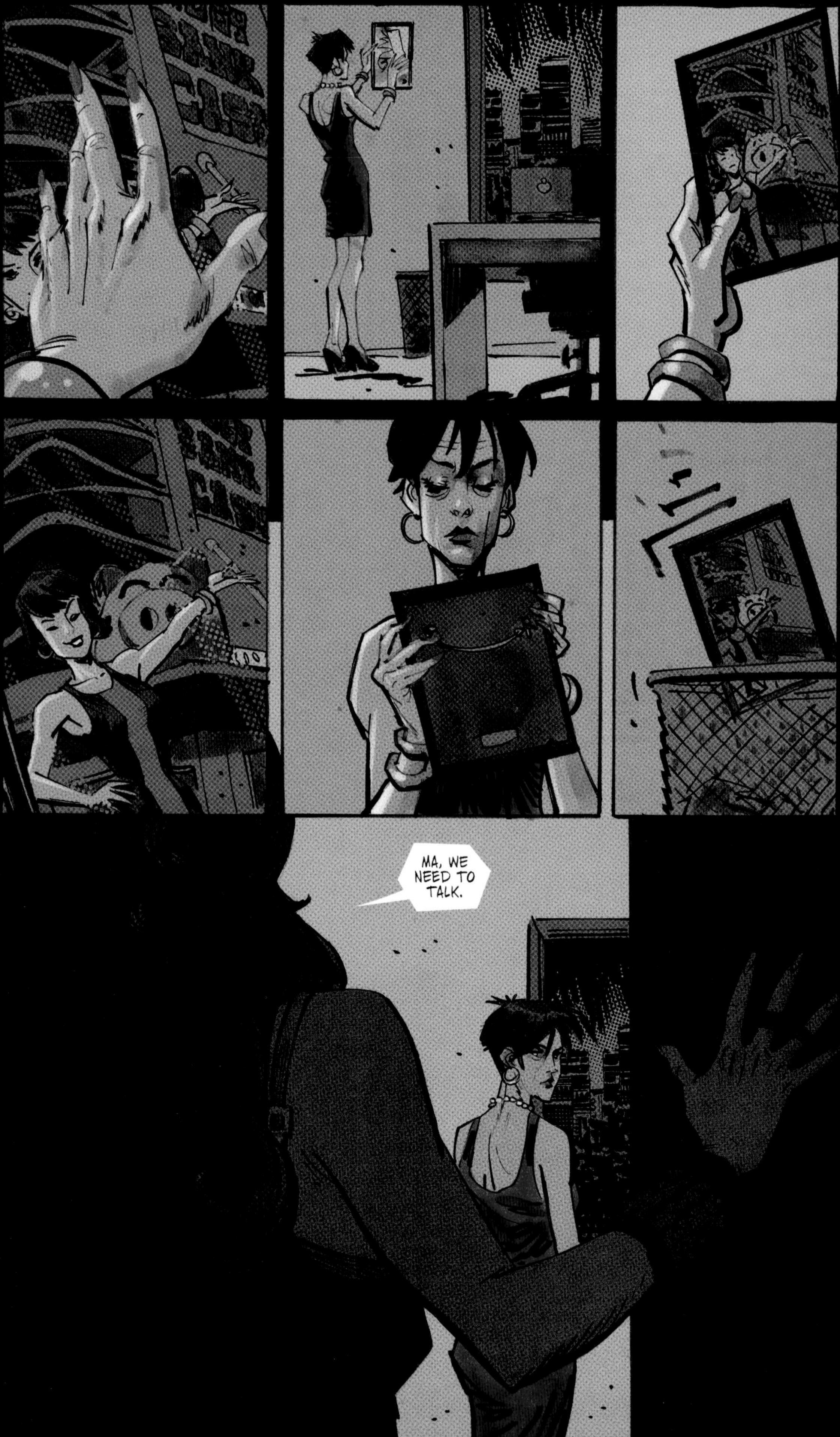
MA, WE NEED TO TALK.

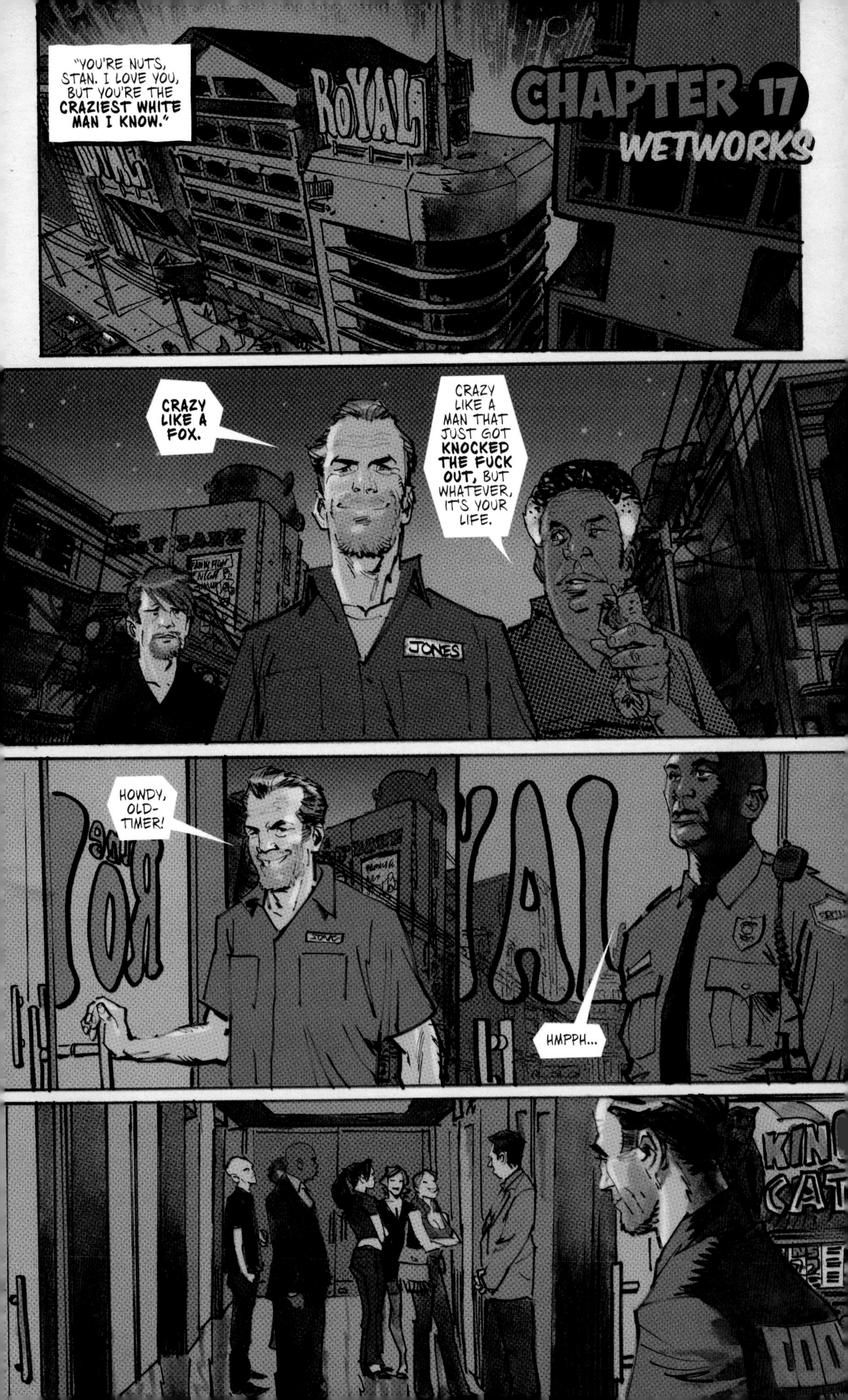
"YOU'RE NUTS, STAN. I LOVE YOU, BUT YOU'RE THE CRAZIEST WHITE MAN I KNOW."
CHAPTER 17
WETWORKS
ROYAL
CRAZY LIKE A FOX.
CRAZY LIKE A MAN THAT JUST GOT KNOCKED THE FUCK OUT, BUT WHATEVER, IT'S YOUR LIFE.
JONES
HOWDY, OLD-TIMER!
HMPPH...

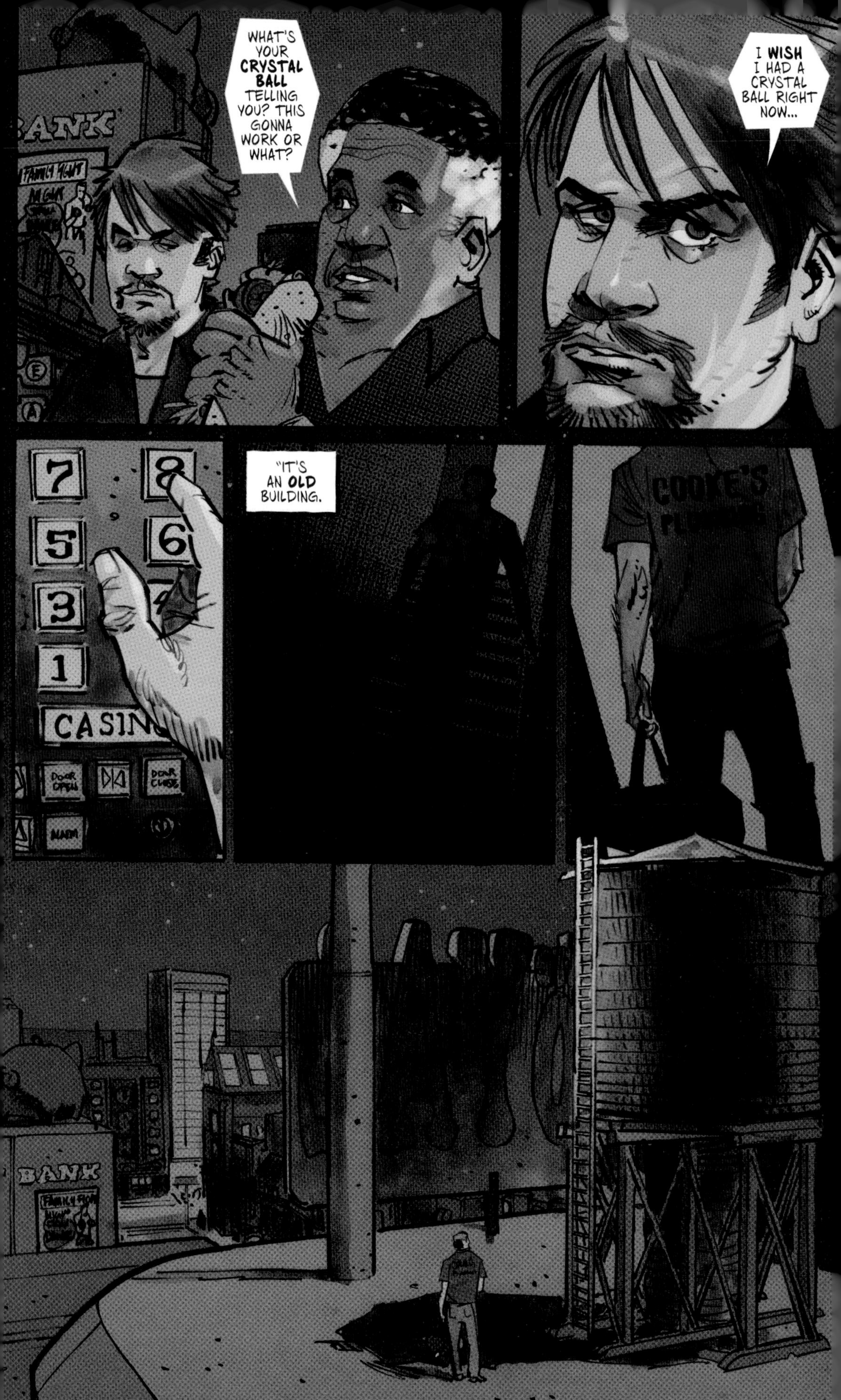

WHAT'S YOUR CRYSTAL BALL TELLING YOU? THIS GONNA WORK OR WHAT?
I WISH I HAD A CRYSTAL BALL RIGHT NOW...
BANK
7
8
5
6
3
1
CASIN
"IT'S AN OLD BUILDING.
COOKE'S
BANK

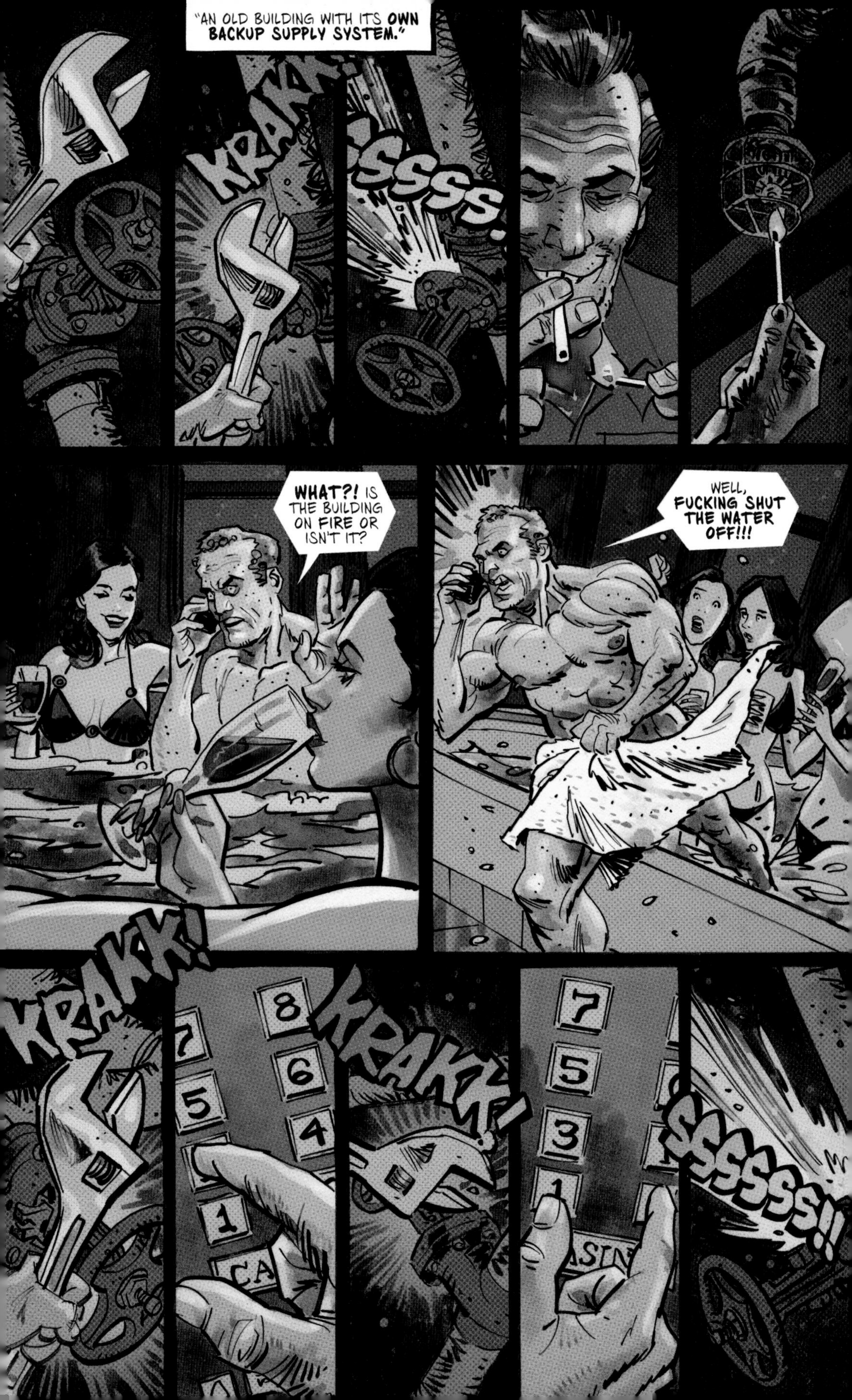
"AN OLD BUILDING WITH ITS OWN BACKUP SUPPLY SYSTEM."
KRAKK!
SSSSS!
WHAT?! IS THE BUILDING ON FIRE OR ISN'T IT?
WELL, FUCKING SHUT THE WATER OFF!!!
KRAKK!
KRAKK!
SSSSSS!!

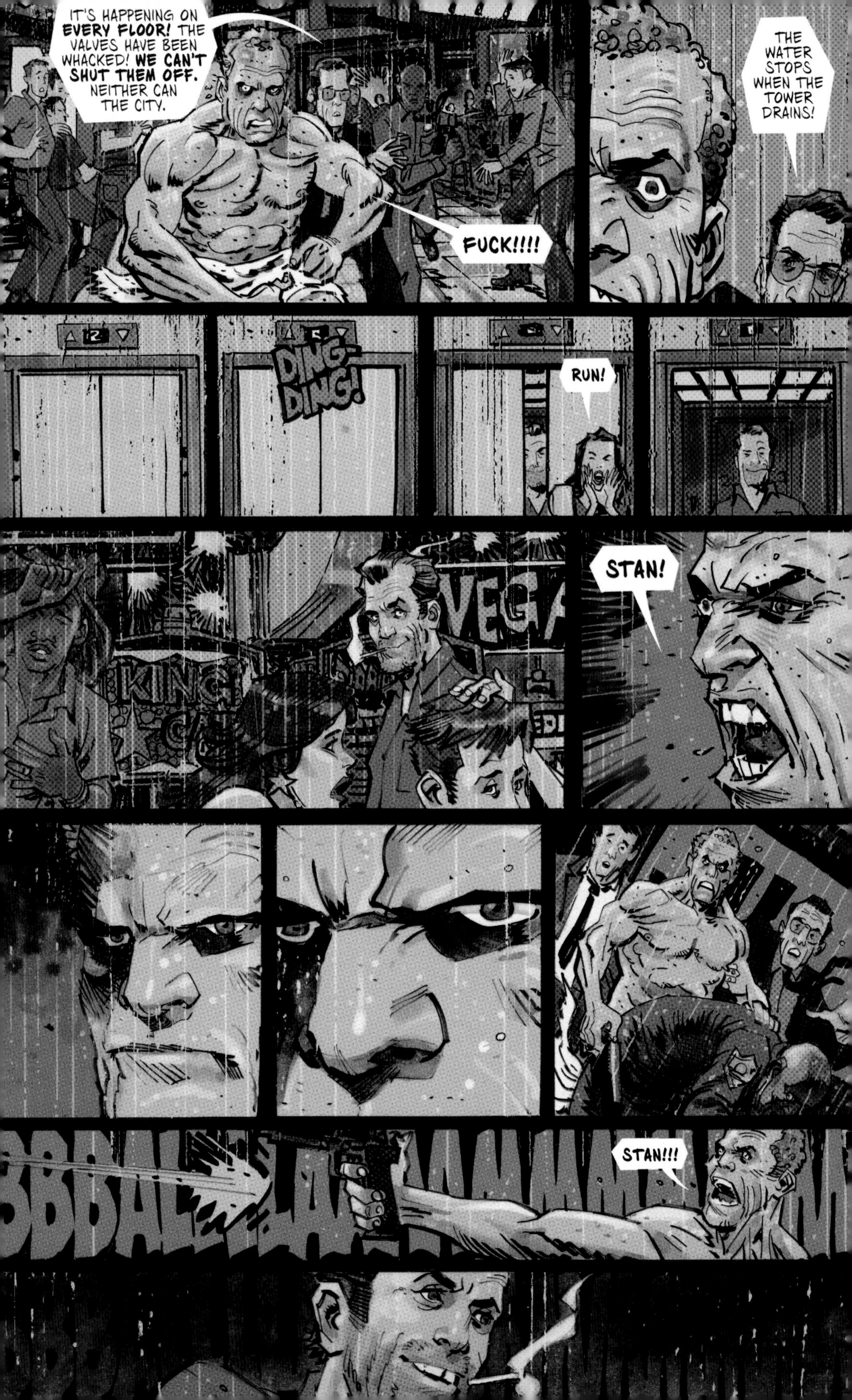
IT'S HAPPENING ON **EVERY FLOOR!** THE VALVES HAVE BEEN WHACKED! **WE CAN'T SHUT THEM OFF.** NEITHER CAN THE CITY.
FUCK!!!!
THE WATER STOPS WHEN THE TOWER DRAINS!
DING-DING!
RUN!
STAN!
STAN!!!

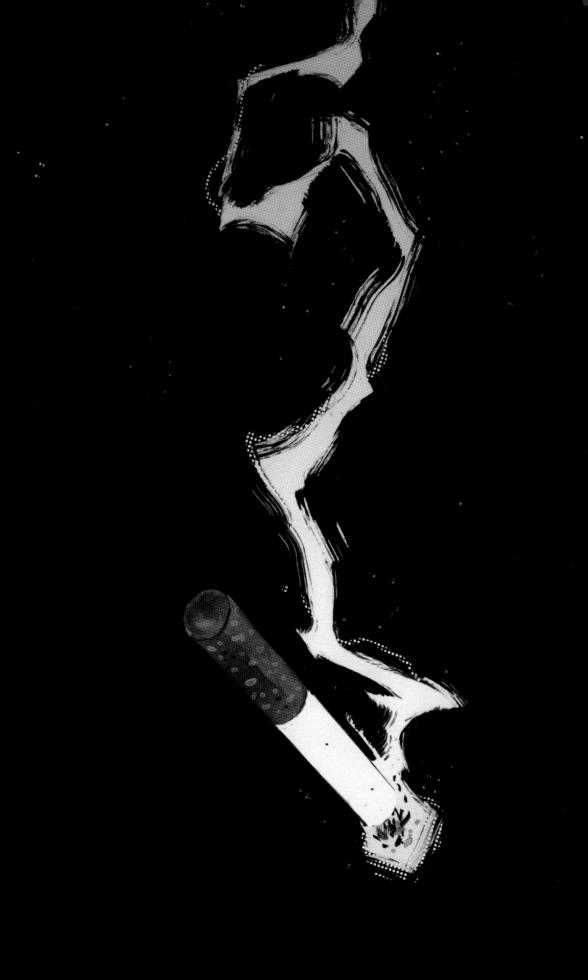

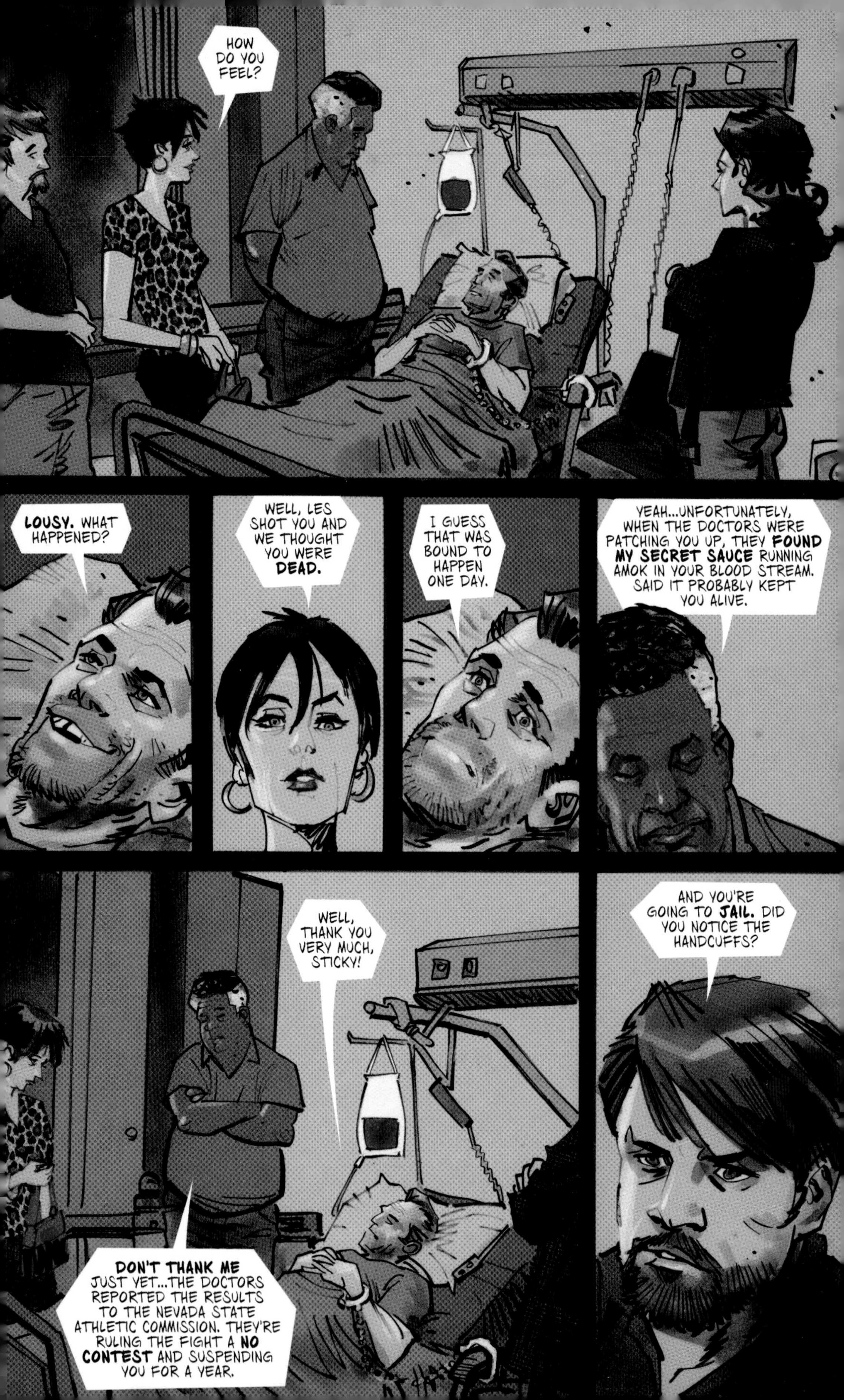
HOW DO YOU FEEL?
LOUSY. WHAT HAPPENED?
WELL, LES SHOT YOU AND WE THOUGHT YOU WERE **DEAD.**
I GUESS THAT WAS BOUND TO HAPPEN ONE DAY.
YEAH...UNFORTUNATELY, WHEN THE DOCTORS WERE PATCHING YOU UP, THEY **FOUND MY SECRET SAUCE** RUNNING AMOK IN YOUR BLOOD STREAM. SAID IT PROBABLY KEPT YOU ALIVE.
WELL, THANK YOU VERY MUCH, STICKY!
DON'T THANK ME JUST YET...THE DOCTORS REPORTED THE RESULTS TO THE NEVADA STATE ATHLETIC COMMISSION. THEY'RE RULING THE FIGHT A **NO CONTEST** AND SUSPENDING YOU FOR A YEAR.
AND YOU'RE GOING TO **JAIL.** DID YOU NOTICE THE HANDCUFFS?

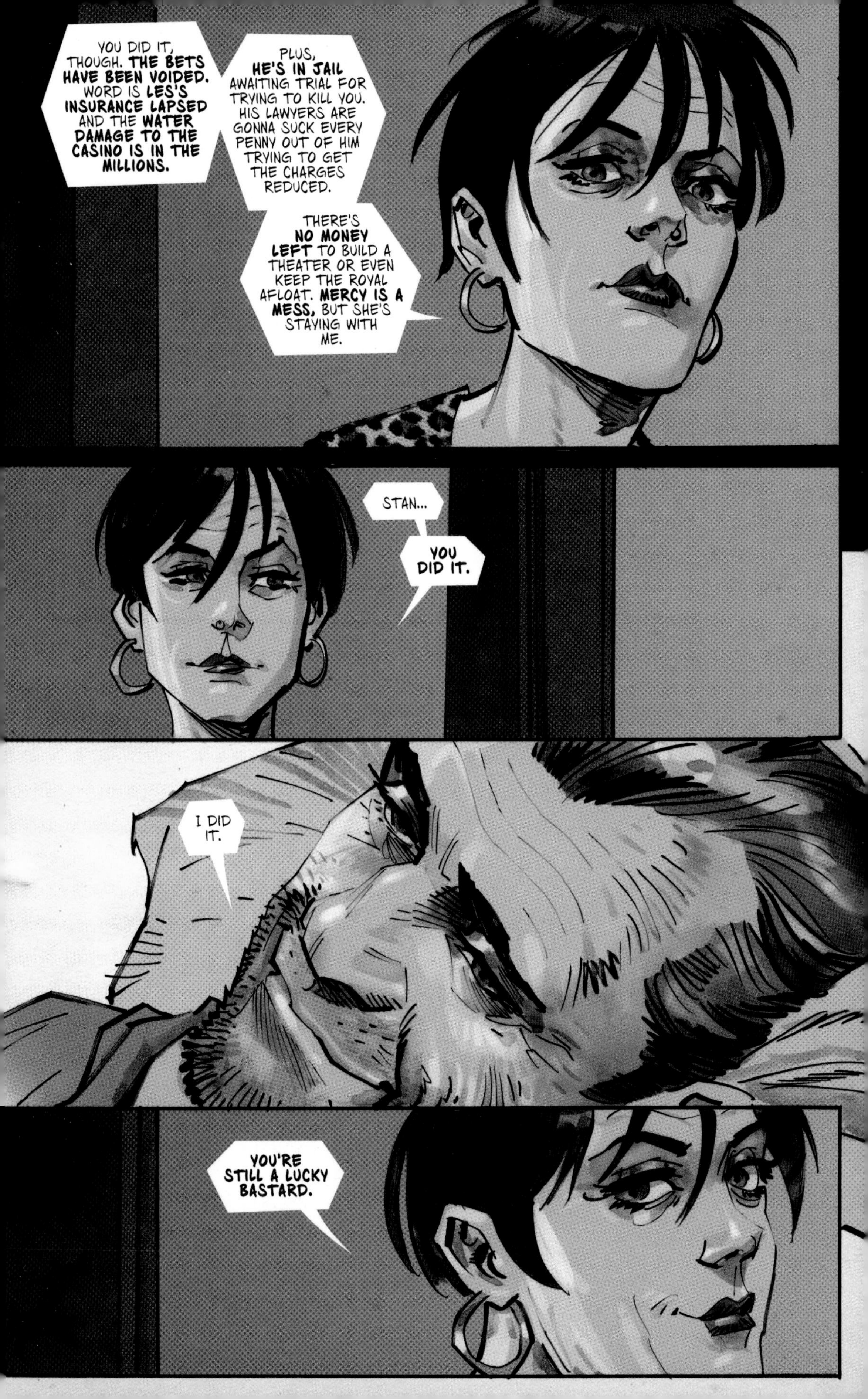
YOU DID IT, THOUGH. THE BETS HAVE BEEN VOIDED. WORD IS LES'S INSURANCE LAPSED AND THE WATER DAMAGE TO THE CASINO IS IN THE MILLIONS.
PLUS, HE'S IN JAIL AWAITING TRIAL FOR TRYING TO KILL YOU. HIS LAWYERS ARE GONNA SUCK EVERY PENNY OUT OF HIM TRYING TO GET THE CHARGES REDUCED.
THERE'S NO MONEY LEFT TO BUILD A THEATER OR EVEN KEEP THE ROYAL AFLOAT. MERCY IS A MESS, BUT SHE'S STAYING WITH ME.
STAN...
YOU DID IT.
I DID IT.
YOU'RE STILL A LUCKY BASTARD.

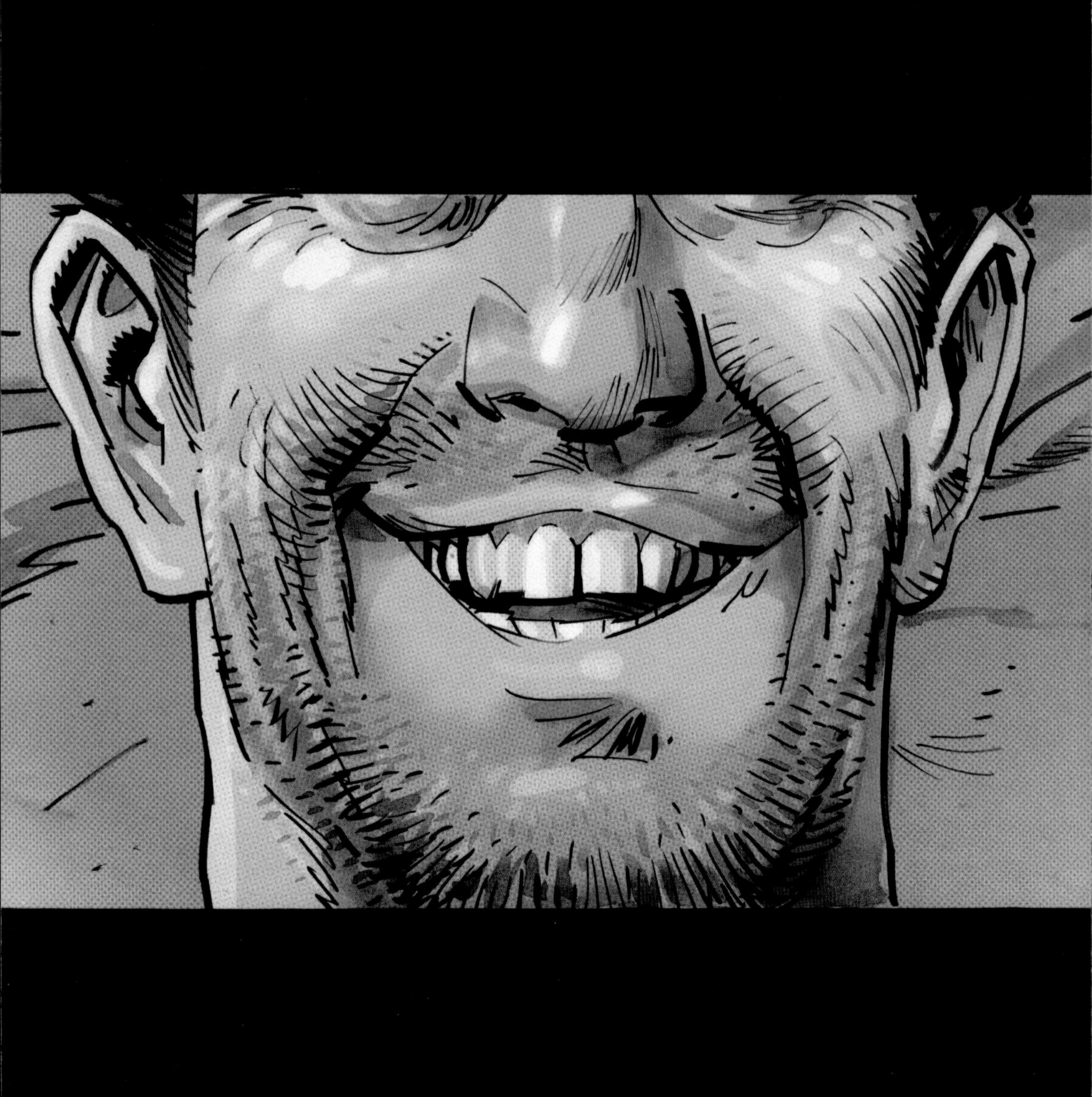

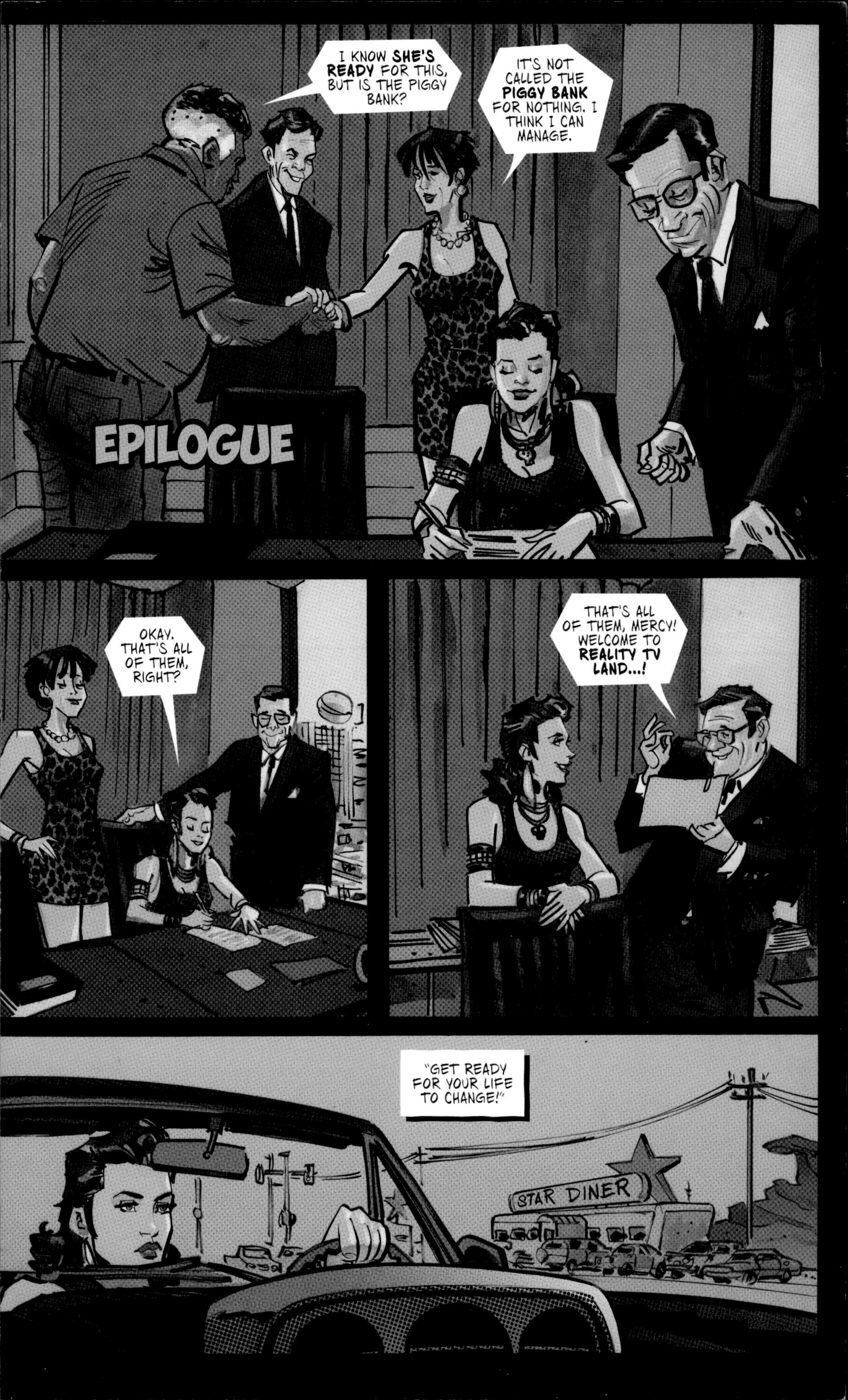
I KNOW SHE'S READY FOR THIS, BUT IS THE PIGGY BANK?
IT'S NOT CALLED THE PIGGY BANK FOR NOTHING. I THINK I CAN MANAGE.
EPILOGUE
OKAY. THAT'S ALL OF THEM, RIGHT?
THAT'S ALL OF THEM, MERCY! WELCOME TO REALITY TV LAND...!
"GET READY FOR YOUR LIFE TO CHANGE!"
STAR DINER

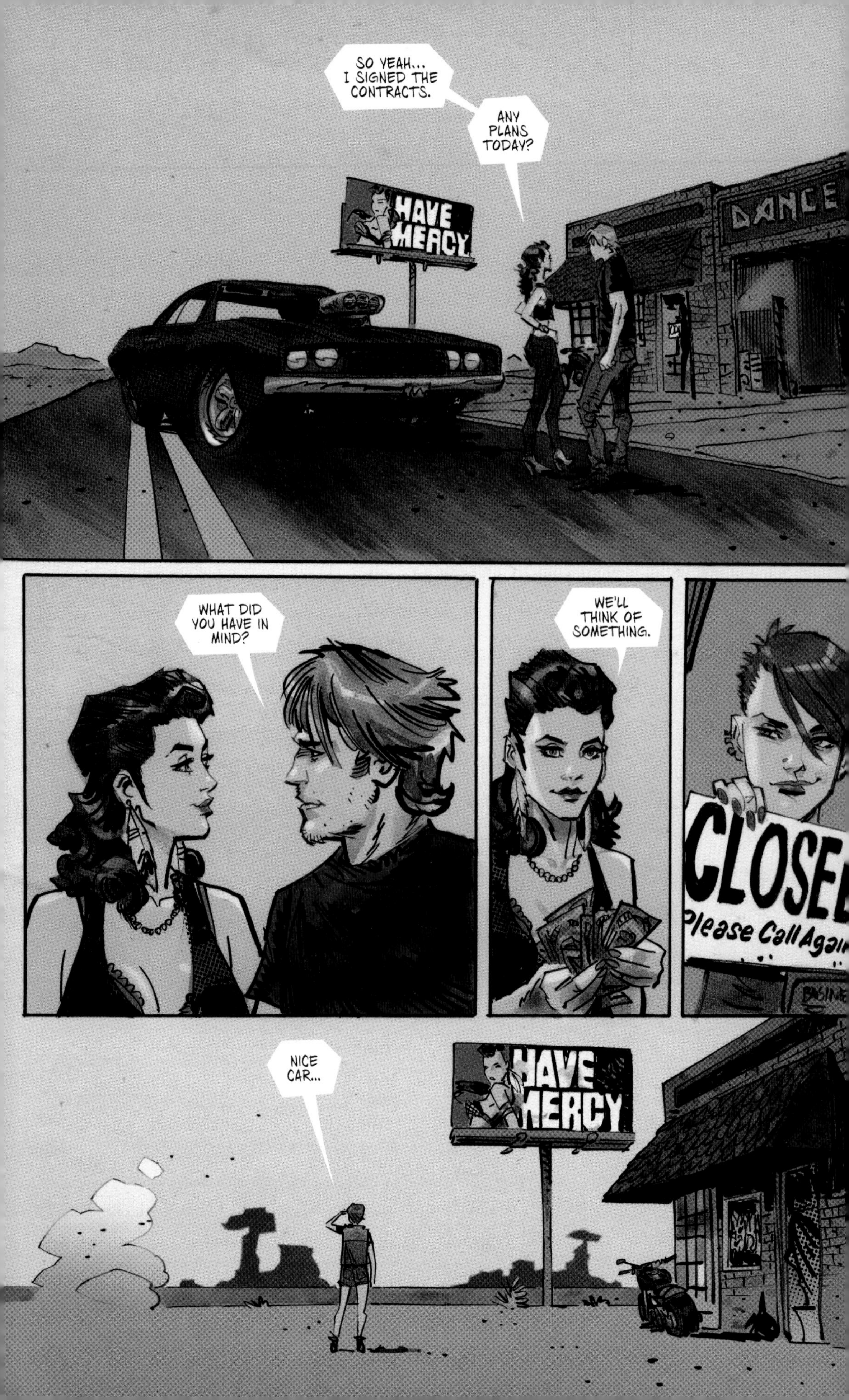
SO YEAH... I SIGNED THE CONTRACTS.
ANY PLANS TODAY?
HAVE MERCY
DANCE
WHAT DID YOU HAVE IN MIND?
WE'LL THINK OF SOMETHING.
NICE CAR...
HAVE MERCY

BACK STORY IS IMPORTANT

When I was five years old, living in Cleveland, Ohio, I would watch my father go through a boxing routine in our cold garage nearly every morning. One day, he put my hands in a guard position, spaced my legs out a bit and told me to imagine that the heavy bag was a real person. A person that had done a terrible thing. A bad guy.

"Is he in your head?" he said.
I nodded yes.
"Good. Now hit the bad guy!"

I remember the rush. I had watched my father pound this huge, heavy, leather trash can day after day. I knew that no matter how hard I hit the bag, it wouldn't break. That was a strange feeling. There's freedom in that. Raw freedom. As a child, you're always being told 'no', or 'be careful'. An opportunity to lash out without consequences? Very rare. That's a weird feeling for a five year old. I stood there a moment and let my feelings fester. Then I yelled something and tore into it.

From then I was hooked. Like every kid, I wanted my father's affection and approval. When he was a young man he boxed professionally until his parents saw his name in the newspapers and told him he had to find another way to make a living. He joined the Army and learned how to draw. He worked for years as an artist and was always submitting his work to newspaper comic strip syndications, usually sports strips. He worked at a lot of different ad agencies, but I could tell his passion was comic book art. Or at least it seemed that way to me. He introduced me to the work of Frank Frazetta, Neal Adams, Joe Kubert, John Buscema and even a young Walt Simonson. He loved movies like *Billy Jack* and anything with Charles Bronson or Clint Eastwood. He could do a mean James Cagney impression.

I wanted to be just like him.

So, of course I wanted to box and draw comic books. But the more I became interested in fighting and drawing, the more he tended to usher me away from them. I wasn't allowed to compete in the Golden Gloves, and he didn't want me to pursue the life of an artist. He warned me passionately that they're both very hard lives. He was right. Being an artist isn't terribly easy. Maybe I should have listened to him. I think about that a lot these days.

In my teens, my father and I drifted apart. He loved kids, but didn't like teenagers. I didn't make it easy, either. All of the stories he told me about his younger days inspired me to try to one-up him. We disagreed on everything, but always enjoyed two subjects: Boxing and comic books. In the end that's all we had in common. I guess that's more than some fathers and sons have. He passed away when I was in my twenties, and by then I was working for Marvel and DC Comics. I moved to California when Image Comics was created and even though he never mentioned it, I would hear from his friends that he was proud of me.

SLOTS is a book I hope he would have enjoyed. I have a lot of mixed feelings about him, but there isn't a day that goes by that I don't think about him. I hope you enjoyed it, too. Stanley Dance doesn't make it easy to love him, but you love him. At times it's hard to tell who is worse, Stanley or Les Royal. But, hell, sometimes it's fun to root for the bad guy. They're the most fun to create. Good guys--they're easy to like. They save the day. Creating a good bad guy can be more important to a story than the protagonist in a lot of ways. Maybe that's why I created so many shady characters for this book.

Speaking of bad guys, I guess the first one I ever created was years ago, back in my father's garage. I asked him when I was older what I yelled before I threw my first punch. He smiled and said:

"You didn't listen to your mommy!"

Back story is important--even to five year olds.

Cheers!

~DAN

ONE LAST THING: Writing and drawing this book has been one of the most rewarding experiences of my career so far. It's also been scary. But scary in that same fun way watching a good horror flick is scary. You don't want it to end. It's a thrill. So I want to thank you for picking SLOTS up. And I want to thank Robert Kirkman for taking a chance on me. He threw me a set of keys to the car I always wanted to drive. He also gave me some of the best damn editors I could have ever hoped for in Sean Mackiewicz and Arielle Basich. Each month they gave me the right amount of rope to hang myself, but made sure I never kicked that chair. Thanks, you two. And thank you, Pat Brosseau, for putting all the words down on the pages. I started my career in this business with your lettering, so it feels like home seeing your name on this book. And lastly, a special thanks to Adam Connolly and his vision for a gritty downtown Las Vegas.

COVERS! COVERS!

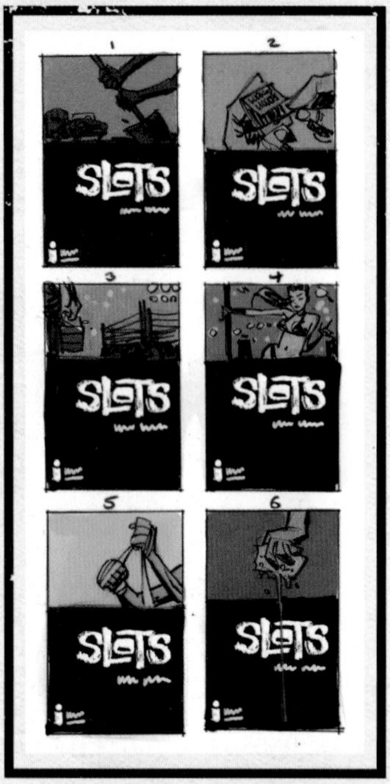
SLOTS
SLOTS
SLOTS
SLOTS
SLOTS
SLOTS

THUMBNAILS

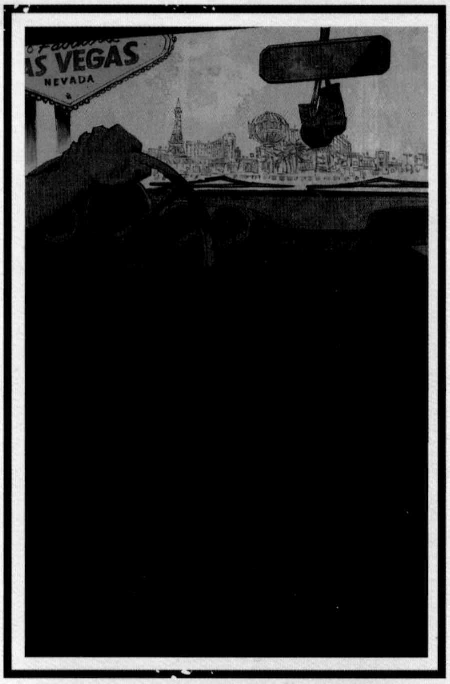
AS VEGAS
NEVADA

COVER #1

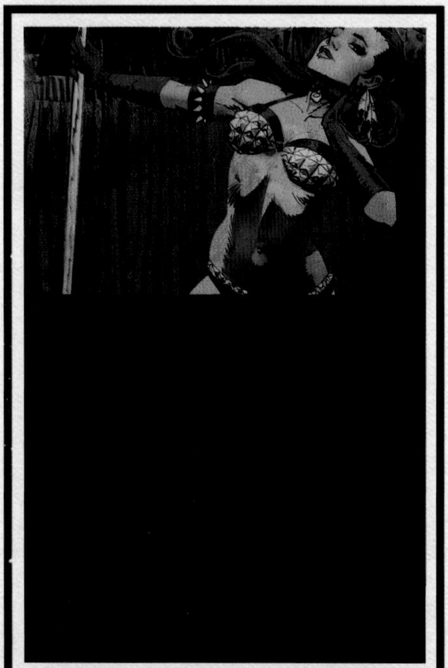

COVER #4

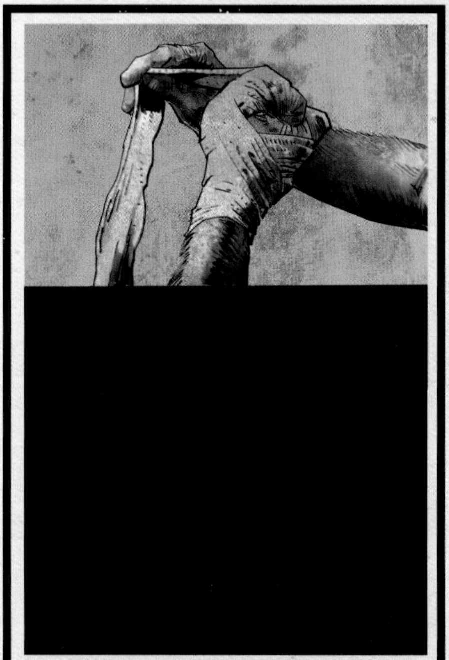

COVER #5

COVERS! COVERS!

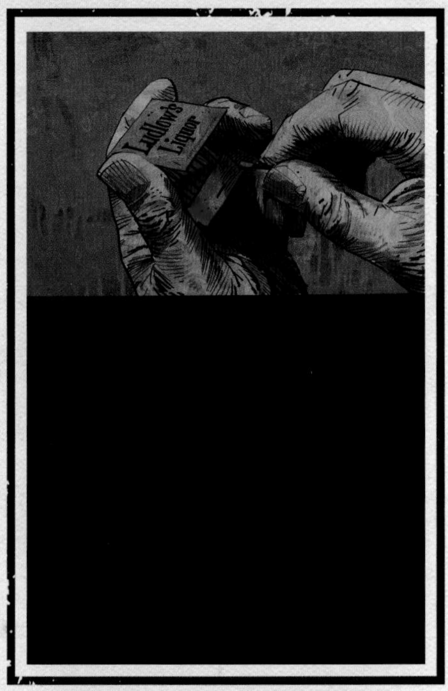
Ludlow's Liquor

COVER #2

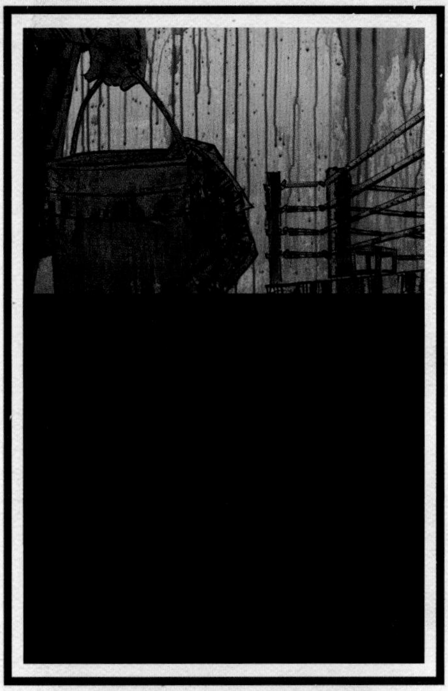

COVER #3

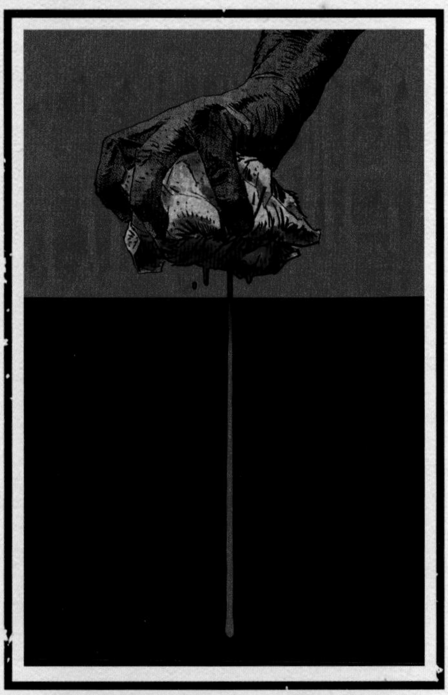

COVER #6

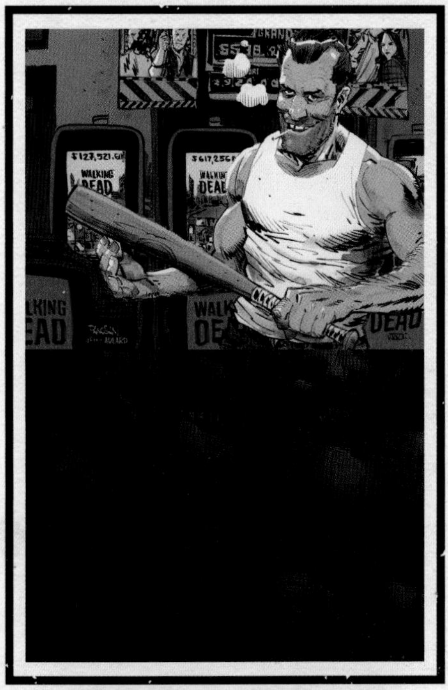
WALKING DEAD
WALKING DEAD
DEAD

TWD VARIANT

For more tales from ROBERT KIRKMAN and SKYBOUND

Daniel Warren Johnson Mike Spicer
EXTREMITY
VOLUME TWO WARRIOR

REDNECK
Donny CATES Lisandro ESTHERREN Dee CUNNIFFE
VOLUME TWO
The Eyes Upon You

VOL. 1: ARTIST TP
ISBN: 978-1-5343-0242-6
$16.99

VOL. 2: WARRIOR TP
ISBN: 978-1-5343-0506-9
$16.99

VOL. 1: DEEP IN THE HEART TP
ISBN: 978-1-5343-0331-7
$16.99

VOL. 2: THE EYES UPON YOU
ISBN: 978-1-5343-0665-3
$16.99

BIRTHRIGHT

VOL. 1: HOMECOMING TP
ISBN: 978-1-63215-231-2
$9.99

VOL. 2: CALL TO ADVENTURE TP
ISBN: 978-1-63215-446-0
$12.99

VOL. 3: ALLIES AND ENEMIES TP
ISBN: 978-1-63215-683-9
$12.99

VOL. 4: FAMILY HISTORY TP
ISBN: 978-1-63215-871-0
$12.99

VOL. 5: BELLY OF THE BEAST TP
ISBN: 978-1-53430-218-1
$12.99

VOL. 6: FATHERHOOD TP
ISBN: 978-1-53430-498-7
$14.99

Gasolina

VOL. 1: BIENVENIDO TP
ISBN: 978-1-5343-0506-9
$16.99

CHRIS DINGESS • MATTHEW ROBERTS • OWEN GIENI
MANIFEST DESTINY
VOLUME 5 • MNEMOPHOBIA & CHRONOPHOBIA

VOL. 1: FLORA & FAUNA TP
ISBN: 978-1-60706-982-9
$9.99

VOL. 2: AMPHIBIA & INSECTA TP
ISBN: 978-1-63215-052-3
$14.99

VOL. 3: CHIROPTERA & CARNIFORMAVES TP
ISBN: 978-1-63215-397-5
$14.99

VOL. 4: SASQUATCH TP
ISBN: 978-1-63215-890-1
$14.99

VOL. 5: MNEMOPHOBIA & CHRONOPHOBIA TP
ISBN: 978-1-5343-0230-3
$16.99

VOLUME 5 THE NEW PATH
BY KIRKMAN AZACETA
OUTCAST

VOL. 1: A DARKNESS SURROUNDS HIM TP
ISBN: 978-1-63215-053-0
$9.99

VOL. 2: A VAST AND UNENDING RUIN TP
ISBN: 978-1-63215-448-4
$14.99

VOL. 3: THIS LITTLE LIGHT TP
ISBN: 978-1-63215-693-8
$14.99

VOL. 4: UNDER DEVIL'S WING TP
ISBN: 978-1-5343-0050-7
$14.99

VOL. 5: THE NEW PATH TP
ISBN: 978-1-5343-0249-5
$16.99

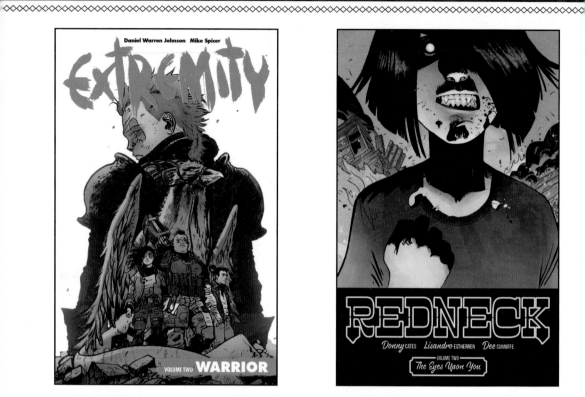